BETTE FORD

CAN'T GET ENOUGH OF YOU

AVON

An Imprint of HarperCollinsPublishers

AVON BOOKS
An Imprint of HarperCollins*Publishers*
10 East 53rd Street
New York, New York 10022-5299

Copyright © 2010 by Bette Ford
ISBN 978-0-06-172881-5
www.avonbooks.com

F
Ford
Bette

First Avon Books paperback printing: July 2010

Avon Trademark Reg. U.S. Pat. Off. and in Other Countries, Marca Registrada, Hecho en U.S.A.
HarperCollins® is a registered trademark of HarperCollins Publishers.

Printed in the U.S.A.

10 9 8 7 6 5 4 3 2 1

To my wonderful agent, Nancy Yost: You are the best

To my editor, Esi Sogah: Thanks for your
invaluable help and insight on this project.

To my mother, Rosena Ford: Your love
and faith keep me strong.

To dear friends, Mary Pittman,
Carla, Fredd, Francis Ray, and
Beverly Jenkins: Your support
and belief that I can do this
one more time mean
the world to me.

Special thanks to Angela Benson Campbell.

Praise the Lord. Give thanks to the Lord, for He is good; His love endures forever.

Psalm 106:1

One

It was a beautiful August day when Jenna Gaines said aloud, "I did it!" Laughing as tears streamed down her face, she slowly mounted the porch stairs not to a brand-new house but to her first real home.

The week had seemed to fly past, first with packing her tiny apartment in Greenwich Village, then going out with coworkers for dinner on Wednesday to celebrate her thirty-first birthday. A tall, striking, African-American beauty with caramel-toned skin, shoulder-length, dark brown, naturally wavy curls that framed her face, and large, hazel eyes, Jenna turned heads wherever she went. What a celebration it had been, her last day as a stockbroker and financial adviser on Wall Street.

She was tired, but it was the best kind of tired, because she had accomplished nearly everything she'd set out to do. With her dated car packed to the brim, she had set out early Thursday morning on the long drive back to her hometown of Detroit, Michigan, hopeful she would arrive ahead of the movers with her things. And she'd made it.

Jenna's hands shook as she tried and failed twice before successfully inserting the key into the locked front door. She raced inside to punch in the alarm's security code.

"I'm home!" she cried as she took in the hardwood floors, the large stone fireplace in the living room, and the curved picture window that faced the street.

But it wasn't about the beauty of a dining room that opened onto a small bricked patio and generous backyard. It wasn't just the small but charming kitchen that put a smile on her face. Jenna loved every square inch of the one-story home's nice-sized bedrooms and the small bonus room she planned to use as her home office.

It had taken years of hard work and sacrifices, all of which she'd done on her own. Having grown up in foster care, she was used to living modestly. What mattered was that she was finally where she belonged. Despite her fatigue, she couldn't hold in her excitement.

Soon she would be starting her dream job, teaching economics as a professor at her former college, University of Detroit-Mercy, where she had obtained both her undergraduate and her master's degrees.

It had taken four tough years in New York to make it happen, working at a well-paid job she'd hated, saving as much as she'd been able while investing wisely and finishing a doctorate. While all those accomplishments were extremely important, they didn't fill her to the point of bursting with happiness. The knowledge that she'd put her final goal into motion before she'd left New York had been like putting the finishing touch on a special cake.

At last Jenna had saved enough money to do what she had been longing to do for most of her life. Finally she would be able to follow her dream of reuniting her family. She hadn't seen her twin sister, Lenna, since they were five, or their older brother, Lincoln, since he was six.

Their father had left the family first, but when the state had been unable to find their mother when she'd left them alone, the Gaines children had been separated and placed in different homes. There hadn't even been a wayward relative to care for them. After years of searching, Jenna had learned that her siblings had both been adopted, while she'd remained in the foster care system until she was eighteen.

Jenna didn't resent her circumstances. In fact, she felt she had been fortunate. She had been placed in a good foster home. Mrs. Frances Green had been a wonderful foster care mother for the three little girls left in her care. Jenna, Sherri Ann Weber, and Laura Murdock had all been blessed with that special woman's care.

Jenna had often wondered why Mrs. Green had not adopted them. She suspected it was because of her advanced age. Most important was that Mrs. Green had loved and cared for them and kept them safe and off the streets. She was a remarkable woman, who had also inspired in them a will to succeed despite the odds against them.

At last, Jenna was back in Detroit, where she could be with her two very best friends and foster care sisters. The three had labeled themselves "fierce and fearless." They'd refused to let their circumstances—being abandoned by the ones who should have cared for them—defeat or define them.

Yes, Jenna had been forced to make sacrifices over the years, including turning her back on the love of her life. She'd concentrated on her education and not letting anything—or anyone, for that matter—prevent her from obtaining her goals. And she wouldn't stop until she found her family. Someday soon there would be a Gaines family reunion.

"It won't be long now," Jenna reassured herself as she went out to the car and found the box of cleaning supplies she'd brought with her. Hard work never hurt anyone, she decided with a determined sigh. Box by box she began unloading her car, bringing everything inside. Then she set to work cleaning.

The move back was only the beginning of a new life. She had so much to look forward to, no reason to look back to the time when she had been young and in love, foolishly listening to her heart and not using her head. She'd made mistakes. But that was all behind her.

When the movers pulled up to the house, she took it as a sign that everything would be fine. Things were going her way. Jenna had no regrets. She'd done what was best for her and not hurt anyone in the process.

She was beat by the time she finally climbed into her own freshly made bed that night. Her joy in her new job and pride in owning her very own home had not diminished. Jenna had come full circle. She was back where it had all begun.

"Jenna? Jenna Gaines, is that really you?"

Jenna didn't immediately move from where she was standing in the busy department store, selecting throw pillows to complement her drapes. Just for an instant, she found herself wondering how she could feel both happiness and dread at the same time.

Slowly, she turned, her smile genuine. "Taylor! How are you?"

Holding onto a baby stroller, Taylor Hendricks-Williams squealed with pleasure as she gave Jenna a one-armed hug. "It's so good to see you. Where have you been? I've tried to reach you so many times over the years. Are you back in Detroit for good?"

Jenna returned the warm squeeze, deeply touched by the other woman's love and thoughtfulness. They'd always had so much in common, both being high achievers who valued family.

"You look wonderful. And yes, I'm back. What about you and Donald? Are you here for a visit? And who is this?"

Thrilled to see each other after so many years, the two women laughed when they realized they were talking at the same time, asking but not answering any questions. At one time, they had been very close.

"You go first," Taylor prompted.

As much as Jenna loved and admired Taylor, she didn't welcome the reminders of the man Taylor brought to mind. Her younger brother, Scott Hendricks, was the man Jenna had once loved with her whole heart.

Jenna knew it wouldn't be long until Taylor asked the question she didn't want to answer, or until she was told details that she would rather not know. Over the years, Jenna had gotten good at pushing away thoughts of her ex-love. She wanted to keep it that way.

"So tell me about this beautiful little doll baby?" Jenna dropped down to get a better look at the sleeping infant.

Taylor beamed. "Our daughter, Brianna. She's four months. We also have a son, Donnie, who's five years old." She practically bubbled with happiness.

Jenna had been Taylor's maid of honor when she'd married the professional basketball player Donald Williams more than ten years ago. It had been a beautiful wedding, but it had taken all Jenna's strength to hide her own unhappiness that day. Since breaking off her relationship with Scott, she'd avoided him as much as possible. She hadn't seen him in years.

"Taylor, that's wonderful. Are you back in Detroit for good?"

She nodded. "Yes, we've been back for almost two

years. After Donald retired from the Bulls, there was nothing keeping us there. The Detroit area has always been home. How about you?"

Jenna admitted, "I recently returned to the city to start teaching economics at our alma mater, University of Detroit-Mercy."

"Oh, Jenna! That is great. You got your PhD?"

"Yes, I'm Dr. Gaines now. I was living, working, and going to school in New York City for the last four years."

"I am so proud of you." Taylor hugged her. "You've reached all your educational goals! And that is saying a lot, having started out as a foster kid."

Jenna beamed, deeply touched, for she knew how sincerely the praise was given. "That means a lot to me coming from you," she replied. "You were always so supportive. I've missed you so much."

"Me, too. It has been so long, too long."

The two looked into each other's eyes with sadness. They'd let the breakup come between them. They'd both missed out on so much of each other's lives. Jenna learned that Taylor had also gotten her master's and PhD. The two beamed, proud of each other.

"Do you have a half hour or so?" Taylor asked hopefully. "Can we go to the food court, to talk and catch up on each other's news?"

Jenna didn't have the heart to say no. She wanted to tell Taylor about her job and her hopes of finding her family. And she wanted to hear about Taylor's time in Chicago, her career goals, and her new home.

This was Taylor. She had always been kind to Jenna and treated her like family, which meant the world to Jenna. The last thing she wanted to do was hurt Taylor's feelings.

"Yes, let's go. But I need to pay for these pillows. Be right back." Jenna headed for the cashier.

The mall was busy with the typical Saturday afternoon crowd, many of whom were shopping for back-to-school clothes. Jenna's mind, however, wasn't on the crowd. Seeing Taylor had been like a warm hug, making Jenna feel as if she really was back home. She'd been away so long and was acutely aware of what she'd left behind. The hug had also left her feeling melancholy.

Memories she'd firmly pushed aside had returned tenfold when she'd driven through the neighborhood where she'd grown up and seen the old elementary and middle school she'd attended.

If only all the memories were that uncomplicated. She'd also seen the apartment building near campus where she had lived with Scott for a short time. Those bittersweet memories had overwhelmed her, until she'd forced herself to keep on driving and not stop. And now she was here with Scott's older sister.

"Ready," Jenna said, even though her thoughts were filled with doubts of a past best left forgotten. Looking back would only bring back the pain and heartache. She didn't want to remember, but instead of making an excuse, she walked at Taylor's side and asked, "How are your parents?"

Taylor slowed before she revealed, "My father passed two years ago."

"I'm so sorry. I had no idea," Jenna said, saddened.

Taylor nodded her understanding. "He had suffered with breathing problems for years. And he went easily in his sleep."

Jenna recalled that Taylor and Scott's parents had moved to Florida because of their father's severe asthma. Taylor, just out of college herself, had taken over caring for the then fifteen-year-old Scott so that he could finish high school in their hometown with his friends.

Jenna couldn't help wondering how Scott had taken

the loss. They had been a close-knit family, and he had been especially close to his father. One of the things that had attracted Jenna to Scott was his love of family. Although she wondered about him, Jenna didn't feel she had the right to ask about Scott, considering she'd been the one to end their engagement.

Taylor went on to say, "My mother has also moved back to Detroit. She refused to move in with us, but she lives right next door. Donald's brother and sister also live nearby. I like the idea of my kids growing up around family."

"That's wonderful." Jenna had to bite her lip to keep from saying Scott's name. Deciding a change of topic was necessary, she approached the entrance to the food court and said, "It looks like we'll be lucky to get a table."

"Do you remember how we used to have lunch at the tiny cafe across from the university? I wonder if it's still there?" Taylor asked with a smile.

Jenna nodded. "Sure is."

They found a table near the outlet of a popular pizza parlor. Both of them ignored their menu and ordered antipasto salad, pizza, and a soft drink.

Once they were seated, Taylor reached into a large tote bag and pulled out a small digital photo album. "I won't bore you, I promise, but I want you to see our son. He looks like his dad."

"Taylor, he's so cute. And you're right, he does look like Donald," Jenna laughed. Glancing through the album, she nearly bit her tongue when she saw a smiling Scott holding his little niece and nephew. Time had been good to him. He was even better-looking, even with a clean-shaven head. Naturally, she'd seen photos of him in news and gossip magazines over the years, but this time was more jarring, perhaps because she knew Taylor was looking on.

Schooling her features, Jenna forced a smile. "The children are beautiful, Taylor. You have a wonderful family."

"Thanks, Jenna," Taylor said. "Tell me about you. You said you're back from New York. Why the Big Apple?"

"You know I've always been goal oriented. New York was just the means to obtain my goal. I needed to make as much money as I could and finish my doctorate. I did both. It was tough, but I landed a job working as a financial adviser and stockbroker on Wall Street."

"Wow, I'm impressed! But I'm not surprised. You've always been a determined young woman."

Jenna laughed, "Some would call it hardheaded. But yes, even when I was little, I loved school and wanted to learn all I could."

Taylor said, "Tell me about you. Have you been able to locate your family?"

"You remembered," Jenna smiled. "Not yet, but I haven't given up on finding my brother or my twin sister. Finally I've been able to take the most important step. I hired a private investigator to help me."

Taylor clasped Jenna's hand. "That is wonderful news. I know it has been a long wait, but I admire the fact you never gave up."

"Giving up was never an option," Jenna replied candidly. She'd always dreamed of being reunited with her siblings. She'd refused to let fears or doubts hold her back. Despite the lost years, she'd clung to hope it was not too late.

She had set her course a long time ago. Now that her education was finally behind her, the future looked bright with promise.

She didn't like to remember the weak moment when she'd wavered. At the time, she had been so caught up in her love for Scott, the college basketball star, that she'd actually considered putting her educational and personal plans on hold in order to follow him around the country like a lost puppy.

He'd just been drafted into the NBA; his dream had come true and his future had soared toward the stars. He'd asked her to come with him to give him a year of her undivided attention. After the year, if she still wanted to return to school, he would pay for her education. Thank goodness her common sense had kicked in before she had actually married the man.

At the time she had told herself that she was glad it had not worked out for them. If she had done what he'd asked, she wouldn't have been true to herself. The last thing she'd needed was to spend her life following a man around while her dreams were being ignored.

How long would it have been before his career goals became more important than hers? What about babies? Everything would change when they came. Jenna had once longed for Scott's babies, a family of her own, but she'd also had her own set of priorities. When he'd decided to join the NBA he had broken his promise to her and his family. She'd finally recognized that they'd no longer shared the same hopes for the future.

Shocked to find she was shaking from the intensity of her emotion, Jenna forced herself to focus on something else. She watched the tender way Taylor bottle-fed her beautiful baby girl. Taylor was a wonderful mother, but her life was vastly different from Jenna's. Taylor had a man who loved her and put her first. Donald hadn't asked her to turn her back on her dreams so he could pursue his own.

When Jenna and Scott had recognized what they'd meant to each other—that they'd wanted to spend their lives together—they'd vowed to wait until after graduation to marry. They'd also vowed to keep their plans between the two of them. Scott's decision to join the NBA had changed all that. Jenna hadn't been the one to break their pledge. She'd only done what had been right for her. Scott hadn't liked her decision any more than she'd liked his.

Well, that was a long time ago. Here she was sitting with his sister, not saying what needed to be said. How long was she going to force Taylor to keep on pretending she didn't have a brother?

Taking a deep breath, Jenna asked, "How is Scott?"

Two

"He's fine. I don't know if you heard that he retired from the NBA. He's put basketball behind him," Taylor replied with a smile.

"It was all over the news last spring. It would be impossible not to know," Jenna said. Suddenly she found herself asking, "Why did he quit? He was still healthy from what I've read." Then Jenna blushed, knowing perfectly well that it wasn't her concern.

"That was the whole point. Scott wanted to stop at the peak of his career. He's reached his goals, got the championship ring. Deciding it was time to leave, he went into business with Donald and his brothers. Plus, he has other successful investments. Scott has done extremely well financially."

Jenna nodded, having heard more than enough. She wanted Taylor to stop before she started on his personal life. Her heart still ached when she heard about the beautiful women in his life. Jenna rushed on to say, "Good for him. I always knew he would be successful. Please give him my best."

Jenna sipped her drink, hoping that subject was closed. She didn't enjoy reading about him in the tabloids or newspapers. Nor did she like to see his photo in some gossip magazine with yet another gorgeous woman on his arm. It was surprising that he hadn't been engaged or married with a house full of babies. She warned herself it was only a matter of time until Scott was taken. He had it all, in one devastatingly handsome package . . . money, fame, and sex appeal.

Thank goodness they'd both moved on with their lives. It would be a wonder if that man even remembered her name, considering the number of women in his life.

Enough! If she wasn't careful, she would be back to recalling the hard strength of his muscular body, his thoughtfulness, and the generous spirit that made him unique.

Back in the day, she had never had to worry about sharing him, because he'd let it be known they'd belonged to each other. Her competition had come not from other coeds but from the NBA. It had all been over for them once the professional basketball league had entered their lives.

No more! Asking about Scott had been a huge mistake. Maybe Laura and Sherri Ann were right. Perhaps it was time for her to stop the casual dates and get serious about finding a new man.

Taylor said candidly, "I know I shouldn't say this, but I'm still disappointed that things didn't work out for you and Scott. You were so good for him, Jenna."

Jenna shifted uncomfortably in her seat. "Let's not go there. What Scott and I had belongs in the past. Thank goodness we've both gotten over it and gone on with our lives."

"I understand. Wouldn't it be great if you two could end up being friends, though? Scott has moved back to Detroit, too, and he'll be working on finishing his degree in chemistry. He wants to keep the promise he made to our parents."

"Scott's going to finish at U of D-Mercy?"

Taylor beamed. "Yes. You might even run into each other on campus."

While Jenna's heart sank, she kept her smile firmly in place. "Good for him. I imagine your mother is pleased."

She wanted to scream. It wasn't fair! He could have finished college anywhere. Why did he have to come back now? She didn't want to have to look over her shoulder, afraid of running into her ex everywhere she went on campus. What a nightmare!

Taylor went on to say, "You aren't wearing an engagement or wedding ring. Are you seeing someone special?"

Jenna hadn't recovered from the news that Scott was in Detroit. It took her a moment to switch subjects. She laughed, saying, "I've only been back in Detroit a few weeks. Give me a little time."

"There are men in New York, you know. I'm sorry, Jenna! It's none of my business." Taylor squeezed her hand. "But I want you to have the same kind of happiness that Donald and I share." It was evident from the contented smile on her face that they were still very much in love.

Knowing she couldn't take much more of this trip down memory lane, Jenna glanced at her wristwatch. "Taylor, it has been great seeing you again. But I'm afraid I have to go." She leaned over and kissed the baby's forehead. "Take care of this precious baby girl. She is beautiful, just like her mama."

Taylor reached into her generous tote bag and pulled out a small notepad and pen. "Don't rush off until you give me your number."

"Of course," Jenna murmured as she quickly jotted down her number and took Taylor's. Then she kissed Taylor's cheek, grabbed her shopping bags, and hurried away, waving good-bye.

* * *

Scott Hendricks was not sure which had awakened him—the pounding in his head or the bitterness of his sour stomach. He groaned. After he managed to open and focus his bloodshot eyes, he realized that it was the banging on his front door, not the pounding in his head, that was the source of the offense.

He swore heatedly, then wished he hadn't bothered. The sound of his own voice made his head hurt even more. One glance around the room confirmed that he hadn't made it to bed last night. Evidently, he'd fallen asleep in the recliner in the den.

Realizing that the noise wasn't going to stop until he did something about it, he dragged himself to his feet to lumber down the hall of the large six-bedroom house.

"Shut up that fuss!" he yelled, then winced in pain. After disengaging the alarm, then the lock, he yanked the front door open. He glared down from his six-feet-eight-inch height at his older sister. "What are you doing here at this time of the morning?"

"Hello, little brother," Taylor frowned at him.

Scott squinted from the bright sunlight. "Don't you have a family to bother?" Not waiting for an answer, he padded on bare feet along the hardwood flooring back toward the den, where he spent most of his time. It was one of the three rooms that had been furnished in the large house; the others were the master bedroom and the kitchen. He fought the urge to cradle his aching head in his hands, knowing it wouldn't help.

After pushing the door closed, Taylor struggled with three grocery bags as she followed her brother toward the back of the gorgeous, but nearly empty, home. "Did you say morning? It is one thirty in the afternoon, Scott Hendricks. What's wrong, little brother? Head hurt?

Good! It serves you right for drinking like there is no tomorrow," she snapped unsympathetically.

One look in the den told Taylor all she needed to know. "You're a cheap drunk," she accused, scanning the empty imported beer bottles on every available surface. "This has got to stop!" she yelled. "It looks as if you didn't even bother to go to bed last night." Then she switched to pleading. "Scott, what's wrong? You've been going downhill ever since you moved back. Why are you throwing your life away like this?"

"If you came over here to preach, go home," he tossed at her as he made his way toward the master suite on the east side of the house.

She yelled, "I'm not going anywhere until I've talked some sense into you!"

"You don't have to buy my groceries. I do know my way to the store."

"Really? My guess is, you don't have a thing in that refrigerator other than beer."

"Go home," he said, slamming his bedroom door behind him. He swore beneath his breath but heard her say that she was putting on some coffee, and he'd better drink it.

Scott's head hurt so bad he could hardly think. Judging by the determination in his sister's voice, he knew she wasn't going anywhere until they'd talked.

He grumbled aloud, "Maybe she'd make herself useful and throw a couple eggs in the skillet."

He didn't bother to glance around his large, disheveled bedroom. Instead he headed to the bathroom. He stripped down and flung his faded jeans and old U of D-Mercy T-shirt onto the growing pile of dirty clothes beside the full hamper. He was grateful when he found a clean bath towel in the nearly empty linen closet.

The impressive, nearly empty house was a mess, and

it suited him just fine. It fit his current lifestyle. After emptying his bladder, he walked into the oversized marble shower stall. He grunted with appreciation when the multi-head feature sent hot water pounding full blast over his tired, aching body. It felt good. He released a sigh as the water soothed the pain in his head and joints. He felt closer to eighty than his thirty years.

"Why can't she stay out of it?" he grumbled aloud, knowing exactly what to expect from his older sister. Taylor was used to taking care of him. But she wasn't going to let it go. What could he say?

He had no excuse for abusing his body this way. Rather than deal with what was bothering him, he'd tried to drown in a tidal wave of imported beer. Talk about stupid! Yeah, he'd known it would be hard, but he hadn't realized just how bad it would be until he'd made the colossal mistake of moving back to his hometown.

Nearly eleven years . . . a long time. He hadn't even seen it coming when he'd sold his house in L.A. He had enough female friends to distract and keep him occupied, so there were no seemingly endless nights. During the past ten years he only came back for public appearances or basketball clinics during the summers for the kids. A quick few days. There had been no reason to return until his father had died and his family had moved back to the area two years ago. Losing his father had forced him to think about the importance of keeping his word. The time was right.

Now that he was back, his life was falling apart, and his big sister wanted to talk about his problem. She acted as if it could be patched with a kiss and a Band-Aid. Unfortunately, he didn't fully understand what was causing him so much pain.

What was he doing? When had he lost control? Why

did he feel as if he'd been run over by a freight train? What in the hell was there to talk about?

He was supposed to be happy! He'd done every single thing he had set out to do. He was retired with more money than he would ever need or want, but most important, he had quit the game he loved while he'd been at the top. He'd gone out a champion. Sure, he had his share of aches and pains, but nothing serious.

From the first, he'd been surprisingly good at both making money and hanging onto it. He'd invested wisely, including putting money into his brother-in-law's business. That investment had turned out to be highly profitable without his having to show his face. Despite the economy, his business interests were doing extremely well. Life was supposed to be good.

Ten years and he still hadn't fulfilled the promise he'd made to his family when he'd signed with the Charlotte Hornets. He hadn't finished what he started, hadn't gotten his degree. It was something he'd always intended to do, and he'd worked toward it during the off-seasons. He was close, only five classes away. He could do it in a year. For sentimental reasons, he'd let his family talk him into returning home and going to U of D-Mercy. His old stomping ground.

Why was being back causing him such problems? He'd gotten over the breakup years ago. Yet since his return, the memories of that failed relationship bombarded him, consuming his daylight hours and entering his dreams. He'd tried, but he couldn't forget what he'd lost when he'd packed his bags and left Detroit.

For so long pro basketball hadn't been just an occupation to him; it was how he had defined himself. Even his dreams of owning his own pharmaceutical company had paled as his basketball career had soared straight to the top. He had been good. He had been named MVP and had an NBA championship ring to prove it.

He'd started as one of the top draft picks at twenty, instinctively knowing it was where he'd belonged. He had no regrets about his choices. When he'd quit college, he hadn't meant to disappoint anyone—certainly not his parents or Taylor. It was his life, his choice.

What he hated was the effect that decision had had on his personal life. It had shattered a future he'd believed was rock solid. The past was what had been haunting him last night, what had him drinking nearly every night since he'd settled in.

A half hour later, he joined his sister in the sunny kitchen. He wasn't surprised to see that she had loaded and started the dishwasher or cleaned the table and granite countertops of the spacious kitchen.

Taylor was nothing if not efficient. She kept her own home running smoothly. Donald was a very lucky man. He had also retired from the game, but Donald had it all. He had two beautiful children and a woman he loved and knew was in love with him, not his bank balance.

Scott had never had that assurance. Well, that was not exactly true. There was a time in his life when he'd known without a doubt that one special woman had loved him—the man and not the basketball star. Unfortunately, it had ended badly.

These days, the women who ran him down were more interested in what he could provide than in what he thought and felt—or even what type of man he'd become. It was okay with him, since marriage was no longer a priority.

"Good, you made coffee," Scott said as he filled a white mug with black coffee. He dropped heavily into one of the chairs positioned around an oak table that sat in front of floor-to-ceiling windows overlooking a spacious backyard and a lake beyond.

"What's with all the drinking? It's not like you.

What's wrong?" Taylor asked from where she cracked eggs into a mixing bowl at the center island.

"Did you come to preach? I've heard it before. Give it a rest."

"I'm serious, Scott. Ever since you returned to Detroit, you haven't been yourself. I don't like it," she cried out, tears slipping from sad, dark eyes.

Scott went over and gave her a hug. "Please, don't! I'm not worth it." He swallowed with difficulty.

"How can you say something like that? You are my brother, and I love you." She brushed away tears.

"Come on, Sis, quit the water works. How are the kids? How is Donald?"

She smiled at the mention of her family. "Donald is at the office, and he is fine."

"Where are the kids? Don't tell me you left them with a sitter?" He went back to the table and retrieved his steaming mug.

"Donnie's in school and Brianna's with Mama." She stared into the bowl of eggs she'd been whipping before she said, "Our mother is also worried about you. We all are."

"Aw, Sis. That's low."

"If you're bored, you can go and work with Donald. You own a sizeable part of the company."

"I'm not bored."

"Then what?"

Brother and sister were close. Time and distance hadn't changed that. Their years of living together while she'd been single, and he a teenager, had strengthened their bond. They weren't just brother and sister; they were also friends.

When he ignored her question and sipped from his cup, Taylor sighed heavily.

"I thought you liked this house, but you haven't done

a thing to it since you moved in. When are you going to buy some furniture? Just look at this place. You're living in a million-dollar pigpen. What happened to that housekeeper you hired?"

"I fired her. I don't need anyone. I can take care of my own home."

"Really? And you are doing a fine job on your own, oink-oink!" she threw back sarcastically, missing her brother's quick grin. "There was not a clean spot in the whole kitchen . . . a beautiful modern kitchen that any woman would love to work in. It's a shame, too. I had to clean before I could cook. Not one clean dish in the entire place." She paused to catch her breath before she asked, "By the way, when was the last time you ate a home-cooked meal? Not recently," she went on to say, "judging by the stack of take-out cartons I shoved into the trash."

"What difference does it make as long as I eat? When did you get so picky?"

Taylor looked as if she wanted to smack him upside his head. Instead, she flipped the bacon frying on the griddle, then began dicing vegetables for an omelet.

"Stop mothering me, I'm fine." He cradled the large coffee mug in his wide palms as he watched the squirrels' antics in the yard.

"Fine? Hardly. Ordering endless cases of beer isn't the answer. You have nothing to eat in your refrigerator, you knucklehead! Not even milk, eggs, bread, or juice . . . the basics! If I didn't know better, I'd think you were raised by wolves."

"Go home, Sis. I'm a big boy, you don't have to take care of me."

"Keep it up, and I will take back not just the food but also the two loaves of banana nut bread I made this morning," Taylor said as she slid the perfectly cooked omelet brimming with cheese and mushrooms—just the way he liked it—onto a plate.

"You brought banana nut bread?" Grinning, Scott kissed her cheek. "Sorry, Taylor, I didn't mean a word. You know I love you."

"Yeah," she said giving him the plate. "Go ahead, eat. I'll get the orange juice."

Scott's stomach growled from hunger. "Mmm, this is good. I hope Donald knows he's a lucky man."

"He knows. That's not the issue." Taylor brought over a plate of sliced banana nut bread and her own mug. Sipping her coffee, she joined him at the table. "You've got to stop drinking. No decent woman would have you." She glanced at him and saw the hurt in his eyes before he turned his face to look outside. Placing her hand on his shoulder and squeezing, she quickly added, "I'm sorry. I didn't mean it that way. I know you still miss Jenna."

"You know nothing about it. There have been plenty of women in my life since we broke up. Why'd you bring her up? That is old news." He went back to eating.

"Is it? I wonder."

"What is that supposed to mean?"

"You haven't been really happy with a woman in years. At least not the way you were with Jenna."

"That was more than ten years ago! Believe me, there have been a lot of women since her." Scott scowled. He was shaking from a deep-seated anger he wouldn't be able to explain if he'd been questioned about it. Why was he getting so worked up? Why should hearing her name throw him?

"It's being back in Detroit without her, isn't it? That's what is bothering you."

Scott shook his head, determined to concentrate on his breakfast. The last thing he wanted to do was talk about Jenna. "You're wrong. I moved on a long time ago. I suggest you do the same."

If Taylor had her doubts, she didn't voice them. She got up and began to empty the dishwasher.

"Stop that. If I need maid service, I'll call one. Why can't you sit down? Tell me about the kids. How's Donnie doing in school?"

"Okay, no housekeeper or maid service. No problem. I'll just call Virgina Hendricks. The next thing you know, she will be moving in with you, little brother, and straightening out your sorry behind. Your mama don't play."

"Yeah, sure."

"I'm serious. You're drinking like a fish, acting like basketball was your entire life, and it wasn't."

"How do you know what's in my life anymore? I've changed, Taylor. I'm not the same kid you helped raise. I'm all grown up."

She huffed, "You haven't changed that much. I'm talking about who you are on the inside. You were never just a ballplayer. You did a lot of community work while you were in Charlotte and L.A."

"Community work? Like hell! What I did was sign a few checks!"

Taylor shook her head. "It was more than that. You worked with the homeless shelters and Habitat for Humanity after Katrina. You went down to New Orleans and not only gave money but worked. You've hosted basketball camps every summer for kids here in Detroit. You did more than sign a few checks.

"Open your eyes, brother dear. The world didn't end when you retired from the NBA. It's still turning each and every day. What? You think Detroit can't use your help? Think again. There are homeless people here and lost boys all over this city, not believing in their own worth. Bored? Go volunteer at the Malcolm X Community Center. Stop feeling sorry for yourself and get out and help somebody. You're not the only one with problems."

"Why don't you go home and take care of your baby?"

"And leave you alone, right?"

"Right! Why can't you get it through your head that there are some things that my big sister can't fix?"

Taylor sighed, then said, "I decided not to tell you, but I can see it will be worse if you hear this from anyone else."

"What?" he asked after a prolonged silence.

"While shopping at the mall, I ran into Jenna. She has moved back to the city and is teaching at U of D-Mercy."

Three

Scott's heart began to race. His mind filled with questions. Back? Back from where? Had she been alone? Or had she found a man she could control? Someone who would let her run his life to suit herself? Did she complete her all-so-important education?

He didn't voice even one of those questions. He had no business even wondering what she'd done over the years. He swore silently. His sister said nothing more but went right on unloading the dishwasher.

Fed up, he couldn't stop himself from asking, "How is she?"

"Jenna is fine. She's done well for herself. She just finished her doctorate."

He nodded in satisfaction, genuinely happy for her. "She did it. Good for her. Why wouldn't I want to know she's well and happy? We parted on friendly terms. We just wanted different things from life. It happens every day of the week, without hard feelings."

"That's not how it looked to me. You two were very much in love and hurt because of the breakup."

"So? It's history. If you see her again, give her my best," he offered.

"Funny, she said the same thing about you . . . her exact words were 'Give him my best.' "

Finished with his plate, he refilled his mug before saying casually, "See, no problems." Deciding to change the topic, he asked, "Did I tell you my classes start next week? I've got all my books. I talked to my old chem professor. I'm really going to have to brush up on my chemistry. It's been awhile since I've worked in a lab. I plan to do this in two terms, not three. Think I can do it?"

Taylor laughed. "Of course, once you've set your mind to the task. Mama is so excited. I'm glad you're doing this. And not just for you, but for the promise you made Daddy." She hugged him. "I'm glad. Classes starting couldn't have come at a better time."

"I don't believe it! We finally agree on something. The drinking was only a minor distraction. I plan to ace all my classes. Come out with a four point o."

"Sounds good. Now about that housekeeper—"

"Do you ever stop?"

"Nope. If you're not going to get help, at least let me and Mama finish furnishing the house. You're living in only three rooms of a twenty-plus-room mansion."

"I tell you what. You'll be the first one I call when I'm ready."

"But—"

"No buts. Now go home. I've got things to do." He tempered his words by giving her a big hug. "Stop worrying."

"How? I've been worrying about you since Mama and Daddy brought you home from the hospital."

"Do me a favor . . . give it a try."

As he kissed his sister good-bye, his thoughts weren't on the planned dinner with his family later in the week. He was struggling to wrap his mind around the fact that Jenna was in Detroit. And she was teaching at U of D-Mercy.

Taylor seemed pleased that Jenna had asked about him, while he expected no less. They'd parted on friendly terms. Jenna was merely being polite. His sister hadn't said so, but he wouldn't be surprised if Jenna was involved or even engaged by now. She'd always wanted a family of her own. Besides, there was no getting around the fact that she was an incredibly beautiful woman. Some things wouldn't change.

What difference did that make at this late date? A lot of time had passed, and what they'd shared was gone. It no longer mattered why they'd broken up. It may be corny, but he cared enough about her to genuinely want her to be happy.

Running into her on campus might prove to be awkward because of what they'd once shared, but that was okay. They had both moved on with their lives.

Since he'd moved back, he'd really indulged in his own pity-party, focusing on what was lost, not on the future. That had to end today. So what if he didn't play in the NBA? He had reasons to look forward, things to do before classes started. It was time he got started and stopped wasting daylight.

Jenna sighed. What had started out as a gorgeous autumn day, with foliage rich in reds and gold and a warm sun bright overhead, had turned out to be a disappointment. The waiting was frustrating. There were still no definite answers from Jack Collagen, the private investigator she'd hired to find her family. She was growing more impatient with each passing day.

Jenna had dressed in a beige tweed pantsuit teamed with dark brown tights and high-heel ankle boots. A crisp white blouse with French cuffs completed the outfit. Busy rifling through her pockets, she held up the line in the crowded cafe a block from the university. Jenna frantically searched a second time, then a third time. Nothing!

Highly embarrassed, she said to the annoyed cashier, "I'm sorry, but I have to put everything back." She'd left her office with a twenty-dollar bill in her pocket and now stood in front of half the campus, unable to pay for her lunch.

"Let me get that for you," a deep masculine voice said from just over her right shoulder.

"I couldn't . . ." She stopped. Recognizing the voice, she didn't have to turn around, but that was exactly what she did. "Scott!"

Although Jenna was tall at five feet eight, she had to look up—way up—to meet his twinkling dark brown eyes. She hadn't seen him in more than a decade, but she had no trouble recalling every inch of the smooth dark chocolate length beneath the dark green shirt and dark brown cords.

"There's nothing wrong with helping out an old friend, is there?" He didn't wait for an answer but handed over the money. He'd collected her tray and given the cashier a generous tip before Jenna had done more than stare at him in shocked dismay.

Jenna didn't know what to say or do, something that was rare for her. Wordlessly, she followed him across the crowded room to a small corner table.

"Please join me," he said with a smile that made her heart skip a beat, ". . . unless you are meeting someone."

Shaking her head no, Jenna finally found her voice. "Thank you for coming to my rescue. I'll pay you back. I can't believe I lost my money on the way over here. I can't figure out how I did it! And I didn't bother to bring a purse, so I don't have a credit card with me." Realizing she was rattling on, she instantly closed her mouth.

"So you'll join me?"

How could she refuse, considering he had just bought her lunch?

"Yes and thank you." She took the seat across from him. Feeling unbelievably awkward, she clasped her shaking hands in her lap. "So how have you been?"

He reclaimed his seat. "I'm well. It's good to see you. It has been a long time." In his rich baritone, he revealed, "You look good, Jenna, professional and successful."

Jenna laughed. "I don't feel very successful, considering I can't pay for my own meal."

"We all have awkward moments. Believe me, I've had my share. I hear you're back in Detroit and are a full-fledged professor here at U of D-Mercy." As if it had been a champagne flute, Scott lifted his soft drink container in a toast. "Congratulations, Jenna." After taking a swallow, he said, "You made it happen."

Jenna blushed. They both knew what sacrifice she'd made in order to make it happen: the dissolution of their relationship. Not about to touch on that subject, she simply said, "Thank you. And congratulations to you. I hear you've retired at the top of your game. And you've moved back to the area."

He grinned. "Don't need to guess the source of your information, now, do we?"

"Taylor!" They laughed as they both said the name at the same time.

Then there was an uncomfortable silence, as if each was searching for something to say, which was ridiculous, considering how well they knew each other. Once, they'd had no secrets.

"How does it feel to be back in college?" She indicated the chemistry books piled on the chair beside him.

Before he could answer, several students came to the table, asking for autographs. Although she wasn't surprised, she was impressed by his ease in handling the situation. He smiled, reached into the inside pocket of his jacket on the chair, pulled out postcard-size basketball cards, then signed before he politely, but firmly, excused himself.

"Sorry about that," he said with a smile as he reclaimed his chair. "What did you say?"

She watched as he casually exercised the familiar move of leaning back in his seat and stretching long legs out in front of him. Scott's six-foot-eight-inch frame was as long and tight through the midsection as she remembered. There were obvious changes. He was packing a lot more muscle after more than ten years in the tough NBA. He'd shaved his head and sported a single diamond stud in his left earlobe. One look at his dark eyes revealed that at thirty, his boyish good looks had been replaced by faint lines near his eyes, on his forehead, and bracketing his lean cheeks. All spoke to the strength and character he'd gained over the years. Without a doubt, he was a confident, sophisticated man, comfortable in his own skin.

"College. How does it feel to be back?" She picked up the turkey and cheese sandwich that had caused so much trouble and began eating. It tasted like sawdust, but she chewed slowly, as if it had been prime rib.

"There are a few adjustments, but basically it's like riding a bike. It all comes back. I especially enjoy being back in the chemistry lab. And it didn't hurt that I've taken classes during my off-seasons. I only need five classes to finish."

Jenna nodded. "I was surprised when Taylor told me you were back at U of D-Mercy. I assumed you preferred the L.A. lifestyle."

"Detroit is home, especially since my family is here. It seemed right to come back to where I started. I have to admit it's taking some adjustments to being back in the city. There have been lots of changes. And I made a promise to my family years ago. It was a promise I intended to keep. Unfortunately, my father has gone, but my mother and sister aren't about to let me forget."

Frowning, Jenna couldn't help recalling how deeply his decision to quit college and enter the NBA draft had hurt her and left a permanent rift between them.

"Something wrong with your sandwich?"

Shaking her head no, she took another bite. When she finished chewing, she said softly, "I was so sorry to hear about your dad's passing. How is your mother holding up?" She reached out to touch his hand where it rested on the table. Momentarily, she smoothed her fingertips over his knuckles in an all-too-familiar gesture. When she realized what she'd done, she jerked her hand back, busying her hands with opening her water bottle. She took a sip and, even though her lunch had lost its appeal, pulled back the peel of her banana, broke off a piece, and popped it into her mouth.

"Thank you. It was rough for all of us, but my mother is doing remarkably well. She loves living next door to her grandbabies. I assume Taylor told you all 'bout that as well."

"Yes, I also had a chance to meet your little niece. She is adorable."

Scott grinned. "A future heartbreaker, that one. I also have a nephew," he said proudly. Then he paused before he went on to say, "Although I've been back for public appearances and basketball camps during the summer, I haven't lived in Detroit in years. How about you?"

Jenna tried not to show her surprise at his interest. "I finished my undergraduate and master's degrees here. Then I moved to New York City. I worked as a financial adviser and stockbroker for four years while finishing up my doctorate."

"I'm impressed, but not surprised. I always knew you

were a fighter. You never hesitated to go after what you wanted." He tapped the third finger on her left hand. "No engagement or wedding rings? Why? Don't tell me the men in the Big Apple are blind."

"Of course not, but like you, I've been concentrating on what was important to me . . . in my case, it was education. Finally I have my dream job and a new home. It's enough for now. If anyone should have settled down, I would have expected it to be you."

Scott shook his head. "Nope. I haven't taken that big step yet. I suppose I haven't met the right woman. And the money has worked against me. Nowadays, I have to take care that it's not the main attraction. But I have no complaints. How about you?"

"None," she echoed, lifting her chin in order to meet his searching gaze. "What's with the shaved head? Got tired of the barber?"

He chuckled. "When I hit twenty-five, I realized I was losing more and more each day. For vanity's sake, I shaved it all off. Do you like it?" He ran his hand over his smooth scalp.

"I do," she replied, refusing to admit how it only added to his sex appeal.

"What about your family? Have you found them?"

Jenna recalled the hours they had done nothing but talk. And how she had shared her deep desire to have her brother and twin sister back in her life. They'd had no secrets.

She shrugged. "That hasn't gone as well as I would like. I've done all I can on my own. I learned that both Lenna and Lincoln were adopted, but I suspect both of them have had their names changed and that's why I haven't been able to locate them. Recently, I was finally able to hire a top private investigator to look for them. So the answer is no, but I haven't given up on finding my family."

"Good for you."

Jenna was disturbed to realize that his show of support touched her. She glanced at her wristwatch. "I have to go. I have a class at two, and I've got to get back to my office to pick up handouts and my computer." She stood up. "It was good seeing you, Scott."

He rose to his feet. "It was good seeing you, Jenna. May I give you a hug?" He displayed one of his boyish grins.

"Of course." She laughed, accepting his warm hug. "And about the money for lunch . . ." She broke off, aware of his clean male scent, mixed with sandalwood and a hint of vanilla.

"Forget the money. As I recall, back in the day, there were many days when you fed me."

Jenna reached into her pocket and took out a business card. "Please stop by the office so I can pay you back."

"It's not necessary."

"I insist."

He surprised her when he said, "Okay. Let's do dinner some night soon." He reached into his back pocket, took out his wallet, and handed her his card. "My home and cell phone numbers. Give me a call when you are free."

Shaking her head, she whispered, "I don't need this. I don't want you to think . . ."

"Keep it," Scott insisted, his full, generous mouth suddenly taut. "Jenna, I'm under no illusions that you want to get back together. I know better."

She shoved it into her jacket pocket, saying, "I don't think it's a good idea for us to see each other."

"Why? Aren't we still old friends?"

"Friendly, yes. But as far as I'm concerned, it ends there."

"What are you afraid of?"

"Nothing. I just think we've hurt each other enough in the past. There is no reason to look back. I'm focused on the future." Before he could say more, she grabbed her lunch tray and quickly said, "Bye, Scott." She paused at the trash container, then hurried out without a backward glance.

She spent the entire walk back to her office telling herself she was grateful that he hadn't followed her.

That evening Jenna was excited. Having her first dinner party in her new home, she looked around to see what she might have forgotten. She had cooked a pot roast with creamed potatoes and glazed carrots, along with lemon meringue tarts. Everything was waiting in the kitchen. She jumped at the sound of her doorbell, then laughed. Nerves! Crazy, considering she was expecting her very best friends—her foster sisters.

Beaming, she flung the door wide. "Welcome! Please come inside."

Laura walked in first, followed by Sherri Ann. Neither had come empty-handed; both brought house-warming presents.

Exchanging warm hugs, Jenna gushed, "You shouldn't have."

"Okay, we'll take them back," Laura teased. A social worker for the Sheppard Women's Crisis Center, she wore a navy business skirt suit that she'd teamed with a bright green ruffled blouse. She looked snazzy, as always.

"Yeah!" Sherri Ann put in. The young lawyer was dressed in a dark green pantsuit and pale yellow tailored blouse. She worked in a prestigious law firm that handled both criminal and corporate cases. None of the three had chosen to straighten their hair. Laura preferred braids, while Sherri Ann wore locks. Jenna's hair was naturally curly.

Jenna shook her head. "Forget it! Whatever is inside those fancy boxes are mine."

As if her foster sisters hadn't helped her move in, Jenna proudly showed them around. She loved decorating, and she was proud of the finishing touches she'd added. They ended the tour in the spacious living room, where they urged Jenna to open her gifts. Laura had given her a set of beautiful crystal wine goblets. Sherri Ann had brought a crystal serving bowl with a matching platter.

Wiping away tears, Jenna laughed, giving them each yet another hug. "I love them! These are things I'm too cheap to buy for myself. I'm so happy. Glad to be back with my two best friends. It's been so long since we've spent any real time together, not since that long weekend in New York when you two came to visit."

"It's great having you home so we can be together," Sherri Ann said.

"We haven't had a good face-to-face chat since Mrs. Green died a year ago," Laura recalled. "I still miss her. She was so good to us."

Mrs. Green had taught them to stand on their own two feet and not wait for a man to take care of them. She'd assured them that with work, they could do whatever they wanted. There were no limits. She had never let them forget that they had good heads on their shoulders. It was a lesson the girls had never forgotten.

They had worked hard to get where they were, and they didn't hesitate to give the credit to the strong, remarkable woman who had raised them. She'd taught them old-fashioned values and skills. She'd taken them to church. She'd also taught them to cook, clean, sew, and knit.

"I miss her, too. But things were not the same when we had to put her in that nursing home. I hated that," Sherri Ann confessed.

"Me, too. That was no place for such a great lady," Jenna insisted sadly.

"We had no other option. With that Alzheimer's, she didn't know where she was, or what was going on. Taking turns caring for her wouldn't change that. She passed quietly in her sleep without suffering. We need to concentrate on remembering the good times," Laura insisted. "She was a wonderful woman, and she knew we loved her. And we know she loved us." Laura raised her tea cup, toasting. "To Mrs. Green! She did good by us."

Frances Green had been an older widow with no children of her own when she'd opened her home to them. She and her late husband had both been educators. Mr. Green had been a college professor, and Mrs. Green had taught high school English and home economics. She had not let her age stop her from doing what she'd felt she had to do. She'd invested her money wisely and had had no need for the money the state had provided for their care. Every dime the state had given her had gone directly to them for their needs and education. Each girl had had her own bank account and had been encouraged to save as much as possible from a young age.

Jenna had taken Mrs. Green's encouragement to heart. She'd wanted a better life, and she'd been willing to work for it. She'd earned scholarship money, along with money from various jobs. She hadn't stopped until her dreams had come true, but it hadn't been easy.

Many times, she'd grown tired of the long hours and endless studying, but she hadn't quit. Jenna was proud that she hadn't let anything or anyone stop her from reaching her goals. And Jenna was so grateful that Mrs. Green had been there to see her college graduation before taking ill.

"I don't want to think what our lives would have been like without our Mrs. Green. She made ladies out of all of us. Even Laura," Sherri Ann teased.

"Very funny. Unfortunately, true." Laura laughed with them. She'd been a tomboy growing up, hating girly skirts and dresses. When they sobered, she said to Jenna, "I'm glad to have you home where you belong. Even though we talked on the phone during the time you were away, Sherri Ann and I missed you so much."

"Amen to that!" Sherri Ann reached out and squeezed Laura's and Jenna's hands. "We can start doing church and Sunday brunch again." They all nodded their agreement.

"I love this house. Jenna, you've done a great job," Laura said over dessert.

The hardwood floors in the living and dining rooms were covered in matching cream floral rugs with touches of pink and purple, which Jenna had found in a hotel liquidation shop. Drapes and pillows were in Jenna's favorite color of vibrant purple. And the sofa, love seat, and two comfortable armchairs were covered with tailored cream slipcovers that Jenna had made herself. The coffee tables and end tables had been rescued from a curb side. Jenna had stripped and varnished them to a rich walnut.

"Thanks. I love it, although I still have a lot to do, but I'll get to it." Just then the telephone rang. "Excuse me."

Jenna hurried into the kitchen and picked up the extension on the wall. When she returned several minutes later, she was shaking.

"What's wrong?" both foster sisters asked at the same time. They waited anxiously, looking into hazel eyes that were filled with tears. All else was forgotten.

Before Jenna could clear her throat of tears enough to respond, Sherri Ann demanded, "Was that your ex?"

"Why would she cry over that jerk?" Laura asked, a surprising comment coming from a woman who adored men and readily admitted that for her only a rich man would do.

"Scott's not a jerk! He's just a liar who didn't keep his promise. Besides, we have to be fair. She left him, not the other way around," Sherri Ann reminded her friend.

"This isn't about Scott!" Jenna interrupted excitedly. "I just got a call from Jack Collagen, the private investigator. He hasn't found my family yet, but he does have some information."

Sherri Ann had recommended Jack Collagen, who had done work for her law firm. "I'm not surprised," she put in. "Collagen is opinionated and macho but good."

"So what did he say?" Laura quizzed.

"Mr. Collagen has some information about my parents. He's e-mailing the report. Sorry, I cried. I'm just a little emotional tonight. Naturally, I've always wanted to know why they left us. All I know is that my father left first. Then my mother tried to care for us, but she disappeared. I don't think there is a reasonable explanation. It hurt then, and it hurts now. I don't care what he says—nothing in his report will change that."

Laura and Sherri Ann nodded in understanding. Each had been disappointed by parents who hadn't lived up to the label. All three had been left to the state's foster care system at far too young an age.

Jenna smiled. "At least I know who my real family is, even if my brother and sister don't share the same last name."

Sherri Ann said, "You're not alone. You will always

have us. We've been each other's family for over twenty-five years. And that's not about to stop now."

They were her sisters of the heart, and they had grown up together, only a few months apart in age. They'd been six when they'd met in Mrs. Green's living room. Both Laura and Sherri Ann had been in other foster homes.

"Let's hope the report will give you some answers," Sherri Ann remarked.

"Sherri Ann is right. No matter what, we have each other. We're not only best friends, we're sisters!"

"Group hug," Laura called out.

Jenna blinked away her tears. Just knowing that both ladies were in her corner was enough. No matter what secrets were revealed in that report, life was good. And hopefully it was only a matter of time until she could find her brother and twin sister.

"No more beating around the bush. Tell us about Scott. I saw that look on your face when I mentioned his name. Have you seen him, Jenna Marie? Talked to him? Did Taylor give him your number?" Laura looked at her pointedly.

Jenna reluctantly admitted, "I saw him." Knowing Laura wasn't going to stop until she had a full explanation, she said, "I ran into Scott at the cafe near campus. I don't think I've ever been more embarrassed in my life." She covered her face with her hands, recalling her shame.

"What do you mean? What do you have to be embarrassed about, young lady? I know you were looking your best. Mrs. Green's girls always look pulled together," Sherri Ann boasted.

Laura huffed, "I know that's right!"

"Believe me, I was mortified. Here I was at the checkout counter, looking good, without a quarter to my name."

"What!" the ladies yelled.

"Stuck a twenty in my pocket, and evidently I lost it on the walk across campus. I was explaining to the cashier why I was leaving without lunch when Scott came up and paid for my meal. He'd been seated at one of the tables and saw the whole pitiful thing." Jenna blushed, shaking her head.

Her dear friends broke into a peal of giggles.

"Well, thanks a lot!" Jenna snapped.

"What did you say?" Sherri Ann asked.

"What could she say but thank you and keep right on stepping with her lunch," Laura quipped.

Sherri Ann said, "For a woman who adores rich men, sometimes you can be so hard. Remind me not to make you mad."

Jenna rolled her eyes. "Do you want to hear this or not?" She didn't bother to wait for a response but went on and told them about her lunch with Scott.

Four

It was Laura who prompted. "So how did he look? Still tall, dark, and absolutely gorgeous?"

Jenna frowned. The man had always been easy on the eye. "He looks older and even better looking. Time has definitely been good to him. He has never had to do without female attention, that's for sure."

"He had to do without you when he broke his promise to finish college and get married. I'd say it was his loss, not the other way around," Laura emphasized.

Jenna was glad to hear the reassurance. "It doesn't really matter anymore. We've been over for a long time. And we both have focused on what we wanted out of life."

"I can't help wondering why he has never married or even gotten engaged," Laura confessed.

"Why bother? We'll never know." Sherri Ann shrugged, "Like you said, he was the one who lost the prize. And what did he gain—fame and fortune. He's been busy buying happiness. He probably can't find a woman who really wants him."

"Why are we rehashing this? There is nothing to discuss!" Jenna snapped, suddenly tired of the discussion.

"Huh-oh. What's gotten into you? Why are you upset?" Sherri Ann quizzed.

"I'm not upset! I'm just tired of this subject. First Taylor showing me pictures of him, then Scott on my case after running into each other, and now you guys want to hear about him. Enough already! I'd much rather discuss something that matters, such as how long before I hear word of Lincoln and Lenna."

Laura patted Jenna's shoulder. "Hopefully it will be soon. Try not to worry."

"It's going to work out. Collagen is the best. He's worth every dime." Sherri Ann surprised Jenna when she asked, "What do you mean Scott was on your case?"

Before Jenna could respond to that question, Laura asked, "Does he want you back?"

"No!" Jenna insisted.

Laura demanded, "Then what?"

"For some strange reason known only to him, he thinks we can go back to being friends. He gave me his cell and home telephone numbers. I guess he wants to hang out, I don't know. Maybe talk about his new lady friends, but my answer was a big fat no. I'm not going backward. Life's too short."

"Maybe he wants to hook up?" Laura surmised.

"Wow!" Sherri Ann said. "From what I understand, the sex between you two was very good!"

Jenna screeched, "I don't believe you said that! I never told either one of you about what happened in bed between Scott and me."

"So what? We're not stupid. We knew what put that sappy smile on your face, girlfriend," Laura teased.

"I repeat, I'm not going backward. Once was enough. Nor do I want to share a man. And with him it's definitely about being added to his long list of conquests," Jenna snapped. She had no regrets. She enjoyed deciding what was best for her, and she was proud of her accomplishments. She had done well without Scott in her life. She didn't need or want him back.

"All I know is, this is the most you talked about the man since you broke up. Did you hear that, Laura? Our girl isn't interested in second place," Sherri Ann said playfully.

"Yeah. You go, Ms. Gaines."

"So now that's settled, let's talk about important stuff. Are there any single men on the faculty?" Sherri Ann quizzed.

Jenna joined in the laughter. "A few," she hedged, certain the last thing she needed right now was a relationship to complicate her life. But male friends were a good thing. She had been pleased to see Jackson Knight, a familiar face, at the faculty dinner party.

Jackson was a few years older, and the two of them had once worked together at the university's computer lab. Jenna had been completing her undergraduate degree while he'd been finishing his master's degree. Over the years, Jackson had gone on to finish his studies, had taught at an Ivy League school, before he obtained tenure and now taught engineering classes at the U of D-Mercy.

"Well?" Laura and Sherri Ann demanded.

"I ran into an old friend at a faculty event." Jenna went on to explain that she and Jackson were merely friends, and they'd gone out a few times. There wasn't really anything to talk about.

Jenna was relieved when Laura changed the subject by telling them about the mentoring project she was starting for teen girls in foster care at the women's center.

After her foster sisters had gone, Jenna went to check her e-mail and found the update the private investigator had left for her. He revealed what she'd long suspected: that both her parents were dead. She was, nonethe-

less, saddened by the details. Fred Gaines and Jennifer
Haynes Gaines had been college lovers. They'd married
because Jennifer had become pregnant, but things had
gone sour for them. Fred had not been prepared to deal
with the responsibility of supporting a family. They'd
both been only children, and both sets of parents—
Jenna's grandparents—had also been deceased. From
what Collagen could find, there had indeed been no
stray aunts and uncles or cousins to be found. Jenna's
father, Fred, had been killed in a car crash less than a
year after he'd walked out on his family.

She also discovered that her mother had died from a
deadly combination of alcohol and pills. No one knew
if her death had been an accident or suicide. Collagen
also reported that Jennifer had been hospitalized for de-
pression a brief time after her husband had left her to
raise their three children alone.

That night Jenna was awake for hours thinking
about her parents and her lost siblings. Even after sharing the news with her foster sisters during their nightly
three-way call, Jenna's heart was heavy. Her thoughts
were filled with so many memories of Scott. On nights
like this, when she'd been sad or awakened from a bad
dream about her family, Scott had simply held her close.
He hadn't made empty promises that it would be alright. He'd held onto her, let her know she was not all
alone in the world. He'd been there for her.

Why was she thinking of him now? It wasn't as if
she missed him. So why did she suddenly feel the need
to share her news with him? It was crazy. They weren't
friends. It was hours before she could push Scott out of
her thoughts and finally fall asleep.

Jenna chewed on the corner of her lip as she waited for
someone to answer the phone. Her glance darted anxiously around her living room. She had put off making

the call as long as she could, but the deciding element had been the arrival of a dozen purple and pink tulips.

She hadn't even had to open the card to know they'd been from Scott. Her hands had been shaking when she had finally gotten around to opening the envelope. She'd been shocked that he'd remembered that she loved tulips more than roses. It had been a simple thank-you for their lunch. He'd had them sent to her office on campus since he hadn't had her home address.

"Hello?"

"Hi, Taylor, it's Jenna."

"Hi, girlfriend. I'm so glad you called. In fact, I was just going to call you. How's it going? Are you all settled in?"

Jenna was frustrated because she couldn't say what she was really thinking. This was a duty call—it had nothing to do with their past friendship. Unfortunately, she cared about Taylor and couldn't bring herself to state the facts. Taylor had always been kind to her, and Jenna loved her and missed her. Why did Taylor have to be Scott's sister?

Jenna shifted, struggling to get comfortable. Then she said, "Things are going well. And I'm all settled into the house and my job."

"Great! Running into you gave me an idea. I have been talking to some of our old coworkers at the campus's old computer lab. We haven't seen each other in so long. Now that you're back in town, I thought it would be great to plan a little get-together in your honor." When Jenna didn't answer, Taylor asked, after a lengthy pause, "Jenna, are you still there?"

Struggling to keep her voice calm, Jenna forced herself to say, "Yes, I'm here. Just surprised."

"Don't worry. You don't have to do a thing but show up. I'm planning it for next Wednesday evening at my house. Please say you can come."

No! Jenna wanted to scream into the telephone. The reason she'd called was to get Scott's address so she could send him back the money she owed him. And thank him for the flowers. That was it. What had she gotten herself into?

Taylor went on to say, "I talked to Richard Hawkins, Sarah Campbell, Margaret Jones, Jane Peters, and Jackson Knight and Janet Hartman. All of us are looking forward to seeing you and each other and catching up on our lives. It's going to be so much fun. Say you can come, Jenna."

Jenna knew she couldn't say no because she was afraid she would run into Scott again. She was turning into a coward, and she knew it. Besides, this get-together had nothing to do with Scott. Just old friends getting reacquainted.

"I don't know, Taylor. I wouldn't want to put you to so much trouble."

"Trouble? Not at all. I love to entertain. Donald, the big tease, would say it was a good excuse for me to show off my cooking skills and the house, but that isn't true. Is Wednesday a bad night for you? I could try Thursday?"

Jenna found herself saying, "No, Wednesday is fine. Yes, I'd love to come. Thanks for asking."

"You're very welcome. Give me your address. I'm going to send an invitation with all the information on how to get to the house."

"I thought you said this was an informal get-together."

"It will be. But my mother taught me to do things the right way. Go ahead. I have a pen." After Jenna complied, Taylor surprised her when she laughed, saying, "I forgot you made the call. Was there something you wanted other than to talk?"

"Nothing important." Jenna took the easy way out. "See you on Wednesday. Bye."

Besides, she didn't want to talk to Taylor about her brother. Why open that can of worms? How could she explain that she wanted to mail a twenty-dollar check to a man who was a multimillionaire? It didn't make a lick of sense. What difference did it make if she didn't thank him for the flowers? Better yet, she would just forget about the whole thing. Scott was no longer a part of her life, regardless of how many nights she stayed awake thinking about him.

Jenna tried to ignore the way she shivered as goose pimples covered her arms. As she stared at the tulips in her best crystal vase on the coffee table, she tried not to think of the man who'd sent them.

She'd done the right thing by agreeing to go to next Wednesday night's get-together. She hadn't hurt a friend, and she wouldn't fool herself any longer; Taylor was her friend, someone she cared about. And she was looking forward to talking to their old friends, some of whom she hadn't seen in years.

It was good she hadn't mentioned Scott. Now all she had to do was convince herself that it really didn't matter whether he came or not. Besides, Scott had never worked at the computer lab. Enough! She wasn't going to live each day worrying every minute that she might run into Scott Hendricks.

She couldn't be happier with her life choices. She had moved beyond trying to please Scott. There was no need to look backward, especially when she had so much to look forward to. The party would be fun.

When Jackson invited her to go with him to the get-together at the Williamses', Jenna firmly pushed any wayward doubts away and said yes without hesitating. She would be pleased to have Jackson at her side.

On the night of the party, she was proud that she

wasn't stressing over what she'd wear or what to do with her hair. She intended to focus on being the confident woman who had achieved many of her goals. She also intended to focus on having a good time.

Her cell phone rang while she smoothed on a plum-colored knit, knee-length dress. She'd filled the V-neckline with a rope of pearls and a gold necklace. Certain it was her date calling to say he was running late, she didn't even glance at the caller ID when she answered, "Hi, Jackson . . ."

"Ms. Gaines?"

"Yes?"

"This is Collagen."

"Yes, Mr. Collagen?" She didn't try to conceal the worry that crept into her voice.

"I think I've found him."

Jenna's heart began to pound loudly in her ears. "My brother? You found Lincoln!" she screamed, nearly dropping the telephone in her excitement. She was shaking so badly that she had to sit down on the bed. It took several moments to get her next words out. "Are you sure?"

"No, I'm not. But you asked me not to approach him. He lives in a suburb outside of Cleveland, Ohio. And he fits the general description. He was adopted when he was seven. His name is Lincoln Nicholas, and he's an attorney."

"Lincoln Nicholas," she whispered, unaware of the tears that trickled down her face, blurring her vision.

"I have to warn you that without approaching him, I can't be certain he was Lincoln Gaines. The circumstances seem perfect, but he might not be your brother. Now, if you'd only let me talk to him even briefly, I might save you a needless trip down here."

"No, please don't talk to him. I want to do this myself. What do your instincts tell you?"

There was a distinct hesitation before he answered, "I believe this is Lincoln Gaines, your brother."

"Thank you, Mr. Collagen."

"Have a pen and paper?"

"Yes. Just a moment." Jenna searched through her nightstand until she found both, then carefully wrote down the address and directions to Lincoln's house. She read them back to Jack Collagen just to make sure she'd gotten it right. He gave her Lincoln Nicholas's work and home addresses and telephone numbers.

"How soon can you get here?"

"I can leave on Friday morning."

"Do you want me to meet you at his home? I can come with you when you approach him."

"Thanks, Mr. Collagen, but I have to do this my way. I'll call you as soon as I know something. Thanks again."

"Don't thank me yet, I might be wrong. Good luck, Ms. Gaines," Jack Collagen said before hanging up.

Jenna didn't know what to think. She was suddenly overwhelmed with emotions, including fear. She closed her eyes, concentrating on breathing evenly and deeply. As her heart rate slowed, she grinned. She simply savored the hope that this could indeed be Lincoln, her long-lost brother. It could be him. It was him. It just had to be. Her head was spinning with excitement as she pressed trembling hands to damp cheeks. Goodness! She would have to redo her makeup. So what if she was going to be late? None of that mattered. She might have found her brother!

Scott had always said she would find her siblings someday. He'd teased that she was too stubborn to give up. Even back then, he'd spent hours on the Internet, helping her sort through information. Years later, he'd made a point of asking if she'd found her family. He was going to be pleased.

As she creamed away her eye makeup and reapplied shadow and eyeliner to swollen lids, she was startled to realize that the first person she'd thought to share the news with was Scott. Why not her foster sisters? Or even Taylor? They'd all supported her efforts to locate her family and knew how much finding them meant to her. Why Scott? They hadn't been close in years.

Yet she couldn't dismiss the many nights that he had held her close, comforting her. He'd listened to her fears and assured her that it was only a matter of time. One of the things that had drawn her to him from the first was his views on the importance of family. She had no doubts that despite their estrangement, Scott would be genuinely happy for her. He would also be the one person she shouldn't tell.

When the doorbell rang, Jenna greeted Jackson with a warm smile. It never occurred to her to share her news with him.

Jenna arrived on the Williamses' doorstep on Jackson's arm, looking forward to the evening ahead. She couldn't count the number of part-time jobs she'd had over the years in her quest to finish her schooling, but the computer lab had been the most pleasant by far. She'd met some wonderful people and formed lasting friendships.

"Jenna!" Donald smiled down at her from his superior height of six-eight. He was just as handsome and warm as she remembered. Without hesitation he swept her into a bear hug. "How are you, little one? It has been too long."

Jenna laughed, feeling confident that she not only looked her best but was also ready for anything. Given the fact that she was wearing three-inch heels, there were very few people who could call her little and mean it. She was glad that her date was above-average height.

Jackson was six-two, an attractive, confident man in his late thirties.

"It's wonderful to see you, Donald. You look great and so fit."

Donald laughed. "Thanks. Jackson, it's good to see you, man." He shook hands. "Come on in." He stepped back, taking her black wool shawl embroidered with colorful butterflies along the borders. "Taylor! Our guest of honor has arrived."

Jenna was quickly swept up in a hug from Taylor. Like her husband, she didn't seem taken aback to see Jenna with Jackson. Then there were hugs from Janet and Sarah, both students when they'd worked in the lab. Like Jenna, they now both worked at the university. Richard Hawkins was with Jane Peters. They had married and now had three young sons. Soon Jenna and Jackson were laughing over old times with the others.

Taylor said, "Come on, Jenna. I want to reintroduce you to my mother."

The house was large and lovely, but Jenna barely had a chance to do more than glance around as Taylor led her into the charming family room, where the beautiful older woman was comfortably seated on the sofa.

"Mama? You remember Jenna Gaines. Jenna, my mother, Virgina Hendricks."

Opening her arms for a hug, Mrs. Hendricks said, "It's good to see you, my dear. How are you?"

Jenna leaned down and returned the welcoming hug. "I'm fine. Thank you. It's a pleasure to see you again. You are looking well." She hadn't forgotten how warm and generous Mrs. Hendricks had been when Jenna had visited her home in Florida years earlier with Scott.

"I understand from Taylor that congratulations are in order."

"Oh, you mean finishing my degree? Thank you. It's taken a while," Jenna said with a laugh.

Mrs. Hendricks said, "And your new job. I can only imagine how challenging it's been for you, doing it all on your own. You should be so proud of yourself."

Jenna smiled, touched by the older woman's sincerity. She had expected to be a bit uncomfortable with Scott's family, considering she'd been the one responsible for the breakup. They'd been estranged for years. Jenna found Taylor and Scott's mother to be warm and genuine. She had no trouble seeing where Taylor got her generous spirit and good looks. Virgina Hendricks was still a lovely woman.

Just then the doorbell sounded and Taylor excused herself. Jenna took the opportunity to offer Mrs. Hendricks condolences over the loss of her husband.

"Thank you, my dear. I appreciate it." She patted the seat cushion beside her. "Sit down. Tell me about your classes."

Jenna nodded and took the seat. "I'm teaching four classes this term. I must admit, I was a little nervous at first. My classes are going well now that I've gained more confidence. I'm enjoying teaching, and my students are learning economics despite their complaints that I give them too much work," she laughed.

"Wonderful. I imagine it has been quite a challenge," the older woman said.

Jenna smiled. "It has been, but you won't hear me finding fault. I love the work."

Just then Scott appeared at their side. He leaned down and kissed his mother's cheek. "Hi, Mama. Jenna," he said, resting his hand on his mother's shoulder.

"You're late," his mother gently scolded, squeezing his fingers. "What happened?"

"I was working in the chemistry lab and lost track of time. I already apologized to Taylor."

"Lucky for you she has plenty of food. For being late, she should make you clean up," Mrs. Hendricks teased.

Jenna dropped her lids, aware of his dark, intense gaze moving over her length to linger on her legs crossed at the knees. Immediately, she felt at a disadvantage. She rose to her full height.

Scott laughed. "It wouldn't be the first time. It's good to see you, Jenna. You are looking beautiful tonight. How are you?"

"Well, thank you." Jenna blinked, suddenly uncomfortable that she had come here with another man. What had seemed like a good idea at the time suddenly felt wrong.

Just then Jackson joined her, placing a possessive arm around her waist. He kissed her cheek before he said to the much taller man, "Hello, Hendricks. How have you been?"

The two men shook hands, then Scott introduced his mother. Jenna was growing more uncomfortable with each passing moment, so she asked Mrs. Hendricks if she could get her something from the buffet in the dining room.

"No, thank you, my dear. Please, you go ahead." The older woman smiled kindly.

Not the least bit hungry, Jenna was nevertheless relieved that she could excuse herself and leave the room. She headed for the dining room, not waiting to see if her date kept pace.

"Oh, my!" Jenna exclaimed when they entered the other room, more for Jackson's benefit than her own. "Taylor has outdone herself tonight. What a spread." Indeed, the sideboard and table were brimming with an elegant array of dishes. "Have you tasted Taylor's stuffed potatoes? Or her prime rib? If you haven't, you are in for a real treat."

Jackson took her hand. When she glanced up at him, he asked pointedly, "Should I ask if I interrupted anything earlier?"

"What do you mean?"

"You and Scott. It is over, isn't it?"

Five

"That's ancient history," was all Jenna managed to get out. She should have expected the inquiry rather than being shocked by it, but things weren't going as expected.

"Glad to hear it. Let's look for those potatoes, they sound good."

Jenna smiled, relieved by the change of topic. "Look, Taylor has filled finger potatoes with cheese and lobster meat tonight," she said as she headed for the stack of plates and silverware. She wasn't hungry, but she planned to fill her plate—anything to avoid answering any more questions about her long-dead relationship with Scott.

As the evening progressed, Jenna was able to relax enough to enjoy herself. Jackson had many of the qualities she was looking for in a man. Besides being single, above average in height, and well educated, he was quite funny, quickly putting others at ease. He also seemed genuinely interested in her and actually listened to her opinions. If only Jenna could just forget about Scott. Every time she glanced up, she expected to see him.

"It's so good to have you both here," Taylor said as she walked up to them. "Can I get you anything?"

"Not a thing. I couldn't ask for better food or company. And you are a wonderful hostess. How could anyone not be having a great time?" Jenna praised.

"I couldn't agree more." Jackson leaned forward to kiss Taylor's cheek. "You throw a slamming party, pretty lady. Tell Donald to watch his back. You, my friend, are a gem."

"Hey, I heard that," the man in question laughed. Donald slid his arm around his wife's waist. "I'm no fool. I know what a lucky man I am."

Blushing, Taylor gazed into her husband's adoring eyes. "I'm the lucky one. Donald is a fabulous husband and father."

Jenna looked on with a thoughtful smile. Taylor deserved true happiness. The deep love the two of them shared was both a genuine joy to observe and an affirmation of what Jenna held dear and longed to have in her life. There had been a time when she'd thought she'd found that remarkable man, but she'd been wrong. Now, she could only dream of sharing such an incredible and enduring love.

"And you, Taylor, are an exceptional mother and wife. I'd say you both are blessed." The male voice was deep, resonating with conviction. Scott went on to say, "What you two share is rare."

Jenna's face suddenly felt warm, flushed with heat. Scott stood directly behind her. Her awareness of him seemed to race along her nerve endings. Although she couldn't see him, that didn't stop her from feeling the power of his personality or the force of his male charm. Even in a well-educated, sophisticated crowd like this, he stood out. And it had nothing to do with his fame or wealth. Both women and men were drawn to Scott. Despite their past failure, Jenna was no exception.

Time had provided a healing balm that had eased

the disappointment of their lost love. Thank goodness it no longer hurt to be in the same room with him. She longed for indifference, where it no longer mattered.

Yet their time together hadn't all been a disappointment. Jenna recalled the number of times she had received Scott's support and encouragement when she'd feared that she would never see her family again. He had never failed her and had always believed. Her call from Jack Collagen suddenly came to mind.

"Scott, that was so sweet. Thank you," Taylor beamed.

"Taylor, everything has been simply wonderful, but those ribs are out of this world. Did you make them yourself?" Barbara McCall asked, joining their group.

Jenna was relieved that the conversation had switched to something other than true love. She wasn't interested in a stroll down memory lane, especially not tonight, of all nights. She was here with a new man, who seemed to care for her. That was what she should be focusing on.

Nonetheless, she was bubbling with excitement at the very real possibility of finding her brother. She'd been holding the news close to her heart all evening and needed to share it with someone. Someone who understood her and what she'd gone through and longed for, for so long. Taylor should have been the logical choice. Why hadn't she pulled her aside?

For some unknown reason her gaze kept returning to Scott. No, that wasn't exactly accurate. Jenna knew why she ached to tell Scott about Lincoln. Scott had been the one who'd held her when she'd woken up crying and shaking from the familiar, yet hated, nightmare. In the dream she'd been continuously searching for and calling out to her family without success. The worst part was that when she'd woken up, she'd known it hadn't been a fantasy but her reality.

During their time together, Scott's soothing touch had eased her pain, and he'd dried her tears. He knew what she'd gone through and would understand the impact this news would have on her life.

When her eyes began filling up with tears, Jenna quickly excused herself and hurried out of the room. She continued on past the kitchen until she could slip out a side door that led to the rear veranda. She had no idea how long she stood outside, taking slow, calming breaths. Although the night air soon chilled her bare arms, she didn't go back inside. Struggling to get her emotions under control, Jenna jumped when she felt a man's jacket, still warm from his body, settle over her shoulders.

Jenna didn't need to turn to recognize the jacket's owner. His clean male scent, combined with the scent of his aftershave, was unforgettable.

Determined to ignore the way her body filled with longing, Jenna refused to turn toward him. Taking a deep breath, Jenna murmured, "Thank you, Scott. I know I should have gone back inside, but I needed a few minutes to get myself together. And thanks for the flowers."

"Something's wrong?"

She shook her head, her lips automatically curving into an engaging smile. "Nothing is wrong. In fact, things could not be better."

"Then why are you out here alone? And not inside showing off your new man."

Jenna heard the censor in his voice and turned to look at him. She shook her head, clarifying, "Jackson is an old friend, just like everyone here tonight."

"There are all kinds of friends, including the ones that sleep together."

Jenna glared at him. "Do you have to be so tacky?"

Not waiting for a response, she blurted out, "I have news. Jack Collagen, the private investigator, called just before I was leaving tonight. He thinks he has found my brother. I still can't believe it!"

Scott let out a loud hoot and swept her up into a tight hug. He easily lifted her off her feet. "Sweet thing, that is fantastic! Are you sure? That it's really Lincoln?"

Laughing, Jenna didn't scold him for using the familiar endearment, but she sobered enough to pull back and say, "At this point, I don't know anything for sure. But I'm excited."

"Why would he call if he weren't sure?"

"Because I asked him not to approach Lincoln. I want to do it myself. Mr. Collagen did the background work. Now the rest is up to me," she said, beaming at Scott.

He shook his head. "Jenna, I don't like the sound of that. You plan to go meet a stranger that . . ."

"It's the way I want it," she said, her chin lifted stubbornly.

"Jenna, you don't know what you may be getting into. Tell me this Collagen will at least be with you."

Jenna laughed. "I could tell you that, but it would be a lie. I'm doing this alone. By Friday evening I should know, one way or the other, if I've found my long-lost brother." She grinned, wrapping her arms around herself. "Wish me luck, Scott. Please."

Scott surprised her when he encircled her waist and brushed his lips against hers in a brief, but tender, caress. "I'm going to do more than that. I am going with you."

"What?"

When she shook her head no, Scott placed his fingertips over her soft, full lips. "No argument. You don't have to do this alone. Let me come with you. Let me be there beside you." He grinned, "I can't count the number of ways you supported me when we were together. You always had my back."

"I don't know what to say," she whispered aloud. "I'm sure you have better things to do this weekend than to drive to Ohio. Cleveland is not exactly around the corner, you know."

"So, he's in Cleveland. You plan to drive? Look, I have a better idea. My buddy Ralph Prescott has a fleet of private planes. It wouldn't be a problem to use one for the weekend. We can be there in less than a half hour in the air."

"No! This isn't some jet-setting, glamorous weekend. This is serious. It's about my brother, whom I have waited most of my life to see again. I planned to drive to Ohio to see him. My car may be old, but it got me from New York. It will get me to Ohio. You do whatever you need to do to get lucky, but keep me out of it."

Scott laughed without humor. "That was low, babe." He took a step back and held his hands up defensively. "It was nothing more than a suggestion. If you feel I'm being too pushy, I will back away. I know how much this means to you, and I only want to ease your way."

Frowning, Jenna realized she was being unfair to him. He was only trying to help. "Sorry, I know I overreacted a little."

"You think," he teased.

She laughed, placing her palm against his heart, then suddenly jerking it away when she realized she was touching him as freely as if they'd still been lovers. "Look, I appreciate the offer, but . . ."

"I know you have your own plans, and I promise not to interfere in any way. I just want to be there, just in case you need a friend to back you up. You want to drive, then we'll drive. Please, Jenna, just let me be there with you."

Jenna knew she didn't need backup. And even if she did, she could ask her foster sisters or Jackson to go with her. Yet for some strange reason, it felt right to have Scott at her side. She tilted her head to the side, unaware of the way she worried her bottom lip.

"Jenna?" he prompted.

"You're an excellent driver. Remember on the drive down to Florida with Taylor for the holidays? We had a great time."

He grinned, "Yeah. With two ladies in the car, we hit every rest stop between here and St. Petersburg. So what time do you want me to pick you up? Or would you rather pick me up?"

"You pick me up. Nine too early?"

"Not for me."

"Hey! You two alright out here? I don't need to call the cops, do I?" Taylor called from the side doorway.

"We're fine. Just sharing news. Come on, Scott. It's getting cold out here." Jenna sent him a teasing smile over her shoulder before she crossed to Taylor. "I've good news. The private investigator I hired thinks he found my brother, Lincoln. Scott has agreed to go with me to check things out."

"Jenna! That's wonderful!" Taylor gave her a quick hug.

Jenna laughed, "I didn't want to say anything in front of the others, not until I know more. It might not be Lincoln. Then I'd have to start all over." Recognizing that she was babbling, she stopped talking.

"I understand." Taylor kissed her cheek. "But I'll have my fingers and toes crossed that it is your Lincoln. Can I tell Donald later?"

"Of course." It wasn't until they were inside that she remembered she still had Scott's jacket draped over her shoulder. Turning back to him, she said, "Thanks, Scott, for everything." She gave back the garment.

He smiled. "Any time."

Just then, Mrs. Hendricks came into the rear hallway with Jackson right behind her. "I was beginning to wonder where everyone ran off to. Is something wrong?"

"Nothing. I was just going to put more cream puffs in the oven." Taylor tucked her arm through her mother's. "Come along, Mama. You can help with the chocolate sauce."

Mrs. Hendricks smiled. "I'd be glad to, dear. Scott, why don't you come also. I have to tell you what that nice Mrs. Roberts said about you."

Scott looked from Jenna to Jackson before he asked Jenna, "You okay?"

"I'm fine." Jenna walked over to Jackson. Smiling, she said, "Were you by any chance looking for me?"

"I wondered where you'd gone off to," Jackson said pointedly.

Jenna looped her arm through his. "I just went out to get some fresh air. It was getting crowded in here."

Jackson nodded, following Jenna back into the living room, where most of the guests were congregated near the impressive fireplace. Flames flickered in the grate, lending a cozy atmosphere to the room.

When he hesitated, Jenna glanced up at him curiously. "Yes?" she prompted.

"Is something going on between you and Hendricks that I should know about? Every time I turn around, you're with him."

"As I told you earlier, Scott and I are just friends. Taylor, Scott, and I were talking. Just like you and I are old friends."

"You and I never lived together," he shot back.

"That's old news, Jackson, and rather boring. Why are we even discussing it?"

"Perhaps because the other guests are talking about it?"

"That's not surprising. Scott is a celebrity. He draws attention wherever he goes. That has nothing to do with me. Can we please talk about something else?"

"Fine with me. I just wanted to make sure I wasn't stepping where I had no business going."

"You're not, Jackson."

He nodded, picked up two wineglasses, and offered her one. She thanked him. She was relieved when he began telling her about a project he was doing with his engineering students.

It was after ten when Jenna said, "It's getting late, and I have class in the morning. Jackson, would you mind if we leave a bit early?"

"No problem. Some of the others have also started making the rounds, saying their goodnights."

By the time they approached Donald and Taylor near the foyer, the crowd had indeed thinned out. As Donald placed her evening wrap around her shoulders, Jenna was glad the evening was drawing to an end. She felt both physically and emotionally drained. She told herself she had no reason to be uneasy as they bid the others goodnight. And she wasn't annoyed by the way Jackson and Scott eyed each other as if they were sworn enemies. They were acting like little boys, fighting over a favorite toy. Men! She was her own person. And she could easily do without both of them.

"Thanks, Taylor. I had a lovely time. It was great seeing everyone again."

"Next time we won't wait ten years," Taylor teased.

"Good idea!" Jenna laughed.

"Come for dinner soon," Donald offered, exchanging a handshake with Jackson.

"Thanks!" Jenna called as she allowed Jackson to take her hand and lead her to his car.

"Enjoy yourself?" Jackson asked as he held the door for her.

Jenna was too tired to do much more than nod. The euphoria she'd felt at the thought that Collagen might have found her brother was wearing off, to be replaced by the real possibility that she might be setting herself up for a major disappointment. What if it wasn't her Lincoln in Ohio? No! She wouldn't let herself think negatively. She had waited and prayed that she would find her family. She wasn't going to let a case of nerves get in the way.

Preoccupied with thoughts of her brother, Jenna was surprised when Jackson pulled to a stop in her drive. She searched through her evening bag for her keys as they mounted the porch stairs.

"You've been awfully quiet on the drive home. Is something wrong?"

Jenna paused, then looked up into her escort's handsome face. She suddenly realized that she hadn't spared him more than a passing thought all evening. He deserved better. Yet she didn't know him well enough to share her family problems with him. She searched for an explanation that wasn't too revealing.

"Nothing is wrong, Jackson." Forcing a smile, she said, "I'm sorry if I seem self-absorbed. A family problem I need to sort out."

"So dating me isn't about you trying to make Hendricks jealous."

Shocked, Jenna quickly shook her head. "No way! Our dating has nothing to do with Scott. I wouldn't be dating you if I wanted to get back at him. That wouldn't be fair. You're a special man, Jackson. I'm looking forward to getting to know you better."

Jackson studied her, courtesy of the porch light that had been left on. He smiled. "Good." Taking her keys, he unlocked her front door.

Jenna stepped inside and quickly punched in the code

for the alarm. Before she could move away, Jackson cupped her shoulders. "You're so beautiful. I can't help being a little jealous. In my opinion, Hendricks was a fool to ever let you go. I won't make that mistake." He leaned down and pressed a kiss on her lips.

Jenna closed her eyes, painfully aware that she didn't feel a thing. Jackson had many of the qualities she admired in a man. He was highly respected at the university. He was single, highly intelligent. He wasn't a womanizer, out for what he could get.

Jenna hadn't cared for his display of jealousy, though. They'd only been out a few times. They'd shared a few lunches on campus and dinners and kisses, but she sensed he was looking for the right woman and wanted to settle down. Jenna also felt he was moving too fast. She couldn't keep up.

She sighed with relief when he didn't deepen the kiss but pulled back. Just because she wasn't ready for the sexual intimacy didn't mean she didn't care about him, though. Jackson was a nice guy.

But Jenna had only shared her body and her heart with one man. When things had gone wrong between them, it had been the worst kind of hurt imaginable. For so long, she'd felt as if she'd lost a vital part of herself that she wouldn't ever get back. Thankfully, that was behind her. Dread was too mild a word to express her doubts about starting over.

Just when she'd thought she was ready to hopefully get her feet wet and get involved with a new man, her ex-love had come back into her world. Now the complication of finding her family had entered into the mix. Plus, she was letting Scott go with her to meet her brother. It was too much.

"Thanks, Jackson. I enjoyed myself. Goodnight."

"Night, Jenna," he smiled and squeezed her hand.

After locking up, Jenna slowly made her way into her bedroom. She pushed away the unanswered questions, the worries and doubts. It was time for bed. She was fresh out of answers. Besides, tomorrow would be here soon enough. She planned to hold onto the real possibility that she could be reunited with her brother, Lincoln, very soon.

Six

Jenna jumped at the sound of the doorbell, then laughed at herself. It was only Scott. He'd invited himself along on this trip because he wanted to help.

"Coming!" Jenna hurried out of the kitchen. "Right on time," she said, unlocking both the screen and front doors. "Wow! It's cold out there," she said, running her hands up and down sweater-covered arms. "I'm going to have to put the storm glass in the door soon." Realizing that she was chattering because she was nervous, she forced a smile. "Come on in. Would you care for a cup of coffee?"

Scott grinned. "Yeah. Some things never change. You still like to talk first thing in the morning."

"And I could never get a word out of you until you had at least one cup of coffee down your throat," she laughed.

"Nice place," Scott said as he looked around.

"Thanks. This way." Jenna was conscious of his dark gaze following her as she led the way into her sunny kitchen. She wore a pair of black, figure-hugging jeans, a purple sweater trimmed in black, and a pair of black pumps. A wide black belt encircled her waist. After filling a mug, she paused and asked, "You still drink it black?"

"Like I said, some things don't change. Mmm," he murmured, taking a fortifying sip. "That's good."

"I made blueberry muffins. Help yourself."

Jenna forced her gaze away from his strong, dark features, powerful shoulders and arms, taut midsection, and long length as she recalled the way he used to wake her with hot, hungry kisses. Dressed in simple navy cords, a blue striped shirt, and a navy leather jacket, he looked too good for her peace of mind. To divert her thoughts, she said, "I'll get my bag."

"Mind if I look around?"

"Not at all."

By the time she was carrying her large duffel bag and black leather jacket and handbag to the foyer, Jenna had calmed down somewhat. She had no reason to be concerned about Scott. Yes, they'd been intimate, but that had been a long time ago. It had been years since they'd spent any time together. What was important was that they were on good terms. There was no reason they couldn't be friendly.

Her cheeks were warm as she recalled the way her foster sisters had teased her, during their nightly three-way call, when she'd explained why she'd agreed to let Scott accompany her on this trip.

"Ready?"

"In a second. I need to wash out the mugs and pour out the coffee before we leave."

"No need. I took care of it."

Blinking in surprise, she said, "Thanks, but let me check the coffeemaker and stove to make sure they're turned off before we leave."

"No problem." When she returned, he said, with a grin, "All set?"

"Yes." Jenna accepted Scott's help with her jacket. He grabbed her case. Looking around, she realized there was nothing left to do before they went out the door but collect her purse and set the alarm.

"You have a very nice home, Jenna. It's warm, comfortable, and charming—but you have that knack. You made our upstairs apartment feel like home even when we had no money."

"Thanks, Scott." Her smile was genuine. "It's a big deal for me to finally be able to afford to buy my own home. I was able to get it before it came on the market. One of Sherri Ann's clients had to relocate and wanted to sell quickly. I was fortunate. The house was in great condition, and the asking price couldn't have been better."

"You have a lot to be proud of," he said as he held the door for her.

Jenna glanced quickly at him but said nothing. She didn't know how to respond. Was it a compliment? Or was it a subtle reminder that she had put her education ahead of their relationship?

Scott walked with her down the stairs. Red and gold leaves covered the lawn as they eliminated the distance to his luxurious Navigator, which was parked in the drive.

After placing her case in the trunk, he turned to her, holding up the keys. "Would you like to drive?"

She was glad to have something to do other than replay old memories over and over again. All of it was better left in the past. Jenna smiled. "Yes, I would. Driving will occupy my thoughts. I didn't sleep well last night . . . too nervous."

Without comment, he held the driver's door open for her. Once she was settled, he crossed to the passenger side and climbed inside.

Jenna frowned as she recalled something else she'd admired about him. He had volunteered for this trip because he wanted to help, but he would have backed away if she'd asked. She would hold him to his promise not to interfere. She liked that he hadn't tried to solve her problems for her or throw platitudes her way in a macho attempt to make it better.

Seat belt in place, Scott silently watched as Jenna adjusted the driver's seat, started the car, and backed out into the street. They were traveling along Interstate 75, which was crowded with morning traffic. It wasn't until they'd left Detroit behind that he raised the question uppermost in his thoughts.

"Why? Are you worried this might not be your brother? That you might have to start over?"

"Yes, and no. I'm hoping this is my Lincoln. The not knowing has me on edge."

"Is that the reason you didn't sleep? You were nervous when I arrived. Or does this have something to do with being with me?"

"Ask me something easy, why don't you?" Jenna blurted out.

He shrugged, "I'm just trying to understand what's going on with you."

"I appreciate your concern, but I'm fine. Well, not exactly fine, but understandably anxious about seeing my brother after close to twenty-five years. I don't know how he will feel about me just showing up at his front door. He might not be pleased to see me." She offered a smile. "But I'm determined to remain positive."

"This has to be hard for you. I can only imagine the emotional roller-coaster ride you're on right now." He shook his head before he added, "Just know that no matter what happens, I've got your back. You're not alone in this. I'll be right there at your side."

Scott was surprised by the soft brush of her fingers on his skin when she reached out to touch the back of his left hand. "Thank you. It helps."

Scott said nothing. He had to force himself to concentrate on the passing scenery. He wanted to study her lovely profile. The heat of awareness traveling along his nerve endings was an unnecessary reminder of how much he enjoyed the sweet caress of her petal-soft skin against his own.

No, he didn't need any reminder to recall how deeply he'd once cared about her. Or how much he'd missed her . . . missed the two of them making love. Swallowing a hefty groan of desire that had his shaft hardening, he tried to focus on what truly mattered.

He was here to make sure that she came out of this okay. The trip had nothing to do with his selfish needs and unfulfilled longings. This trip was about Jenna. She'd been without a family of her own for a long time. It was time she caught a break. He wanted that for her. She deserved some happiness. He could only imagine the heartache she'd suffered growing up without her siblings. He'd always had his parents and his sister to keep him grounded. It was her time. He prayed it turned out the way she wanted.

"Tell me about this PI. What do you know about him?" Shifting his long legs, Scott kept his tone light as they passed the sign welcoming them to Ohio, the Buckeye State.

"Jack Collagen came highly recommended. The lawyers in Sherri Ann's firm have used him to find background information on their cases. And I looked him up online. Everything I found supported her view that he's good. He was able to find out things about my family that I'd never known."

"Such as?"

"That both my parents are dead. I assumed, but I didn't know. Now I have both their death certificates. I even know my grandparents' names, on both sides."

"There is no doubt?"

"None."

"Wow," he said, then quickly added, "I'm sorry, Jenna, for your loss."

"Me, too. But it's okay. I never knew why my mother disappeared out of our lives. I learned from Mr. Collagen's report that one night she mixed booze with pills. She evidently was upset because my father had walked out on us. I learned that my parents were college sweethearts. Mr. Collagen also found out my father was killed in a car crash less than a year after he left us. He died in Jacksonville, Florida."

Scott frowned. "That's rough. How are you handling all this?"

"Naturally, I was sad when I read the report, but I was also relieved. There aren't any more unanswered questions. I finally understand why I was left in Mrs. Green's care."

"Do you think your mother committed suicide?" Scott asked carefully.

"I don't know, but it sounds like it. Perhaps she simply couldn't handle raising three little kids on her own? We were so young at the time. There's no way of knowing how she was really feeling the night she died. All I remember about my father is his voice raised in anger. I don't really remember him. I do have memories of my mother caring for us, and tucking my sister and me into bed. I also remember her reading to us . . . things like that. Most of my memories are of my twin and big brother. Mainly, I just remember the three of us playing together." She smiled, then released a soft sigh. "I was only six when I went to live at Mrs. Green's house. I was so upset and missed my twin. I didn't like not having her beside me when I went to bed. It didn't feel right. For a long time, I blamed myself for not being able to keep our family together. I couldn't help feeling as if I did something wrong. And I was the oldest twin. I was supposed to take care of Lenna."

"Sweet thing, that's crazy. You were a baby."

Scott recalled the nightmares she used to have of looking for her brother and her twin and not being able to find them. Jenna would wake up crying. He thought of the times he'd just held her through the night. Later, he'd wondered how she'd managed the nightmares on her own.

"I haven't seen my siblings in over twenty years."

There was such a wealth of sadness in her voice that it made him want to reach out and take her in his arms. He longed to ease her hurt, hold her as he had while they'd still been a couple. It had meant so much to him to be able to share those private moments with her. He acknowledged that the impact of that loss still bothered him. He no longer had the right to be there for her.

Clearing the lump of emotions from his throat, Scott said, "Hopefully you'll find your brother today."

"Yes. Sometimes I wonder why I couldn't just give up. Why I had to keep trying. I'm too darn stubborn, I guess."

Scott laughed. "I can't argue with that. Once you've made up your mind, it's set. There's no turning back."

"That's not true!"

"Tell me one time you changed your mind," he challenged.

"I ordered steak the other night, then changed my mind and got the crab legs. So there!"

Scott laughed. "Food doesn't count. I'm talking about important stuff."

"What important stuff? Like my hair? I no longer bother with trying to straighten it. I'm going natural these days. It saves a lot of time in the hair salon."

He shook his head, "Okay . . . okay. Let's just say when it comes to some things, once your mind is made up, that's it."

"Let's not say that at all. State your case and be specific."

"When we were taking Dr. Woodridge's world history class, I told you he had a thing for you. No matter how I tried to convince you, you wouldn't listen. It wasn't until the guy actually hit on you that you took me seriously."

"That's so weak! I told you at the time you were right. Now, admit it. I'm right and you're wrong."

He chuckled, "And that's not how I remember it. You denied it even with the truth staring you in the face. As I recall, you had to slap the guy."

"I did. And your memory, Mr. Hendricks, is flawed. You must be getting old." She giggled, then she said, "Are you ready to stop for lunch? I need food."

"Any preference?" he asked, the sweet sound of her laughter warming his heart. Oh, he was hungry alright, but not for food. He ached for all the things he'd lost and had never stopped missing. Her laughter was only one of those things. There was so much more he yearned for, including the delectable taste of her soft, lush mouth.

"You decide," she said with a smile.

Scott began to wonder if his being with her was a good idea. His desire seemed to mushroom with each passing mile. At this rate, he would be trying to hide a hard-on all weekend.

After stopping to refuel, they found window seats in a popular restaurant. Before they could examine the menu, Scott was approached by fans wanting his autograph. Although not thrilled by the interruption, he handled it with ease, quickly signing and giving out the basketball cards he always carried.

"Sorry about that," he shrugged. "I can't seem to get away from it."

"No need to apologize. I should have expected it. I'm not used to being with a celebrity."

He frowned. "It's a part of the deal I made when I entered the NBA. It's not my favorite part of the package, but I have no problem with it as long as it's not too intrusive." Scott didn't tell her how much he'd rather be alone with her, with no prying eyes watching their every move. Instead of studying her captivating beauty, Scott opened his menu. "Anything look appealing?"

"The salad topped with grilled chicken sounds appealing."

"I thought you said you were hungry. Now, a double order of meat loaf and mashed potatoes sounds good. Wonder if the pies are homemade?"

Although hungry, Scott had to force himself not to simply stare at Jenna. He was fascinated by the way her hazel eyes danced with humor and her lush lips, tinted a dark pink, were so seductively full and soft.

"Double order, huh?" She shook her head. "And there is no fat on you. It isn't fair."

He laughed, and the waitress came to take their order.

Once they were alone again, he asked, "You never said if part of your nerves had to do with the two of us traveling together. Are you finding it to be uncomfortable?"

He could tell by the look on her face that she hadn't expected the question. He wasn't trying to make things difficult, yet he had to know how she really felt. He didn't like to think she was shying away from him, as if things were so wrong between them that they couldn't be in each other's company. They'd loved so deeply and shared so much at one time. There was no getting around the fact that there had been fundamental changes since they'd separated.

"Come on, Scott. It's been over ten years. We've both changed. The years have a way of doing that to you. We aren't the same people who fell in love and planned to marry long ago. Yes, I'm a bit uneasy around you." Jenna studied him while nibbling the corner of her lip. Then she said, "You should have expected it."

"You're right. Our lives aren't the same. But deep down inside, we're still the same two people who once shared everything. Babe, you agreed to let me tag along on this trip because you know you could trust me to be in your corner . . . to be there for you."

He hesitated, then he revealed, "I trust you to be open and straight with me, for you to tell me what you really think. You're not like other women. I know you don't have a hidden agenda. I also know that you aren't interested in my bank balance." He sighed, then said, "Just knowing that means a great deal to me. It allows me to relax and be myself." He smiled at her before he said candidly, "Jenna, I don't like the idea that you might be uncomfortable around me."

"There are levels of comfort, Scott. I'm not leery of you. I know you'd never hurt me physically. Yet we've hurt each other. Furthermore, we haven't been privy to each other's thoughts and secrets for a long time. I don't know the sophisticated, famous man you've become. And you don't know the confident woman I've become. We're not those same kids anymore who fell in love at U of D's computer lab."

He nodded, hoping it was only a matter of time until she was able to be completely relaxed in his presence. He believed deep down where it counts that she was wrong. They were still the same two people who had once loved deeply.

When he'd invited himself along on this trip he hadn't taken his physical reaction to her closeness into consideration. His sole purpose had been to be helpful to her. He hadn't given much thought to the number of hours that they'd be required to spend in each other's company. Time that served to remind him how long it had been since he'd sampled her lips, filled his hands with her soft breasts and squeezed her lush hips. His awareness of her was as keen as it had been the day they'd met. Nothing could block from his memory what it felt like to be a part of her.

If only he'd convinced her to fly. Besides being faster, the flight would have provided some much-needed distractions. Right now, he'd give his last dime to be able to get his mind off how it felt to be inside Jenna . . . once again be surrounded by her wet, feminine heat. Ten, even twenty years wouldn't be enough time to wipe that sweet memory from his mind. Holding back a groan of frustration, he shifted uncomfortably, hoping to ease the pressure of his pulsating shaft. He drank the glass of ice water in front of him rather than pouring it over his head, where it might have done some good.

This trip was about Jenna's family. He needed to concentrate on that single detail. Jenna was counting on his support. The trip had nothing to do with their long-dead, non-existent relationship.

"Here you are, Mr. Hendricks. Mashed potatoes and meat loaf, just the way you wanted it. Can I get you anything else?" The beaming waitress put the heaping plate down in front of him. She barely glanced at Jenna as she put her plate down.

"Thanks," he said absently. He waited until they were alone, then asked, "Do you have enough food?"

"Plenty. I'm not six feet eight with a hollow leg," she teased.

"Very funny," he grinned. "Want some?"

"Nope, but you enjoy. Have you decided what you're going to do with a degree in chemistry?"

"I'm considering going into research, searching out new drugs. I'm interested in developing a drug to counteract asthma symptoms. My father suffered from a severe form of the disorder. I'd like to eradicate it."

"Really? That would be wonderful."

He nodded. "Randol Pharmaceutical has been doing extensive research on a promising formula. It's exciting. I've been doing my own research. I know it can be done. But it's going to take time and a lot of money. I'd need at least a master's degree to do the work I'm interested in doing."

"That's great, Scott. At least you don't have to worry about getting a job to support yourself while you're going to college."

"Basketball did that for me." Scott grinned, while marveling at her ability to get him to open up. He rarely shared his private thoughts with anyone, outside of family.

Jenna had him singing like a canary. It was a combination of her genuine interest and beguiling smiles. He stopped eating, recognizing that if he wasn't extremely careful, she'd have him falling in love with her all over again.

He swore silently at the mere thought. That was all he needed, to fall under her sweet spell again. He'd been there . . . done that. He'd survived once, losing this opinionated, determined, hardheaded, incredibly beautiful and caring woman. There was no doubt about it. Twice would kill him, he surmised, hiding a grimace.

Seven

Basketball! Jenna silently fumed as she ate her lunch. There was that word again. Because of it, every eye in the room was zeroed in on their table, especially the women. If not for basketball, they'd still be together.

No, that wasn't exactly true. It wasn't the game that had come between them. The problem had been that he'd chosen basketball over her. Even after all this time, it still hurt. She wasn't quite sure why. Goodness, she should have been over it, as well as him, by now.

Was that it? Was that why she was so uncomfortable around him? Was she worried that she still had feelings for him? Impossible! Until a few weeks ago, she hadn't spoken to or seen him in years. Scott hadn't been a threat to her.

"So what's new with Sherri Ann and Laura? Has Laura found that rich husband yet? Has Sherri Ann managed to master the legal system?" Scott teased.

Jenna laughed. To know Jenna was to know her foster sisters. "They're both doing well. Laura has no wedding plans, but she's a social worker, has her Masters, and has become a champion for abused women and children. Sherri Ann finished law school, passed the bar in one try, and works at a highly respected and profitable law firm. She's determined to become a partner before she's thirty-five."

"I've no doubt she'll do it. All three of Mrs. Green's girls are winners."

"Thanks. Sherri Ann and I have been helping Laura by volunteering at the Sheppard's Women's Crisis Center. We've been mentoring teen girls who are in the foster care system but living on their own."

"What do you mean? If they're in foster care, aren't they with a family?"

"Not always. Some older kids live alone in rented rooms, under supervision of a state-appointed monitoring agency."

"I had no idea."

"Most people don't."

"How old are these kids?" he asked.

"At least sixteen."

"That seems awfully young to be on their own," he ventured.

"I agree. Not everyone has a Mrs. Green in their lives, like Sherri Ann, Laura, and I had. Because of her, we especially want to help teen girls without foster parents."

"I can't get over the fact they are allowed to live independently."

She nodded. "Each child must meet with a social worker, attend school, plus take classes for independent living skills with the agencies. It's hard just growing up, but without some adult taking an interest in you . . ." She smiled. "Well, you understand why Sherri Ann and I decided to become mentors. Laura is the strong one. She's out there every day, trying to make a difference in so many lives."

Scott reached over and moved a finger along her cheek. "Laura's strong, but so are you. You're a remarkable lady, with a warm and generous spirit. Those girls are lucky to have you in their corner. Like I said earlier, when you set your mind to something, it gets done. Just look how you've moved heaven and earth to find your siblings."

Jenna smiled, touched by his understanding and display of support.

"How's the salad?"

She'd been poking at her food, but now she began to eat in earnest. "Good." She looked away, wondering if she should be alarmed by the ease of their discourse.

When the waitress placed the check facedown on the table, Jenna grabbed it.

Looking amused, Scott quizzed, "In a hurry?"

"Just making sure you didn't take it. I already owe you twenty dollars. This should even things out," she said, getting to her feet. Jenna didn't wait for him but headed toward the cashier. He didn't say a word as she paid for their meal and even bought him a chocolate mint.

"You don't owe me a thing," he said into her ear as they headed toward the door, making her jump. "But if paying for lunch makes you feel better, I'm all for it." Then he swept her hair aside and placed a kiss on her nape. "All set?"

She trembled as desire raced along her nerve endings. Instantly, her nipples began to harden and her feminine core tightened. She whirled around to see a satisfied smile on his face. She clenched her hands, wanting to smack him, but she knew he'd only laugh.

He had accomplished so much in such a short amount of time. He'd met every goal and then some. He was so darn sure of himself. Even though he was a very successful man, that didn't give him the right to rub his success in her face. Had he forgotten that she had also reached her own goals?

"What's wrong?" he said once they were outside. The sun was warm overhead, and they'd left their jackets in the car. "I let you . . ."

"That's just it. You didn't let me do anything. I'm the one who planned this trip and let you come along, not the other way around. So why do you think you're supposed to pay for everything? We took your car."

Scott blinked rapidly, as if she'd caught him off balance. "Babe, I'm sorry. It may look as if I'm trying to take over, but I'm really not. You're calling the shots." He shrugged large, muscular shoulders. "As for paying for things, I'm used to doing it. It's automatic."

She warned, "Keep your wallet in your pocket. You're here to offer support, not financial help. Got it!"

Scott grinned, spreading his large hands in a defensive gesture. "Got it." With his arm around her shoulders, they began walking to the parking lot. "Please answer one question for me."

"What?"

"Is it my turn to drive?" he teased.

Blushing, she quickly put in, "Naturally. It's your car."

"I don't want to mess with your plans." When she stuck out her tongue at him, Scott laughed. "I was only playing with you, babe. Loosen up. You're taking this much too seriously. I get what you're telling me. I know you're not quite yourself today. You have a lot riding on the outcome of this trip." He assured her, "It's going to work out. You'll see. And you're right. In the past when I was with a woman, I expected her to sit back and let me pay for everything. It's nice knowing you think that I'm worth more than the number of zeros in my portfolio."

Jenna frowned. She couldn't help speculating how it must have made him feel to be valued for his hefty income rather than being an intelligent, resourceful man. There was no doubt about it. Life wasn't always fair. Evidently, his situation made it difficult for him to trust the women who chased after him. Doggone it! She didn't want to feel sympathy for him . . . didn't want to feel anything at all for him.

Glad that they'd reached the car and eager to put space between them, Jenna tossed him the keys. He opened the passenger door for her. She mumbled an automatic thank-you.

All the masculine attention was driving her up the wall, but Jenna held in a protest. What exactly could she say? That she preferred not be treated like a lady? Hardly! She was clearly looking for a reason to keep him at a distance. It was her way of protecting herself.

Furious with herself, she clasped her hands in her lap while staring without really seeing the beauty of the trees around her. What was her problem? She should have been enjoying nature's kaleidoscope of autumn colors. Didn't she have enough to deal with, without worrying about her every response to her ex? There was a reason that he was her ex. Besides, in a few short hours she could be seeing her brother for the first time in a very long time. Hoping for a distraction, Jenna turned on the CD player. Soon Alicia Keys's sultry voice filled the car's interior.

They were a little over thirty miles outside of Cleveland when Scott switched on his turn signal and left the freeway. He merged onto a secondary road and stopped at a strip mall with a convenience store, gas station, car wash, and fast-food restaurant.

"We need gas," he volunteered. "Need to go inside?"

"Yes, but I can wait until we've paid." She grabbed her purse and hurried to catch up with him. After she'd given him the cash to pay for the gas, she called, "I won't be long."

While washing her hands after using the facilities, she realized how badly her hands were shaking. "Nerves," she mumbled aloud. It took two attempts to apply lip gloss. After smoothing her hair, she stared at herself. The closer they came to Cleveland, the more her doubts escalated. If she didn't calm down, she wouldn't be worth a nickel when she came face-to-face with Lincoln Nicholas.

What would she say to him? That she was his long-lost sister? Then ask if he remembered her? And what if he didn't remember her? What if he didn't have a sister? She grimaced at the thought. She didn't want to even think about starting over again. Mr. Collagen had proven to be reliable. And as far as he could tell, this was her Lincoln. No . . . she wouldn't start doubting now. With that decided, she turned to leave.

"Ready to roll?"

Jenna nearly screamed at the sound of Scott's voice as she emerged from the ladies' room. Pressing a hand over her heart, she said, "You startled me. Yes, I'm ready."

He casually clasped her small, cold hand in his large warm palm. "Would you care for a snack? Ice cream cone? Cookie?"

"I'm not hungry, but if you'd like . . ." Her stomach was taut with tension.

"I'm fine. We're almost there. How are you holding up?"

"No problems," she lied badly.

Although he looked skeptical, he made no comment but gave her hand a reassuring squeeze. When they reached the car, Scott asked, "Care to drive?"

Jenna found herself saying, "I'd better not. I'm too nervous to focus on much of anything, including staying on the road. I lied. The closer we get to Cleveland, the worse I feel." She confessed, "I'm going to be so disappointed if this isn't my Lincoln."

Scott gave her a hug, then pulled back. "If it's not your brother, then we'll check into a hotel and have a nice dinner. Perhaps go out clubbing for a few hours to forget our troubles. On the way back to Detroit, we will figure out where to start looking next." He kissed her temple. "You're going to find him, Jenna Gaines."

"Mr. Collagen is expensive. I can't keep paying him to come up with nothing. This could take years, with no guarantees that I'll ever find my family. I have to be realistic," she ended in a sigh.

"Hold on, sweet thing. Let's take this one step at a time. We don't know if this man is your brother. But if it isn't, you have no reason to worry about paying for the PI. If and when you need financial help, you've got it. We're friends . . . remember?"

Jenna didn't respond; she simply went and got into the car. Overcome with emotions, she couldn't respond, not without breaking down. She was incredibly touched by Scott's generosity. They'd been estranged for years, yet he meant what he said. All she had to do was ask.

By the time they were both buckled in, she reached across the console and placed her hand on his arm. "Thanks, Scott. You've no idea how much your offer means to me. Although I could never ask you to do something like that, I appreciate your offer. And you're right. I'm getting ahead of myself. We don't know if this is my Lincoln. I'm going to have to calm down or I won't be able to ask if he's my brother."

"That's right, sweet thing. One step at a time." He started the engine and put the car into gear.

It was late afternoon when they reached University Heights. Scott tried to convince Jenna to at least check into a hotel, where she could relax for a few moments and freshen up . . . perhaps call Lincoln ahead of time rather than just showing up at his doorstep without warning. Jenna flatly refused. At her insistence, they went straight to Lincoln Nicholas's home—no detours. She told herself she was relieved when Scott stopped arguing with her.

"This is it?" she asked as he eased to a stop in front of a large, sprawling, older Victorian-style home. Sheers covered the large front picture windows and small orange pumpkins lined the stairs leading up to a covered porch. The late-model SUV was parked in a wide drive in front of the two-car detached garage. A child's tricycle had been left in the yard.

Before Scott could open his door, Jenna grabbed his arm, as if she could hold him in place. She was quaking with dread. Her large, hazel eyes pleaded for his understanding. Suddenly, she needed time . . . lots of it. For so many years, she'd dreamed about this moment, even mapped out every detail in her head. Now that the time had come, she wasn't sure she could actually go through with it.

Tenderly, Scott cupped her cheek. "Frightened?"

She nodded, her eyes glistening with unshed tears. "I'm not sure I can do this."

He lifted her chin until he was gazing into her eyes. "You've been waiting for this for a very long time, sweetheart. If you back out now, you'll never know if that's Lincoln Gaines living here. Are you going to let a little fear stop you?"

"Absolutely not!" she snapped.

"That's my girl," he chuckled, then he leaned down to place a gentle kiss on her lips. "Ready?"

Jenna blinked back tears, then looked at him in dismay.

"Jenna?"

After a quick nod, she reached for her door handle.

She stood for a moment, taking in every detail of the house. A large wooden porch swing was positioned near the arched oak door that sported a stained-glass window.

It didn't matter that she was so numb she couldn't feel her feet as she began moving up the walkway. She was grateful for Scott's supportive arm around her waist as they mounted the porch stairs together.

When he would have reached for the doorbell, Jenna shook her head. She didn't want to rush this moment. She wanted to savor every second, lock it away in her memory to be replayed again and again. She looked through the bright-colored glass into a wide foyer. She thought she heard a male voice coming from the back of the house, but she couldn't be sure, because her heart was pounding wildly.

"It's going to be alright, Jenna. You're going to be fine whether this is your Lincoln or not," Scott said quietly.

She mouthed the word "thank you," unaware of slipping her left hand into his while she reached to press the doorbell. As they waited, Jenna was so glad to have Scott at her side.

She froze at the sound of approaching footsteps. Unconsciously, she held her breath, her eyes closed while she silently prayed for strength.

"Take a deep breath, babe," Scott urged.

Jenna did just that as she stared at the tall man who'd opened the front door. A screen door separated them. His long frame was shadowed by the mesh frame.

"Can I help you?"

Jenna felt the reassuring squeeze of Scott's hand on her waist just before she found her voice. "Hello. We're looking for Lincoln Nicholas. Is this his home?"

"I'm Lincoln Nicholas. What can I do for you?"

Jenna's heart pounded like a steel drum as she fought
to collect scattered thoughts and an avalanche of emotions. She didn't speak because she couldn't. She stared
at Lincoln Nicholas. He was well above six feet tall,
with dark bronze skin and close-cut, dark brown wavy
hair. As she studied his African features, she realized he
reminded her of someone, only she didn't know who.

"I'm Scott Hendricks and . . ."

"The NBA player?" Lincoln asked.

Scott nodded. "And this is Jenna Gaines. May we
come inside?"

"Did you say Jenna Gaines?" Lincoln asked, his
voice barely above a whisper. "It can't be . . ." His voice
suddenly trailed away.

"May we come inside? Just for a few moments,
please," Jenna asked softly.

Lincoln nodded, unlocking the screened door and
pushing it wide to allow them entrance.

Jenna had no recollection of entering the foyer, or
viewing the living room as he closed the door behind
them. They followed him down the central hall to a
large family room. Lincoln Nicholas had a handsome,
strong, square-jawed face. As she studied him, she acknowledged that while he didn't look like anyone she'd
ever met before, he seemed incredibly familiar. There
was something about the shape of his forehead and his
wide mouth that tugged at her.

"Lincoln, who was at the door?" a woman's voice
came from over his right shoulder.

It was when he turned toward the sound that Jenna
saw the mole at his jawline, below his right earlobe.
Suddenly, she knew why he looked so familiar. He
looked like her father. Her legs began to shake so badly
that she had to grab Scott's arm to steady herself.

Just then, a beautiful woman with dark brown skin

and a short natural entered the room. On her hip she carried a little girl with dark brown curls. The child's denim-clad legs were wrapped around her mother's small waist, and her bronze cheek rested on her shoulder with her thumb firmly in her mouth.

"I'm not sure," he said as he turned back to them. But he didn't take his eyes off Jenna. "Did you say your name was Jenna?"

There was no hesitation on her part; Jenna lifted her chin, stared up into her brother's brown eyes, and declared, "I'm Jenna Marie Gaines. I have a sister, Lenna Marie Gaines. I also have a brother, who's a year older. His nickname was Sonny. My parents were . . ."

Lincoln quickly bridged the space that separated them. "Fred and Jennifer Gaines," he finished for her.

With tears in her eyes, Jenna nodded, then whispered, "Are you my . . ."

"Yes, I believe I'm your brother." Lincoln reached out to touch her cheek. "It's you, isn't it, Jenna? After so many years."

She couldn't push the words past the swell of emotions in her throat. She merely nodded, "Yes, Lincoln. You still have the mole, just like Daddy. You look so much like him."

Jenna wasn't aware of the tears that trickled down her cheeks. She wrapped her arms around her brother for the first time since they were young children. Her cheek rested against his chest. "Oh, Lincoln . . ." she sobbed, "finally I found you." She was flooded with so many emotions, mostly joy and heartfelt relief.

The siblings held on to each other for a while, neither of them moving from the comfort of the long, welcoming hug. Eventually, Lincoln and Jenna drew apart, but brother and sister were unable to look away for some time.

Eventually Lincoln said, "Jenna, this is my wife, Carolyn. And our daughter, Corrie, she's two." He grinned as he urged his wife forward. "Carolyn, this is my sister Jenna."

Jenna accepted the other woman's hug and looked with adoring eyes at the beautiful toddler. "It's nice to meet you, Carolyn," she said, reaching back and linking her fingers with Scott's. "Carolyn, Lincoln, I'd like you to meet my friend, Scott Hendricks. We've driven down from Detroit."

As the two men shook hands, Jenna noted that while Lincoln was tall—close to six-three—Scott towered over him by a good five inches. When Jenna's gaze locked with Scott's, her eyes sparkled with happiness and excitement. With a radiant smile, she thanked him. Yes, she could have done this without him, but she was relieved that she hadn't had to.

"I can't believe it!" Lincoln exclaimed. "Jenna, my beautiful sister, is all grown up!"

"This is incredible. Sit down, please," Carolyn urged, indicating the two blue sofas facing each other adjacent to a navy leather armchair and ottoman. There was a large flat-screen television mounted on the wall above a fireplace and a child-size padded armchair, along with a collection of toys, in the corner of the room.

Once they were all seated, Lincoln and Jenna were busy smiling and holding hands while Carolyn and Scott looked on affectionately.

"You said that you finally found him. Have you been looking long?" Carolyn asked with her little daughter on her lap.

Jenna laughed. "It seems like forever. For as long as I can remember, I've wanted my brother back. For years, I've searched online for information about my family. I couldn't find Lincoln Gaines anywhere. It's only recently that I've been able to afford to hire a private investigator to help me. I knew you were out there somewhere."

"I was privately adopted when I was seven. I took my parents' last name. Tell me about Lenna," Lincoln asked.

Jenna's eyes lost some of their sparkle. "I haven't been able to locate her yet. I think she might have been privately adopted, like you. Her name must have been changed. My investigator is still searching. I've got to call him and let him know that you are indeed my brother. I wouldn't let him approach you when he first located you. I wanted to do that myself."

"I'm glad you cared enough to look." He gave her a hug. "What about you, Jenna? Has this been hard on you?"

She smiled, blinking back tears. "It's something I felt compelled to do for a long time."

"Tell us about your life," Carolyn encouraged.

Still shaken by strong emotions, Jenna took a deep breath before saying, "I live in the Detroit area. I have a house in the city. I finished my doctorate in the spring and began teaching economics this fall at the University of Detroit-Mercy."

"That's great, Jenna. Congratulations. So you were also adopted," Lincoln surmised.

Eight

"No, Lincoln. I was never adopted. I stayed in foster care after Mama left us."

Lincoln exchanged a concerned look with Carolyn before he said earnestly, "What? But . . ." He paused as if shocked. "I'm so sorry. That had to be difficult for you. How did you manage on your own?"

Jenna quickly added, "It wasn't difficult or hard on me. I am blessed. I was placed in a wonderful home with two other little girls. We had a truly wonderful older woman, Mrs. Green, to look after us. She was good to us. It wasn't like those horrible stories you hear about. We weren't shifted from home to home. Mrs. Green raised us. We stayed with her until we were eighteen and old enough to go on to college. All three of us finished college. We beat the odds," Jenna ended proudly. She glanced at Scott, and he smiled back at her.

"That's wonderful, Jenna." Lincoln beamed and squeezed her hand, truly happy for her. "You flourished in spite of the circumstances. I'm proud of you."

"I am, too," Scott put in. "With the help of scholarship money and grants, Jenna worked her way through school. And she went all the way through."

Lincoln marveled, "And you two are friends. I can't

get over it. Scott Hendricks is sitting in my house. I watched you win that last championship where you were the MVP. I bet you can't go anywhere without being recognized."

Scott laughed good-naturedly. "The height thing always gives me away. Now that I'm retired, the attention gets to be a little old."

"You're a celebrity!" Carolyn exclaimed as her daughter crawled off her lap and climbed on her dad's. "How did you two meet?"

Scott leaned back and waited for Jenna to answer.

"We met years ago in college," she smiled.

Carolyn jumped up. "I forgot all about dinner. I'd better check on it. You two haven't eaten yet, have you? Please say you'll stay and eat with us."

Jenna glanced at Scott. He smiled back. She nodded. "We'd like that. Do you need any help?"

"Nope. You visit with Lincoln. I'm sure he's dying to know everything you've done in the last twenty years," Carolyn called as she hurried toward the kitchen with Corrie in her arms.

"It's truly incredible," Lincoln said, shaking his head in amazement.

"Incredible," Jenna repeated.

Scott asked for directions to the restroom and excused himself. When he didn't return, Jenna smiled, realizing he'd gone into the kitchen to visit with Carolyn to give them an opportunity to talk privately.

Jenna asked, "Lincoln, did you ever try to find me or Lenna?"

Lincoln looked away, obviously uncomfortable. He pulled on his chin thoughtfully before he revealed, "It wasn't because I didn't care. I thought about both of you every day while growing up. I hoped you two were alright. I always assumed you two had been adopted together. It never occurred to me that they might split you two up."

He frowned when he said, "No, I never searched for you two. I believed you two were happy and doing well. I don't really know why I never tried to find you. Maybe I felt a little guilty because I had been adopted into a wonderful, loving family. I wanted for nothing. My parents are wealthy, prominent attorneys, as are my two older sisters. I'm the only boy. It was important to my dad that I took the family name. And it's expected I will take over the firm someday."

He paused before he confessed, "My father offered to find out what he could about our family when I was a teenager, but I refused. I'd closed that door and didn't want it opened. I thought it was better if I didn't intrude in your lives." He paused, then admitted, "I couldn't bear it if one of you had suffered while I was living the life." Taking her hand in his, he whispered, "I'm sorry, Jenna. I know it was wrong."

Jenna patted his hand, seeing the shame in his eyes. "You have nothing to be ashamed of or even embarrassed about, Lincoln. I'm glad you grew up as part of such a loving family. You deserved to be happy. There is nothing wrong with that. None of it was your fault. You didn't make the mess our parents created. They left us, not the other way around."

"I know that."

"Do you? Then stop blaming yourself. You and I were both blessed to be raised by people who loved us. I can only pray that Lenna has been as fortunate."

"Amen to that," Lincoln echoed, releasing a sigh of relief.

Carolyn called, "Dinner's ready, you two. Lincoln, please help the baby wash her hands."

Once they were all seated in the dining room, Jenna

said, "Carolyn, everything looks wonderful." She eyed the serving plates filled with a glazed ham along with a large bowl of creamy mashed sweet potatoes.

"Thanks, Jenna. You and Scott are to relax and enjoy yourselves. We are so happy to have you with us."

"That's right," Lincoln beamed. "Shall we say grace?" After blessing the food, he began circulating a serving bowl of mixed greens and a platter of cornbread muffins.

"Delicious," Scott said, sampling his brimming plate. "You're not only beautiful, Carolyn, but you're also a great cook."

"She's that, as well as a wonderful mother," Lincoln added as he gave Corrie a buttered muffin.

Carolyn blushed at the compliment and smiled at Corrie, who was seated between her parents in her high chair.

"How did you two meet?" Jenna asked.

"We were high school sweethearts. I think we fell in love in tenth grade," Carolyn laughed.

Lincoln smiled, "I proposed the night of the prom. We waited until I finished law school to marry, though."

"The men are right. Carolyn, you are a fabulous cook," Jenna said.

"Thank you, one and all. I'm lucky to be able to stay home with our daughter. Lincoln and I just found out we're expecting another baby in the spring."

"That's wonderful," Jenna laughed. "Carolyn, how are you feeling?"

"No problems so far," she smiled.

"Congratulations. Lincoln, you're a lucky man," Scott grinned.

"That I am," he beamed.

"Lincoln, tell us about your parents," Scott asked.

"They're great. Both warm and loving. It didn't matter that I was Black. Like I told Jenna, they are both attorneys. I have two sisters. No, I have four sisters. There's Linda, Candace, Jenna, and Lenna. Wow, I am a lucky man, surrounded by strong, beautiful women."

Lincoln went on to explain that the family's firm specialized in corporate law. He and his father practiced contract law, managing pro athletics all over the Midwest. Jenna could tell that Scott's interest was piqued when Lincoln began naming the men they represented from the Green Bay Packers, Cleveland Redskins, the Chicago Bears, and the Bulls.

Lincoln took a sip from his glass before he said, "Both Candace and Linda are married, and both have two sons. Corrie is the only girl in the family."

"Her aunts and both sets of grandparents are determined to spoil her. If I didn't put my foot down, she'd get everything she wanted from both sides of the family," Carolyn revealed.

"Well, I am pleased to have sweet little Corrie as my niece." Jenna smiled, reaching out to caress the baby's soft cheek, which earned her a smile from her little niece.

It was while they were eating slices of Carolyn's lemon pound cake that the couple invited them to stay overnight with them.

"We wouldn't want to impose," Jenna insisted.

"Nonsense. We can bring Corrie in with us and Jenna can have her bed. It's a double bed. And Scott, the sofa in the family room opens into a king-sized bed. Say you will stay . . . please!" Carolyn encouraged.

Scott looked over at Jenna. "It's up to you."

"Please say yes," Lincoln urged. "I like the idea of you being close. We still have so much to catch up on."

Jenna laughed, saying, "Yes. We can stay."

It wasn't until they were in the kitchen, helping with

the cleanup, that Scott and Jenna had a chance to talk privately.

"You don't mind staying? Or using the sofa bed?" she asked as she rinsed a plate and handed it to him to load into the dishwasher.

"Jenna, will you stop? As long as you're happy, I'm fine." Lifting her chin so he could look into her eyes, he quizzed, "You're happy, aren't you, babe?"

Barely able to contain her joy, Jenna laughed through her tears. "I'm more than happy. I'm thrilled to have finally found my brother." She surprised them both when she threw her arms around his neck and pulled his head down so she could press her lips to his. "Thank you for tagging along with me. I haven't been myself since Mr. Collagen called to tell me about Lincoln. The not knowing was the worst part of it all. Thanks for putting up with me."

"You're welcome." He tightened his arms around her.

With her breasts pillowed on his chest, her senses quickly soared. His unique masculine scent was working its own special magic on her senses. She yearned to rub the aching tips of her breasts against his wide chest, to ease her hips forward until they were against his muscular thighs. The planes and angles of his strong body were both arousing and familiar.

She closed her eyes against the sudden rush of sensual emotions flooding her system. It took all her strength not to rub against his hardness or suckle his full bottom lip. His nearness was like a potent aphrodisiac. As she stared into his dark, sultry eyes she decided ten years wasn't nearly enough to forget what it felt like to be his. She rose up on her toes for another kiss, but before they could connect she heard someone approaching.

"Were you able to find everything?" Carolyn called

before she came through the kitchen's swinging doors.

"No problem," Scott answered, taking a step back, forcing Jenna's arms to drop to her sides.

Jenna's face felt hot from a combination of embarrassment and disbelief. Goodness! What had happened to her common sense? Had she lost her mind as well as her sense of self-preservation?

"We're nearly done," Jenna volunteered, hoping to fill the void.

Suddenly she was furious with herself and Scott. How easily he made her feel what was best forgotten. She shook with the force of her emotions. She had no business recalling the special promise she'd made to him the night he'd proposed. What difference did it make now if she'd promised to be his . . . always? They were not connected. The past no longer mattered.

"You're our guests. You shouldn't be working," Carolyn insisted.

"Just be glad you got a night off," Jenna teased as she struggled to regain control.

Carolyn laughed. "I'm going to like having you for a sister."

"Good, because I'm looking forward to it. Will you show us the rest of the house?"

Carolyn beamed. "I'd love to."

While Lincoln got Corrie ready for bed, Carolyn gave them a tour of the rambling, older home. The couple had been slowly renovating the house. Although there was still work to do, they were proud of what they'd accomplished. Three of the five bedrooms needed work, as did the living room, library, and home office. Carolyn explained they'd turned over the renovation of the three bathrooms to the professionals.

It wasn't until Jenna was preparing for bed that she recalled the kiss she and Scott had shared in the kitchen. Although angry with herself for wanting more, she firmly pushed the thought away, refusing to dwell on it. It had been a mistake and didn't mean anything.

Jenna woke to the soft giggles of her little niece, Corrie, standing at the foot of the bed.

"Morning, baby girl. Did you come to wake me up?"

Corrie nodded, then dropped to hide behind the footboard of the double bed.

Jenna smiled, sitting up. "You have such a pretty room, Corrie," she said, trying to coax her out of hiding. "And so many books." Jenna pointed to the child-sized shelf filled with picture books. "Which one is your favorite?"

Corrie popped up, giggling. She raced over and pulled out a large book with a bear on the cover. She brought it over to Jenna to see, but she was too shy to stay and was soon racing out of the room.

Jenna laughed, shaking her head. She hugged herself, so happy to have found her brother. Not prepared to waste time in bed, she quickly got up and grabbed her robe and toiletry bag before she headed to the hall bathroom.

The day flew by in a whirl of activity. Jenna got to know her sister-in-law while pitching in to steam the aged wallpaper from the living room walls. Lincoln and Scott painted an upstairs bedroom.

Later in the day, David and Marleen Nicholas stopped by, as did their daughters, Candace and Linda, who came with their families. Jenna had a chance to visit with Lincoln's adopted family during an impromptu dinner. The men grilled steaks and corn on the cob on the patio while the ladies prepared mixed green salad and baked potatoes with all the fixings.

When the festivities were done, and the families had

said goodnight, Jenna assured herself that she was relieved that she hadn't had an opportunity to exchange
more than a few words with Scott the entire day. It was
better that way. She didn't want to magnify the kiss
they'd shared in the kitchen, a kiss that never should have
happened. She couldn't afford the complications, she
told herself as she pulled her nightgown over her head.

Friendship was one thing, but hungry kisses were
entirely different. Longing for the taste of his mouth
wasn't acceptable. How had it happened? One minute
she'd been thanking him, the next they'd locked lips. A
mistake! She had to make sure it didn't happen again.

If she started feeling weak, she only had to recall all
the things she had done on her own. She hadn't needed
his kisses then; she certainly didn't need them now.

Regardless of how grateful she was to him for his
support, she wasn't about to forget what had gone
wrong between them. As long as she kept that firmly
fixed in her mind, she couldn't make another wrong
move. Satisfied with that conclusion, she curled on her
side in Corrie's bed and quickly fell asleep.

On Sunday the temperature dropped. The overcast
sky suited Jenna's mood. She couldn't help feeling a little sad as she hugged her brother and his family good-
bye, but she was cheered by the knowledge that they'd
agreed to spend the Thanksgiving holidays with her in
Detroit.

"You okay?" Scott asked once they were under way.
Although he hadn't taken his gaze from the road, his
concern was evident in his deep voice.

Surprised, she quickly gave him a reassuring smile.
"Are you kidding? I couldn't be happier. I've finally
found my brother after years of searching for him."

"A dream come true."

"Absolutely."

Jenna quickly looked away. She refused to study the subtle changes in his dark, masculine profile. The years had certainly been good to him. And yes, in a sense, he was back in her life. So much had changed, and so quickly, that she was having trouble figuring out how she felt about it all.

"I still can't believe it!" she whispered aloud. "I found my brother. I have to pinch myself to make sure it's real. I know I could have done this alone, but I'm glad I didn't have to. *Overwhelmed* is too mild a word to explain how I feel. I have my family back. My life has just changed forever."

"You deserve to be happy," he said quietly.

"Thank you."

"I'm glad we're friends again," he said quietly.

"We both know that's not exactly true. It was the simplest way to explain our being together to my brother and Carolyn—there was no reason to go into our history. But it doesn't matter, since we've both moved on with our lives."

"So you don't plan to explain us to your brother?"

"There's no need. You two will probably never see each other again." Jenna wasn't trying to be rude, yet she was determined to keep the past where it belonged . . . buried and forgotten. She rushed on to say, "Did I tell you I talked to Mr. Collagen, thanked him for finding Lincoln? He was able to do what I couldn't do on my own. He will be concentrating on finding Lenna."

"That's good."

"It helps knowing Lincoln wants to find Lenna as much as I do."

"Don't you think it's odd that he never tried to find you? After all, you never changed your name. Except for four years in New York, you even lived in the city where the three of you were born," Scott said thoughtfully.

"He has his reasons."

Scott said, "You asked him?"

"Yeah, I wondered about it. Besides, he admitted he felt guilty because he'd been adopted. He believed that Lenna and I were still together and had also been adopted. He assumed we were doing well and had gone on with our lives. It never occurred to him that we had been separated. Or that I was in foster care." She ended with, "He apologized for not looking for us."

"How do you feel about it?"

"I was disappointed, but I don't hold him responsible. He was only a kid like me, caught up in grown-folks' business."

"Meaning . . ." he prompted.

"It's all water under the bridge. It's over and can't be changed. I prefer to concentrate on what's important. We've found each other. That's what matters."

"Jenna, why are you letting him off the hook so easily? He's a lawyer. He had the wherewithal and money to search for both of his sisters, yet he didn't." Scott seemed genuinely perturbed.

"You think I should be upset?" She shook her head in disagreement, then went on to say, "We all make choices. How can I fault his? Lincoln's successful and has a wonderful family backing him up. I'm happy about all those things," she insisted. "I'm sure he would have eventually gotten around to searching for me and Lenna."

"Hey, I know you are happy for him. And you're probably right about him getting around to looking for you and your twin. This situation, at least to me, points out the special person you are, Jenna Gaines. You wanted your family back. And you were willing to move heaven and earth to make that happen regardless of the personal cost." Scott paused, then said, "No one loves like you, Jenna. You give your whole heart. I have no doubts that you will find your twin sister. It's only a matter of time."

Jenna's heartbeat pounded in her ears. For an instant, when he'd said "love," she'd thought he'd been talking about the two of them.

"Thanks, Scott," she said with a hopeful smile. "All I can say is from your mouth to God's ear."

Jenna was surprised at how tired she was when, hours later, Scott turned into her driveway. It had been an eventful trip. Finally it was over. Stretching tight muscles as she got out of the car, Jenna moved slowly around to the back of the car to get her bag.

Scott merely smiled as he hefted it into his left hand and pulled down the hood of the trunk. With a hand on the small of her back, he urged her up the rain-dampened walkway.

"Scott, I want to thank you for all you've done this weekend." While searching in her purse for her keys, she said, "I'm sure there were a hundred and one things you could have been doing."

He shrugged wide shoulders as he held the screen door open so she could slide her key into the lock.

"I'm glad you took me up on the offer," he replied. "It was a pleasure for me to see you so happy." He followed her inside as she quickly punched in the alarm code.

After flicking on the lights, she turned and looked up into his dark, searching eyes. Her breath quickened in her throat.

"Well . . ." She stopped abruptly, feeling awkward.

"It's late. And I'm sure you'd like to get some rest. Tomorrow is a workday," Scott said, putting her case down on the rug beneath the table in the foyer, then going to stand before her. "There is no reason for us to be uncomfortable with each other. I know your secrets and you know mine. We've both seen and heard the best and worst from each other." He leaned down to kiss her cheek. "Jenna, I'm thrilled that things worked out for you and Lincoln. Let's go out one day this week to celebrate. What evening is good for you?"

She hesitated. She didn't want to seem ungrateful. Yet, at the same time, she doubted the wisdom of seeing each other socially.

He lifted her chin until they were gazing into each other's eyes. "If you're wondering if I have ulterior motives, then you're correct. I've missed having you in my life. I really enjoyed being with you this weekend. I hope you don't think I'm trying to take advantage here, but I also have to be honest with you. If it's too soon to talk about us, then I'll back off."

"There's nothing to talk about," she said.

He studied her for a few moments, then said, "I'm a straightforward guy. That hasn't changed. There's no game playing or intent to capitalize on a weak moment. Jenna, all I'm asking for is another chance with you. But tonight we are both tired, so let's leave this discussion for another day." He ended with that, but his engaging smile had her staring at his firm lips.

"Scott, I don't know what you expect me to say or even know how I feel," she hesitated.

"No pressure. Let's take this one small step at a time. If you'd like to go out to dinner to celebrate finding your brother, please give me a call."

"I'm not changing my mind about us just because you went with me to Ohio to find Lincoln. I could have gone on my own. I'm used to taking care of myself and proud of my accomplishments."

He chuckled. "I'm proud of you, also. You did what you set out to do. Sweet thing, I'm talking about dinner, not a lifelong commitment. Okay?" Then he teased, "What are you afraid of? I promise I won't embarrass you by using the wrong fork."

"I'm not afraid of anything," she was quick to clarify, deeply touched by his sincerity and acknowledgement of her success. It shouldn't matter, yet it did.

"Then there's no reason why we can't go out to celebrate? Who knows? By the end of the week, you may have news from the private investigator about your twin. Jenna, if you need me to be patient, I can do that, also."

She couldn't help smiling. She found herself teasing him, "I don't recall you ever being patient about anything. When you learned you were eligible for the NBA draft, you didn't hesitate to go after what you wanted."

He shrugged. "I was nineteen. If nothing else, give me some credit for learning a few things over the years. I'm not the same man. Stuff happened. So how about Wednesday night? Or are you afraid your new boyfriend Jackson will object?"

"I told you I'm not afraid!" she snapped. "Okay, okay, I'll go, but don't make me regret this change of heart. And it has to be on Thursday."

"Thursday is fine. See you around eight. I'll leave it up to you to decide the particulars. I'm open." With that, he called goodnight an instant before he closed the door behind him.

Nine

"I can't remember when I laughed so hard," Sherri Ann said, taking the last sip of her soft drink. "Any more popcorn, Laura?"

"Nope, Jenna ate it all," Laura teased. She sat between her two foster sisters in the back row of the crowded multiplex theater. The three had opted to indulge in a Sunday afternoon viewing of Tyler Perry's latest movie.

"So? I was hungry. I told you two I wanted to eat first. I was late for service this morning, so I missed breakfast," Jenna said as she watched the end credits roll.

"Any more secrets?" Sherri Ann quizzed. "I still haven't gotten over the fact you allowed Scott to go along with you to meet Lincoln."

"Neither could Jackson. I mentioned it in passing on our date last night, and wow. You'd think I committed some grievous wrong, the way he reacted. It's a good thing I didn't tell him that I went out to dinner with Scott on Thursday night to celebrate finding my brother. He probably would have hit the ceiling. I don't get why he's so upset. Jackson and I are only friends. Just like Scott and I. Nothing serious."

Laura laughed, "Can you imagine, Sherri Ann? Her new boyfriend isn't overjoyed that she's still seeing her ex-fiancé?"

"Stop exaggerating, Laura. Scott and I are history and everyone knows it. I was worrying if Scott would pull something at dinner, but he turned out to be a perfect gentleman. Jackson acted like we really had something going on. Men!"

Laura mocked, "Oh, dear! You poor, pitiful thing. You have two gorgeous men after your smart-mouth behind while Sherri Ann and I stay home eating bonbons and knitting! Pardon me if I don't feel sorry for you, Jenna Marie."

"Shut up, Laura! You have more men trying to date you than Sherri Ann and I can count," Jenna put in.

"Not me. You mean Sherri Ann. She has her choice of those single, gorgeous lawyers she meets in court all the time." Laura pushed her arms into her leather jacket. "Let's get out of here. I'm hungry."

"Will you two hush up!" Sherri Ann stated emphatically. "I'm not going anywhere until I find out what is going on between Jenna and Scott. And don't you dare tell me nothing. You're seeing him again. That has to mean something."

"The operative word is *seeing*—we aren't dating. We're friends . . . sorta." Jenna grabbed her own jacket. "I'm with Laura. Where are we going to eat?"

"Can you two focus on something besides your stomachs? You have some explaining to do. Sort-of-friends? Laura and I are your friends and neither one of us is interested in getting into bed with you. Scott's another matter. That man wants you back," Sherri Ann announced with her hands on her hips.

"Hush!" Jenna said as the theater lights came on.

"Well?" Sherri Ann prompted.

"I know," Jenna agreed.

"That's all you have to say, 'I know'?" Laura huffed. "Sherri Ann is right. You're keeping secrets."

"No, I'm not. What's the point of making a big deal over what Scott Hendricks wants? I'm not going backward. Just in case no one has noticed, I've moved on. Now, can we talk about something else? Where are we going to eat, ladies?" Jenna demanded.

Sherri Ann and Laura exchanged a concerned look before Laura said, "You're glossing over this. You need to pay attention to what's right in front of your nose. Scott's not wasting time trying to be your friend. And he's not messing around, either. When he's ready to make his move, you'd better be prepared. He knows your weaknesses. That man still has feelings for you."

"That doesn't mean I have any for him! It takes two, and I'm not interested." Jenna linked arms with both her foster sisters, urging them out into the aisle. "Let's go."

Sherri Ann looked doubtful. "Okay, but don't say Laura and I didn't warn you. You're not going to know what hit you when Scott turns that sexual charm loose on your 'I'm-not-interested' self."

"Forget Scott. Jackson is the man I want to talk about," Jenna claimed as they headed toward the exit.

"Yeah, sure," Sherri Ann tossed back.

"I'm serious. Jackson has got so much going for him. He's good looking, intelligent, and really seems interested in how I think and feel about things. That's huge."

"Have you even considered sleeping with him?" Laura wanted to know.

"No! I've only been dating Jackson a few weeks."

"That's my point! Admit it. You aren't even thinking about him in that way. There's no chemistry . . . no sex appeal . . . no nothin'." Laura wrinkled her nose as if in distaste.

"I never said that!" Jenna snapped.

"You don't need to," Sherri Ann said as they crossed the lobby. "It's obvious."

"To whom?" Jenna asked.

"Everyone but you," Laura teased, pushing the glass door open. "Burgers or pizza?"

"Pizza," Jenna said absently, not pleased with her foster sisters' assumptions. So what if she wasn't ready to sleep with Jackson? Sexual chemistry would come naturally, given enough time. Sherri Ann and Laura were merely anticipating problems when there weren't any. Jackson was a good man. And she was enjoying getting to know him. There was nothing wrong with that.

As for Scott, she could handle him, too. He knew the score, so there wouldn't be any surprises. If he pushed too hard, she wouldn't be afraid to push back or set the record straight. Besides, he was only trying to help her find her twin. He knew how much it meant to her. Sherri Ann and Laura were overreacting. Why go looking for trouble?

After class on Wednesday evening, a student told Jenna that Scott Hendricks was waiting in the hallway for her. Although he'd come the previous week to walk her to her car, Jenna hadn't expected him this week. Even though it was late and the parking lot was nearly deserted, she hadn't asked for his help. If he offered, she wouldn't refuse the company.

She also noted the number of students who recognized Scott and stopped to speak with him or asked for his autograph. She took time to answer questions about the next assignment and to pack up her things. She was the last to leave. She found him lounging on a padded bench near the rear glass doors.

"Hey," she smiled, briefcase in hand. She wore navy trousers, a pink pleated blouse, and a cranberry-and-pink argyle patterned vest and sweater.

He smiled, rising to his full height. "Hey, yourself. Pretty. You make it yourself?" He fingered the soft wool of her knee-length cardigan.

Jenna shook her head in surprise. "You remembered I like to knit."

He fell into step beside her, taking her heavy case. "Yeah. I still have the gray-and-blue argyle scarf you made for me. Ready?"

"I know you're used to that kind of thing. I mean, people stopping you, vying for your attention. Do you ever get tired of it?"

"Frequently, but it goes with the wealth and fame," he said as they moved toward the double doors. "As long as they stay clear of my personal life, I can manage the imposition. How was your class?"

"Good," she said quietly. It was a clear autumn night, but the wind was brisk as they made their way through the parking lot. "You have lots to do, taking a full schedule of classes and your business interest. You don't have to walk me to my car, Scott."

Suddenly, Jenna recalled her foster sisters' claim that she wasn't sexually attracted to Jackson. Unfortunately that had never been the case when it had come to Scott Hendricks. From day one, she'd been aware of his intense masculinity. She'd spent years trying to forget what it had been like to be in Scott's arms. Even though he'd only been nineteen when they'd fallen in love, he'd been an unselfish lover. He'd put her needs ahead of his own pleasure. Nor could she forget that he'd been her first love.

Scott was frowning when he said, "I've been in the chemistry lab all day. Stopping to check in on you, Jenna, doesn't inconvenience me." With that said, he went on to ask, "How are things going with you? Any news from Collagen?"

Jenna flashed him a quick smile. "Yes, I got the call right before class." Then she rushed on to say, "The woman he thinks might be Lenna has been working in Las Vegas for the past six months. Before that she lived in L.A. trying to break into acting. Besides the fact that she looks a lot like me, she's originally from Michigan." Squeezing his hand, Jenna said, "Isn't that good news?"

"I sure hope so. How soon will you know?"

"Mr. Collagen's e-mailing photos of her with background information. I'm so excited! I can't wait to get home and study them and read about her. It could be my twin."

"Why wait? I have my laptop with me. Let's check it out."

They reached her car. While she slid into the driver's seat, he took the passenger seat and turned on his laptop. Balancing the machine on the console between their seats, Jenna keyed in her e-mail information. When she opened the attachment with the photos, both Scott and Jenna gasped. The likeness was startling.

Jenna's eyes quickly filled with tears as she struggled to accept the truth. Swiping at the tears, she whispered, "That has to be my twin sister!"

"Wow! It's incredible. How can that not be your twin? She looks exactly like you, babe." He cupped her chin, then brushed his mouth over hers. "Congratulations."

"It's too soon to celebrate." Jenna quickly read the e-mail. "It says that her name is Leah Bennett. She was adopted by Keith and Angela Bennett. She grew up in Grand Rapids, Michigan. No wonder I couldn't locate her on the Internet. I was looking for Lenna Marie Gaines."

"When are we leaving? I'm assuming you don't want to drive all the way to Vegas?"

Her hazel eyes went wide for a moment as she con-

sidered her response. "Friday after classes. Do you
think we'll have a problem getting a flight out with so
little notice?"

"Leave the arrangements to me. With any luck we
should meet Leah on Friday night. Saturday morning at
the very latest. I'll call with the details." After snapping
his briefcase closed, Scott cradled her chin in his wide
palm. "You've waited a long time for this moment,
babe. It's almost over." He placed a hard kiss on her
lips, and with a tender flick of his tongue, he tasted her
before he released her. "Lock up," he cautioned. After
a wave, he was gone.

Unaware of the way she ran her tongue over her tin-
gling lips, Jenna just sat. Still reeling from the impact of
his kiss, along with the recent discovery, it was several
moments before she realized she was just sitting there
staring at nothing. After locking the doors, she clicked
her seat belt into place. Yet she waited, making no effort to start the car.

"What just happened?" she whispered aloud.

Scott Hendricks was what happened. One touch
of his tongue had sent her senses soaring toward the
heavens and had her body sizzling from the sudden heat
of desire and longing for the unforgettable feel of his
tongue on other parts of her body.

It wasn't until she was nearly home that she realized
that she had not only accepted his offer to go with her
to Las Vegas but had also agreed to let him handle the
arrangements. There was no doubt that Scott was back
in her life. That didn't mean she should let her defenses
lag or allow him free rein of her life. Had she done
that? Surely not! Perhaps in her excitement at finding
her twin she'd simply failed to reinforce her limits? A
congratulatory kiss was one thing, but tongue action
was taking it too far. No more!

* * *

Jenna had just turned out her beside lamp when the telephone rang. "Hello?"

"Can you be ready to leave Friday afternoon, around four?" His rich baritone voice had her heart racing.

"Of course, I'm not going to let anything get in my way."

"Shall I pick you up at your office or at home?"

"At home."

He chuckled. "Rather not be seen leaving campus with an overnight case and me?"

She giggled. "Let's just say I'm not looking for trouble. The less said about my personal life the better. Besides, everyone knows who you are, Mr. NBA."

"There was a time when you didn't mind being seen with me, young lady."

She quickly clarified, "I don't have a problem being seen with you. Nonetheless, it would be nice not to have everyone on campus in my business. I'm working toward tenure, not to end up in the tabloids as your new lady. You're news, Hendricks."

"At one time, yeah, but not anymore. I'm simply a college student, trying to get his degree in the next year or so. See you on Friday, Jenna."

"See you," she said softly as she put down the telephone. She worried her bottom lip, wondering if she was wrong for not mentioning the kiss. There hadn't been a bit of sexuality in the conversation. No reason to bring it up. Maybe she was overreacting.

It wasn't until she was snuggled against her pillows that she noticed she'd forgotten to ask for details about their flight. Well, she'd have to make sure that she reimbursed him on Friday. This trip was not some romantic getaway.

She giggled, imagining his face when she handed him a check for both their tickets.

"Friday." Lenna was in for a huge surprise! Jenna hugged herself in delight. She couldn't wait.

* * *

Jenna's jaw dropped when their limousine stopped beside the private jet waiting on the tarmac. She watched as steps were lowered and a smiling, uniformed flight attendant waited in the open doorway.

"What's going on, Scott? Tell me you didn't hire a private plane to take us to Las Vegas. I'm supposed to pay for this trip. And this is way out of my price range."

She'd been proud of herself for not making a comment when he'd arrived at her place in a chauffeur-driven limousine. But now he'd gone too far.

Scott didn't wait for the driver to do the honors. He hopped out of the car and held a hand out to her.

Annoyed, she tucked her handbag beneath her arm and got out without assistance. "You didn't answer my question. How much is this trip going to cost me? Do I need to put my house on the market?"

"Very funny, Jenna. The airplane's not going to cost you a dime. A friend of mine, Ralph Prescott, owns a fleet of private jets. It's a favor to me."

"Some favor. What do you have to do to pay him back?"

Scott chuckled, "Nothing. Friends help each other out."

"And he just happened to have a jet doing nothing?"

"Ralph's not the issue. Come on. The driver's waiting for us to board so he can carry on our luggage." He placed his hand on the small of her back.

Jenna frowned at the way she was dressed in simple black slacks and a black ruffled blouse, which she'd teamed with a collarless leather jacket, belt, and a small brimmed hat, all in yellow. Her only jewelry was a pair of large, gold hoop earrings. Nothing fancy—a work outfit. But deep down, she knew that clothes weren't the real issue. The culprit was being with Scott and having the vast difference in their lifestyles thrown in her face.

"Jenna?"

"What?" she asked as she mounted the stairs to the beautifully appointed jet, done in rich bronze tones with lush cream leather armchairs and a gleaming galley.

The pretty flight attendant greeted them by name.

Forcing a smile, Jenna nodded politely.

"What is wrong? Why are you letting this bother you? You'll be seeing your sister in a few hours. That's all you should be concerned about," Scott said close to her ear.

Jenna silently sank into one of the plush armchairs and watched as Scott took the seat beside her. A desk had been built into one corner, and a flat-screen television was mounted on the wall. It looked like a tastefully decorated study, with its plush leather armchairs and marble-topped tables. Glancing around, she couldn't help wondering if the rear door led into a private bedroom and bath. Naturally, she'd heard of such opulence; she just hadn't experienced it.

Clasping shaking hands in her lap, she decided he was right. She had no reason to be upset. Scott's jet-setting lifestyle had nothing to do with her. He'd lived beyond her reach for a long time. Having it blatantly pointed out shouldn't hurt. So why was she smarting?

Struggling to regain her equilibrium, Jenna admitted it really didn't matter that they were taking a private jet to Las Vegas. Scott was right. She would see her twin sister in a few short hours, and that was what was important. She needed to keep her priorities straight.

"Welcome to Prescott Air. My name is Joan. Please let me know if you need anything before we take off. Ms. Gaines? Mr. Hendricks? Would you care for something to read?"

Jenna was presented with an array of popular magazines. Deciding she needed a distraction, she picked out the new issue of *Vogue* magazine.

Just then the pilot, Anthony Watts, came out. Scott had evidently flown with him before and quickly made the introductions. After describing the altitude at which they would be flying, the weather conditions, and the approximate time they would reach Las Vegas, Captain Watts asked if they had any questions. Then he wished them a good flight and returned to the cockpit.

"I can't get over all this." Jenna's hands fluttered restlessly.

"Are you afraid of flying in a smaller plane?"

Jenna lifted her shoulders helplessly. "There's nothing small about this Learjet."

Soon the seat belt sign was turned on, and they were buckled in as they taxied along the runway.

"Talk to me, Jenna."

"I've never liked flying," she confessed. "When we were poor college students, we didn't have many opportunities to fly." She laughed. "You used to pick me up from my late-night class in a beat-up old car."

Back then they hadn't had secrets. They'd talked about everything. They'd truly been friends as well as lovers.

"That was a long time ago. At the time it didn't feel like a hardship." He chuckled. "It's a wonder we went anywhere, considering the shape that old Camaro was in."

"We were young and in love. Everything was fun. But to answer your question, I'm a much better flyer now, even though I still don't enjoy the takeoffs." She pressed a hand to her stomach. "I've got butterflies."

Scott reached out and clasped her hand, giving it a reassuring squeeze. "You really don't have anything to worry about. Prescott Air has a great safety record."

She nodded, a bit uneasy. "I'll take your word for that, even if I know you're only trying to get me to relax."

"How am I doing?" he teased, moving his thumb over the back of her hand.

"No complaints," she smiled. She couldn't help being conscious of the touch of his hand and the scent of his teakwood body. His aftershave was a heady mixture of sandalwood and a hint of vanilla along with his clean male skin.

"Good."

Once they were in the air and the plane had leveled off, the flight attendant unsnapped her seat belt. She asked, "Ms. Gaines, would you care for something to drink? You have your pick of soft drinks, a selection of cocktails, wine, and champagne."

Jenna glanced at Scott, suddenly realizing she was still holding his hand. Quickly releasing his fingers, she said, "Yes, thank you. I'd like some iced tea, if you have it."

"Of course. Mr. Hendricks?"

"Vernors, please."

"Coming right up," the flight attendant said with a smile before disappearing into a small galley kitchen.

"Champagne?" Jenna laughed. "I could get used to this. Are they going to serve us dinner, too?"

"Whatever your heart desires." He grinned, leaning back in his seat and crossing his long legs at the ankles.

"I think I'll pass on dinner. I'm too nervous to eat. I keep wondering if this Leah Bennett is really my sister. The pictures are remarkable."

"Try to relax. You'll have your answer soon."

"That's easier said than done. Despite my best efforts, I can't seem to relax. Maybe I should have ordered a drink."

"Hoping for a bit of liquid courage?" he teased.

"It can't hurt." Then she said seriously, "I won't be able to calm down until I know one way or the other if she's my twin."

He ran a gentle finger down her soft cheek. "You already know the answer, babe. How can Leah Bennett be anyone else but your sister? I'd be shocked if she wasn't."

She shrugged. "I'm trying not to get my hopes up. I don't want to be disappointed. I've waited so long for this." She looked pointedly at him. "Let's talk about something else . . . anything."

Just then Joan returned with their drinks. She placed them on the small polished table between their seats, then returned with a silver tray of finger sandwiches and petits fours.

Jenna had meant it when she'd said her stomach was a bit uneasy. She shook her head. Once they were alone again, she crossed her legs and began flipping through the fashion magazine. Unable to concentrate, she watched as Scott munched on a cracker piled with cheese and cold cuts.

"Good?"

"It should hold me until dinner." After taking a sip of his drink, he said, "I wish you could relax."

"This is about as relaxed as I'm likely to get. You're used to this kind of opulence." She gestured wildly.

"I wouldn't say I'm used to it. If you're asking if I've been on private planes before, then the answer is yes. And I've had my share of limousine rides, slept in costly hotels . . . that kind of thing."

"Does that include wild parties, drugs, and women throwing themselves at you?" she blurted out.

Ten

He looked pointedly at her. "No, Jenna. I've never been into drugs or wild partying. I'm no saint. But money has nothing to do with it."

"Scott, I'm not stupid. How can you say having money hasn't changed you?"

"Expensive toys don't make the man or woman. I'm still the same guy you met more than ten years ago on campus. I wasn't into drugs or partying back then. Yes, I don't have to worry about money, but I'm still Virgina and George Hendricks's son. I want the same things out of life that I wanted back when we first fell in love." He paused, touched by her interest, then said, "I'm flattered that you're curious about my life over the years."

"You're grinning," she accused.

"Yeah," he said, rubbing his jaw.

Jenna looked down, as if suddenly fascinated by her fingernails. "I didn't intend to pry. Maybe I'm interested because your life has been very different from mine. While I was poor and studying, you were living in the lap of luxury."

"Not that different. I suppose I did my share of clubbing when I first was drafted. I enjoyed being able to afford nice things, cars, clothes, and that kind of stuff.

And yes, I enjoyed the female attention fame brought me, but I've never taken it to heart. You see, I've always known it was the money and lifestyle they were attracted to, not me."

"What makes you say that?"

"Because it's true. The women I dated weren't genuinely interested in getting to know me. And that was okay, because I wasn't ready to settle down. I've gone out with all kinds of women, successful in their own fields . . . actresses, models, and businesswomen." He shrugged. "I've always known I wasn't the attraction."

He took a long swallow of his drink before he said, "Having been in a relationship that ended in disappointment, I didn't want to go down that same road. Yet I've grown tired of the carefree lifestyle with an endless string of the same type of women. So I moved on to more important things."

"Such as . . ." she prompted.

"Such as family. I regret not keeping my promise to get my degree. I took classes during the off-seasons but never put forth the effort needed to get the job done." He hesitated before he said candidly, "I hit a rough patch when I first retired from the game, and I moved back to Detroit. Did some heavy drinking and scared my sister a bit before I got myself back on track."

"Why are you telling me all this?"

"You know why."

Jenna shook her head. "I don't."

He sighed and picked up another cracker piled high with cheese. He took his time eating it. Finally he swallowed, then answered, "You know. You just don't want to talk about it." At the continued shake of her head, he revealed, "I want you back in my life, sweet thing."

She surprised him when she asked, "Haven't you forgotten something? I was the one who broke up with you. I broke your heart." She tapped his chin with a slender finger. "So why are you smiling? It isn't funny."

"I'm smiling because I can. Yes, you broke my heart, but I'm aware of the fact I also broke yours, as well as disappointed you. We were both young and did a fine job of making each other miserable. But we survived it. For that I'm glad. And we can even talk about it."

"It only took nearly eleven years," she pointed out.

"Yeah, that's true. But when I look at you, I see a successful woman who is real, genuine, and very special. Jenna, when you love, you give it your all. I miss that . . . I miss you." He leaned forward before he asked, "I know I promised not to push, but have you thought about us?"

She shook her head. "I've tried my best not to think about the two of us and the mistakes we made. I'm not like you. I don't want to repeat past mistakes. It hurts too much."

"That's not fair. You gave us no more than, what, half of a second's worth of thought?" he quipped.

Just then a soft bell chimed and the pilot's voice came over the speakers. They were approaching Las Vegas's McCarran International Airport and would be landing soon.

Jenna worried her bottom lip while quickly fastening her seat belt. "Now isn't the best time to talk about this."

With his seat belt secure, he nodded. "You're right. You've enough on your mind with seeing your twin sister again." He reminded himself to slow it down . . . to just relax and simply enjoy being with her. This trip was not about him or his needs. This was for Jenna and getting her family back. He wanted it for her. She deserved that and so much more.

Yet her closeness challenged his resolve. Scott was no saint. He couldn't stop himself from wanting her. He'd limited himself to occasional touches and kisses. More than that was up to her. Aware of her vulnerability, he had to be careful not to take advantage of her. Jenna's happiness mattered to him above all.

Jenna stared out the window, studying the landscape below, then she met his gaze. "Scott, I wasn't being flippant or callous, but I know . . ." She stopped abruptly when he brushed his lips over hers.

"Let's agree to leave it for now without any qualifiers."

"What do you mean?"

"I don't think you know how you really feel about me. You've been too busy avoiding the subject."

When she would have voiced her objections, he kissed her again. This time it was a deep, hungry kiss. The slow flick of his tongue was a tantalizing reminder of what they'd once enjoyed. They were both breathing hard by the time the jolt of the jet's wheels touching down separated them.

Alarmed by the potency of that sizzling-hot kiss, Jenna didn't dare look at him. She returned her gaze to the sparkling lights rushing past. When the plane finally rolled to a stop beside an empty hangar, a limousine stood waiting nearby.

"You arranged for a car to take us to the hotel?"

"Mmm. Ready?" He released his seat belt.

"Yes." Suddenly she began wondering about their hotel arrangements.

"How are you holding up?"

The question immediately reminded her why they were together. She didn't bother to object when Scott helped her with her jacket.

After thanking and saying good-bye to their flight crew, Jenna was rushed along to their limousine.

"Nervous?" The inquiry broke the silence as the car was soon caught up in the evening traffic.

"I can't say that I'm nervous like I was when I met my brother, but I'm excited. I can't help wondering how she'll react when she sees me. It's been a long time coming, and I feel as if a part of me has been missing . . . an essential part that no one else knows is gone. Does that sound crazy?"

"Makes sense to me. Have you ever been to Las Vegas before?"

"No, this is my first time. How about you?"

"Many times."

When he smiled but didn't elaborate, Jenna almost questioned him, but she caught herself in time. What he'd done in Las Vegas or anywhere else wasn't her concern. What was she thinking? They'd lived separate lives. The fact that she was even curious was downright annoying. She'd shown too much interest in his love life. So what if he'd traveled the world with beautiful, glamorous women? She might not like hearing about his involvements. Besides, it had nothing to do with her.

Their sole reason for being together was to find her sister. As long as she kept that thought in mind and didn't let him back into her life in any meaningful way, she would be fine. She must remember that this trip wasn't about the two of them.

"You're awfully quiet," Scott mused as the limousine eased to a stop in the luxury hotel's impressive curved drive.

"I'm fine," Jenna said, a bit too quickly. "I hope it doesn't take too long to check into our rooms. I'm anxious to see Lenna."

"All the doubts behind you?" he asked as he got out of the car.

"Pretty much," she replied absently, taking his hand

to let him help her out. Once their luggage had been handed to the hotel's bellman, Scott casually tipped the limousine driver before he urged her into the well-lit lobby of the impressive hotel.

Her first thought was that she couldn't afford to stay here. Perhaps she should have discussed her budget with Scott? Fortunately for him, he no longer had to be concerned about money. No, she suddenly decided that she wasn't going to worry about anything either. She was here in Las Vegas to locate her sister. So what if she had to exceed her budget along the way? It didn't matter, because her goal was to locate Lenna. She'd have to make arrangements to pay him back later.

Jenna noted that Scott was greeted by name. There was no delay at the check-in desk. They were escorted through the elaborately decorated lobby to a bank of glass elevators, where they were whisked up to one of the top floor's penthouse suites.

As Jenna stood in the center of the luxuriously furnished living room of a two-bedroom suite, she muttered to herself, "Go with the flow." She looked around in utter disbelief. She'd planned to pay him for the traveling expenses. How? She'd have to cash in her 401(k) to cover the cost of this trip. This was no two-hundred-a-night hotel room! It was more like ten thousand a night, and that didn't include the private jet or the limousine service.

"What? Not going to check out your bedroom? Make sure it's okay?" Scott stood near the floor-to-ceiling window that overlooked twinkling lights and lush hotel grounds.

She confessed, "I didn't expect anything this lavish."

"It's only for the weekend. Think of it as a mini-vacation." He waited, as if expecting more protests.

She forced a smile. "Excuse me while I get freshened up. I'll only be a few minutes." Carrying her jacket and purse, she headed to the open bedroom where her luggage had been placed.

"Take your time. According to Mr. Collagen's report, Lenna or Leah Bennett should be working at the Starlight Lounge tonight. Are you hungry? Would you like me to order something to eat?"

"You go ahead. I'm too nervous to eat."

"Sweet love, you didn't eat anything on the plane. How about a grilled turkey and cheese sandwich? Is it still your favorite?"

She stopped so suddenly that she nearly tripped on the lush carpet. The tender endearment caused her breath to catch in her throat. It brought back memories . . . detailed, intimate moments of a time best forgotten. Alarmed by her emotional reaction, she had to struggle to maintain her composure.

"That will be fine. Thanks," she said shakily.

She couldn't breathe easily until the bedroom door was closed behind her. On trembling legs, she sank onto the end of the queen-size bed, grateful for the support. It was too much, all of it: the opulence of the trip, the prospect of seeing her twin, and now the bittersweet memories of when they were lovers came rushing back. Shakened, Jenna simply sat watching the desert sun set in the distance.

"I don't want to go back," she whispered.

It would have been easier to cope if the memories had all been bad. Unfortunately, some were so sweet and achingly tender that they brought back a wealth of emotions. Emotions she preferred to remain locked away forever. It hurt recalling the good times. She didn't want to remember the sweet magic of being in Scott's arms . . . being on the receiving end of his hot, hungry kisses and intense lovemaking.

"I won't do it!" she muttered aloud, wrapping her arms protectively around herself.

It had taken years to learn how to push away those memories. Why now? None of it mattered anymore! What she needed was a few minutes to calm down. Her focus should be on what she'd come here to do . . . find her twin sister. So what if she was caught up in Scott's world? It wouldn't last beyond the weekend. His life had nothing to do with hers. Their connection wouldn't extend beyond the loose boundaries of friendship.

With that settled, she collected her toiletries and went into the connecting bathroom. "No worries," she repeated as she took care of the necessities. Learning the details of his life didn't mean she was softening toward him.

She wasn't reckless enough to dismiss the way he'd hurt her or welcome him back for more of the same. She was no longer the naïve twenty-year-old who had fallen in love with the campus basketball player. She was a career woman who had her priorities straight and clear goals that couldn't be swayed by a fancy trip into fantasy land.

Jenna had thought she was prepared for the loud music blaring from the sound system, the dim lights, the overdone glitz of the club's interior—which leaned more toward sleaze than glamour in her estimation—but she'd been wrong.

Even though she wasn't the only woman seated at the small tables, she was extremely uncomfortable. The room wasn't packed, but there was a sizeable number of men surrounding the well-lit stage. All eyes were on the nearly nude woman gyrating around in a pair of glittery panties and stilettos.

She reminded herself that she wasn't there to judge. Yet she couldn't help feeling relieved that it wasn't her twin up there topless. Bored by the dancing, she looked around, noting that there weren't any clocks mounted on the walls, not even near the bar. Thankful that she wasn't on her own, she wondered what Scott was thinking. He looked as bored as she was. To his credit, he'd suggested she might be more comfortable waiting in the limousine or the lobby, but she'd refused, insisting that if Lenna could put up with it, so could she.

After searching the room yet again, she let out a disappointed sigh before she said in Scott's ear, "I don't see her."

"Don't worry. If she's here, we will find her." He signaled to one of the barmaids dressed in bright blue hot pants and bra.

"What can I get you, gorgeous?" The barmaid leaned in close to Scott, all smiles as she looked him over appreciatively.

He had to speak into her ear to be heard over the music. Jenna anxiously looked around once again while he ordered their drinks. Scott pulled out a fifty-dollar bill when he asked about Leah Bennett. Although Jenna could not hear his exact words, she watched the barmaid nod, pocket the money, then stop at the bar to place their orders before she went through a rear door, labeled Private.

Scott reached over to gently squeeze Jenna's hand. He said into her ear, "She's here tonight. Evidently, she just finished dancing. Hopefully, it won't be much longer."

"Good." Jenna forced a smile, unaware of the way she clung to his hand. She found the whole situation disconcerting. She wasn't a prude, yet she would have wished for so much more for her twin. If this was indeed her sister, Jenna wanted to understand why she'd decided to strip for a living. She had so many questions, but for now she had to cope with the endless wait.

Even though Mr. Collagen's report had detailed what Lenna did and where she worked, it hadn't stopped Jenna from wanting to see her sister again. Nor had it prevented Jenna from wanting Lenna in her life. The job didn't define her twin. Losing their parents had been devastating for all three Gaines siblings.

Ignoring the drink in front of her, she continued to anxiously scan the room. She gasped the instant she spotted Leah Bennett. The barmaid who'd waited on them pointed in their direction. Jenna didn't recall moving, but suddenly she was on her feet and hurrying to the woman who was without doubt her twin.

"Lenna!" Jenna whispered the name, then grabbed her sister and held on to her. Tears of triumph and sheer joy spilled down her cheeks. "I can't believe it's you!"

Her twin pulled back far enough so she could study her in disbelief. "Jenna? Is it really you!"

"Yes!" Jenna was barely able to contain her excitement as she clung to her little sister. It wasn't a dream. Her twin sister, Lenna, was real and right there!

"Come on, ladies," Scott said. "Let's go out into the lobby, where we can hear each other without shouting." He ushered them out, away from the blaring music and noise of the dark club.

"Who's this?"

"Scott Hendricks." He introduced himself as he stared down at Jenna's twin. "You're the mirror images of each other!" He laughed, looking from one to the other.

And they were incredibly alike, even after living apart for twenty-five years. They were the same height and nearly the same weight; even their long, dark-brown hair was parted in the center. The obvious difference was in their makeup and the way they dressed.

Lenna had on tight black leggings and a low-cut blue blouse. Her naturally wavy hair had been straightened and flowed down to her shoulder blades. She also wore considerably more makeup and chunky jewelry than Jenna did.

Cradling her twin's face, Jenna said, "Oh, Lenna Marie. You're beautiful. You look so much like Mama."

"I'm Leah now. I can't believe it's really you, Jenna Marie. What are you doing here? How did you find me? How did you even know where to look?"

Thrilled, Jenna laughed happily. "Believe me, it wasn't easy. I tried on my own to find you for years, then I finally broke down and hired a private detective to do it for me. It's been too long coming, little sis."

Scott interjected, "What time do you get off work, Leah? Can we take you somewhere so the two of you can talk? Perhaps go out and get some dinner? Jenna has been so excited, she's barely eaten the entire trip."

"I can't leave until two. But I'd love to go out to eat," Leah beamed.

"Wonderful!" Jenna said eagerly. "We'll meet back here at two."

The twins exchanged another hug, then Leah pulled free. "I've got to get ready for my next set." She hurried away, past the bouncer guarding the door that evidently led to the rear dressing rooms.

"Ready to go? Get some fresh air?" Scott carried Jenna's things, forgotten in the excitement.

"I can't believe it!" Jenna exclaimed, taking time to slip into her jacket and tuck her satchel purse over her arm before going out into the crisp night air. She linked her arm through his. "Pinch me! Tell me I'm not dreaming." Her eyes were glistening from tears as she looked up at him.

"I can do better than that," he said huskily, pulling

her into his arms. His kiss was tender, brimming with emotion. "It's real. You did it! You have your family back. Congratulations, babe."

Jenna clung to him, knees shaking. "If this isn't real, don't wake me. I don't want it to ever stop."

Scott chuckled. "Come on. Let's get inside the car before you collapse."

"Good idea," she laughed.

Their driver spotted them and instantly had the passenger door open and waiting for them. Once they were inside, they both laughed like two happy children.

When the driver started the engine, Jenna panicked. "Scott, we can't leave. We have to wait for Lenna."

"Calm down. We aren't going far, just killing time until she's ready to leave for the night."

Jenna sighed, realizing she'd overreacted. "I'm a mess. For a moment there, I was scared of losing my sister after finally finding her." She shuddered at the thought.

"Will you stop worrying? Nothing bad is going to happen." Scott placed a kiss in the center of her right hand.

"My emotions are in an uproar. I'm not sure I know what I'm feeling."

"Sit back. Try to relax and enjoy this special time."

"You're right." She leaned her head back against the soft leather cushions while gazing out the window, not really seeing anything. Lost in thought, she absently moved a caressing thumb over the back of one of his large hands.

It was true. She was overcome with feelings, so many that she couldn't begin to sort them out. Along with the pure joy, she was thrown by the deep sense of gratitude she felt that Scott had shared it with her. Bombarded by emotions, Jenna knew she had no choice but to deal with those feelings.

She'd fought against being vulnerable to him and lost. Being near him had caused her awareness to grow, not lessen. She should be savoring the sweetness of her reunion with her twin, not wondering how she was going to protect herself from Scott. Her foster sisters had warned her, but she hadn't listened. Now that he had come right out and said he wanted her back, it was up to her to decide what to do.

She should have asked Sherri Ann and Laura to accompany her on these trips. But no, she'd allowed Scott to tag along with her. In the midst of finding her family, she'd realized she'd wanted him with her. What she hadn't done was look too closely at the reason behind that decision.

Lost in thought, Jenna jumped at the caress of his lean finger down the side of her cheek. Instantly her eyes locked with his and her heart began to race. She was immediately caught in the warmth and tenderness of his dark, intense eyes. And she couldn't look away.

He flashed a wide, quick smile, pointing out the tinted windows. They were back at the club. "See, I told you there was nothing to worry about."

Jenna turned to see her twin walking out the door. Before she could voice her relief, Scott had gotten out and was escorting Lenna—no, Leah—to the limousine.

"Wow, I have to hand it to you, big sis. You folks know how to travel in style," Leah crooned.

Jenna laughed, too happy to bother with an explanation. Clasping her twin's hand, she asked, "Did you have any problems getting away?"

"Nope, I'm fine. I called my boyfriend to let him know my plans, but he isn't home to miss me." She ran a hand over the soft leather seat. "I could easily get used to this. Where are we going?"

Scott smiled. "You pick. This is your city."

Clearly excited, Leah laughed, leaned back, and crossed her long legs. "Man, this is the life! Let's see." Then she named the well-known real estate tycoon's hotel and casino that catered to the very rich. The hotel's restaurant was rumored to serve only the best in the world.

Before Jenna could protest that it was too expensive, Scott chuckled. "Let's do it." He lowered the window between the compartments and gave their destination to the driver.

Jenna touched his arm. "Don't we need reservations?"

He kissed Jenna's cheek. "No worries, babe."

Jenna nodded, determined to do just that—forget her worries and focus on getting reacquainted with her twin. Somehow, she'd find a way to pay him back. She had no intention of taking advantage of his generosity.

Leah surprised her twin when she said, "Scott, I can't believe I didn't recognize you immediately."

He stretched out his long legs, then said with a grin, "My height gives me away."

Leah laughed, exclaiming, "Big sis, you've done well for yourself. So how did you two lovebirds meet?"

Before Jenna could clarify they weren't a couple, Scott said, "We met in college before I entered the NBA. But we want to hear about you, Leah. It has taken Jenna years to find you."

Eager to hear her sister's story, Jenna nodded. "Yes, please tell us. How long have you worked at the club?"

"Less than a year. I came to Vegas for the money. There are lots of opportunities in this town if you can meet the right people." Leah explained, "I wanted to be a famous actress since I was a little girl. When I left Michigan and moved to L.A., I was eighteen. Unfortunately, L.A. is a tough town. I had all kinds of jobs, but I couldn't get a break, no matter how hard I tried."

Leah let out an excited squeal when they eased to a stop in front of the well-known hotel-casino. Bubbling with excitement, she hopped out the instant the chauffeur opened the door.

Jenna whispered urgently in Scott's ear, "I'm sorry about this. I had no idea she'd pick something so expensive."

Scott brushed his lips against hers. "Remember, no worries tonight. Savor the experience. Okay?"

Jenna nodded before she followed her twin. Scott was right. There would be plenty of time later to sort it all out.

Eleven

Scott was captivated by the similarities between the Gaines twins. They hadn't seen each other since they were kids, yet they were still identical. It was uncanny how alike they were, from the husky tenor in their voices to the way they moved and finished each other's sentences. It was nearly impossible to believe that Leah could be as eye-catchingly beautiful as his Jenna, yet the proof was staring him in the face.

His gaze lingered on a beaming Jenna. The tide had finally changed for her. She had her family back. She was happy and looking forward to getting to know her siblings.

They'd been seated at the best table in one of the most opulent restaurants in Las Vegas. No expense had been spared. Pristine white linen, fine bone china, and gleaming silverware graced the tables, while fresh flowers perfumed the air and candlelight glowed inside crystal lanterns.

Leah laughed loudly. "I can't believe I'm here. This place reeks of money." She looked pointedly at her twin. "I suppose you're used to places like this. Judging by your designer outfit, your shoes and that bag you're carrying must have cost the earth." She winked at Jenna.

"Scott evidently takes very good care of you, big sis."

Shifting uncomfortably in her seat, Jenna hastily denied, "Scott doesn't take care of me. I buy my own clothes. And I love hunting for a bargain. My foster sisters claim fifty-percent-off is my middle name. The purse was a gift."

"Foster sisters? You weren't adopted?" Leah seemed shocked. She rushed to say, "I never would have guessed, with that perfect speech. If Scott doesn't take care of you, what exactly do you do to earn your keep?"

Stunned by the question, Scott wondered if Leah had meant to put Jenna down. Or had she recklessly tossed out the comment without due thought?

Jenna volunteered, "I'm a college professor. I teach economics at the University of Detroit-Mercy. I just finished my doctorate, which took me awhile, but I worked my way through college."

Scott boasted, "She has reason to be proud of herself. She did it all on her own . . . college and grad school. She even had a gig on Wall Street."

Leah seemed stunned, dismissing all but one point. "It's true? You weren't adopted? I thought you were teasing."

"No, I was put into the foster care system, but I was lucky to have a wonderful foster mother. Mrs. Green raised me with two other little girls, Sherri Ann and Laura . . . my foster sisters," Jenna said proudly. "Enough about me. Tell me about your adopted family. Did you have brothers and sisters? What was it like for you?"

"No brothers or sisters. The Bennetts couldn't have children of their own. I still can't figure out why they didn't take both of us. They knew we were twins, but it didn't seem to matter to them. All I remember is that one day we were together and then you were gone, and

I was alone with them. When I was little, they were nice to me, but I felt so lost without you and Lincoln. I cried every night for months."

Jenna reached out to take her twin's hands. "Me, too. It was awful. I missed you so much."

Just then, their waiter introduced himself and asked if they were ready to order.

Jenna looked stunned when Leah ordered the most expensive item on the menu. Her worried gaze went to Scott. He merely smiled, squeezing her soft hand reassuringly.

Once they'd placed their orders, Jenna prompted, "You said the Bennetts were nice when you were little. Were you happy with them?"

"No," Leah said bluntly. "They were very strict and religious. They had their own ideas of how a kid should be raised. Things were okay until I started noticing boys. Then everything changed. Nothing I did seemed to please them, that's for damn sure." She shrugged, draining her glass of wine. "After a while, I gave up trying to be a good girl. I was tired of restrictions. I just wanted to do my own thing. The only thing I liked in high school was the drama club. Yet they insisted I go to college and study to be a teacher. No way! I couldn't wait until I graduated and was free to move out."

"Oh, Lenna! I'm so sorry." Jenna's voice brimmed with compassion. "That had to have been hard for you."

"It's Leah now," her twin reminded her. "I never went back. Once I was able to leave, hell, I ran. I have no tender memories." She laughed. "I'm sure the Bennetts were pleased to see the back of my fast tail."

Just then the waiter brought an array of appetizers. Savoring her jumbo shrimp in cocktail sauce, Leah asked for details of Jenna's growing-up years.

After a bite of bacon-and-cheese-covered potato

skins, Jenna put down her fork and told her twin about Mrs. Green and how happy she'd been growing up with Laura and Sherri Ann.

Between his soup and salad, Scott stopped marveling at the sisters' similarities and began taking note of their differences. There were more distinctions between them than the way they dressed, applied makeup, and styled their thick, dark-brown locks.

"So, while I was adopted, supposedly living the good life, you came out smelling like a damn rose. Don't that beat all?" Leah seemed genuinely perplexed.

Jenna blushed, as if she was embarrassed. Even though, in Scott's opinion, she had done nothing to be embarrassed about, Jenna ducked her head, as if she'd been guilty of some unnamed crime. She seemed relieved when their waiter arrived with their entrees.

They concentrated on the meal for a time.

"My man isn't going to believe me when I tell him that I ate at The Tower! His jaw will drop when he hears I met you, Scott. He's a real sports nut. He's seen all your games. He put money on your championship game," Leah giggled.

Scott acknowledged her comment with a smile. "It's a treat for us to be here with you, Leah. Jenna has been talking about finding her family since the day we met. It's a dream come true for her." Scott kissed Jenna's cheek. "Right, sweet thing?"

Jenna gushed, "Yeah. I can't wait to tell our big brother that we found you. He is going to be over the moon."

"You found Lincoln!" Leah yelled, flinging up her hands in surprise.

Overcome with emotion, Jenna could only nod her head. Her lovely hazel eyes shimmered with tears. Scott decided she'd never looked happier or more beautiful.

And he was thrilled for her. She deserved it. He so admired what she'd done on her own, and all of it from such humble beginnings.

He couldn't ignore his selfish hopes. He wanted nothing more than to make all her dreams come true. If only she'd let him back into her life, give them another chance at happiness. He just knew that this time, if they put their minds and hearts into it, they could make it work.

"Tell me about Lincoln!" Leah begged.

Unable to speak through her tears, Jenna looked pleadingly at Scott. He began telling Leah about Jenna's tireless efforts to find her siblings. He explained how she'd saved for years in order to hire a private investigator to find them. He went on to tell about their trip to Ohio. By then Jenna had recovered enough to talk about the weekend visit with Lincoln and his family.

Jenna ended with, "Our little niece, Corrie, is so adorable. Just wait until you meet her. And they are expecting a new baby in the spring."

"I can't wait. Does he know you found me?"

"Not yet," Jenna clapped her hands together excitedly.

Scott reached into his jacket and pulled out his cell phone. He showed Leah photos he'd taken of Jenna with the family in Ohio.

Then he asked, "Shall we?"

"Yes, please!" the twins said at the same time, then giggled.

Scott made the call and handed the phone over to Jenna. She was laughing and crying as she apologized to Lincoln for calling so late, then explained who was with her. Soon Leah and Lincoln were talking while Jenna looked on from the shelter of Scott's arm around her shoulders. He was thankful that he didn't have to put into words his deep appreciation for being allowed to share this special moment with Jenna. It meant the world to him.

By the time Lincoln and Leah had hung up, both twins were wiping away tears. They excused themselves to freshen up. While they were gone, Scott ordered an array of desserts for the ladies to sample, plus a bottle of the best champagne to mark the occasion. When they returned, he took note that while Leah was thrilled by the extravagance, Jenna was concerned about the cost.

After they'd clinked flute glasses in celebration, Jenna invited Leah to join her and Lincoln for Thanksgiving in Detroit.

Leah shook her head. "I can't see my way clear to come. I can't afford it. I only just got settled here in Las Vegas."

"But you have to come," Jenna insisted. "Don't worry about the money. I'll take care of it for you."

"Are you serious?" Leah exclaimed.

"Absolutely. I can hardly wait for all three of us to be together again."

Scott said nothing, but he was aware that Leah hadn't bothered to thank Jenna for the generous offer. After topping off their champagne glasses, he lifted his glass. He toasted, "To the Gaines family reunion!"

Scott soon realized he had to stop comparing the twins. What difference did it make that Jenna was regal and poised, while Leah was assertive and not afraid to ask for what she wanted? Both sisters had suffered because of their parents' failings and loss, but they carried themselves well and held their heads high, emphasizing their tall stature. While Jenna had struggled to educate herself, Leah had turned her back on the opportunities her adopted family had offered. Because of that, Leah had had to fight to make a place for herself in the often ruthless entertainment industry. Scott didn't envy her. Becoming an accomplished actress was no small feat. It would take years of study and hard work with no guarantees. The Gaines twins might look alike, but they were vastly different from each other.

While waiting for the check, he wondered if he was being judgmental. He was coming up with some strong assumptions about Leah after being with her for only a short time. He didn't really know her. After all, she was Jenna's twin and deserved his consideration and friendship.

He nearly chuckled aloud as he acknowledged that when it came to his lady, he was decidedly biased. His lady? When had he started claiming her as his own? Who was he kidding? Jenna had always been special to him. She deserved the best that life had to offer.

He'd been surprised when Jenna hadn't clarified their situation to her twin but had let her believe they were a couple. He couldn't wait to find out why Jenna hadn't taken time to explain. Sure their relationship was complicated, but so what? Life was full of complications.

Scott sighed, recognizing that his time would be better spent trying to figure out a way of convincing Jenna he was worthy of her trust. Perhaps he was relying too heavily on the fact that she hadn't rejected his hugs or his kisses? It had been a struggle not to push for more, to give her time to adjust to having him in her life. He reaffirmed that this was about Jenna. She was what mattered. Yet he was also keenly aware that he hadn't been invited to Thanksgiving dinner.

It was close to five in the morning by the time they dropped Leah off at her apartment. It was in a run-down area that had Jenna worrying about Leah's safety, but Jenna wisely kept quiet about it.

She was thrilled when Leah agreed to take the next night off. Scott planned to celebrate the twins' reunion by taking them out on the town. He also encouraged Leah to bring along her live-in boyfriend.

While their driver dealt with the traffic, Jenna covered a yawn. Despite the late hour, she couldn't help speculating on what Scott expected once they were back in the suite.

They'd kissed several times. And Scott had been so kind to her. Perhaps too generous? Did he expect more kisses or for her to make love with him? With her head down and eyes closed, Jenna wondered if she was being naïve about all this. It looked as if she was about to find out exactly how much Scott had changed during the time they'd been apart. The possibility that she might have been wrong to trust him had her stomach tight with tension. Many things about him had changed, but she doubted his keen sexual appetite had lessened over time.

"It's way past your bedtime, young lady," Scott crooned close to her ear as the car slowed to a stop in front of the hotel.

"I'll be ready to sleep the moment my head hits the pillow." Jenna shifted to put more space between them.

"It's been one eventful day." His voice was low and sexy. When he got out, he held a hand out to her.

Too tired to protest, she graciously accepted his help from the car, keenly aware of his masculine charm. All too soon they were back in their suite with the door locked behind them.

Suddenly, Jenna was angry with herself for agreeing to stay. She should have said no to a suite. Now she would have to put on a brave face to get out of what might be a sticky situation.

Forcing a smile, she said, "I need to go shopping in

the morning. I didn't bring a dress for a night out on the town. So I'll say good-night. And thank you for everything, including that wonderful meal."

Cupping her shoulders, he looked down at her for a long moment, making her heartbeat speed up. "There is no need for thanks. Some things remain unchanged between us. I love seeing you happy. Sleep well, sweet Jenna." He brushed his lips against her forehead. Then he dropped his hands before moving toward his bedroom door down the short hall.

She was weak with relief when she closed her door quietly behind her. Leaning against it for support, she scolded herself for letting her fears get the best of her. She was ashamed of her wayward thoughts. Scott had never given her reason to doubt his sincerity or his self-control. He'd offered to help her find her family, and that was exactly what he had done.

How could she let her fear of falling for him all over again cause her to make such a terrible mistake? Thank goodness he didn't know what she'd been thinking. Jenna was so upset by her lack of faith in him that she purposely left her bedroom door unlocked.

Even after hours of much-needed sleep, she felt guilty for the way she'd misjudged Scott. She suspected that her lack of faith came from a well of fear . . . fear that was generated by her increasing awareness of his masculine charm.

Awareness could lead to hunger . . . hunger to once again experience his lovemaking. Furious with herself, she punched her pillow. Just who did she think she was kidding?

She still desired Scott Hendricks. She wanted the fierce heat and sizzling sexuality that was so much a part of the strong, intense man she'd once loved with all her heart. Despite her best efforts, she could no longer avoid what was right in her face. Every time he was near, she recalled the passion they'd shared.

Although young, Scott had been a tender lover, considerate of her needs. Jenna had been a virgin when they'd first come together. Even though he'd never said so, she'd suspected that his experiences in the bedroom had also been limited. He'd been nineteen to her twenty. There had been a few awkward moments, even a bit of embarrassment, that had quickly given way to the intensity of making love. There had also been tenderness fueled by how they'd felt about each other. They'd loved so deeply that they hadn't been able to get enough. There had been no worry about unwanted pregnancy, though. They'd used protection to safeguard themselves and their future.

Last night, as Jenna had watched Scott with her twin sister, she'd been shocked by feelings of insecurity. Lenna was outgoing and had the confidence that Jenna had longed for growing up. Her twin wasn't afraid of her sexuality. She didn't just embrace it, she drew men to her like a sponge. Every man in the room had at one time or another stared at her twin's striking beauty. Lenna—no, Leah—had been in her element. She was accustomed to male attention. She'd even flirted with Scott.

Scott's awareness of Leah's beauty hadn't been lost on Jenna. She hated that she'd felt threatened enough to be jealous. Why else had she let her sister think there was more going on between her and Scott?

Jenna was not only embarrassed, but also disappointed in herself. There was no point in trying to sugarcoat her behavior. The green monster had gotten the best of her. What was next? Her only recourse was to move forward and not repeat the mistake.

She showered and dressed in jeans, tucking in a

pink-and-plum print blouse. When she'd packed, she
hadn't expected to be going out on the town. Her favorite black cocktail dress was tucked away in her closet
at home, so she had to find something pretty without
breaking her budget.

On her way into the kitchen she spotted a note from
Scott propped against a bowl of fresh flowers on the
dining table. He'd gone to the hotel's gym for a workout
and would be meeting an old teammate for lunch in
one of the hotel's restaurants. She was welcome to join
them. He reminded her that their driver, Josh Barnes,
was at her disposal—all she had to do was ask for him
at the desk. She smiled, imagining her twin's reaction.

She found a selection of French toast, scrambled
eggs, and breakfast meats warming in the kitchen, as
well as coffee and an array of fresh fruit.

"I could easily become spoiled by all this." She shook
her head at the extravagance while filling a plate. It was
nearly eleven when she jotted her thanks for the lunch
invitation on the back of his note, along with a warning
not to expect her back until late afternoon.

The driver took her to the Fashion Show Mall, which
included major department stores such as Nordstrom,
Bloomingdale's, and Saks Fifth Avenue, where she'd
spent many enjoyable hours hunting for bargains while
living in New York.

It took a few hours, but she was delighted when she
found a cranberry cocktail dress on sale. She loved the
sequined straps that crossed beneath the bodice, and
the full, flirty silk skirt. After more hunting, Jenna discovered the perfect pair of peep-toe cranberry pumps.
She was glad she'd brought along an ivory cashmere
shawl, a small ivory purse, and her pearls. She scolded
herself when she splurged on a black lace-edged strap-
less bra and boy-cut lace panties.

Jenna was disappointed when she returned to an empty suite. She needed to explain why she'd let her twin believe they were a couple. But how could she without admitting to being jealous? No . . . no. Stretching out on the chaise longue, she dozed off.

When she awakened, for a few seconds she had no idea where she was, until she spotted Scott lounging in the armchair with his laptop open. The room was in shadow, and lamps had been turned on.

Twelve

Smiling, she stretched. "Hi. I hope I wasn't snoring."

Chuckling, Scott tugged on his ear. "Was that rumble coming from you?"

She tried to give him a glare, but her infectious laugh got in the way. Despite her inclination to deny it, she was glad to see him. She was just so happy. She'd found her twin. She had her family back, and Scott had shared it with her.

"What are you doing? Don't tell me you're working?"

"Working? Me? Never. I'm retired, remember?"

"Then what are you studying with such concentration? Never mind!" she exclaimed, covering her face as she eased up to a sitting position. "Forget I asked. Tell me to mind my own business."

He laughed. "There is no big secret. I'm just online checking to see what was going on with my portfolio."

"You don't hire someone to do that for you?"

"Why? Do I look stupid?" He laughed. "No, seriously, I have money I play around with. It allows me to invest in some unusual ventures. It's a hobby of mine."

"It could be a risky hobby, especially considering the recent plunges of the market," she surmised, but her interest was piqued.

"I only risk what I can afford to lose," he grinned. "I work within my limits."

"Can you?"

"Without a doubt. My odds are better than any of the casinos here in Las Vegas. In the past four years, I've invested in six minority companies, and all but one has shown profits. In the past year, I've invested in three new companies that I think have potential."

She grinned, clearly intrigued. "Tell me more."

He released a deep chuckle. "How could I forget? This is your thing. Tell me how you're doing. Any big losses?"

"A few hits, but I'm doing relatively well. I believe in diversification, and I've got time on my side. When you consider the downturns, the problems with the banks, and the economy, it can be scary. Please, tell me about the start-up companies and how they're doing?"

"Last spring, I read about a new security company that had some novel ideas on how to derail identity theft. It's a huge problem that I don't think we've fully addressed." He seemed enthused by her interest and went on to explain why he was willing to take the risk. When he glanced at his watch, he said, "Hold up. I had our chef prepare something to hold us over until our late dinner."

"This suite comes with a chef?" She watched him go into the kitchen.

"Yes," he said from over his shoulder. "And anything else you might like."

"Such as?"

"You know about the car and driver. The chef, a personal trainer, and massage therapist. Your imagination is the limit." He came back in carrying a tray loaded with sandwiches, which he placed on the wide leather ottoman. He held up bottles of juice for her inspection.

Jenna took the apple juice. "Thanks." Sampling crab salad on a toasted bun, she decided she was hopelessly lost when it came to the lifestyle of the super rich. There were more perks than she could ever come up with on any given day. Evidently, she was destined, like most folks, to be on the outside looking in, while hoping to win the lottery. She almost giggled out loud. It might help if she bothered to buy a ticket once in a while.

Impatient to hear more, she urged, "Finish telling me about this company. You said the owner used to work in military intelligence?"

"Oh, yeah," he said, settling back in the chair, a roast beef sandwich in one hand and a bottle of cranberry juice in the other. He told her about the company and why he'd decided to invest. Then he went on to tell her about the Jacobs brothers in Detroit. With his backing, they would soon be opening a supper club in the city.

She was so engrossed that she was surprised when he finished by saying, "We'd better get moving or we're going to be late picking up Leah and her guy."

"You're right!" She jumped up, hurrying to her bedroom with his deep laughter vibrating in the background.

Jenna had been looking forward to this evening and had dressed with care. She was secretly thrilled by Scott's long whistle and compliment when she emerged from her room.

"Thank you," she said softly as he draped her shawl around her shoulders. "You look very handsome," she admitted, taking the time to straighten his silk tie.

She dropped her hands, curling them at her sides to keep from smoothing them over his pristine white shirt and across the broad expanse of his shoulders, covered in an expertly tailored charcoal gray suit. Considering the superb fit, it had to have been made for him alone. Handsome was an understatement, considering his flawless, dark skin, long, powerful frame, and good looks.

Scott smiled, placing his hand at the small of her back and urging her forward. "We need to get moving."

Eager to see her twin, Jenna merely nodded her consent. Despite her best efforts to neutralize her feelings, she hadn't figured out how to deal with her keen awareness of him. Every second spent alone with him seemed to heighten her senses and weaken her resolve to keep her distance. Jenna was terrified of falling in love with him all over again. Plus, she was playing this dangerous game of pretense.

"You okay?" Scott asked as he helped her inside the limo.

She hedged, "Just looking forward to spending time with Lenna." Changing the subject, Jenna said, "I'm glad she was able to take the night off. I just wish she didn't have to take her clothes off for a living. She's not taking advantage of the fact that she's smart."

"Why are you going there? Leah doesn't seem to be bothered by her choices. She's doing what she wants to do. You're twins, but you two aren't the same."

"No, Scott. In this, we are the same. She just decided to take the easy way out of a bad situation. She's a smart girl. There is no reason she can't use her mind to get ahead. I want to help her reach her potential," Jenna insisted, gazing out at the bright lights.

He cautioned, "Sweet thing, are you listening to yourself? You just found her. Don't start trying to change her. Get to know her first."

She sighed. "I'm not saying there's anything wrong with dancing for a living. But in her case, we're not talking about art."

"I can't argue with that, but I don't think you need to rush in criticizing. It's only natural that you want a better life for her, but the choice has to be hers. It's too soon to push."

"You're right," she consented around a frustrated sigh. "I just hate to see her wasting her life this way, especially if I can help."

Squeezing her hand, he urged, "Relax, sweet thing. Enjoy being together. There will be time enough later for that serious discussion. Tonight is a celebration, right?"

"Yes . . ." she echoed, watching as they slowed to a stop, parking in front of her sister's apartment building.

Evidently, the couple, both dressed in black, had been waiting for them. Within moments, the two were making their way to the car. Jenna and Leah reached out to clasp hands, while the men nodded to each other as they made themselves comfortable on the adjacent seat. Leah was in a short, tight dress and quickly made the introduction.

John Norton, tall, light-skinned, and very good looking, had left his black silk shirt opened to the middle of his broad chest. He was all smiles as he kissed the back of Jenna's hand and shook Scott's hand. "I have been eager to meet you two ever since Leah got home last night. Twins? Who would believe it? But one look is all it takes to seal the deal." He laughed heartily, as if he had told a joke. "This car is nice," he went on. "Scott, you sure know how to travel in style. That's what I'm talking about," he said as he patted Leah's thigh, seeming pleased as he looked around. "Man, is that . . ." he trailed off as he leaned forward to study the array of liquor inside a glass-encased built-in compartment.

"Are you from Vegas, John?" Scott asked.

"Hell, no. I'm from L.A., like my bit—" He stopped

and corrected himself. "I mean, like my lady. She and I met at a club. We've been together ever since." He took out a bottle of aged scotch. "Hey, this is the good stuff. Do you mind, my man?"

"Help yourself. You and Leah are our guests." Scott showed him where the crystal tumblers and ice cubes were stored.

"Thanks. I could get used to this, fast," John said, helping himself but neglecting to inquire if anyone else would care for something to drink.

Scott asked, "Would either of you ladies care for champagne?"

Jenna shook her head. "I'll wait until I've eaten."

Leah smiled. "I can wait, too. Where are we going, Scott?"

"Why, that's up to you ladies. I thought we might start the evening out at Wolfgang Puck's restaurant, then take in the show at Cirque du Soleil's KÀ. Then follow that by stopping in at Planet Hollywood and Tryst."

Leah squealed with delight, clapping her hands. "I can't wait!"

"Sounds like a plan to me," John put in, emptying his glass in one long swallow. "Man, this is sweet. You riding around in a limo, living the life of the rich and famous. I'm not surprised. I've seen your moves on the basketball court, Hendricks."

"What do you do for a living, John?" Jenna asked.

"Well, baby, I'm in between gigs." He nodded. "Leah tells me you teach at a college. You're smart and beautiful. I like that." He refilled his glass, saying, "My man, when you guys played for the championship, you were on fire. Hit that hoop from all over the damn court." He laughed boisterously. "I put my money on you that night. Talk about a great game. How many bitches did you guys take on that night? Ten? Twenty?" He laughed even louder while draining another drink.

Jenna decided right then that she did not like the man. She'd tried to withhold her opinion until she'd gotten to know him, but she suspected that his being in between jobs was not a recent setback. He was unemployed while Leah danced and stripped down to a G-string to keep a roof over their heads and food on the table. Jenna had to bite her tongue to hold back an angry retort. Just who did he think he was, casually referring to any female by that foul name.

"Glad you enjoyed the game," Scott said smoothly, then changed the subject, "Leah, have you been to any of the Cirque du Soleil's shows?"

"Not in this lifetime," Leah giggled. "I've been dying to go."

Jenna smiled at her sister. "Sounds like we're in for a treat."

"Classy," John joked. "My baby don't know the difference between first class and a ten-dollar bill, man. She barely makes enough to keep a roof over our heads."

Jenna swallowed a gasp while Leah giggled, as if he'd told a joke.

Scott said evenly, "Leah didn't have any problems sipping champagne or dining at the best table last night."

"The food was fabulous," Leah piped in. "I can't wait to sample Wolfgang's food. I read about it in the newspaper."

Scott nodded. "John, you say you're between jobs. What exactly is your specialty?"

"I'm a businessman. I've been in a little of this and that. I've been trying to get enough cash together to start up my own club to showcase the ladies. If you're interested in investing, let me know. I can hook you up on the ground floor with a real sweet deal."

Scott smiled. "Thanks, John. I'll keep that in mind. Hope everyone is hungry. I know I'm ready for a thick steak," he said as the chauffeur turned into the drive.

He didn't wait for the driver to open the door but slid out and held out his hand to first Jenna, then Leah.

He placed an arm around Jenna's waist, pausing to allow the other couple to enter the building first. He said close to her ear, "You okay?"

"Hardly. What does she see in that jerk?"

"Good question. Try not to let it get to you. We have an entire night to get through."

"Exactly," she whispered back.

Jenna was not just angry; she was also upset with herself for letting another person influence her mood. Their night of celebration seemed to move in painfully slow motion. She wanted it over. It wasn't that she didn't enjoy the wonderful meal or the viewing of the show in a private VIP box at the theater. Or that she didn't relish every moment of being with her twin sister. John, Leah's boyfriend, was the problem.

It was impossible to ignore the way he tried to take advantage of everything and everyone that came within his grasp. He made no secret that he was out for number one and that it didn't matter whom he hurt in the process. Jenna wondered if that included her sister.

She was disgusted by the way John spent as much of Scott's money as he could. He ordered the thickest steak and the most expensive liquor available. They'd barely sat down in the exclusive nightclub Tryst before John was busy ordering drinks. Jenna had to give him credit. He could hold his liquor. It didn't seem to bother Leah that the more he drank, the louder he became. Or that he ordered drinks for his new friends at the next table on Scott's tab.

Frustrated, she wanted to shake some sense into Leah, force her twin to take a long, hard look at what was right there for all to see. Forget about love. John Norton wasn't enamored with her sister. Jenna feared that he would use Leah until she was all used up. Only then would he move on to his next pretty victim.

Jenna was also surprised by the number of people, even among the club's elite clientele, who came up to Scott to either shake his hand or ask for an autograph.

While out on the dance floor with Scott, Jenna struggled to let go and simply enjoy. Even the breathtaking beauty of the ninety-foot waterfall and the lavish surroundings couldn't keep her from fuming. Scott's whispered assurance that it didn't matter hadn't helped. The hours were slipping away and her mood hadn't mellowed. Scott might be able to shrug it off, stating that it was only one night out on the town and insisting that it wasn't about to break him, but Jenna couldn't let it go.

She barely held onto her temper. She fumed silently, telling herself it was better if she kept her mouth shut—that was the only way to get through the rest of the night without spoiling her sister's enjoyment. Jenna was genuinely pleased to see her twin so happy. While Leah didn't seem to mind John's selfishness—she was evidently used to it—Jenna thought it was a shame, because Leah deserved so much more.

Later, when it was time to part, Jenna found it nearly impossible to say good-bye to her sister. Only the knowledge that they would see each other during the Thanksgiving holidays kept Jenna from bursting into tears. To Jenna's delight, Leah had agreed to come for a visit.

On their way back to the hotel, Jenna worried that Leah might change her mind and not want to leave John behind. Scott had offered to fly them both to Detroit. Although touched by his willingness to help, Jenna flatly refused. Scott had done enough just by coming with her to Las Vegas. When she thought about all he'd done to make her reunion with her twin memorable, Jenna was overwhelmed. It would be unconscionable to ask for more.

"You've been brooding all night, babe. Keeping it locked inside won't help. You might as well spit it out," he encouraged her as he let them into their suite.

Jenna was carrying her pumps, having kicked them off in the elevator. "You know what's wrong. I've had it up to here"—she gestured wildly above her head—"with that man. I don't understand what my sister sees in him. John Norton is nothing but a hustler."

"You let him spoil the celebration for you. He isn't worth it."

"I know," she sighed. "What I don't understand is, why doesn't it bother you? It was bad enough spending an entire night with that loudmouthed drunk." She tossed her shoes onto the carpet and draped her wrap over the nearby armchair, then went to the French doors, where she stared out at the twinkling lights, her small hands balled into fists. "Why did he have to take advantage of you that way? It was too much!"

"Let it go, Jenna."

"I can't," she hissed, blinking away tears. "It's just plain wrong!"

Scott went over and cupped her shoulders, turning her to face him. "Why? Why do you care so much?"

Jenna's entire body suddenly went taut with tension as she struggled to sort out her emotions. Her damp eyes collided with his. She tried to look away but couldn't.

Reluctantly, she quietly admitted, "We're friends. I don't dislike you."

"You haven't said you cared about me, either. Yet you've been acting that way tonight."

"Any decent human being would be upset."

"But would she brood over it for hours? And would she be outraged to the point of tears even after claiming she has no feelings for him?"

"You are reading too much into it."

"What does that mean? Do you still have feelings for me, Jenna?"

Thirteen

It means I didn't like sitting back and watching what happened tonight," she snapped. She was not about to put a label on her emotions. Nor was she prepared to examine them too closely or to explain them to him.

"I'm really struggling here not to . . ." He stopped. His voice was barely above a whisper, his frustration evident.

"What?" She watched as he closed his eyes and took a deep breath.

When he opened them again, he moved a caressing hand along the side of her face. "Does it help knowing I still care about you, sweet Jenna?" He pressed a kiss against her cheek, a series of kisses along her jawline. "You're important to me—that has never changed." His mouth covered hers. The kiss was hot, yet incredibly tender, as he sponged, then suckled, her bottom lip. "Something has changed with you tonight. I'd like to know what."

Her breathing was quick and uneven as she fought for control. Desire danced along her nerve endings, adding to the confusion. "It doesn't matter, Scott."

"It matters, Jenna. Everything about you matters to me. I promised myself before we left the city that

I wouldn't pressure you this weekend. You're dealing with enough changes in your life. You don't need me trying to seduce you into doing something you're not ready to do. I've tried to limit myself to a few touches and kisses.

"But tonight, sweet girl, you have my senses soaring and need riding me hard. I'd like nothing better than to make love to you until dawn lightens the sky." His hands were curled into fists at his side. "Forget I said that. I'm going to keep that promise, if it kills me. I suggest you do us both a favor and go into your bedroom and lock the door. Now!"

Annoyed by his take-charge attitude, she hissed, "When did you get the job of deciding what is best for me?" Her voice shook with emotion while her body ached with need. "I'm not a little girl in need of your protection." She lifted her chin while folding her arms beneath her breasts. "In case you haven't noticed, I'm all grown up. I make my own decisions."

Scott quirked a dark brow. "Oh, yeah, I noticed." His voice rasped with need and impatience. "I'm warning you, I'm not some superhuman with extraordinary abilities and ironclad control, like that doll they put my name on a few years back."

Her eyes went wide before she giggled, "The Scott Hendricks doll?"

He nodded, his mouth taut and his gaze smoldering with desire. "I mean it, Jenna. Go!"

"Stop ordering me around."

"Then don't blame me if you find yourself on your back with your soft thighs wrapped around me."

"Nothing is going to happen. We both know what went wrong the first time around."

"Why, Jenna? Why are you acting as if what we shared ended years ago? Something's happening right now . . . between the two of us. I'm not going to pretend it's nothing. The feelings are there, and they're real."

She stared up into the molten heat of his dark eyes, wanting to deny his claim, but she couldn't—not in good conscience. He was correct. Something very powerful was going on between them. Even though it scared her and she might have regrets later, she was not running from it or him.

"Admit it, Jenna," he said urgently between deep, tongue-stroking kisses. "Admit you still have feelings for me. That you still want me."

Jenna didn't say anything. She couldn't find the words. Overcome with desire and powerful emotions, she allowed her senses free rein as she inhaled his clean male scent. She luxuriated in the heat of his long, hard length pressed against her soft curves.

"Have you missed me as much as I've missed you?" he asked, his voice rough with need.

"Oh, yes," she nearly sobbed, opening her mouth for more of the sizzling, hot thrusts of his tongue against hers.

"I need you," Scott growled into her ear.

There was no doubt in her mind that he meant every word. She could feel the heavy pressure of his hard shaft against her. He needed her as desperately as she needed him. Her inner core pulsed with desire. She wanted him deep inside, filling the emptiness.

"Hurry," she begged as she slid her hands under his coat to the buttons lining his shirt. Her fingers shook as she struggled to get beneath the cloth. She longed to feel his dark skin. She was breathing heavily by the time she freed the top buttons and slid her hand inside. They both trembled at the feel and fierce heat of his skin against her palms.

"It's been too long." His voice was husky with need.

He shrugged out of the jacket and yanked the shirt out of his trousers, ripping the remaining buttons off with one quick jerk of the wrist.

She was beyond protest. She needed to touch him. Her hands trembled as she caressed his chest, teasing his taut, ebony nipples. He growled his pleasure as he leaned down to issue a tongue-stroking kiss. He explored the roof of her mouth, her sharp teeth, then he suckled her tongue heatedly. She quivered with need as his tongue slid down the length of her neck to lick the fragrant hollow at the base of her throat.

Finally, she was back in his arms. This was no dream or even a memory. It was real. His large hands boldly cupped her aching breasts, gently squeezing them. It felt so good . . . so right. She sighed when he worried her hard, sensitive nipples.

Lost in a sensual daze, Jenna didn't offer a single protest when Scott swung her off her feet and carried her into his bedroom. She trembled with desire as he unzipped her dress, unhooked her bra, and eased down her lace panties. Before she could inhale, she was draped across his bed with her arms wrapped around his strong neck.

She kissed him, pushing bothersome worries and doubts aside to concentrate on giving and receiving long-awaited pleasure. Sizzling flames of passion traveled along her nerve endings as he warmed her soft flesh. His tongue felt like rough velvet on her skin. Had anything ever felt better?

He didn't stop there. He followed the silky lines of her dark skin but slowed when he reached the swell of her breasts. Jenna cried aloud when Scott tantalized her with the streaming hot wash of his tongue over her softness. He licked the entire globe until she ached with need and trembled as desire built with each flick of his tongue. His entire focus was on her as he laved her highly sensitive nipple. She whimpered when he applied the hard suction she adored. It had been so long since he'd indulged her this way, and it was as deliciously sweet as she remembered.

Just when she thought she couldn't tolerate more, he moved to her other breast and repeated the titillation. Jenna sobbed out her enjoyment, not wanting the sizzling-hot magic to ever stop.

Being with him this way was both achingly familiar and incredibly new. He cradled her in his arms as he pleasured her. No one made her feel the way he did. He alone touched that special place deep inside that both frightened and thrilled her.

He lifted his head, whispering into her ear, "You feel so good in my arms."

Resting her cheek on his shoulder, she gave free rein to the yearnings she'd been pretending didn't matter since he'd reentered her life. Moving her hands over his bare chest with her eyes closed, she indulged herself, allowing her other senses to take control.

Padded with muscle, his chest was heavier than she remembered. She worried his taut nipples until his breath quickened and he released a throaty groan. Traveling down to his tight, firm midsection, she marveled at the intense heat of his dark skin.

Realizing that he was still wearing trousers, she quickly unfastened them, unzipping and pushing away fabric until she could touch only him. Jenna sighed in pleasure as she stroked Scott's firm stomach, caressing his belly button and hard core muscles. She heard his sharp indrawn breath when she lingered, relishing the texture and smell of his skin.

He moaned huskily when she caressed the jutting length of his aroused sex. She used both hands to encircle his shaft, paying particular attention to the sensitive crest. Encouraged by his guttural moans as she stroked his entire length, she shifted to gently squeeze his heaviness below, then she moved to suckle a taut nipple.

Suddenly, Scott jerked her up until their mouths connected. The kiss was deep, ravenous, making them both shake from the intensity of the exchange.

"Sweet Jenna . . . tell me that you want me. That you need me as much as I want and need you," he rasped into her ear.

"Yes, oh yes. Scott, I need you now," she said without hesitation.

He rolled her over until she lay beneath him. His open mouth was scorching hot against the side of her throat. Large hands cupped full breasts, then smoothed down over her flat stomach. He spread her thighs so he could palm her feminine mound. After cupping and then rhythmically squeezing her damp heat, he parted dark curls to finger her fleshy, slick folds. She moaned, unable to contain her desire.

Scott slid a long finger into Jenna's moist sheath. Sobbing his name, she clung to him as the pleasure mushroomed. He eased in a second finger while circling her opening. She trembled in response as he slowly caressed her highly sensitive feminine bud . . . tantalizing her with gentle strokes.

"You are so wet and incredibly tight," he whispered as he quickened the pace.

Caught up in a maze of sensual delight, she could barely form a coherent thought. Each new sensation spiraled upward, sending her to an even higher level of enjoyment. Close to climaxing, she whimpered in protest when he removed his fingers, but she issued a heartfelt sigh of relief when he tantalized her with his tongue. The pleasure quickly spun beyond her control, and she shuddered from an intense release. It was sharp and poignant but not enough. She needed more. She needed him . . . inside of her . . . a part of her.

"Oh, Scott! It has been so long. Please hurry, I need you deep inside," she said urgently.

He gave her a hard kiss before he reached into the nightstand for a box of condoms. Her heart raced with anticipation as he ripped the packet and quickly covered his shaft. The moment he came close, she pulled him back to her.

"Hurry . . ." She was fed up with being without him.

Scott ignored her dictate to rush. He clenched his teeth as he slowly eased forward, stretching her with his rock-hard sex. They both shuddered from the long-awaited, sizzling-hot contact. He groaned her name and tightened his arms around her as she whimpered his name, pressing even closer to him and draping her legs over his muscular thighs.

Jenna moaned from a mixture of pain and pleasure, glorying in the sheer joy of being one with him. Her senses were raw and fully engaged. Slowly, he filled the emptiness, bridging the gap that separated them.

When he remained still, giving her time to adjust to his entry, she was frustrated by the delay. She moved despite the burning pressure. She wanted him, now. He clasped her hips, holding her still.

She pleaded, "Scott . . ."

"No, I'm hurting you." His entire body was taut with tension and damp from perspiration. He cradled her face. "How long has it been?"

She shook her head. "It doesn't matter. Please . . . don't stop."

Although his breathing was rapid and uneven, he remained still. Frustrated, she licked the side of his throat down to the base, then down further to worry his nipple. Scott's nostrils flared, as if he was inhaling her scent, but he kept a firm hold on her hips.

"Don't," he said between clenched teeth. "I don't want to hurt you."

"Scott," she crooned as the burning pain receded, giving way to pulsating need. She'd done without him so long . . . too long. She wanted him . . . every hard inch. Closing her eyes, she tightened her inner muscles around him and stroked his engorged shaft while rocking her hips from side to side.

Scott groaned as his control shattered. He moved in earnest, in and out of her damp heat. All too soon they were caught up in his rhythmic thrusts and the incredible pleasure of finally being connected. She gasped for breath, marveling at his incredible masculinity. Each of his steel-hard strokes was sheathed in tenderness. He kissed her as if to soothe her earlier hurt, and she returned his kisses as overwhelming need turned into unparalleled enjoyment.

"You feel so good . . . so right," he said close to her ear. Perspiration beaded his face and upper body as he held himself back, his body taut from the strain.

Desperate for the full force of his lovemaking, she whispered, "Stop treating me as if I'll break. I'm not a porcelain doll."

Jenna lifted her legs, wrapping them around his waist, opening herself for his full penetration. Scott growled her name as the last thread of his control snapped. He pulled out only to quickly plunge deep inside, giving her his entire length again and again. She was swiftly caught up in his powerful thrusts. Wrapped in each other's arms as insurmountable pleasure engulfed them, hurling them toward completion. She screamed as her frame shook from mind-numbing pleasure that overwhelmed her senses. Her last coherent thought was that it was even better than she remembered. Scott's shout of exultation immediately followed Jenna's. They clung to each other, their hearts pounding with excitement, gradually returning to normal.

His warm, tender kisses moved across her forehead, down the bridge of her nose to the tip, then over each cheek. Jenna focused on taking slow, fortifying breaths, her body damp from perspiration.

Much had changed over the years, but one thing had not. Despite her best efforts, she hadn't forgotten that intense heat and soaring passion were as much a part of their lovemaking as sweetness and tenderness.

She had to be careful not to confuse the past with the present. Yes, it had been incredible. It was also glaringly obvious that she'd cared too much back then . . . had loved too deeply. The loss of that love had nearly destroyed her. It was a mistake that she didn't intend to repeat.

Keenly aware of their intimate connection, she pressed her palms against his chest. He moaned as he pulled back and rolled onto his side.

"Sorry. I didn't mean to crush you."

She didn't explain that his weight wasn't the problem. Once her amour had cooled, she'd pushed him away because she'd been uncomfortable with their intimacy.

"Are you okay? I'm sorry I hurt you."

Embarrassed, she shook her head. "I'm fine. How about you?"

His response was to gather her close, kissing her temple. "I know I have no right to ask, but that doesn't stop me from wondering how long it has . . ."

Not about to answer, Jenna pressed her fingers against Scott's full lips as if she could hold back the question. "Let's leave the past right where it belongs."

He sighed, then yawned. "Excuse me. You're right. We're making new memories."

Vastly relieved at not having to answer his question, she relaxed against him, murmuring, "I'm exhausted. I don't know about you, but three nights of very little sleep have caught up to me."

Unfortunately, she couldn't disarm her fears, or forget the broken promise, or the years of lonely nights, plus the numerous beautiful women in his life who had been captured for all time by the press. Naturally, her life had gone on after they'd parted. The one thing that hadn't changed was her core belief: She couldn't share her body with someone she didn't care about. And she'd never cared enough to let another man get that close to her, something she couldn't share with him.

His long fingers gently massaged her nape and her shoulders. "Sleep, sweet girl. Trust me to keep you safe for a few hours. Leave the worries to me. Okay?"

"Mm," she murmured, covering a yawn.

If only life were that simple and problems that easily solved. He wasn't the same man she'd met and fallen in love with in college. He was sophisticated, worldly, and an accomplished lover. If she wasn't extremely cautious, she could find herself falling in love with him all over again.

How exactly could she stop that from happening? She already cared more than she could comfortably admit. How else had she ended up in bed with him? She'd turned her carefully constructed world upside down when she'd let him make love to her. Now what? Pretend it didn't change anything? Better yet, pretend it hadn't happened?

"Can't sleep?" he asked, pressing a slow, drugging kiss against her swollen lips.

Suddenly trembling with renewed desire, she kissed him back. She was giving and receiving tongue-stroking kisses.

"Again?"

"Again . . ." he growled deep in his throat.

* * *

The sun was high in the sky before either one of them got any sleep.

"Wake up, sweet thing. We have to get moving if we want to stop by your sister's on our way to the airport."

Jenna jumped at the sound of Scott's voice. She issued a weary moan. Resting on her stomach, she hugged the pillow.

"I'm sorry, babe. I didn't mean to scare you." He smoothed her thick waves. "You do want to see Leah again, don't you?"

Jenna would have liked to pull the pillow over her head and shut the world out. Instead she said, "If I ask nicely, will you go away and let me sleep?"

Scott's response was a deep, throaty chuckle. "I could call and change our flight until this evening, but we will get in very late."

"No, don't do that. That will only make it worse. After a good night's sleep, I can manage work and my classes tomorrow." Using the sheet to cover her nudity, she rolled onto her back and sat up. "How come you're so wide awake?"

"Hot shower and two cups of coffee." He handed her a hot mug.

Jenna sipped, murmuring her appreciation. "Thank you."

"Better?"

"Much." Finally able to open her eyes, she was disturbed by what she saw.

He looked so good with a towel wrapped low on his taut hips, barely covering the prominent ridge of his sex and thick, powerful thighs. His dark chest rippled with muscles.

She was suddenly conscious of her tousled hair, kiss-swollen lips, sensitive breasts, and sore femininity due to his thorough lovemaking.

Flushed with embarrassment as she recalled what they'd done together, she found she couldn't meet his gaze. She'd acted like a kid in a candy shop. One taste had been all it took to have her hungry for more. If she didn't watch her step, she would be reaching for him yet again. Goodness! Giving in to cravings, especially one that was bad for her peace of mind, was a weakness she couldn't afford.

After a few more sips of coffee, she pointed to his white dress shirt draped along with her dress and underthings on the armchair.

"Mind if I borrow your shirt?"

He grabbed the shirt and held it for her.

She hurried into it, overlapping the front. Once she was decently covered, she grabbed her things, promising she wouldn't be long. She dashed into the other bedroom.

They were in the limousine on the way to her sister's place when Scott asked, "Are you still angry with John?"

Jenna shrugged. "Wasted energy. He is what he is. I just hope Lenna—uh, I mean, Leah—takes a hard look at him before he disappoints her." She sighed. "What a weekend. It's almost gone. And I have to leave my sister behind."

Scott gave her hand a squeeze. "What's important was that you finally found her. Right?"

She smiled. "Thanks for the reminder. It's going to be so hard saying good-bye."

That proved to be an understatement. Jenna was close to tears when she hugged her twin for the last time. She clung to the promise that Leah would be coming to Detroit for the upcoming Thanksgiving holiday weekend.

Fourteen

A brooding and silent Scott studied Jenna as she napped on the flight back to the Motor City. She was incredibly beautiful both inside and out. Her ease on the eyes wasn't the issue, though. If only she was as easy to figure out as one of the chemical compounds he routinely worked with in the lab. Science was basic, simple systematized knowledge that came from study and observation. The most complicated chemical formulas and theories he thrived on didn't even compare to the challenge of trying to understand the intricacies of the female mind.

He still couldn't believe she had made love to him last night. He'd really tried to hold back, had tried not to rush her, and he'd failed miserably. Although ashamed of his weakness, he couldn't deny the deep satisfaction that came from their loving. It had eased some of the heartache of living without her for so many years. Having her back in his arms had also shown him how deeply he still loved her.

A great deal had changed over the years they'd been apart, yet his feelings for her had remained constant. He loved her, and because he loved, he knew what had been missing in the wee hours of the morning as they'd made love.

Jenna might have given her body, but she'd closed off her heart. Whenever he'd brought up their lovemaking, she'd changed the subject. She was acting as if nothing had changed between them. He was left wondering if she regretted what they'd shared.

Was that the problem? Was that why she had been so distant? Did she wish she hadn't given in to their passion? The thought really grated on him, so much so that it left him feeling hurt and disappointed.

It was pointless to recall the sweet magic of having her back in his arms, his body deep within hers. Yet he could think of nothing else. Nor was it beneficial to remember how unbelievably tight she'd been and that he'd hurt her because of it. He was no doctor, but he suspected it had been a long dry spell. How long and how dry was the question he wanted answered. He couldn't stop wondering why she'd done without for so long. Why him and why now?

He shook his head, wishful thinking. He couldn't blame her if she had been with a dozen men. They'd been separated for more than a decade. It was none of his damned business.

"What now?" he muttered, shifting restlessly. Should he keep silent? Or should he confront her and hope for an explanation? And then do what? He couldn't make her forgive him. Nor could he demand she take him back. Life didn't work that way.

He could only hope that given time, seeing each other and spending time together would . . . what? Cause her to fall in love with him all over again? Well, that was unlikely. They were still playing the blame game. She needed a lot more time. Maybe then she would realize that all wasn't lost?

He assured himself that he wasn't completely off the mark. She cared enough about him to let him make love to her. More than once. That had to mean something. Unfortunately, beyond the obvious, he wasn't sure what it meant.

One thing was certain. He would accomplish nothing if he wimped out and gave up. Absently fingering the championship ring on his right hand, he silently vowed he wasn't about to give up on her or them. If there was another way, he'd just have to find it. In the meantime, he would keep on doing what he did best: loving her. Jenna would wear his ring . . . one day.

After punching in the code to disengage the house alarm, Jenna was forced to cover yet another yawn. "Excuse me. After that nap I had on the plane, you'd think I'd be all caught up."

"Evidently not," Scott smiled.

"What are you doing?" she asked, watching as he went through the house.

Emerging from the kitchen, he walked down the hall that led to the bedrooms. "Just checking to make sure everything is fine. Doesn't hurt to be cautious," he said when he returned to the foyer.

Jenna wasn't surprised when he pulled her against him, but she certainly hadn't been expecting it. But then the entire weekend had been one new experience after another, from the private plane to a topless nightclub. Then she'd gone and slept with Scott. What had she been thinking? That was the problem. She had not been.

"Scott, we shouldn't—"

"Shouldn't what? Talk about what happened after we went back to the hotel?"

"What purpose would it serve? We were caught up in the moment and made love."

Scott pressed a kiss against the sensitive place on

the side of her neck, sending shivers up and down her spine. "I have no regrets, sweetheart. I missed you, and I want you back in my life. Regret won't change what we shared."

As she looked at him, she realized everything he said was true. She had missed him. And she'd welcomed his lovemaking. Regrets? Wasn't that what she'd been doing?

"You're right. Regrets are a waste of time," she said thoughtfully. "Things aren't the same. We're two different people. We shouldn't expect it to be the same. This time we both know what we want, what to expect."

They weren't in love, as they had been back when they'd been living together. They weren't working toward a shared future. There would be no high expectations, no romantic fantasy. Jenna wasn't the young girl with her head in the clouds and mostly in love with love.

Despite the strides she'd made over the years, she'd slept with him during a time of weakness. Last night she'd given in to the craving for his lovemaking. So what? She was human.

"Mmm," he moaned deep in his throat as he gave her a tongue-stroking kiss. "If you ask, I'll stay the night."

Trembling with desire, Jenna hedged, "It's late. We're both tired and have a busy day ahead of us."

"What are you doing tomorrow night?"

"Picking out paint for the spare bedrooms? Why? Are you offering to help?"

He chuckled, "Why not? If I volunteer, it will save you the trouble of climbing a ladder. I'll see you around seven."

Walking with him to the door, she said, "You've got a deal. I can't thank you enough for all you've done this week, especially going with me to find my sister."

"You're welcome." Briefly touching her cheek with his, he whispered, "Sleep well."

"Good night." She waved, then locked the door behind him.

Frowning, she had no business being disappointed at not letting him stay. They both needed time to regroup and sort out what had happened. She didn't like feeling as if she'd rushed headfirst into something without giving it proper thought before acting.

For so long, she'd concentrated on protecting her heart and keeping her emotions under control. She'd been careful not to repeat past mistakes. And then she'd gone to bed with Scott.

"There's no point in beating myself up about it. It's over!" she chided herself aloud. Grabbing her bags, she headed for her bedroom.

Unfortunately, unpacking, sorting through laundry, and getting ready for bed weren't enough to take her mind off Scott and what they'd shared. Searching for a diversion, Jenna put in a three-way call to Laura and Sherri Ann. She told them about finding her sister. When she found herself admitting that she'd temporarily lost her mind and slept with Scott, they were not surprised. Her best friends had predicted it and hadn't told her. By the time she got off the telephone, she felt as if the weekend was finally over. She'd put it behind her and moved on.

Her siblings were coming for Thanksgiving. Soon her family would be together. Jenna couldn't stop grinning. There was quite a bit left to do to get the house ready for company. She was looking forward to the work. It would be the final step in making the dream of having her family together come true. She wouldn't let anything come before that, not even her libido.

* * *

Ten days later, Jenna had nearly finished the guest bedrooms. She looked around the largest room, trying to
examine the results with critical eyes. The late afternoon sun provided little warmth, but it brightened the
room by bouncing off the forest green-accented wall,
where the queen-size bed had been positioned. The
other walls were painted apple green. The bed had been
dressed in crisp white sheets and covered with a deep
green comforter.

She hadn't been able to afford covering the padded
headboard in cream leather, like she'd seen on one of
her favorite home decorating shows. So, armed with her
staple gun, foam padding, and a precut plywood headboard, she'd settled for covering it in a yellow and green
floral poly-cotton pattern fabric she'd found marked
down in the fabric store. She'd sewn a matching valance
and trimmed the white curtains. And she'd made three
accent pillows in the same floral fabric.

As she smoothed the pillows, she decided the room
had turned out well, despite her limited budget. She
admired the round table she'd found on a curb years
ago that she'd stripped, sanded, and stained in a rich
mahogany. The finishing touches pulling it all together
were the cream ceramic lamps with white shades and a
yellow Queen Anne chair she'd found on sale in a home
decorating store.

Jenna walked across the hall to the small bedroom.
It had been painted cream. The double bed had been
dressed in crisp white sheets, and a cranberry-and-
white comforter covered the bed. She'd bought the oak
headboard and night table from a hotel liquidation
store. The cream curtains were topped with the matching cranberry valance. The small armchair's seat and
back cushions, upholstered in ivory damask, had been
Jenna's first upholstery project. She'd taken the class as
an undergrad.

Jenna liked the way the rooms had turned out despite her financial limitations. And she hoped her siblings would be comfortable with what she'd created in such a short time.

Sighing, she preferred not to think of the man who'd volunteered to paint the rooms for her, leaving her free to sew and search for what she needed to complete the project.

She was pleased that she hadn't repeated the mistake she'd made in Las Vegas. She'd kept Scott out of her bed and away from her vulnerable heart. He hadn't been thrilled, but he hadn't pressured her to change her mind.

The stack of term papers waiting to be read and evaluated forced Jenna into her small home office that held her oak desk and comfortable black desk chair. The wall across from her desk was lined with two floor-to-ceiling bookshelves, brimming with books about economics, home decorating, and business, as well as a wide selection of novels. The small purple sofa bed that she'd had since her undergraduate days was tucked beneath two small windows covered by wooden blinds. They provided the only source of natural light.

Switching on the desktop lamp, Jenna ignored her hunger pains and settled in to concentrate on the work. She'd had a late lunch, so dinner would have to wait. When the telephone rang a few minutes before nine o'clock, she stretched, arching her back and raising her arms over her head.

Some of her students' views on why the economy was important to the masses were limited, to say the least. What annoyed her was that most of the information they'd collected on John Nash, the brilliant mathematician and Nobel Prize winner in economics, had been obtained from the Internet or the Hollywood version of his life.

Removing her reading glasses, she reached for the cordless telephone. A quick glance at the caller ID had her saying with delight, "Hi, Leah. What a nice surprise. I was grading term papers and could use a break. Did you get the check I sent for your ticket?" Not waiting for a response, she rushed ahead with, "Have you called the airlines?"

"Not exactly. I've got some bad news." Leah paused before she went on to explain why she wasn't coming to Detroit for the upcoming Thanksgiving holiday.

A healthy dose of frustration, combined with disappointment, had Scott debating the wisdom of stopping at Jenna's tonight. Instead of approaching the front door, he sat brooding in the car.

Jenna had done an outstanding job of keeping him at a distance since they'd returned from Las Vegas. She'd gotten so good at pretending their night together hadn't taken place that she almost had him convinced. The big question was why. Frustrated, he pounded a fist against the padded console.

She said she had no regrets, but she didn't act that way. He was lucky if he got a kiss. Was she trying to drive him out of his mind? Or was she merely trying to drive him out of her life? Perhaps she was waiting for him to give up and walk away?

"Well, I'm no quitter," he snapped. He realized his hands were unsteady when he tugged on a snug knit hat.

She couldn't change what had happened. They'd made love until the sun had been high in the sky. It had been good for the both of them. No, more like a slice of heaven that he badly wanted to repeat.

Grabbing a large bag of take-out food from the floorboard behind the driver's seat, he slammed the door and activated the power locks. His long legs quickly eliminated the distance to the front porch. Ms. Gaines was about to discover that she could run, but no matter how fast she moved, she couldn't outdistance his determination to win back her heart. Love didn't stop just because it was inconvenient or deemed no longer necessary.

Brushing impatiently at her tears, Jenna reluctantly went to answer the doorbell. She didn't need the porch light to recognize Scott.

"Hi, why are you here?" she asked as she unlocked both the front and the storm doors. She folded her arms to stop herself from reaching for him but stepped back to allow him inside.

"I hope you haven't eaten. I brought dinner," he said as he lifted the bag, which sported the name of a restaurant they both enjoyed. Frowning, he asked, "What's wrong, sweet thing?"

She waited for him to place the bag on the entrance table, then practically threw her arms around his waist. She nudged his open leather jacket aside to press damp cheeks against the soft knit of his navy-and-gray-checked cashmere sweater. She held onto him as stormy emotions raged beyond her control.

He held onto her while his large hand cradled the back of her head. He moved a caressing hand up and down her back. He murmured soothing words in her ear as he tenderly rocked her.

When the worst had passed, she sniffed while struggling to regain a measure of control. "I'm sorry. I've gotten you all wet."

"Forget about me, sweet thing." He shed his jacket, then guided her under the archway into the living room. Once they were seated on the sofa, he took her hands into his. "Tell me what has you so upset."

Struggling to mop her tears with her fingers, Jenna said, "I need a tissue."

"I'll get it." He came back with a box he'd found in the bathroom.

"Thanks." Suddenly she felt self-conscious. "I'm sorry. I didn't mean . . ." She stopped tugging her form-fitting lavender cardigan sweater down to the gray slacks she'd worn all day. She must have looked like a wrinkled, crying mess.

"Tell me."

"I just got off the phone with Lenna. I mean Leah. She's not coming for Thanksgiving." Fresh tears filled Jenna's hazel eyes. "I know it's not the end of the world, but it sure feels like it. I was so looking forward to having my family all together again. The bedrooms are ready." She threw her hands up in a helpless gesture. "Now this."

"Oh, babe. I'm so sorry." He took her into his arms, cradling her face against his broad shoulder. "But why? You sent her the money for the ticket, right?"

Jenna snuggled close. "Her low-life boyfriend is what happened. John not only left her for another woman but he took all her money with him."

"What!"

"You heard right. I'd say good riddance except that Leah is devastated. She's in love with the dirty dog."

"You mean he found another fool to take care of him?" Then he quickly said, "Sorry, I didn't mean to call your sister a fool."

"It's okay," Jenna sniffed. "She was a fool to trust him. I'm glad he is gone, but I hate how unhappy she is."

"Why can't she come? If you can't afford to send her another ticket, then I can arrange for a plane." He stopped. "Why are you shaking your head no?"

"Besides the fact that I couldn't let you go to the expense, Leah said she won't come—not under these circumstances. She's embarrassed. I tried to change her mind, but I didn't have any luck," she sighed unhappily.

"Oh, Jenna, I'm so sorry. I know how much having her here meant to you." He kissed her forehead and her damp cheeks, then brushed her lips with his.

She swallowed back tears. "I know. And I thank you for your generous offer to help. It was so kind of you."

"This has nothing to do with being kind. I care about you. I want you to be happy." He kissed her again, only this time, he lingered, taking his time. He caressed her bottom lip with the slow stroke of his tongue. When he pulled back, his voice was huskier with need. "You've waited a long time to have your siblings together. Maybe, if I called, I could convince her to change her mind?"

She shook her head. "No. We have to respect her wishes. I'm going to have to tell Lincoln. He's going to be so disappointed." She wiped away more tears. "I'm sorry. I can't believe I'm being a big baby about this."

"Shush." He dried her tears with a tissue, then kissed her cheek. "I'm so sorry, Jenna. I hate to see you hurting this way."

She sighed, resting against Scott, relishing the feel of his arms around her and his hard length against her side. When he kissed her, she parted her lips and countered by stroking his tongue with hers. The sound of her stomach rumbling made them both pull back and laugh.

"Someone is hungry. Good thing I brought food."

"I took advantage of having a late lunch by skipping dinner and going to work on the pile of term papers in my office. What's your excuse?"

"For not eating? I got so involved with my project in

the lab that I forgot the time. So, is the beautiful, smart, and efficient Dr. Gaines ready to chow down?"

She teased, "You won't have to ask me twice." She was up and going back into the foyer for the food. "What did you bring?"

Following her into the kitchen, he said, "I wasn't sure what you wanted, so I brought a little bit of everything."

"Uh-oh. That may not be a good thing," she laughed. After placing the bag on the center island, she went over to the sink to wash her hands while trying not to notice the way his dark eyes moved over her. She was conscious of her messy hair and the fact that she'd cried away what had remained of her makeup. Yet she didn't rush to repair the damage. He'd seen her looking worse.

Leaning a shoulder against the refrigerator, he smiled, crossing his arms over his chest. He was so tall, dark, and incredibly handsome that she would have had to be dead not to notice his masculine charms. Rather than stare at the way his jeans hugged his muscular thighs and cradled his prominent sex or the way his sweater clung to his broad chest and powerful biceps, she busied herself with opening cartons.

"Barbecued ribs and chicken, cole slaw, steak fries, salad, and garlic toast. Wow! Scott, there is enough for six people. What were you thinking?"

He chuckled. "I wasn't thinking. I was hungry. What do you need me to do to help?"

"Nothing. While you wash up, I'll set the table and we can start dishing up the food and heating it in the microwave."

"Sounds like a plan," he said with a grin, heading into the small half bath between the kitchen and the home office.

While berating herself for recalling every detail of the night they'd shared, Jenna collected plates, glasses, silverware, and napkins. He took a seat at the center island.

"I almost started without you," she teased, handing him a serving spoon.

"That hungry?" he grinned.

Soon they were absorbed in eating dinner. When they finished, Scott reached out to tuck a thick curl behind her ear.

"Feeling better?"

"Much. That was delicious. What made you take the chance that I hadn't eaten?"

"It wasn't that much of a risk. If you weren't hungry, you could watch me make a pig of myself."

"Very funny," she said, pushing back her chair.

Working together, they cleared the counters, put the food away, and loaded the dishwasher, reminiscent of their college days—only back in the day, they hadn't been able to afford the luxury of a dishwasher.

When they returned to the living room, she pressed a finger into his chest. "Don't forget. When you leave, you're taking most of the food with you. These hips can't handle a slab of ribs."

"Judging by what I've seen"—he encircled her waist, resting his long fingers on the top swell of her hips— "you won't hear any complaints from me." He cupped and squeezed her full buttocks. "You're packing some danger curves, sweet thing."

He pushed her hair aside to place a lingering kiss on her neck, close to her ear, before he laced his fingers with hers and tugged her down onto the sofa.

Gazing at their hands, she said, "Thanks for coming by. I'm sorry I fell apart the way I did."

He nodded, disengaging their fingers. He began kneading her taut shoulder muscles and the back of her neck. "Jenna, are you sure I can't help? I don't mind . . ."

"No, Scott. I don't need you to fix it for me. What I needed was for you to hold me and let me cry it out and listen to me. You did all three perfectly, and I thank you for that." As his fingers massaged the tension from her muscles, she purred deep in her throat. "Oh, that feels wonderful. You'd better stop while you still have feelings in your fingers. At the rate you're going, I may never want you to stop."

"I don't intend to stop, not until my lady begs for mercy," he teased. Taking her lobe in his mouth, he warmed it with his tongue, making goose pimples form on her skin. She moaned her enjoyment when he began to suckle.

Fifteen

"Scott . . . what are you doing?"

"You know exactly what I'm doing. I've missed you, babe," he said an instant before he covered her mouth with his. His kiss was long . . . hungry. It was the first of many—each hotter, wetter than the last.

Jenna was no longer sure why it was important that she resist his sweet magic. All she knew was that she needed him. Her heart fluttered with excitement as she wrapped her arms around his strong neck, pressing her suddenly heavy breasts into the muscular plane of his chest.

He felt so good, but it was not enough. She wanted more. She wanted him deep inside, filling her emptiness. Rubbing her aching nipples against him, Jenna trembled with desire.

Sliding a hand beneath his sweater, she slowly moved it over his taut stomach, up over his well-muscled chest. His skin was hot to her touch. Encouraged by his sigh of enjoyment, she began caressing his taut nipples. His sigh quickly became a moan.

She wrapped her arms around him, inhaling his unique, intoxicating scent. The heat of his open mouth journeying down her throat caused her to tremble. He tongued the sensitive place below her earlobe, and her resistance melted like snow on a heated walkway.

"I want you . . . now," she said urgently, pressing her lips to his throat, pulling his head down to reach her full lips.

Scott's response was immediate. His kisses were filled with desire and urgency. Jenna was breathless with longing when he lifted his head.

She caught his hand in hers and led the way to her bedroom. It was her private sanctuary, where she came to relax, to think and to dream. She flicked on the floor lamp, then turned to face him. They stood at the foot of a brass king-sized bed covered with a purple, plum, and mauve quilt she and her foster sisters had made and piled high with white lace-edged pillows. The walls were painted a rich mauve. The bed dominated the room. The same bed they'd saved for and picked out to-gether back in their college days. Back then, it had been a major investment for their relationship and future.

"You still have it." His surprise was unmistakable.

Not wanting to dwell on the past or her inability to let the bed go, Jenna ignored the comment, kicking off her shoes.

Having yanked his sweater over his head, Scott reached for her. He began unbuttoning her cardigan, wasting no time in stripping her bare. After a series of tantalizing kisses, Scott shoved down the covers. He lifted her onto the bed and came down beside her.

"Jenna," he crooned, cradling her face in his wide palms. "I hope you don't feel like I'm taking advantage of your upset. The truth is I need you."

As she looked into his dark, hungry eyes, she accepted that she felt the same. At that moment, she not only wanted him but she also needed to be with him. She was glad he felt the same.

"No need to apologize. I want you, too." She wrapped her arms around his neck and hugged him tight. She closed her eyes, savoring the feel of his long, strong body. It felt so right to have him here in her special place.

After sharing a long, hot kiss, Jenna began moving her hands up and down his spine, his taut buttocks. At the sound of his husky groan, she knew he was enjoying her touch as much as she loved touching him. But she was hungry for more. She slid a hand between their bodies to palm his engorged sex.

His breath quickened and he growled his enjoyment. He husked into her ear, "It feels good, babe. Don't stop."

She stroked his rock-hard shaft starting at the thick base, paying particular attention to the ultrasensitive head. She didn't stop until he caught her hands. When she protested, he distracted her by cupping her breasts and squeezing her softness. She moaned as he worried the pebble-hard tips, tugging them repeatedly.

When Scott began to pull back, Jenna tightened her arms around his torso. "Don't . . . Come inside me. Hurry," she begged.

They were both breathing heavily, skin damp with perspiration.

He chuckled. "Not yet, but soon. I want you hot and so wet that you won't want me to stop. And I won't stop until we're both spent."

"I'm ready now," she complained, moving her damp sex against his hard, muscular thigh.

His response was a deep, throaty moan. Then he kissed his way down her body. He warmed the side of her neck, pausing to lave the scented base of her throat. Dropping his head, he slowly took a peak into his mouth. When she was weak with longing and calling out his name, he covered her mound, squeezing her softness, then opened her to his long, stroking fingers. As he caressed her ultra-sensitive bud, her heart pounded with excitement.

When she called out his name, he kissed her before sliding a finger into her moist sheath. His caress was firm and insistent, and soon he replaced his finger with his mouth. He laved her fleshy softness before he found and repeatedly licked her sensitive bud. Then he applied the sweetest suction. Eyes closed, Jenna tossed her head from side to side, crying out as she reached completion. The pleasure was sharp and intense.

She dug her fingers into his shoulders, holding on until the whirlwind stopped. But before she could recover, he dropped his head and swiftly took her back to the point of no return.

"You're so sweet," he said as he gathered her close. He soothed her, stroking her soft hair and kissing her tenderly as she recovered.

"You enjoyed that, didn't you?" she whispered. "Driving me out of my mind?"

He chuckled, clearly pleased with himself. "Be right back." He retrieved his jeans from the floor to pull out several foiled packets.

Although weak from pleasure, Jenna's heart raced with anticipation.

His dark eyes smoldered with desire as he flashed a wide grin steeped in male pride. Rejoining her, he placed a kiss on each temple and whispered, "Ready Jenna?" He didn't wait for an answer. His lips covered hers.

What began as a tender kiss on the mouth quickly turned into something both spellbinding and deeply erotic. Jenna pushed against his chest until he was flat on his back, then she straddled his hips. He cradled her nape and pulled her head down for yet another hungry kiss. They were both panting by the time their lips parted. She shifted, pressing her aching flesh onto the broad crest of his engorged sex. Closing her eyes, Jenna shivered as she sank onto his shaft, taking him deep inside her sheath.

"Yes . . . oh, yes," he groaned into her ear, his big body taut with tension.

For a time neither of them moved, savoring their connection. Then the sheer magic of their joining quickly sent them into a wildly provocative dance of a mind-numbing enjoyment. The excitement was impossible to contain and swiftly sparked into white-hot flames of unparalleled pleasure. The force of his relentless strokes quickly had her heightened senses soaring into the heavens, and she experienced an agonizingly sweet orgasm.

Her release caused her inner muscle to tighten around him, sending shock waves rippling through his system. His big body convulsed from the power of his mind-blowing climax. Jenna and Scott clung to each other as their breathing slowly returned to normal and their sweat-drenched bodies cooled.

"That was unbelievable," she sighed, smoothing her hands over his chest and shoulders.

"You're what's unbelievable," he crooned into her ear. "No one has ever given me so much pleasure, sweet Jenna." He punctuated each word with a kiss.

She stiffened. She didn't like being reminded that he'd had lovers since their breakup. She was jealous. "Unlike you, I haven't . . ." She stopped abruptly, shocked by what she'd nearly revealed. His past relationships had nothing to do with her.

His dark eyes locked with hers. "Why, Jenna? Why haven't you been with another man since we broke up?"

She immediately dropped her lids. "It doesn't matter."

"It matters to me."

"No, it's part of my past, therefore it's none of your business," Jenna snapped.

She pushed away and hurried into the connecting bath.

"She's right," Scott grudgingly admitted, staring at the closed door.

How badly had he overstepped? He felt as if he'd been balancing on a tightrope. He didn't dare take a step too far to the right or left, for fear of giving her a reason to put even more distance between them.

Hearing her confirm his selfish hope left him reeling. Suddenly he had to know why Jenna had held such a vital part of herself back for so long. He hadn't needed her confession. He'd suspected the moment he'd entered her lush body in Las Vegas. There was no getting around that he'd hurt her despite his best efforts. He'd been so absorbed in his responses to being with her again that he hadn't taken a hard look at her reason for remaining celibate. Maybe he hadn't looked closely because he hadn't wanted to know the answer. Yet the question haunted him for days.

Making love to her had proven what he'd always known. Scott didn't just want her back in his life—he wanted it all, including the closeness and the connection they'd once shared. Unfortunately, it wasn't up to him.

"Why, Jenna?" he whispered aloud.

There was no shortage of willing men in Detroit or New York. Jenna was a breathtakingly beautiful woman, both on the inside and out. If she'd wanted a man, she could have had several. She'd chosen to remain celibate. Her reason was the question that he had no right to ask, but that didn't stop him from wondering if she'd been so caught up in reaching her personal goals that she'd overlooked her feminine needs. More important, why had she allowed him back into her bed? She'd been dating Jackson Knight since she'd returned. Was she still seeing him?

Scott was on shaky ground. He'd taken a huge risk by coming here tonight. If not for her disappointment over her twin, Jenna wouldn't have welcomed him into her bed tonight. He wasn't proud of taking advantage of her temporary weakness.

The sound of the door opening instantly caught his attention. Although disappointed that she'd covered her lush curves with an oversized U of D T-shirt, he was glad that it was one of his old jerseys. He watched as she crossed the floor on bare feet and climbed into bed.

He smiled when he felt her snuggle against his side, resting her head on his shoulder. Stroking her soft curls, he pressed a lingering kiss at her temple.

"Sleepy?"

"Mmm," she murmured. "I'm sorry I was a mess when you arrived."

"I'm the one that should be sorry. I know how much you were looking forward to spending Thanksgiving with both your siblings."

She nodded. "I haven't given up hope. There's always Christmas. I still have to tell Lincoln. He's going to be disappointed. I assumed that John leaving with the money caused the breakup."

"The guy was a loser. Leah's better off without him. Given time, she will realize that."

"I hope so. But it's not going to happen overnight. And she still has to strip tonight to pay her rent."

Scott predicted, "Leah's going to need you to help her see that John was in love with himself, not her. And that she has other options."

"Ain't that the truth! I'm hoping to convince her that there's more in life besides dancing and taking her clothes off to entertain a bunch of strangers. Lenna's very bright. There're so many opportunities out there for her. She doesn't need to use her body to get ahead. That's what her brain is for."

Scott caressed her shoulder. "Who's better than her older sister to help her see the possibilities?"

Jenna brushed her swollen lips over the base of his throat. "I suspect it's not going to be that simple. Lenna . . ." She sighed, "I mean Leah. I keep forgetting. Anyway, we're only just getting to know each other again. I'd like to help, but I don't see how I can, unless she's ready to make a change."

"Maybe John's leaving will help her see the need?"

"I hope you're right." Jenna admitted excitedly, "I'd love to offer her a fresh start. She's more than welcome to come live with me until she can find a better job. Why not? I have two empty bedrooms. If she wants to go back to college and get her degree, I can help with that, too." She looked up at him expectantly. "What do you think?"

"Doesn't matter what I think. It's up to you and Leah." He kissed her soft, parted lips. "Are you sure you want to do this?"

"I've thought of little else since I got back home. I hate the way she's living. It's such a waste. Besides, that's what I've been trained to do . . . help others reach their potential. Why shouldn't I want that for my own flesh and blood?"

He chuckled. "You don't have to convince me. Have you considered that Leah may not want a new career? She may want to stay in Las Vegas? She's interested in acting."

"What does exotic dancing have to do with acting?"

Jenna quipped. "We have theater right here in Detroit. We also have classes in drama and the arts."

"Calm down," he soothed, smoothing her soft curls. "I'm not disagreeing with you, babe. I just want you to consider that your sister may not want to change. Most important, I don't want to see you hurt."

"Me?" Jenna laughed. "How could I be hurt? Moving to Detroit will be good for her. Lenn-Leah didn't have a Mrs. Green in her life, but she has me. I plan to give her the love and support she needs to get on her feet."

He smiled. "I'm sure Leah will realize she's lucky to have you back in her life." Just then Jenna covered a yawn. Scott teased, "Are you going to sleep on me?"

She giggled. "Afraid so. I suppose you have to get up early?"

"I do. I have an early lab."

"Then don't wake me. I plan to sleep at least until ten. I don't have any classes tomorrow, but I do have those blasted term papers waiting for me."

He laughed, then switched off the lamp, plunging the room into darkness. He wasn't smiling, though, as he thought of the obstacles separating them. He had his work cut out for him just to get her to look beyond their past.

As he held her, asleep and cradled against his heart, he couldn't deny they'd done a fine job of hurting each other badly. But damn it, he wasn't going to let their past destroy their chance at making a go of it. They deserved a second chance.

Jenna might not be ready to admit it, but he believed she still had feelings for him. Why else had she let him make love to her? Lovemaking wasn't the deep love and connection he craved, but it was a starting point. For that, he was grateful.

* * *

Jenna pushed her disappointment aside to throw herself into her plans to make this Thanksgiving one to remember. After a long talk with Carolyn, she was confident she had the menu under control.

She was in her office on campus, talking to Sherri Ann on her cell phone, when there was a knock on the open door. She smiled at Jackson Knight, motioning for him to come in.

She said into the phone, "I have company. Are you sure you want to go to Farmer's Market with me tomorrow morning? It's going to be crowded, especially on the Saturday before the holiday."

"No, but I want to eat on Thursday," Sherri Ann teased.

Jenna laughed. "Sherri Ann, I have to go. I'll talk to you later." She smiled, tucking the phone into her jacket pocket. "Jackson, what a nice surprise. How have you been?"

Feeling a combination of embarrassment and guilt, she sighed. Even though she didn't owe him an explanation, she knew she should have called him when she'd returned from Las Vegas.

"I'm well and very busy just like you," he smiled, leaning over the desk to place a kiss on her cheek.

She kept a smile firmly in place.

"I've missed you. What do you say we take in a play this weekend?" Jackson asked, making himself comfortable on the edge of her desk.

Jenna, who shared the office with another professor, was glad they didn't have an audience. "I'm sorry, Jackson. I can't. I should have told you earlier, but . . ." She stopped, struggling to find the right words.

"So the rumors are true," he surmised.

"Rumors?"

"It's all over campus that you're seeing Hendricks. Why didn't you just call and tell me? Why did I have to hear it from someone else?" He rose, folding his arms.

"I didn't realize there were rumors about Scott and me," she replied. Then she paused, and said with a frown, "Yes. We're seeing each other. I apologize. I should have told you."

"Do you think it's wise to flaunt the fact that you're sleeping with a student?"

"Is that what they're saying around campus?"

He shrugged. "Look, it's none of my business, but—"

"You're right. It isn't anyone's business, only Scott's and mine."

"Jenna, I'm trying to give you some advice. You're just starting out and want tenure. How's it going to look if it gets back to the head of the university? You think he's going to turn a blind eye?"

Taken aback, she stiffened. "I've done nothing wrong. Technically, Scott's an undergraduate, but he's hardly a minor. And he isn't one of my students. We're not even in the same department."

Jackson scowled. "I'm just trying to help. How serious are you about Hendricks? We all know he has his pick of the ladies. Have you considered he might have gone after you to prove he still has what it takes? Once he's gotten his degree under his belt, he'll probably move back to L.A. You're just starting your career here at the university. Why put yourself at risk with this kind of notoriety? Have your picture splashed in some tabloid. I'd hate to see you hurt."

"I appreciate your concern, but I'm not getting into this with you. I've heard more than enough on the subject." She folded her arms beneath her breasts.

He gazed down at her for a long moment, thoughtful. Then he said, "I wish things could have been different. I enjoy your company. Jenna, you never gave us a real chance. Hendricks was always in the background."

She remained silent, but she agreed with him. She'd enjoyed his friendship but hadn't looked for or expected more. When she'd started seeing Jackson, she'd made a point not to closely examine her feelings for Scott. And she most certainly hadn't given any thought to how her colleagues or her department head might view her involvement with Scott.

"Jenna?"

Realizing he was waiting for a response, she lifted her chin. "I'm sorry you feel that way, Jackson. You're right. I should have told you when my situation changed. We only dated for a short time, but I hope we can remain friends."

He nodded. "You should have." Taking her hand, he gave it a squeeze. "You're a very special lady. If he can't give you the loyalty and commitment you deserve, remember you can find those qualities in someone else. I was willing to put you first." He paused before he added, "Take care of yourself."

She nodded.

"Good-bye." He walked out.

Jenna was touched by his sincerity. Jackson was a good man. He deserved a woman whose heart was whole. When she'd first met Jackson, fighting her feelings for Scott had been a full-time endeavor. She'd lost that war. Letting Scott into her bed hadn't been the smartest thing she'd ever done. Sex had brought with it a whole new set of complications. When she wasn't working to find ways of convincing her sister to move to Detroit, she was thinking about Scott and the host of new problems their involvement generated.

There was a knock on the open door. Tanya Gray, one of her students, rushed into the room. "Professor

Gaines, I'm sorry I'm late. My babysitter was sick this morning and I had to drop my daughter off with my mother." Tanya was a single mother working her way through college. Dropping into the chair in front of the desk, the younger woman reached into an overstuffed backpack. "I'm not happy with my grade on my last essay test. I was wondering what I can do to improve my grades. I want an A out of this course."

Jenna nodded, reaching for her reading glasses. After studying her computer screen, she said, "You got As on your first two tests, but on this one you dropped down to a C. What happened?"

Sixteen

Jenna threw herself into the preparations for the Thanksgiving holiday. She was striving for perfection and wasn't leaving anything to chance.

She was ready when her brother and his family arrived on Wednesday evening. She welcomed them into her home with warm hugs.

"I love what you've done to the house, Jenna. And you've only been here since the summer. It's beautiful," Carolyn exclaimed from where she sat beside Lincoln on the sofa.

"Carolyn's right. You've made a wonderful home for yourself. And you did it all on your own. I'm proud of you," Lincoln said. Corrie, their tired little daughter, was curled up in her dad's lap.

Blinking away happy tears, Jenna blushed. "Stop. You're embarrassing me. I'm just so pleased to finally have the three of you here. It's after eight and past the dinner hour, but if you're hungry, I've prepared a little something just in case."

Carolyn and Lincoln exchanged a smile before he teased, "I could eat a little something."

"I hope you haven't gone to a lot of extra work," Carolyn said.

"Not at all." Jenna rose to her feet.

"Let me help you."

Jenna shook her head. "No need. It won't take me long."

Carolyn called, "Are you sure I can't help?"

"Positive. Tonight you can relax. Tomorrow, I'll come looking for you," Jenna warned, hurrying to the kitchen.

A little something consisted of grilled salmon, rice medley with mixed vegetables, and a fruit salad. Jenna was laughing until Lincoln brought up their sister.

"Have you spoken to Leah recently?"

Somber, she shook her head. "Only once since she told me about the breakup and that she wasn't coming for Thanksgiving."

"We were so disappointed. We'd hoped she'd change her mind and come after all," Carolyn said.

"No such luck," Jenna sighed.

"Carolyn and I wondered if we should have offered to pay for her ticket. It's too late now . . ." Lincoln's voice trailed away.

"I don't think she would have come. She wasn't just upset, but embarrassed that her boyfriend left her for someone else and stole from her."

"But why?" Lincoln quickly asked. "She's not responsible for his bad behavior."

"No, but Leah picked him. She doesn't want us to think badly about her because of him," Jenna surmised.

"Everyone makes mistakes. I sure kissed a few frogs before I fell in love with Lincoln." Carolyn smiled before returning to coaxing Corrie into eating.

"We all have," Jenna acknowledged. "It was kind of you and Carolyn to want to help Leah."

"Leah and I have only talked a few times, but I hope she decides to leave Las Vegas. I don't know what she makes, but from what you told me it doesn't sound as if she's a show dancer working for one of the big hotels."

"Far from it." Jenna took a sip from her water glass. "I've also been trying to finds ways to help. I'm not sure she's even willing to listen to what I have in mind." When they looked at her expectantly, she said, "I'd like her to move in here with me. It would be a fresh start. Leah could stay until she finds a new job. Or she could go to college, if she'd like." She looked anxiously at her brother. "Well?"

Smiling, Lincoln got up and kissed Jenna's cheek. "I think it's a generous offer. Leah's lucky to have you back in her life."

"Lincoln's right. That's so kind of you," Carolyn said with a smile.

"I've been incredibly blessed. I've had to work hard, but I didn't do it all on my own. I had a helping hand. And that's what I'd like to do for Leah." She reluctantly admitted, "I'm worried that she might be offended by my offer."

Before Lincoln or Carolyn could respond, Corrie began to whimper as she climbed into her mother's lap. "Sleepy, Mommy."

"I know, baby," Carolyn soothed, kissing her cheek.

"I'll carry her," Lincoln volunteered.

"Excuse us?" Carolyn said.

"Of course. Let me know if you need anything."

"Be right back, Sis."

Jenna had cleared the table and was putting the food away when Lincoln returned.

"Carolyn will be back as soon as she gets Corrie settled." He rolled up his shirtsleeves as he went over to the sink and began rinsing off the plates.

"You don't have to—"

"You've done enough. Sit down while I load the dishwasher."

Jenna had just made herself comfortable at the counter when he asked, "Why are you so worried? Why wouldn't Leah be thrilled by your offer to help?"

"She might take it as a criticism of her."

"That's ridiculous," he said as he filled the top rack.

"But it's a possibility that I can't ignore. Lincoln, all three of us have been living apart for over twenty years. Leah doesn't really know me."

"You're her twin."

"Long lost. Just think how you'd feel if I came in and tried to change you. You wouldn't like it or me very much. And I couldn't blame you."

He paused for a moment before he nodded. "You have a point, but that doesn't mean you shouldn't make the offer. She might surprise you."

"Maybe?"

"You sound doubtful. You aren't having second thoughts, are you?" Lincoln asked as he dried his hands on a dish towel.

"Second thoughts about what?" Carolyn joined them.

Lincoln smiled. "Is the baby asleep?" Carolyn nodded, and then he went on to say, "Jenna's worried that Leah might consider her offer to help as a criticism of her lifestyle. I didn't want Jenna to change her mind about helping."

"Surely not." Carolyn gazed at her sister-in-law, her hand resting absently on her swollen stomach. Her pregnancy was starting to show.

"I'm not changing my mind. It's too important to me to give up. But I have to make sure I'm going about this in the correct way. I can't jump in with both feet."

After taking in the spotless kitchen, Carolyn quizzed, "You didn't let Jenna do any of the cleanup, did you?"

Lincoln chuckled as he laced his fingers with his wife's. "Not one dish."

Laughing, Jenna teased, "You've trained him well." She led the way back into the living room.

Once they were all seated, Carolyn asked, "What's the plan for tomorrow? Do we need to start cooking tonight? Or are we waiting for first light?"

"Neither. No work for you, young lady. You're my guest."

Carolyn wasn't pleased by that response. "I don't intend to watch our hostess work her way into exhaustion. I tried that last Christmas in an effort to impress Lincoln's mother. I was so tired by the end of the evening, I was in tears. Poor Lincoln had to put up with me. Believe me when I say it wasn't pretty. Never again."

"Wow," Jenna exclaimed.

"Carolyn is right. The aim is not to do you in, Sis."

Jenna laughed, "Not to worry. I have it all under control. Both of my foster sisters are coming and bringing side dishes. I made the sweet potato pies last night. The turkey is cleaned and waiting to be tossed into the roaster oven. The vegetables are prepared and ready to go into the dressing. I cleaned the chitlins earlier in the week. All that's left is to make the yeast rolls and the finishing touches."

"We're having chitlins?" Lincoln gushed.

She laughed. "I remember how much you used to like them when we were little. I was going to try to keep them as a surprise, but the cooking smell will perfume the house and give it away."

"Love them, but I haven't had them in years. I'm looking forward to it," he grinned.

Carolyn joined in the laughter. Shaking her head, she said, "None for me."

"Isn't it funny how people love them or hate them? No in between," Jenna mused before she said, "I'm looking forward to you meeting Sherri Ann and Laura. We've been close since we were little girls."

Lincoln asked, "What about Scott? He's coming, isn't he? You two haven't had a falling out, have you?"

Flustered, Jenna swiftly explained, "You'll see Scott tomorrow. We're still friends." She didn't elaborate on the drastic changes since they'd traveled to Cleveland.

"Friends?" Lincoln questioned. "Come on, Sis. There was more going on than friendship."

Jenna admitted, "We have a complicated history." She went on to give them the overview of their relationship. She ended with, "I wouldn't say we're back together, but we're not estranged, either."

Lincoln and Carolyn exchanged a look before Carolyn said, "Both Lincoln and I like Scott, but only you can decide if he's worth risking your heart."

That in a nutshell was what bothered Jenna the most. She feared she'd given him her heart a long time ago but hadn't gotten it back.

"Nothing ventured, nothing gained," her brother advised. "Scott's a great guy, and he seems to really care about you. Well, enough said on that subject. It's been a long day."

"If you need anything, knock on my door," Jenna insisted.

"Night, Sis." Lincoln kissed her cheek.

"I'll meet you in the kitchen around eight," Carolyn promised, giving Jenna a hug. "No arguments."

Jenna laughed. "Deal. Sleep well."

Satisfied that all was ready in the kitchen for the busy day ahead, Jenna checked the locks on the doors and set the alarm before she went to her bedroom. She whispered a prayer of gratitude before she climbed into bed. She couldn't stop smiling or thinking of her family in the guest rooms. It was what she considered to be a miracle. She wouldn't be satisfied until her family circle was complete . . . until their sister was back in the family fold.

Just then her bedside telephone rang. She didn't bother looking at the caller ID. "Hi, Scott. Can't sleep?"

He chuckled. "I wouldn't say that, but it helps hearing your voice. How was it? Lincoln and his family arrive safely?"

"Oh, yes. We had a nice dinner and visit. They liked the house."

"Good. I can hear the happiness in your voice. Congratulations. It's been a long time coming."

"Yeah," she said around a sigh. "I won't say it was worth the wait."

They shared an understanding laugh.

"You sound tired," she said candidly. "How many hours did you put in at the lab?"

"Too many," he admitted.

"Well, tomorrow you have no choice but to take it easy."

"There are always notes to review and planning for the next experiment," he said around a yawn. "Sorry about that."

"Why are you pushing yourself so hard?"

"I intend to get an A in my instrumental lab course and on my final project."

"Have you given more thought to going for that master's of science in chemistry?"

"Some, but I'm still undecided. It's late. I'd better let you get some sleep. You have a big meal to prepare tomorrow."

Even though she knew he was expected to eat with his own family, she said, "Don't forget. You promised to stop by."

"I wouldn't miss it for the world. Sleep well, sweet thing. I wish you were in my arms," he ended huskily.

"Me too. Bye." After pressing the off button, Jenna reluctantly admitted how much she missed him. She'd taken to reassuring herself she could handle him in her bed without emotional repercussions.

They were grown-ups, without fairy-tale expectations getting in the way. Yes, she cared about him and had slept with him. That didn't mean she would fall in love with him again. Love was a huge gamble that she was unwilling to take on.

What if she was already on shaky ground but was too stupid to know it? Jenna moaned at the thought. She was too smart to fall into the same deep hole. So what if she preferred his seductive brand of lovemaking? She was older, knew the pitfalls.

"Enough!" she whispered aloud. If she wanted to look better than the golden-brown turkey she intended to pull from the roaster oven in a few short hours, she had to get some sleep.

"It's about time we met," Sherri Ann exclaimed as she and Laura welcomed Lincoln and Carolyn into the fold.

"We've been waiting so long to meet you, little brother," Laura teased, wiping away tears. "You might as well get ready, because as far as Sherri Ann and I are concerned, you have two new sisters."

Lincoln threw back his head with a hearty laugh, giving each a hug. "The pleasure is all mine. It's a relief to know Jenna was not alone and had you two in her corner."

Carolyn was soon engulfed in their exuberant display of affection. Shy, baby Corrie was cooed over, playfully teased until she was all giggles as she got to know her adoring new aunts. Just in case she wasn't won over by all the attention, the teddy bear and doll the two loving aunts had brought did the trick.

When Lincoln cautioned that they were going to spoil her, Laura fought back, saying, "There was no such thing as too much love. Besides, we had two birth-days and Christmases to make up for."

Sherri Ann asked, "Where's Scott?"

The inquiry caused Jenna to momentarily lose her smile. "He's running late."

Jenna was annoyed with herself for caring. She had every reason to be over the moon because she was shar-ing the holiday with her family. The people she cared about were all here. Why was she letting a man she didn't love spoil her pleasure? Shame on her!

"He's coming, right?" Laura persisted.

"Any minute now. Poor Lincoln has been watch-ing the football games with only Corrie for company," Jenna teased, hoping to change the subject.

"Poor Lincoln will get cleanup duty later," Carolyn teased. "Come on, ladies. You have to see the pies Jenna made. I had no idea she was such a good cook."

"Oh, yes. Mrs. Green made sure our education was complete." Sherri Ann linked arms with Jenna. She whispered, "Smile. He'll be here. He knows how im-portant this day is to you."

Jenna complied, grateful for the support. Evidently all the planning and anticipation of this big day, along with the disappointment that her sister hadn't been able to come, had left her feeling a bit emotional.

"Jenna, these are fabulous!" Laura exclaimed as she admired the two golden-brown sweet potato pies, a deep dish apple cobbler, and a lemon meringue pie. Jenna had just that morning made the apple as a special thank-you for Scott.

"When did you have time to do all this?" Sherri Ann gushed. "The house is spotless, and the dining room table is fabulous. I see you brought out Mrs. Green's tablecloth."

Jenna laughed, deeply touched by the compliments.

The foster sisters cherished the heirloom that had been passed down to them from their beloved foster mother.

"Thank you, Laura and Sherri Ann. I'll admit I've been working hard to . . ." Just then the doorbell chimed. "I'll get it," she called, hurrying out of the kitchen, unaware of the knowing smiles the ladies exchanged.

Seventeen

Jenna's heart was racing when she opened the front door. "It's about time," she scolded, determined to hold on to her frown.

"Sorry I'm late, babe," Scott said, taking her into his arms for a hug.

With her cheeks pressed against his chest, she inhaled his favorite special scent of sandalwood soap with a hint of vanilla, mixed with his warm scent. For the first time that day she completely relaxed.

"I thought you weren't coming," she reluctantly admitted, close to tears.

He lifted her chin so he could see her face, but she kept her lids lowered. She didn't want him to see the doubt that she'd been harboring, the irrational worry lingering deep inside that she couldn't count on him to be there for her. She had no idea where the fear came from or why it had hit now, when she was in the midst of her party. Nonetheless it was there.

She'd tried so hard to guard against exposing the vulnerable core deep inside, and the well of emotions. She thought she'd put aside the countless nights when he hadn't heard her awake alone after that awful dream of being abandoned. The dream always left her shaken and feeling all alone in the world. It was a reminder that she had no one to care if she lived or died. In the dream she walked down a long hallway filled with doors. She opened door after door, endlessly searching for her family. During the time she and Scott had been together, he had been there to hold her, dry her tears, and remind her that she was not alone.

As Jenna clung to him, she knew she was over-reacting. Yes, she'd had the dream last night, but when Laura had asked if Scott was coming, it had triggered the memory.

"Sorry, I was delayed. I was stuck over at Donald's folks, where they were showing the video of their recent trip to Africa." He kissed her cheeks and her lids until she opened her eyes and looked at him.

Jenna sighed as he brushed his lips over hers, then lingered.

"With so many people here, I hoped you wouldn't notice I was late," he teased.

"Will you look who the cat dragged in out of the cold," Laura laughed.

Embarrassed to be caught clinging, Jenna quickly stepped back. "Just for being late, you get cleanup duty, and it won't be pretty."

Laughing, Scott gave Laura a hug. "Hey, short stuff. How are you?"

"You'd better stop. I brought the macaroni and cheese, and the cranberry and orange relish. Be careful or you won't get any," Laura teased.

Sherri Ann said, "Don't worry, Scott. I brought the collard greens and cream corn, so you won't starve. Move over, Laura. It's my turn." She also received a welcoming hug from Scott.

"You made it," Lincoln greeted him from where he stood with an arm over Carolyn's shoulders.

"Glad to see that you two made it." Scott shook hands with Lincoln and gave Carolyn a kiss on the cheek. "What's the score? Are the Lions still behind?"

The ladies groaned at the mention of the football game.

"What?" Scott asked.

Shaking her head, Jenna said, "Come on, ladies. Let's get this show on the road. We've got food to get on the table."

Jenna couldn't have asked for a better culmination to the long-awaited day. Her heart was full as she took in the ready smiles and laughter around the table, including little Corrie. When it was her turn to give thanks, her eyes filled with happy tears. Everyone smiled in complete understanding. Going around the table expressing thanks was one of the family traditions that she remembered from her and Lincoln's childhood and had wanted to preserve.

Sherri Ann and Jenna told stories about Thanksgivings with Mrs. Green. Laura laughed as her foster sisters told about her refusal to clean or eat chitlins.

Lincoln talked about growing up in the Nicholas household. He'd been adopted into a white family, who'd loved and accepted him completely. Unfortunately, he'd been the only black child in the neighborhood and elementary school. David Nicholas, his adopted father, had understood and had made sure that Lincoln had had blacks in his life. He'd attended private but racially mixed middle and high schools. David's best friend and law partner was African American and was like an uncle to him. Lincoln considered himself blessed to have grown up surrounded by love.

Scott told a story about being on the road during Thanksgiving. He and his teammates had ended up eating at a Chinese restaurant in San Francisco. He'd really missed his mother's candied sweet potatoes and corn-bread dressing that year.

Jenna's pies were a real hit. She had no idea how he managed it, but Scott ate two helpings of her apple cobbler with ice cream.

After the meal Lincoln and Jenna excused themselves and went into the home office to place a call to their sister. On the speaker phone the three siblings were overcome with emotions as they talked, so thrilled to have finally found each other after so many years apart.

The highlight of the call was when Lincoln and Jenna managed to convince their sister to consider relocating in Detroit, even though Leah would only commit to an extended visit. Lincoln promised to send an airplane ticket. And Jenna promised to have her room ready and waiting for her. Jenna assured Leah that she was welcome to stay as long as she liked.

Delighted with the outcome, brother and sister rejoined the others, eager to share the exciting news. It wasn't long after that that Laura turned on the sound system and Scott started a fire in the fireplace.

It was close to midnight by the time Jenna's house was put to rights, her guests had gone, and Lincoln and his wife had gone to bed.

Exhausted, Jenna soaked in a hot tub. She was baffled as she recalled her emotional meltdown at Scott's being late. And she was too tired to even try and figure it out. She roused herself enough to dry off before she climbed into bed and fell asleep.

The Thanksgiving weekend passed so swiftly that Jenna could hardly keep up with all they said and did. One of the most poignant moments came on Saturday afternoon, when she and Lincoln pored over old photo albums. Carolyn had thoughtfully brought one of Lincoln with his adopted family, and Jenna shared the ones from her elementary, middle, and high school years.

She couldn't help being sad on Sunday when she waved good-bye to Lincoln and his family. But mostly she was happy, grateful for what they'd been given.

She called Laura and Sherri Ann for a three-way chat. She admitted how much she was looking forward to spending the Christmas holidays with both her siblings. The three laughingly recalled the holidays they'd spent growing up.

A little later, Jenna said into the telephone, "I've got to go. The doorbell just rang."

"Are you expecting company?" Sherri Ann asked.

"Naturally, it's Scott. They haven't seen each other all day," Laura insisted.

"How do you know it's Scott? He didn't say anything about coming over this evening," Jenna said, getting up from where she had been curled on the love seat.

"Laura's right. It has to be Scott. You two haven't been alone during the long weekend," Sherri Ann teased.

"It's him. Got to go. Talk to you tomorrow." She left the cordless telephone on the table in the foyer and unlocked the door. "Hey!"

"I know I should have called first," Scott said, wrapping his arms around her waist.

"It doesn't matter." She tilted her head up for his kiss and lifted her arms to encircle his neck.

He dropped his head, covering her full lips with his own. He groaned deep in his throat as she welcomed him, giving him access to her soft, sweet mouth.

She had no idea how he'd known that she needed him. She was just glad he was here.

"Hurry," she urged as she began unbuttoning the tan-and-black plaid flannel shirt he'd worn beneath a dark brown leather jacket.

Caught up in desire, she'd forgotten they were standing in the open front doorway. Anyone passing by could see them. Scott moved them inside and closed the door. All she wanted and needed at the moment was in her arms.

Scott chuckled as she pushed and pulled off the jacket and shirt. Then he groaned heavily when her soft hand caressed his bare chest, then slid over his hard, cloth-covered shaft. Her hands trembled as she unfastened his belt, opened his jeans, and eased down the zipper.

Jenna felt his big body shake as she slid a hand inside his black knit briefs. She traced the prominent crown of his sex, smoothing moisture over the crest with a fingertip. She heard his surprised gasp when she dropped to her knees to pleasure him the way he'd generously pleasured her in the past. It was something she'd never gotten up the courage to do until now. Tonight was special, and she wanted to please him.

She was determined not to spoil the moment by rushing. Scott groaned her name when she moved from laving the head of his shaft to suckle. Hoping to increase his pleasure, she intensified the suction.

Suddenly, he was pulling her up until he was ravishing her mouth. He didn't slow until they were both gasping for air. With her arms wrapped around his neck and his arms around her, her gaze locked with his.

"Why did you stop me?"

He shuddered, releasing a throaty laugh. Against her lips, he said, "Isn't it obvious? I couldn't take more. Thank you." He gave her yet another slow, deep kiss, then lifted her to carry her into the bedroom.

Jenna vaguely considered protesting that she was too heavy, but in truth, she was oblivious to everything but him as he placed her on her feet. Her black blouse, jeans, and underthings hit the floor, along with his jeans and briefs, socks and athletic shoes.

She barely had time to push the top sheet, blanket, and quilt down before he was there, giving her yet another toe-curling kiss.

"If you kiss me like that again, I think I'll die," she gasped.

"Then prepare yourself for heaven, sweet thing. I plan to do a lot more than kiss your lips."

Jenna didn't try to control her shivers as Scott kissed his way down her body. He left nothing to chance. He was thorough as he warmed every inch of her body until she was close to screaming from sexual frustration.

"No more," she begged, reaching for one of the condoms he'd dropped on the nightstand.

"It's called sweet torment," he whispered into her ear.

Even though she was trembling from relentless need, she managed to get the packet open and cover his erection. His large frame shook when she stroked his steel-hard length, then gently squeezed his heaviness below.

Before she could take her next breath, he had her beneath him, filling her completely. She cried out her enjoyment as his long, rhythmic thrusts quickly took her to the point of no return. A heart-pounding climax sent her senses soaring and left her numb from exquisite pleasure. He shuddered with the force of his powerful release. With arms and legs wrapped around him, she clung to him, focusing on the sheer beauty of their closeness. Nothing could be more intense or feel better.

When he rolled onto his back, he took her with him. The sound of the clock was the only noise in the room as the minutes ticked away. Leisurely, Scott caressed Jenna from her nape to the base of her spine and round hips and back again.

"Wow!" He pressed a kiss to her forehead.

"Yeah . . ." she echoed.

"You liked it when I lost control."

She giggled, pressed her lips to his. "Do it again."

He laughed, giving her a hard kiss. All too soon, they were caught up in each other again. It was late when they were raiding the refrigerator to make turkey sandwiches smeared with cranberry and orange relish. While they polished off the last piece of the sweet potato pie, Scott asked about her twin.

"Does she still plan to come for a long visit?"

"We talked to her again on Saturday. She sounds excited about the trip to Detroit. Lenn—I mean Leah—made no mention of how long she plans to stay. But you better believe I'm going to do everything I can to convince her to stay indefinitely."

He nodded. "She may not realize it yet, but it will do her a world of good to take advantage of the opportunity you're giving her. It's no small thing, Jenna. Are you prepared to disrupt your life to help her?"

"It's not a sacrifice. We're talking about my twin sister. Besides, I don't see it as a disruption. I'm looking forward to sharing my home with her." Placing the empty plates in the sink, she went back to where he sat in only a pair of briefs. She was wearing a thigh-length, lavender silk robe.

Lifting her arms to encircle his neck, she whispered, "Are you concerned that her being here will cut into our time together?"

His dark gaze locked with hers. "I'd be lying if I didn't admit I've thought about it, but only in passing. Neither of us has a lot of idle time. You're busy establishing yourself at the university, and I'm busy trying to finish up my degree. We will find a way to work around our hectic schedules, include Leah in our lives, as well as find time to be alone." He boasted, "No worries."

Jenna brushed her lips against his. "I'm glad you feel

that way. And you're right. It may get a bit crazy trying to get everything done and finding time to see each
other.

"We've only been involved a short time, but we're
resourceful enough to come up with a way to do it all,
though. Lenna might not realize it yet, but she needs
help. I'm sure she'd do the same for me if the situation
were reversed." She covered a yawn. "Sorry."

"It's Leah," he reminded her, tugging her along with
him. "Let's get some sleep."

"I know it's Leah. I'm just exhausted."

"I bet. You've been working nonstop for weeks,
babe. First you worked to find your siblings, and then
getting ready for Thanksgiving." He urged her past the
bed into the bathroom. "We'll sleep a lot better after a
hot shower."

Jenna was too tired to argue. The hot water left her
feeling almost boneless. She let him take care of her.
Luxuriating in the feel of his soapy hands gliding over
her skin, she could only sigh when Scott dried her off
and carried her to bed.

Cradled against his side, she pushed away fear that
she was becoming too dependent on him and it was a
mistake to let her guard down. When he left her—and
she had no doubt that one day he would leave—she was
going to once again be alone. She would be left with
even more memories to mark their time together. Jenna
sighed soberly. Letting him back into her life was a risk
she'd been willing to take. Falling in love was not something she was willing to chance.

She couldn't forget the euphoria she'd felt when he'd
asked her to be his wife all those years ago. Nor had she
forgotten how much she'd yearned to have his babies.
The dream might have died a slow, painful death, but
for some strange reason the longing hadn't disappeared.

For a moment, she wondered what it would be like to have his child. Her heart filled at the giddy thought. All her life she had desperately longed for a family of her own. In a sense, she had that now that her siblings were back in her life. If only she could forget about the children she and Scott had talked about having during the happy times. It had been nothing more than a sweet fantasy. She'd never seriously considered raising a child alone. But she'd always hoped their baby would have every advantage, which, in her estimation, meant growing up in a loving home with two adoring parents.

Even now, as she recalled her dream of lifelong commitment, Jenna accepted that she wouldn't settle. She could never be happy with less, both for her own sake and her baby's. Too bad: she'd always been an all-or-nothing kind of girl.

So why, then, was she lying in the arms of the man she knew she couldn't trust with her heart and her future? It made no sense. Yet Jenna didn't have a sensible answer. When it came to Scott Hendricks, she was shamefully weak.

No, she hadn't completely lost her mind. But for now she wanted what she wanted . . . which happened to be Scott. When they were done, they'd go their separate ways. She might be a little worse for wear, but her spirit and her heart wouldn't be broken.

Eighteen

Jenna couldn't stop smiling as she hugged her twin sister. They were surrounded by the hustle and bustle of Detroit's Metropolitan Airport.

"I can't believe you're here," she said, reluctantly letting her sister go.

"Believe it." Leah laughed. "You are stuck with me for awhile. I gave up my apartment and job."

"You're going to stay?" Jenna exclaimed, picking up her sister's heavy carry-on bag.

"For a few weeks. I don't remember much about Detroit. I'm willing to give it a shot. That's if you haven't changed your mind about putting me up?"

Jenna laughed as they walked toward the set of escalators that would take them to the luggage claim area. "I won't change my mind. It had to have been a difficult decision for you to give up your place and your job."

Leah laughed. "Jobs like that aren't hard to get. As long as I stay in shape and keep my weight down, I shouldn't have problems getting another one. Besides, I was ready to move out the day John walked out on me. He picked out that place, not me. I was tired of struggling to pay that jacked-up rent. I can live without a pool and a gym. John wanted to impress all his friends. I was the one working long hours to keep us off the streets." Leah swore, calling him a particularly foul name. "I don't even know what I saw in him!"

Jenna's face heated with embarrassment, aware of the way heads turned as they passed. They were both dressed casually in jeans and sweaters, but Leah's jeans were skintight and hugged her curves like a second skin, and her red V-neck pullover was low cut and clung to her full breasts. Jenna's jeans flattered her figure, and her lavender turtleneck just skimmed her curves and highlighted her creamy brown complexion.

There was no doubt that the two were identical twins, but there were differences. Jenna's lips were tinted in dark magenta, and her shoulder-length, wavy hair framed her face. Leah was heavily made up, her eyes outlined with thick black liner. She'd added fake lashes for drama, and her lips were painted a bright crimson and were shiny with gloss. Her straightened hair flowed to the middle of her back. Jenna's nails were polished with white French tips, and she wore two-inch heels. Leah's nails were long, painted a dark red, and she wore four-inch platform heels.

Jenna encouraged her sister, "You're better off without John. You'll see once you're settled. You've got time to relax and get your bearings before you decide what you want to do next."

Once they'd collected four large cases, Jenna paid a porter to carry them outside.

"Leah, you wait here while I go get the car. It won't take long."

"What happened to Mr. Tall, Dark, and Rich? And the limousine service? You didn't break it off with him, did you?" Leah quizzed.

"His name is Scott. And he's got a class. Besides, I wanted to pick you up myself. Be right back." Jenna hurried away.

It was early evening by the time Jenna got Leah home

and settled into the largest guest bedroom. Looking at the piles of clothes spread out on the bed and armchair, Jenna asked, "Are you sure you don't need my help?"

"We've done enough for now. It will keep. I'm thirsty. Let's get something to drink," Leah urged.

Jenna led the way into the kitchen and asked, "What would you like? Fruit juice? A soft drink?"

"Got any beer?"

Jenna blinked in surprise. "Of course. I keep a few bottles in the refrigerator for Scott." Grabbing a bottle of the imported beer and a can of Vernors, she opened a cabinet and brought down glasses. "Are you hungry? Would you like something to eat?"

"No glass," Leah said, reaching for the bottle. "Mm, the good stuff." She pointed to the label. "Got any snacks?"

Jenna smiled, opening a bag of potato chips and dumping them in a large bowl. She also opened a can of salted mixed nuts and poured them into a small bowl before collecting napkins.

"You have a gorgeous home. What I don't get is why you live here and not with Scott?"

In the living room the twins sat side by side on the sofa, food on the coffee table. Leah had turned on the flat-screen television beside the fireplace.

"Well?" Leah prompted.

Amused, Jenna asked, "What makes you think we don't live together?"

"Look around. No men's coats in the hall closet. No men's gear in the bathroom. Nothing's out of place. Nothing related to sports, specifically basketball. I've seen nothing that could possibly belong to a man, except for a few bottles of beer," Leah remarked as she tipped her drink for a swallow.

Jenna munched on a chip. "I'm proud that I can

take care of myself. I've been on my own since I was eighteen. There was only one time in my life when I lived with a man, and I was a kid, in love for the first time. I take pride in having put myself through college and paying my own rent all these years. With the help of scholarships, grant money, and part-time jobs until grad school, I can honestly say I did it on my own. This house might be modest, but it's all mine."

Leah ignored the comment. "Tell me about Scott."

Trying not to let it show that her feelings were hurt, Jenna asked, "What about him?"

"He's your man. So why do you live like everybody else when you could be living the life? From what I saw, the man's loaded, for God's sake!"

Jenna scolded, "Don't take the Lord's name in vain."

Leah rolled her eyes, helping herself to more chips. "Are you going to answer my question, Jenna Marie Gaines?"

"I thought it was obvious, Lenna Marie Gaines."

"Not to me."

"I wasn't raised to expect someone else to do what I can do for myself," Jenna explained. She'd worked her butt off to make a good life for herself. Why couldn't her sister appreciate that?

"Neither was I, but that didn't mean I bought into that sh—"

"Leah! Please watch your mouth!"

"Okay! Okay! You are too much. A real lady. Can we get back to you and Scott? Why did you go after Mr. NBA if you didn't want the entire package? You could have settled for any old dude working on the assembly line."

"It was never about money with Scott. I fell in love with a poor nineteen-year-old college student who just happened to play basketball. Neither one of us had any money. We used to pool our money just to go out for a movie and hamburgers. We'd lived together less than a year when he quit school and decided to play basketball. He went his way, and I went mine."

"You broke up just when the brother was about to make some cash?"

"Yes. Scott made money. Lots of it, but that had nothing to do with me." Jenna went on to explain her decision to pursue her goals and how they'd met again on campus.

"So you two were apart all those years. And only recently got back together," Leah said, incredulous. "I still don't get it. Tell me why you have not moved into his big old mansion? I bet it's gorgeous."

"He knows better than to ask." Jenna was too embarrassed to admit she hadn't even seen his home. She had no idea how big it was. When they'd slept together, it had always been at her place. For all she knew, he could be living in a cave in the heart of the city.

"Stupid, if you ask me. What's the point of having all that money if you can't take advantage of it?"

"That's where you and I are different, little sis. I'm really not interested in what Scott owns. It's the man I'm attracted to." Determined to change the subject, Jenna said, "Detroit has a lot to offer. Once you have settled in, I'd like to show you the city and where I work. I'd also like you to meet my foster sisters. We grew up together. Do you remember me telling you about them?"

"Yeah, yeah. The very successful Laura and Sherri Ann. I can hardly wait. So, what do you do for fun in this city? I'm talking about clubs and casinos. Where do you and Scott go when you go out?"

"Scott and I spend time with family and friends. And we're both busy with our careers. I'm a real homebody, but don't worry. We'll take you wherever you want to go. Plus, we're not far from Windsor, Canada."

"Do you and Scott plan to get married?" Leah quizzed.

"Why are you so interested in my relationship with Scott?"

"Just wondering how serious you are about him."

"Why?"

Leah shrugged. "Who knows? When you get tired of him, you can pass him along to me. You know what they say about twins."

"What?"

"Why, they share everything, including men," Leah joked.

"What?" Jenna said in disbelief.

"It was a joke!"

Jenna wasn't amused, but she dismissed it. "I'm surprised that you're even thinking about men, especially after what you've been through."

"What does that mean . . . 'been through'? John was a real jerk, but he didn't beat me or anything drastic like that. I'm not stupid. I wouldn't put up with that. One of the girls at the club was always coming in with a fresh set of bruises. We all tried to talk some sense into her, but she wouldn't listen."

"Well, I'm glad to hear you didn't have to deal with that. No, I meant I thought you would be turned off men for awhile. John disrespected you and took advantage of you. That hurt."

"That's what life's about. Do unto others before they can do it to you. This girl likes men. And I plan to take after my big sis. Find a man with a fat wallet." Leah giggled. "Be right back." She went into the kitchen.

Jenna laughed, shaking her head. Life was full of surprises. She was thrilled to have her twin with her, even if they didn't exactly agree on everything.

When Leah returned with another bottle of beer, Jenna teased, "You and Laura are going to get along just fine. She's always saying the right man is a rich man."

Laughing, Leah said, "I like her already. She and I are going to have to get Scott to introduce us to some of his professional ball-playing friends. I bet you can talk him into throwing a party. Invite some of his wealthy friends. The only females invited will be me and you, and Laura and Sherri Ann. It sounds like a plan to me."

Jenna was laughing so hard that she nearly fell off the sofa.

"I'm serious!"

That sent Jenna into another bout of giggles.

"Do you remember when we dared Lincoln to eat that bug and he did it?" Leah responded, giggling herself. "We told Mama, and she nearly turned him upside down trying to shake it out of him." Leah was laughing so hard that she was holding her side.

"Oh, I remember! We ended up spending most of the night in the emergency room because she didn't believe him when he said he didn't really eat it. And I wasn't the one who dared him. That was your doing, little sis."

"So it was. But I didn't think he'd really do it," Leah confessed.

"Neither did I."

"You haven't changed. Look at this place, beautifully decorated. You always kept your dolls looking like new. They always had hair, clothes, and the shoes, while mine were naked and bald in no time. I hated that about you."

"I know, you used to complain about it," Jenna said.

"How'd you do it? We were little kids."

"I don't know. I just tried to take care of my things. I even tried to take care of you and even Lincoln when Mama wasn't around. He was older, but I was always such a little mother hen."

Leah nodded. "I remember. I was so scared. I hated it

when she left us alone in the house, especially at night," Leah admitted.

"Me, too. Especially after Daddy left."

"Do you remember him?" Leah asked.

"I didn't think so, until I saw Lincoln. He looks like Daddy," Jenna said sadly. "We were so young when he left."

"I remember her crying all the time. She was always so sad," Leah said.

Jenna said, "It had to have been hard on her with three little kids to take care of on her own."

Leah scowled. "She had no business going off and leaving us alone to fend for ourselves."

"You still blame her for not coming back?" Jenna asked.

"I do. What about you? Don't you blame her for leaving us the way she did? If she'd have just stayed, we wouldn't have been separated. We would have grown up together."

Jenna was surprised by the level of resentment in her twin's voice. "I try not to blame her. What good can it do? I only end up feeling guilty and sad when I do." She put her arm around her twin's shoulder. They sat with their heads touching, like they did when they were little. "I honestly think she did her best. It just wasn't enough to keep us together."

"I suppose she was no worse than the Bennetts. They never kept their promises. They said they'd take care of me, but they never loved me. Do you think Lincoln blames Mama?"

"I honestly don't know, Leah. But for his sake, I hope not," Jenna said sadly.

Hoping to lift her twin's spirits, Jenna began telling her about their little neice, Corrie. She soon had Leah laughing and cooing over the pictures Jenna had taken at Thanksgiving.

Nineteen

"*Scott, it's about time* you showed your face," Leah laughed, throwing her arms around his neck and kissing him on the mouth. "I've been here two days already." Leah clung to his arm. She wore a short, skintight black dress.

Clasping her by the shoulders, he held her at arm's length. Smiling, he said, "It's good to see you, Leah. How do you like the Motor City?"

"It's not Vegas!" she laughed. "Jenna and her foster sisters took me out clubbing last night. We had a good time."

"Hi. Sorry, I'm running late." Jenna hurried into the foyer and went to Scott. She blinked in surprise when he wrapped her in a tight hug and gave her a lingering kiss.

"You look good," he said, admiring the dark purple knit that smoothed over her curves. His hand rested at the small of her back.

"Thanks. Doesn't Leah look nice?" She beamed proudly at her twin.

"Absolutely," he said quickly.

With a wide smile, Leah linked her arm through Scott's. "Where are we going?"

"Bradley's. The grand opening is tonight. It's a very classy supper club. It's in a great location on the water, not far from Sinbads restaurant. The Jacobs brothers are the owners."

"Who?" Leah asked.

"Brad and Brian Jacobs are from the Detroit area. They are determined to do their part in revitalizing the city. They renovated an old warehouse. Wait until you ladies see it. I think you will be impressed. They had a difficult time finding backing until I decided to help them out."

"Really," Leah practically bounced with excitement. "Congratulations, Scott. Are you excited?"

"For them, yes. It's a dream come true."

"Are they single?" Leah asked.

"They are both married," Scott said, moving to help Jenna into her coat. Then he helped Leah. "There should be plenty of single men out tonight. Two of my friends from the Pistons are planning to attend."

"Really," Leah and Jenna said at the same time and laughed.

"Taylor and Donald also plan to come." He explained to Leah, "My sister and her husband. Shall we?" he asked, opening the door.

"You don't have to ask me twice," Leah laughed.

Scott ushered Leah to the waiting limousine parked at the curb. He hurried back to wait for Jenna as she finished locking up and setting the alarm. He clasped her hand as he quizzed, "You okay?"

She smiled. "I'm fine, although I've missed you this week."

He kissed her temple. "Me, too. Spend the night with me," he whispered.

Jenna shivered from the cold. It had snowed and the ground was coated. She whispered, "I can't leave my sister on her own. She's only been here a few days. Please, don't be angry."

"I'm not." He gave her fingers a gentle squeeze. "Maybe she'll get lucky tonight and won't need you."

Jenna couldn't help laughing. "Shame on you," she teased, then she sobered. "Scott, you didn't have to go through all this expense for us."

He didn't wait for the driver but opened the door for her. "I thought you might enjoy the change."

"Me?" She slid onto the lush dove-gray seats.

Getting in, he whispered close to her ear, "Yes, you. I haven't had a chance to spoil you since Vegas."

Jenna blushed. Although she said nothing more, she was secretly pleased by the thought. It was an unusual concept. No one had ever attempted to spoil her. It made her feel warm inside . . . cared about.

Leah urged, "So tell me about these friends of yours, Scott. How long have they been playing in the pros?"

"Doug and his twin, Neal Dunn, have only been with the Pistons a year. We met while I played with their older brother, Matt, a few years back. They are considered to be a double threat and will take Detroit all the way to the championship."

Jenna couldn't figure out why it mattered how long they'd been playing. They were NBA, so that should please Leah. She frowned as she stared out the window. Why was she upset by the way Leah had clung to Scott? It didn't mean anything. Leah flirted with every man within her vicinity.

Jenna was surprised by the crowd. The television cameras and crews were out. There were lines of limousines waiting their turn. It was unlike anything Jenna had ever seen. It reminded her of the Hollywood red carpet events she saw on television.

Leah was clearly excited when it was their turn to exit

the limo. She linked her arm through Scott's, laughing and smiling as if she expected to be on the late-night news.

Bradley's was bound to be a hit, judging by the enthusiastic crowd and impressive facility. Jenna waved to Sherri Ann and Laura when she spotted them in the crowded foyer.

"Do you think we're going to be able to get seats?" Jenna asked.

"No worries. We have reservations," Scott said, nodding to people he knew in the crowd. He grinned when he spotted the owners. The Jacobs brothers were tall, but Scott towered above them.

"Scott, I'm glad you could make it," Brian said, shaking his hand.

"Looks like you guys have a success on your hands," Scott grinned.

"Let's hope so," Brad said. "We owe you, Mr. Hendricks. We couldn't have done it without you."

"You came through for us." Brian grinned. "This is my wife, Sheila, and Brad's wife, Joan." He introduced the two ladies.

"Nice to meet you both," Scott smiled, shaking hands. "This is my lady, Jenna Gaines." His arm was around her shoulders. "And this is Leah Bennett, Jenna's twin sister."

"Two beautiful ladies," Brian laughed. "Welcome to Bradley's. It's a pleasure to meet you both."

Scott smiled. "And this is Sherri Ann Weber and Laura Murdock, Jenna's best friends. Brian and Brad Jacobs, the owners of the club."

Sherri Ann and Laura had come with dates. They took turns introducing them as they waited to be seated.

"I hope you're all ready for a good time." Brian signaled the hostess. "This is Karen. She will show you to your table."

"Thanks. Congratulations again. We'll talk later," Scott nodded.

Karen smiled. "This way, ladies and gentlemen." She moved past the grand staircase into the beautifully appointed dining room, where there were gleaming crystal chandeliers overhead.

Bradley's was tastefully decorated, upscale and classy. The service was excellent, even on opening night. Jenna wasn't surprised, considering the fact that Scott was the silent backer. He'd clearly picked a winner.

He'd undoubtedly had the Jacobs brothers thoroughly investigated before he'd agreed to help them. Jenna liked that he valued his name, guarded his reputation, and kept his word. She also admired the fact that despite the hard economic times he was willing to offer a helping hand.

Jenna was impressed by the celebrities and community leaders that stopped by their table to shake hands with Scott. Judge Quinn Montgomery and his beautiful wife, Heather, stopped to say hello, as well as the head of the Malcolm X Community Center, Dexter Washington, and his wife, Anthia.

Scott's mentor and old friend, Charles Randol, and his wife, Diane, also took time to talk. Charles owned Randol Pharmaceutical, one of the most successful drug companies in the country. Jenna recalled Scott's enthusiasm over the cutting-edge research they were doing in HIV and respiratory medications.

Scott was greeted by NFL player Wesley Prescott and his wife, Kelli, and ex-NBA player Ralph Prescott and his bride, Vanessa.

The impressive nightclub was on the third level. A live band performed on stage in the front of the room. A crystal fountain sparkled in the center of a gleaming mirrored curved bar. The music was going full blast when they were shown to their table. The Jacobs brothers sent over a complimentary bottle of champagne.

"This is a nice boss man," Leah teased as she playfully stroked Scott's arm. He was seated between the twins. "This place is on jam! It reminds me of Vegas."

"Looks like everyone turned out to celebrate the grand opening," Laura said from where she sat with her date. "I don't think I've been in such a crowd since the festivals during the summer."

"You've got that right," Sherri Ann said. "Isn't that Wesley and Kelli on the dance floor?"

"It is." Laura waved to them.

"Enjoying yourself?" Scott asked close to Jenna's ear.

Jenna smiled, sipping from her glass. "Absolutely." After watching her twin snapping her fingers in time to the music, she whispered to him, "Dance with her. She's dying to get on the dance floor."

Scott whispered back, "I'd rather dance with you."

Jenna smiled but softly urged, "Please."

He sighed heavily, then said into her ear, "The next slow dance is mine. Okay?"

"Okay." She watched as Scott escorted Leah out on the dance floor.

"Are you nuts?" Laura hissed, moving to the empty chair beside Jenna.

"What?"

"You know what! Sending Scott to dance with her. He should be dancing with you. The girl is practically in his lap as it is. And don't tell me you haven't noticed the way she flirts with your man every chance she gets," Laura snapped.

"Hush, keep your voice down. That's Leah's way. She doesn't mean anything by it," Jenna defended.

Laura whispered, "Just because she makes a habit of flirting with every man that comes under her radar doesn't mean she's harmless. Will you open your eyes? Leah is not just beautiful. She looks exactly like you. That girl could be a threat."

"She is also my family. She would never do anything to hurt me," Jenna insisted.

"You know that?"

"Yes. Just like I know you and Sherri Ann wouldn't do anything to hurt me. Come on, Laura." Jenna squeezed her hand. "Leah didn't have Mrs. Green teaching her how to behave. Give her the benefit of the doubt. Please."

Laura sighed impatiently. "Okay, but be careful. Scott is a decent man, but he's no saint."

Jenna laughed. "I trust him. If I didn't, I wouldn't have let him in the front door. Besides, he knows that I don't play."

"Okay." Laura gave her a quick hug. "Love you."

"I love you, too. Stop worrying."

"Something wrong?" Sherri Ann joined them.

"I'll tell you later," Laura promised. To her date, she said, "Come on, Sam. Let's break in this brand-new floor."

"It sounds good to me." He took her hand.

"Jenna?"

"Nothing wrong, Sherri Ann. Relax," she said with a smile.

"Come on, Sherri Ann. Let's hit it." Her date—Ross Turner, a coworker—rose to his feet.

"I can't leave Jenna alone."

"Sure you can. Enjoy yourself," Jenna said and waved her away. "Go!"

Sherri Ann reluctantly let her date pull her onto the crowded dance floor.

Jenna sipped her soft drink. Laura was being protective. She was wrong about her twin. It didn't matter that they were just getting to know each other all over again. Deep down where it counted, they were connected. They weren't just sisters, they shared the same DNA. They were identical inside and out. For so long, Jenna had felt as if a vital part of her had been missing, but she hadn't felt that way since she'd found Leah.

Their differences came from circumstances they could not control. Leah hadn't grown up with a Mrs. Green in her life. She hadn't received the love and care that Mrs. Green had given the three of them—or the polish. That didn't mean Leah didn't have a good heart or that she didn't love her family. Jenna was confident that time would prove to Laura that she was mistaken.

The music stopped and the others came back to the table.

"You've been sitting here all alone?" Scott quizzed with a frown.

"Only for a few minutes. The band is wonderful. The food is fabulous. I'd say, Mr. Hendricks, that you have a hit on your hands," Jenna enthused.

"Scott, I didn't think I'd ever find you in the crowd."

He looked up at the sound of his sister's voice. Grinning, he kissed her cheek, then introduced Taylor and her husband, Donald, to everyone.

Taylor and Jenna hugged. "I'm so glad to see you here tonight. Scott has been telling us about this place. I thought my baby brother was exaggerating."

"You were wrong, sweetheart." Donald patted Scott on the back. "I have to say, brother-in-law, this deal was sweet. The place is great. You've got a big moneymaker on your hands."

Scott threw back his head and laughed. "That's high praise indeed, coming from you. Did you meet the Jacobs brothers?" He motioned to the waiter to bring more chairs.

"Yes, Taylor and I were impressed."

"We're going to have to bring Mama and the kids for an early dinner. The food was wonderful. Jenna, what do you think?" Taylor asked Leah.

"Everything is over the top. Scott has a gold mine on his hands," Leah answered with a grin.

Realizing her mistake, Taylor laughed. "I can't believe I did that."

"It happens all the time, especially in low light." Jenna giggled.

Encircling his arm around Jenna's waist, Scott said, "The first time I saw them together, I couldn't believe my eyes." He laughed. "Thought I was seeing double."

Laura said candidly, "They look alike, but we all know our Jenna. She's the one trying to soothe everyone while keeping us on the straight and narrow. No messing up allowed. She doesn't suffer fools well."

"Are you saying I'm bossy?"

"You said that, not me. But if the shoe fits, Professor Gaines . . ." Laura teased.

Everyone laughed at that retort.

"Laura is saying we love you." Scott brushed his lips with hers.

Jenna's breath quickened, despite her best efforts not to take the innocent comment to heart.

Just then two very tall men approached their table. Scott grinned, offering his hand. "Everyone, this is Doug and Neal Dunn," he said, making the introductions.

The two·men were fraternal twins—similar, but not identical. They were two of the best NBA players and were making the league step back and take notice. While the men at the table were ready to discuss in detail the Pistons' chances of taking the Eastern Conference this season, the ladies weren't having it.

When the band came back from their break, the tables quickly emptied.

Out on the dance floor, Jenna said to Scott, "Thanks for dancing with my sister." She rested her cheek against his chest as they moved in time to a slow ballad. "Did you see Leah's face when you introduced her to the Dunn twins? She was on top of the world with two handsome brothers competing for her attention."

He chuckled, tightening his arm around her as he swayed from one foot to the other. "As long as you're happy, that's what I care about." Pressing his lips to her temple, he said, "I'm glad to finally have you to myself. I missed you, babe."

She shivered from the deep, husky timbre of his voice and his raw sexuality. He asked, "Have you given any more thought to spending the night with me?" When she didn't respond, he quizzed, "Jenna?"

Reluctantly, she revealed, "I can't. I told you why. Nothing has changed. It's too soon for me to leave Leah on her own. I'm sorry."

"So am I."

Just then the music changed to an upbeat song. Scott surprised her when he didn't keep dancing but cupped her elbow and started back to the table.

"You're angry," she accused.

"A little disappointed, that's all."

It wasn't all. Knowing she'd let him down upset Jenna. She hated disappointing him. As much as she wanted to be with him, she couldn't ignore her decision to make her sister a priority. She assured herself that he understood and there would be other nights.

As the evening drew to a close, Jenna was surprised when her sister said a hasty good-bye and left with the Dunn brothers. Everyone seemed surprised by it, although no one made a comment. The club was closing when Jenna and Scott said their good nights to the others.

* * *

"Looks like you're stuck with me," Scott broke into the silence. He shifted against the expensive leather seat as their limousine sped through the quiet streets.

Jenna offered a weak smile. Her large hazel eyes were concealed by her thick lashes. "Hardly stuck." Raising and dropping her hands in a gesture of dismay, she said, "I'm still in shock. I don't believe what happened."

"You mean Leah leaving with the Dunn brothers?"

"Yeah!"

"Believe it," Scott chuckled, moving his thumb over the back of her balled-up hands.

"It's not funny."

"Babe, it's not the end of the world. Leah's a big girl. And she chose to spend what was left of the night with Neal Dunn."

"It's just that . . ." Jenna paused. "I don't know why I'm so surprised."

"Leah may be your twin, but she's not you," he said in an attempt to soothe her.

"You're right. She did something I'd never even consider." Then she looked pointedly at him. "What do you know about this Neal Dunn?"

"Enough. As I told you, I played ball with their older brother, Matt. The two of us were teammates with the Charlotte Hornets until he was traded."

"That's it?"

"Jenna, Leah's only going out with him, not going down the aisle with the man."

"She's sleeping with him. And she doesn't really know him. He could be a serial killer for all we know."

"Not likely. Besides, we really don't know what they're doing. They may stay up all night talking."

She poked him in the middle with her elbow. "Even I'm not that naïve. I might not have known my sister long, but I don't think she is sporting a halo."

He placed a tender kiss on her lips, savoring their softness. Not liking the worry he saw in her pretty hazel eyes, he decided a change of topic was in order. "What did you think of Bradley's?"

"Very nice, elegant. Everyone seemed to be having a good time. It was good to see Taylor and Donald. Your mom doing the babysitting honors?"

"Yeah. She's crazy about her grandbabies." He laughed. "This will be your first visit to my house. I'm in Bloomfield Hills."

"Yes, I've wondered why you haven't invited me before." She gazed pointedly at him.

Scott laughed, confessing, "My reason for not inviting you sooner had nothing to do with you. I'm embarrassed to say that until recently, the only person who came by was my sister. And she only stopped by to yell at me. The place was a mess. And so was I."

"What do you mean?" She slipped her hand into his.

"When I moved back to the area I only brought my clothes, kitchen basics, and mementos. As for furniture, I had my bedroom set, leather sofa and recliner, a few lamps, not much. Throw in towels and sheets, and that was about it. The extent of my shopping for the new house was getting a television, DVD player, and my favorite sound system. In short, I used my bedroom, the kitchen, and den. The rest of the rooms remained empty."

"But why?"

"When I sold the house in L.A., the buyer wanted everything." He shrugged, taking a few moments before he reluctantly said, "I wanted to make a fresh start, only I fell into a slump. I did a lot of drinking and brooding, wondering if I'd made a big mistake in returning to Detroit. I was also missing you badly and not handling it well."

"I had no idea."

He said candidly, "It was a tough couple of weeks. I had poor Taylor worried. She gave me a jolt when she told me you were back. My getting back into college and the lab, and then seeing you, was the kick in the butt that I needed." He grinned sheepishly. "When I saw your place, I decided to get it together. I hired a housekeeper and interior decorator. I finally felt as if I can invite you over."

"Goodness. I assumed you were living in a show-place, something like Taylor and Donald's." Jenna took him by surprise when she asked, "What was your place like in Charlotte and L.A.?"

They'd made a point of not questioning each other about the lost years. It seemed easier not to delve too deeply into each other's lives. He didn't want to hear about the men she'd dated, especially not the ones who'd tried to get close to her. He especially hadn't liked seeing her with Jackson Knight.

"I had a condo in Charlotte, and I bought a house in L.A. Both places were done by decorators." He shrugged. "All I cared about was that I was comfortable." For some reason his places had never felt like home, only a place to sleep and dump his stuff. As for the women in his life, he'd been careful not to let any one of them get too close.

Jenna laughed. "That tells me nothing about your personal sense of style."

He chuckled. "I don't believe I have one."

Giggling, she said, "Everyone has a personal style. You look very good tonight," she said, smoothing his dove-gray dress shirt and charcoal-gray silk tie, which he'd teamed with a beautifully tailored black suit.

Pleased, he said, "I'm only a few miles from Taylor and my mother." The limousine turned onto a long, curved drive paved with cream-colored brick. It eased to a stop beneath the portico of an impressive house.

While Scott settled with the driver, Jenna studied the old-world charm of the Venetian-inspired home. Mounted sconces lit the cream stucco exterior and framed the arched double doors.

"It's beautiful." She smiled up at him as he put his key in the lock.

He grinned. "You may want to reserve judgment until you've seen the interior." Pushing the door wide, he stepped back for her to proceed.

They stood in the wide marble foyer, furnished in a traditional fashion with a heavy oak chest flanked by two straight-back, wheat-colored padded chairs.

"This way." With a hand at her spine, he urged her down the long hall and through the open doorway on the right. "This is the den, where I spend most of my time."

Jenna took in the taupe walls and drapes, the deep-cushioned bronze leather sofa and armchair with matching ottoman, and the dark brown leather recliner that dominated the room. His laptop sat open on the mahogany desk with its comfortable, wheat-patterned chair. A huge flat-screen television was mounted above a console table that served as a bar. The rich teak hardwood floor was covered by a large bronze, taupe, caramel, and ivory patterned area rug.

"Well?" he prompted.

"It's strong, masculine, and comfortable. I like it. Show me more."

Relieved, Scott took her across the hall to the large dining room. "I can't take credit for anything other than picking out the taupe for the walls and drapes."

Jenna admired the rich, dark cherrywood traditional dining room set with high-back wheat-colored upholstered slipper chairs. "It's lovely."

Scott showed her the spacious living room done in shades of cream. Twin taupe suede armchairs were separated by a round end table, and two cream velvet sofas faced each other. They were positioned on either side of the impressive marble fireplace. The large, wingback chair, covered in a striped silk cream and taupe, faced the fireplace, its matching padded bench positioned in front of an oversized glass-topped coffee table.

He explained that the double French doors on each side of the fireplace opened onto the covered veranda that wrapped around the back of the house. "Beyond the garden is an outdoor pool and tennis court. I've hired a contractor to add on an indoor pool, gym, and basketball court." Smiling, he took her hand. "Come on. I want to show you the kitchen and family room."

The kitchen was beautiful and spacious, with stainless steel appliances, taupe and bronze granite countertops, and a huge center island. Before she could comment, he took her next door to the empty family media room. He even showed her the five empty guest bedrooms with connecting baths.

"Still impressed?" He waited for her response. He had no idea why her approval was so important to him. It just was.

Jenna laughed. "Well, there's still a lot to do, but you've made remarkable progress. I can only imagine your sister's and mother's reactions."

With an arm around her shoulders, he said, "They were pleased that I'd finally settled in." He guided her past the kitchen and living room to the east wing, where he paused in front of a set of double doors. "This is the master suite," he said as he pushed opened the doors.

He watched her closely as she took in the oversized bed that had been custom made to accommodate his height. The taupe suede, padded headboard stretched to the ceiling, while two beautifully crafted, granite topped nightstands held a pair of bronze table lamps. The bed was covered with a plush, dark-brown velvet comforter and pristine white sheets. It was piled high with white pillows. A long, bronze padded bench was positioned at the foot of the bed. A large flat-screen television was mounted on the wall across from the bed, while bronze leather armchairs faced each other and shared a matching ottoman. The door on the left opened into an enormous walk-in closet, and the door on the right led to the luxurious spa-like bathroom, also done in shades of bronze.

"Well?"

She slid her arms beneath his jacket and wrapped them around his waist. "Your home is a showplace . . . exceptional."

He frowned. "Does that mean it feels like a home?"

"Absolutely."

He grinned, pleased with her response. "You are exhausted," he whispered, kissing her forehead. "My invitation is still open. You are welcome to spend the night."

Snuggling against him, she sighed softly, then said, "Yes, I'll stay, but I doubt I'll have the energy to do more than sleep. Is that okay?"

"As long as I get to hold you, you won't hear any complaints out of me," he confessed. He brushed her lips with his. "Need any help getting undressed?" he asked, confident that her being here with him tonight was enough as long as she continued to have room for him in her life.

He was a patient man. He could wait for her to realize she still had feelings for him . . . that their love was not a thing of the past.

"If that means I don't have to move, I'm all for it," she said wearily.

Ignoring his pulsating need, Scott undressed them both. They shared a soothing, hot shower. Jenna could hardly keep her eyes open by the time they cuddled in the center of his large, comfortable bed. After she kissed the place where his neck and shoulders joined, causing shivers to race over his heated skin, she mumbled good-night, then drifted off into a deep, restorative sleep.

Although he was tired, sleep didn't come. He rested on his back, with Jenna's head tucked beneath his chin, while she slept on him. Her lush curves were covered by one of his old L. A. Lakers T-shirts. He gently smoothed a palm down her back. Her shapely long legs were tucked between his.

Savoring their closeness, his focus was entirely on her. Determined to enjoy every single moment they shared like this, he closed his eyes and gave his other senses free rein. He relished Jenna's softness while he inhaled her unique womanly scent. He indulged his sense of taste by dropping his head to momentarily lave her neck . . . no more. She needed rest, and that was exactly what he'd give her. All the while he listened to her deep, slow breathing.

Scott refused to dwell on his earlier disappointment when Jenna had flatly refused to consider his invitation. She'd swept it aside, just as he'd ignored his body's natural reaction to her sweet curves and closeness. As fatigue caught up with him, he acknowledged that he held his world in his arms.

Twenty

Jenna was sleeping so soundly that Scott didn't have the heart to wake her. The urgency of his throbbing arousal forced him out of his comfortable bed and into a cold shower. He smiled despite his selfish need. Having her here was worth any amount of temporary discomfort.

He dressed in gray sweats, then went outside to begin his run. He smiled as he ran, leather gloves and a knit skull cap being his only concession to the bitterly cold morning. As his long, powerful legs ate the miles, he mulled over the chemical compounds and formulas he planned to work with in the lab the next day. Five miles later he was barely winded, his muscles loose. He took another shower, this one hot and soothing, then dressed in faded jeans and a black crew-neck, cashmere sweater.

He allowed himself only a few minutes to admire his lady snuggled against a pillow. Feet encased in athletic socks, he padded into the kitchen and began preparing breakfast. Pleased with his efforts, he carried the heavily laden tray down the hall. He was brought up short when he reentered the bedroom to find Jenna not in bed but nearly dressed.

She looked up, offering him a pretty smile as she

eased her dress up over her luscious hips and plump breasts and onto her shoulders. She pushed back her thick, wavy hair.

"Good morning, I was coming to look for you." Her hazel eyes twinkled. "You've been busy. It smells divine."

Smiling, Scott placed the tray on the leather ottoman between the armchairs. "I'd planned to surprise you with breakfast in bed." With a hand on a lean hip, he complained, "You're dressed."

"If I'd known, I would have stayed put." She stretched up on tiptoe to place a kiss on his lips. "How'd you sleep?"

"Not as well as you did. You looked so pretty asleep in my bed. I didn't have the heart to wake you so you could run with me." He gave her a squeeze before he asked, "Hungry?"

"I could eat a small bite," she hedged, then laughed at his frown. Rubbing her hands together she said, "What did you make? Cereal? Pop-Tarts?"

Chuckling, he said, "More like waffles with strawberries, turkey bacon, and coffee." Discarding the dome, he held up a plate. "Did I mention the waffles were frozen, the bacon microwaved, but the coffee was freshly brewed."

"It's the thought that matters." Collecting a plate and silverware wrapped in a napkin, she settled in an armchair. "Smells good." She said grace before she dug in. "Mmm, delicious."

He couldn't stop grinning. "You must really be hungry." He took the other chair, then passed her a glass of orange juice before he took his own plate. "I could have cracked a few eggs, but I didn't want to chance messing that up."

Smiling, Jenna didn't stop eating. "Is it really ten?

I didn't realize it was so late. Leah's probably at home wondering . . ."

"If Leah is back, she knows you're with me."

"You think I'm overreacting, don't you?"

"I didn't say that." He tucked a wavy lock behind her ear before he went back to his own breakfast.

Jenna swallowed. "You didn't answer my question."

Scott didn't respond immediately. Reluctantly, he admitted, "I think you should ease up a bit. Stop worrying about every little bump in the road. I'd like to see you relaxed so you can enjoy this time with your sister."

There was an extended silence as he waited for her response.

Sighing, she said, "I just want things to go smoothly as we get to know each other again. What's wrong with that?"

"There's no such thing as perfection, not in this lifetime."

"I don't expect perfection," she defended, sipping her coffee.

"You were shaken when your sister went with Neal Dunn."

"I know. She surprised me, that's all. No biggy."

"You sure?"

"Absolutely." She flashed him a reassuring smile. Returning her nearly empty plate to the tray, she said, "I'll help you clean up before I leave."

"You don't have to rush off. I'd like nothing better than to spend the day with you." Finished with his plate, he came over to cradle her chin. "I haven't seen much of you since your sister arrived."

Jenna stared at him for a long moment. "I know, but we talked about this, remember?"

"Yeah, I know. I'm not complaining, just missing you." He held her close. "It's easier said than done," he said with a shrug. When she reached for the tray, he said, "It's heavy. I'll get it."

Once the kitchen was clean, she said, "I should get back."

He opened his mouth to protest but thought better of it. Then he nodded his agreement.

They both were quiet on the drive to her place. Even after he stopped the car, they looked thoughtfully at each other.

Jenna broke the silence when she said, "What are you going to do with the rest of your day?"

"I've got enough work to do on my project to keep me busy. I also promised to stop by and see my mom. Probably take her out to dinner. We haven't done that in a while and she likes that kind of stuff."

He smiled, determined to conceal his disappointment. He consoled himself with the thought that there would be time later for the two of them to be alone together. He would wait until Leah had settled in and Jenna had more time to devote to him.

This was a special time for her, and he wouldn't burden her with a host of personal demands to cement their relationship. He prided himself on being a patient man. Besides, his lady was more than worth the inconvenience.

Introducing Leah to the Dunn brothers had turned out better than he'd hoped. He hadn't expected her to take off with them, but unlike Jenna, he wasn't surprised. Leah's body language screamed that she was ripe for the taking. His single goal had been to keep Leah occupied with any man she'd wanted, just not him.

He didn't appreciate the way Leah had clung to him last night. It had bordered on disrespect to him and Jenna. And he wasn't about to let Jenna's sister come between them. He'd really tried to withhold judgment for his lady's sake. It hadn't worked. Before they'd left Las Vegas, he'd found Leah to be extremely self-centered, but he'd wisely kept his opinion to himself. Jenna adored her sister and expected those close to her to do the same.

As Scott leaned down to briefly cover her mouth with his, he said, "I'll call tonight." Then he got out and opened her door. He held his hand out to her, but he didn't trust himself to do more. He wanted her too badly.

"Having fun?" Sherri Ann said over the loud music pouring out of the club's sound system. She paid for the next round of drinks the waitress had plopped down in front of them.

"I left fun two clubs ago," Laura complained, kicking off her heels. Glaring at Jenna, she hissed, "This is our third night out this week, but does your sister appreciate our sacrifices? No! She's living it up on the dance floor with yet another guy. Only for you, sister girl."

"Shut up, Laura. You're just tired," Sherri Ann huffed. "None of this is Jenna's fault. She's only trying to entertain Leah. There's nothing wrong with that."

"Laura's right," Jenna admitted unhappily. "I shouldn't have dragged you two into my mess just because I'm having trouble saying no to my sister."

Laura snapped, "I suggest you get over it before we all lose our jobs while Ms. Thing catches up on her beauty sleep during the day."

Jenna sighed heavily. "Leave it to Laura not to mince words. Things aren't going as I'd hoped. Instead of Leah poring over college catalogues and planning her future, she has been burning the candle at both ends. And she's running me ragged." She threw up her hands helplessly. "I've done everything I can think of to get her to see that there are other options open to her besides dancing nearly nude for a living. I've even dragged you two into it. I'm so sorry. This stops tonight."

"Scott's going to celebrate!" Sherri Ann said.

"Has he said something to you?" Jenna asked, aware that she hadn't seen much of him lately.

"Of course not. I'm just saying he has to be sick of it."

"We're all sick of it . . . that is, everyone except Ms. Leah," Laura said, picking up her club soda with lime.

"I'm sorry. I shouldn't—"

"Jenna, will you stop with the guilt? You didn't drag us into anything. Laura and I don't want you to be out here alone, fending off some drunk while Leah's living it up."

"That's right. Are you prepared to let her go out on her own, if it comes to that?" Laura quizzed.

Jenna took a swallow of her diet cola, then said, "I'm tired of her bad habits invading my life. If she insists on clubbing every night, then so be it. We all have better things to do."

"Like sleeping," Laura remarked dryly, causing all three of them to laugh.

"What's funny?" Leah asked. She picked up Jenna's glass but quickly made a face and put it down when she realized it was a soft drink.

"We're leaving. We have to get up early in the morning," Jenna announced.

"It's not even midnight!" Leah complained.

"This pumpkin is tapped out." Jenna began collecting her things.

"Just like that you're going to leave me stranded in a strange city?" Leah glared at her twin.

"Leah, it's late. We've got work in the morning," Sherri Ann defended.

Leah, clearly put out, swore. "I don't believe this—"

"What I don't believe is you!" Laura snapped. "Jenna has practically bent over backward trying to please your selfish behind."

"That's enough out of both of you. Leah, you're welcome to stay, but we're leaving." Jenna had had enough. She wasn't about to get into a shouting match in public. "Let's go, ladies."

Leah was mumbling beneath her breath, but she grabbed her coat and purse before she followed them.

It was a bitterly cold night. The moon shone bright overhead. They were forced to let the engine run before they could get underway. Jenna was behind the wheel.

Sherri Ann broke the strained silence. "Laura is right, Leah. You're acting like a spoiled brat. Jenna adores you and has gone out of her way to please you."

As she guided the car onto the expressway, Jenna said, "Can we drop this, please? We are all tired. And I don't know about anyone else, but I've had all I can take for one night."

It was starting to snow. Jenna was forced to slow her speed and switch on the windshield wipers. They dropped off Sherri Ann first, then Laura. As they turned out of the driveway of Laura's condo, the snow was really coming down, and Jenna was forced to slow down even more.

Jenna was concerned about Leah's continued silence. She didn't want her sister to feel as if they were picking on her. She tried to lighten the mood by saying, "It's really coming down. I'm glad we left early."

The lack of response caused Jenna to glance at her twin in the passenger seat. Leah sat with both arms crossed beneath her breasts, staring straight ahead.

"Leah, I'm sorry you're upset. Laura and Sherri Ann can be very protective at times, but they didn't mean to hurt your feelings."

"What was calling me names meant to do? Make it all better?" Leah said in a huff.

"No, but we were all tired and upset. Perhaps some things were best left unsaid. No one meant to call you names. Can we please leave it at that?"

"Fine!" Leah snapped.

Jenna worried her bottom lip, trying not to feel as if she was caught in the middle of a war. She did her best to concentrate on getting them home safely. She didn't relax until she eased to a stop in her drive.

Jenna didn't say anything more until they were inside. On her way to the kitchen, she asked, "Would you like some hot chocolate?"

"No," Leah snapped.

"Please, don't go to bed angry."

"What do you expect, Jenna? You and your friends ganged up on me tonight, and I didn't like it."

"It wasn't like that. We were only trying—"

Leah held up her hand, palm up. "That's the way it seemed to me. It's time I moved back to Vegas."

"No, Leah! You're more than welcome to stay here."

"You mean as long as I do things your way, don't you, big sis?"

"That is not what I said. That's the last thing I want. You've just moved here. You haven't given yourself enough time to get on your feet after your breakup with John. I know money is tight, and you're used to doing your own thing. But why move back and get yourself into a financial bind? Stay here with me. It will give you time to decide what you want to do next. Look at the college catalogues. You don't have to dance in clubs to make a living."

"I know that," Leah said, crossing her arms.

"Good. I've also learned a lesson. I'm stepping back and letting you do your thing. My friends and I won't be following you from one club to the next."

"Fair enough, except I don't have any transportation."

"That's one problem I can't help you with."

"You could always ask your man. A rich guy like Scott, I'm sure he has more than one car."

Jenna shook her head. "It doesn't matter. I'm not asking."

"Why not?"

"It's not his problem. Maybe you can call your friend Neal Dunn," Jenna said. She had no idea what had happened between the two of them. After the club opening, Leah hadn't mentioned the man's name. "Maybe he will loan you one of his cars?"

"Not likely. The man was interested in one thing. Once he got that, he moved on," Leah said dryly.

Jenna covered a yawn. "I'm beat. Good night, Sis." She changed direction, heading toward her bedroom. "See you in the morning. Sleep well."

Fuming, Leah made her way into the kitchen. Retrieving a bottle of sauvignon blanc cooling in the refrigerator, she lifted a brow at the costly label, then expertly uncorked it. After pouring a generous portion, she made herself comfortable in the living room.

Everywhere she looked showed the expert care and attention to detail her twin had put into making her home a showplace. Not even a throw pillow was out of place. From the paint colors and drapes to the furnishings, rugs, and accessories, all was meant to impress. The house might have been modest, but it was beautiful. Nothing had been left to chance. It was just like her big sister . . . perfect.

Had the girl ever taken a wrong step in her entire
life? From what Leah had observed, it was highly unlikely. Jenna had worked her way through college. Little
Miss Perfect hadn't stopped there. Despite the odds, she
had made it through graduate school with top grades,
all the while holding a job on Wall Street. When she'd
graduated, she'd gotten her dream job and bought her
own home. She might have had an old car, but she had
expensive clothes. Her good luck hadn't stopped there.
Hell, no!

Jenna had reunited with her lost love, who just happened to be a very rich and good-looking pro athlete
that still adored her. Little Ms. Perfect had it all . . .
the house, the job, and the man. Damn her! She'd even
replaced her own family with those goody-goody foster
sisters.

Who gave her the right to pass judgment on her own
flesh and blood? She was just plain wrong to embarrass
her own sister in front of her high-class friends, who
thought they were better than ordinary folk.

"It's wrong!" Leah grumbled aloud as she drained
her glass. Resentment bubbled inside of her.

Every room in this place pointed to her twin's success. To make matters worse, whenever Leah looked
into the mirror, she didn't see herself. She saw Jenna
mocking her and pointing out her failures. Jenna had
big plans for Leah to go to college, make a new life for
herself. If left up to her twin, she wouldn't be satisfied
until Leah was exactly like her.

"It's not fair," Leah grumbled unhappily. She was
the one who had been adopted. She was the one who
was supposed to have the advantages, not the other way
around.

While Jenna had grown up with two best friends,
Leah had been alone. There had been no one to turn to,

no one to talk to, and no one to understand what she'd gone through growing up in that cold, strict home. The Bennetts hadn't loved her. They'd wanted to control her, had ruled her every waking hour. When she hadn't been in school, she'd been in church. Every minute of the day had been supervised and monitored. It had been horrible.

She hadn't been allowed to talk on the phone. She hadn't been able to choose her own friends or pick out her own clothes. Every aspect of her life had had to meet with her adopted parents' approval. By the time Leah was sixteen, all she'd wanted was out. They'd offered to send her to college if she'd lived at home with them. Leah shuddered at the memory.

When she was eighteen, she took every dime she'd saved, packed her clothes, and bought a bus ticket out of town. She'd run as far and as fast as she'd been able, promising herself she'd never go back.

Only Leah hadn't ended up in the cushy life, like her twin. She'd gone to L.A., determined to have all the glitz and glamour of the Hollywood lifestyle she'd dreamed about as a kid. After years of trying to break into the business, Leah had nothing to show for it but a few commercials and sore feet from waiting tables to keep a roof over her head.

She'd met John in a club. He had talked her into dancing for a living, insisting she'd be seen by the movie producers and television moguls, but that hadn't panned out.

Las Vegas had turned out to be one disappointment after another. Leah had landed jobs, but not on the Strip or in one of the big hotel chorus lines, as she'd planned. Each new club had been further from the Strip and sleazier than the last.

The stripping had been another of John's moneymaking schemes. It might have been worth it if she could have snagged one of the high rollers that frequented the top casinos. Instead of attracting the rich, young, sports figures, rap stars, or even older corporate heads, she had fallen in love with a man who'd been out for what she'd been able to do for him.

Leah swore unhappily. She should have ditched him a long time ago. Sex and good looks did not pay the bills. Never again. She'd learned her lessons with John when he'd left with all her money.

"It's my turn to get what I want," she mumbled to herself as she refilled her glass.

Well at least she had given her a place to stay until she figured out her next move. The one thing Leah had learned from being around her sister and her uppity friends was that there were wealthy men in the Motor City ripe for the taking. She only needed one.

It was a damn shame she hadn't met Scott first. He'd picked the wrong twin. Jenna didn't appreciate the man. She was too caught up in her precious career. Poor Scott needed a woman who knew how to put him first.

"A woman like me," Leah said aloud.

Leah could see the mistake Jenna was making with her man. Leah loved her sister, and she'd tried to warn her, pointing out on more than one occasion that Jenna should be living with the man, but her twin wouldn't listen. Jenna was leaving Scott open for another woman to step right in. Leah shook her head. At the very least, Jenna should be making herself available to him. How long did she expect to hold onto a man with his qualities . . . money, good looking, with a hot, gorgeous body?

"She won't. Not for long," Leah surmised, helping herself to more wine.

Twenty-one

Scott silently fumed. He was still ticked off over the mix-up that had taken place when he'd arrived at Jenna's earlier that evening. He'd tried to let it go, but it still rankled. As far as he was concerned, the evening had gone downhill from that point on.

As he followed the Gaines twins into the living room, the clock on the mantel confirmed the late hour. But he didn't plan on leaving, not until he had some time alone with his love. Rather than taking a seat on the sofa, as was his custom, he rested a shoulder against the mantel in front of a log-filled grate.

He'd always considered himself to be an easygoing guy. Yet tonight he'd lost his temper and nearly said something he would no doubt regret later. Scott swore silently. He didn't appreciate the trick Leah had played on him, pretending to be Jenna. She'd answered the door in Jenna's purple silk top with jeans. She'd even done her hair and makeup like his lady.

He'd been so hungry for Jenna that he hadn't realized it wasn't her until he'd tightened his arms around her and he'd lowered his head for her kiss. Suddenly, his instincts had kicked in. Her hazel eyes had been hard with intent, not filled with the warmth and humor he'd been expecting. The breathy welcome in Jenna's voice when she said his name also hadn't been there. Thankfully he'd recognized Leah in the knick of time and hadn't done more than brush his lips against hers.

"Would you care for something to drink?" Leah asked playfully, her full lips sporting a provocative smile.

Concealing his annoyance at her attempt to take over Jenna's hostessing duties, Scott muttered a frosty, "No, thanks." His resentment had been building. He knew he had to gain control over it before Jenna caught on. He didn't dare voice his feelings.

Was nothing off-limits with Leah? Tonight was hardly the first time that Jenna's twin had managed to include herself in their evenings out. To be fair, the blame didn't entirely rest with Leah. Jenna was reluctant to leave her sister on her own, even for a few hours.

Frustrated, Scott craved time alone with his lady. They needed time for just the two of them to be together . . . to finalize their connection. If he was completely honest, he'd admit that he longed to give into selfish needs. He was tired of doing without, fed up with waiting. He wanted to taste every sweet inch of Jenna's curvy frame. It had been too blasted long since he'd been inside her . . . since she'd fit him like a second skin, silky soft, and damp with need. How he missed his sweet love.

The last time they'd slept together he'd done nothing beyond holding her close. He could kick himself for the missed opportunity. Aware that she'd been on an emotional roller-coaster ride the past few weeks, he hadn't wanted to make demands. It was important that he show her they didn't need to make love each and every time they were together. What they had was more than their sexual needs. He'd done everything within his power to make her feel happy, protected, and loved.

Now he felt like a selfish bastard for even entertaining thoughts of wanting more. Jenna deserved the peace and comfort he'd provided that night. He didn't exactly regret not making love to her. As long as he had her, he had enough.

As he walked purposefully toward Jenna, who had just switched on the floor lamp, he knew he had to find a way for them to spend quality time alone. Placing a possessive arm around her waist, he said, "Leah, will you excuse us, please? I'd like to speak to my lady . . . privately."

"Scott!" Jenna exclaimed.

He quirked a dark brow and tightened his hold on her waist.

"Sure. Good night." Leah flounced off.

"Finally," Scott whispered into Jenna's ear.

"That wasn't very nice and certainly not subtle," she scolded. Then she teased, "You're still angry about that trick Leah pulled on you earlier. Honey, admit it. She fooled you for a moment."

Ignoring the dig, he sat down with her beside him on the sofa, dropping an arm over her shoulders. "I'm sure Leah understands we wanted to be alone. It hasn't been that long since she had a man," he said gently.

He wasn't about to voice his belief that her twin had done more than play a joke on him but had indeed gone after him. He was no one's fool. He could handle the flirting and vying for attention. But if he was right about her intentions, it could possibly harm their relationship. It was a risk he was unwilling to take.

He could be wrong. Was Leah simply being thoughtless and wasn't out to do harm? Had he overreacted? Had it only been a childish prank that twins play on each other and unsuspecting family and friends? Perhaps the twins were making up for the innocent fun they'd missed out on growing up apart? Suddenly he wondered if he should give Leah a well-meaning warning. But then he'd run the risk of its getting back to Jenna. His beloved was touchy when it came to her family.

Frustration warred with need and made his kiss rough. Realizing he was bruising her lips, Scott immediately softened, soothing her luscious mouth with a gentle wash of his tongue. Jenna released an encouraging moan deep in her throat. She welcomed his bold thrusts and met each with her own sweetness as she suckled his tongue.

Desire quickly flamed into raging, hot need. With her wonderfully soft breasts pillowed on his chest, he easily lifted and pulled her around until she sat facing him, straddling his thighs, her sex flush against his aching shaft. Scott growled his enjoyment and deepened the kiss until they were both filled with hunger and breathless from lack of air. They sat grinning at each other as if they'd reached some lofty goal.

Chuckling, he said into her ear, "Should I apologize for forgetting and being carried away?" He placed a hot kiss against the sensitive place on her throat.

"Absolutely not." Jenna shivered, whispering, "I missed being like this with you."

He didn't say that all she had to do was go home with him. Rather than get into an argument, he pressed his mouth against hers. "It goes without saying how badly I want you." There was no way of concealing his rock-hard shaft. His entire body pulsed with desire. Resting his forehead against hers, he said, "Let's go away for the weekend. Just the two of us. I'd love to show you Charleston. Say you will come?"

"What about Leah?"

He held back the automatic retort. Instead, he said, "She's a big girl. She can look after herself for two nights. If you'd like, I'll provide limo service for her. She can ride in style while we're gone."

Jenna shook her head vehemently. "You don't have to do that."

"Believe me when I say it will be worth it, just to have you to myself for a little while."

"Honey, I'd love to go, but it's so close to Christmas and the end of the semester. You have as much to do as I have. I plan to make this Christmas the best ever, all about family and friends. If you think the food was good on Thanksgiving, wait until you see my table on Christmas Day." She rubbed her hands together, a big smile on her face. "Unfortunately, I haven't even come close to finishing shopping. Let's go after Christmas."

"Please." He kissed her to silence her protest. "We can still go skiing in Aspen after the holiday. But if we work together now, we can get it all done. I'll help in any way you need. Say yes, babe. We need this time alone now. Charleston is so romantic this time of year. I suppose I could be nice and give us a little time to do a little sightseeing. You're going to love seeing the Avery Research Center, the African-American museum is phenomenal. And the Gullah cuisine can't be missed. Say yes, sweet thing." He gave her a lingering kiss.

Giggling, she nodded. "I'd love to go. Thank you."

"Thank you." After a series of long, sweet kisses, he whispered, "I'd better get out of here before I lose what little control I have." Cupping her hips, he rose with her to his feet, letting her body slowly slide down his.

"You're welcome to stay the night," she urged softly.

He shook his head. "You wouldn't be comfortable letting me make love to you with Leah so close. It will have to wait until I have you all to myself. I won't be

satisfied until I've made you scream when you come."
He laughed as she blushed.

Jenna said in a whisper, "Hush! Leah might hear you."

"See what I mean." With his arm around her waist,
they walked to the door.

Turning, Jenna wrapped her arms around his waist,
saying softly, "I'm sorry. Leah's move here hasn't turned
out the way I expected."

"That's called life, babe. It doesn't ever go exactly as
planned."

"I know, but I thought I'd do a better job of handling
things."

"What things?"

"Managing our time together. I didn't realize it
would be this difficult. The blame rests with me. It's
just that I've waited so long to be reunited with her. I'm
so glad that she's here. I know I let her get away with
too much. I shouldn't have let her play that trick on you.
I'm sorry about that. But she honestly didn't mean any
harm." She sighed wearily. "I hate to disappoint her.
Sometimes I feel as if I'm being pulled in two directions.
Like tonight, I want to go home with you, but I also
feel guilty, as if I'd be neglecting my sister." Biting her
trembling bottom lip, she looked up into his eyes, confessing, "I don't want to hurt or lose either one of you."

"Shush." He placed a silencing finger against her
lips. "You aren't hurting or losing anyone, especially
not me. Sweet thing, we're about more than sex. We
will work it out. Our weekend away will go a long way
toward easing the situation."

"What about tonight?" She brushed against him,
rubbing his erection.

"I can wait. How about you?" he teased.

The sound of her laugh was sweet and welcome. "I
have no choice."

"Neither do I. Just because I have a hard-on doesn't mean I'm not particular. I want only you, Jenna Gaines." He leaned down, taking a quick, hard kiss. "Pack light. You're not going to need sleepwear. I plan to keep you warm. Night."

Scott waited until she set the dead bolt and key in the alarm before he made his way down the porch steps and to his car. Jenna had a point. Things hadn't gone as either of them had expected. He had assumed Leah would be like Jenna. He had had no idea that the resemblance would have more to do with their physical appearance than their personalities. He hadn't known Leah long, but from what he observed, she was nothing like his Jenna.

He smiled. "My Jenna . . . my love." He liked the sound of it so much that he repeated it to himself. He wouldn't stop until there was no doubt that they were a couple and in love.

He didn't mind sharing Jenna with her work, her friends, or even her family, but he did mind having to worry that her twin didn't have her welfare at heart. He also couldn't quietly sit back and let Leah take advantage of or possibly hurt his Jenna.

What if he was wrong? Leah hadn't exactly done anything to Jenna that he knew of. When she'd pretended to be Jenna she hadn't been underhanded about it. Jenna had known about the prank. But then Leah was used to being the center of male attention. Yeah, maybe he was looking for a problem when there really wasn't one.

Scott frowned. Life was unpredictable. His and Jenna's situation was a prime example. They should have been married by now. Their careers would have been on track and they would have been getting around to starting their family. Unfortunately, they hadn't stuck to the plan. He'd chosen the NBA, and she'd chosen her studies. They'd separated and spent so many empty years apart.

On the drive home, he marveled over how fortunate they had been to have found their way back to each other. He wouldn't be satisfied until they had it all back. He'd come to terms with his feelings for Jenna. Despite their separation and time apart, his feelings hadn't changed. He was still very much in love with Jenna, and he wanted her love. For weeks, he'd been working hard to convince her he wasn't the same man who had tossed their love away. He was going to prove to her he was worthy of her love and trust.

Lately, it seemed as if every single time he saw a softening in her, something would happen to throw them off course yet again. He worried that he was losing ground. Naturally self-reliant and on guard, Jenna hadn't been easy to win over. But he'd done it. They were almost back. They just had a few critical steps to make to move forward. And this time they would make it work. Even though she hadn't said the L word, he was encouraged that she was close. She wanted to be with him as much as he wanted to be with her.

Leah had really put a kink in his plans. Instead of concentrating on getting reacquainted with her twin, she was forever flirting with him. Because she made him uncomfortable, he'd done everything he could think of to avoid being alone with her, which meant he saw less of Jenna.

He was a straightforward kind of guy, but his frustration level was off the charts. It was a shame that he couldn't share his concerns with Jenna. In her eyes, Leah could do no wrong. Until he was certain he had Jenna's complete trust, he couldn't tell her what he most feared. Leah was jealous of her twin. Was she capable of hurting Jenna?

Feeling as if his hands were tied, he swore impatiently as he turned into his drive. If he was right, he would have to warn Jenna about her twin. It was the only way to protect his love. But not yet; there was still time for her to enjoy getting to know her sister. It could keep until after Christmas and the special things she was so excited about sharing with family and friends. In the meantime, he had plans of his own. He would turn their getaway into a wildly romantic weekend that neither one of them would soon forget.

Things didn't go as planned. Jenna's work forced them to postpone their trip to Charleston. She hated disappointing Scott, even though he insisted that he understood.

He surprised her on Saturday. He called early and asked her to spend the day with him, warning her not to eat.

Scott took her to one of their old favorite places, the Pancake House, where they shared a huge breakfast, starting with a stack of pecan pancakes, fluffy scrambled eggs, crispy bacon and sausage, and freshly squeezed orange juice with plenty of coffee.

By the time she put down her fork, Jenna was holding her stomach. "I can't believe I ate all that."

"Believe it!" Scott teased, holding his own stomach.

Jenna laughed when they arrived at the Detroit Zoo. Despite the cold, the sun was bright overhead as they enjoyed the animals' antics and recalled the lazy afternoons they'd spent walking hand and hand through the park.

From there they stopped to tour another of their favorite old haunts, the Charles H. Wright Museum of African American History. It was Jenna's first visit since she'd been back in the city. She was glad to see that her favorite exhibits were on display, along with many new acquisitions. The Middle Passage displays were heart-wrenching.

"I love coming to this place. It's like visiting a dear friend." Jenna smiled, lacing her fingers with his. "Thank you for bringing me back."

"I love it here, too. It was something we could do without spending much money. Back then that was important," Scott chuckled.

"You liked to visit the Science Museum, too."

"I practically lived in that place growing up." He smiled, tucking a wavy lock behind her ear. "Life was good back then. We didn't have much as far as material things, but it didn't really matter. We were happy just being together. We didn't need anything more."

"We were so young and in love," she said around a sigh. "Full of hopes and dreams. We thought we had all the answers."

"Some things have changed, but not everything." He steered her away from a group of high school students until they were between displays. He bent until his forehead rested on hers. "Do you ever wish we could go back?"

"To being nineteen and twenty?"

"To being deeply in love. Before the hurt and separation?" he asked, his dark brown eyes searching her hazel eyes.

Jenna shook her head, smiling up at him. "Why are you being so serious all of a sudden? We were having so much fun."

"A lot of things have been left unsaid."

"Maybe it's best that way. Rehashing the past will only bring back things I'd rather forget about. It certainly can't change what happened." Jenna grabbed his hand, giving it a bit of a tug. "Let's keep going. There is still so much to see."

She was relieved when he let her lead the way. She sent him a playful grin over her shoulder. Jenna was having fun. She didn't want to remember the pain-filled part of the past and all that had been lost.

She was surprised by the change in him. He was way too serious, considering they had made a point of focusing on the here and now. Today was about leaving their problems behind and enjoying themselves. She didn't want to rehash past mistakes.

It was late afternoon, and the shortened winter sun began to set as they walked to the parking lot.

"How long do you need to get ready for dinner?" he asked, starting the car. "Should I drop you off now and come back around—"

She shook her head. Laughing, she held up her full tote bag. "I don't need to go home. I've got everything I need with me. You don't mind if I use your guest room to shower and dress?"

He grinned. "You're welcome to use anything of mine you'd like."

Jenna said playfully, "Thank you, sweet man."

His eyes locked with hers for a few moments. "My pleasure, sweet Jenna." That said, he set the car into motion.

Neither spoke on the drive to his place, but there wasn't much that needed to be said. They both were looking forward to the time that stretched ahead of them . . . time for just the two of them.

Twenty-two

Jenna grinned for all she was worth. "The evening has been nothing short of spectacular!" Her arms were wrapped around Scott's lean waist as they moved in time to the music on the crowded dance floor.

He had surprised her by taking her back to Bradley's. This time it was vastly different from the supper club's grand opening. They'd been shown to a candlelit table tucked into the corner. The glass walls overlooked the river and provided a lovely view of the star-filled winter night. A grand piano being played in the background added to the romantic ambience.

They shared bites of his lobster tail dripping in clarified butter and her ginger-glazed, grilled salmon while enjoying the creamy, buttermilk mashed potatoes and grilled mixed vegetables. They sipped rich, fruity Pinot Grigio. They lingered over the exquisite meal, then finished with plum tart, topped with homemade French vanilla ice cream. After he paid the tab, they walked hand and hand up to the nightclub.

Scott's voice was deep and raspy when he said, "A night to remember."

Refusing to worry about anything, including the calories she'd consumed that day, Jenna closed her eyes, indulging her other senses. Moving with him on the dance floor, she inhaled his clean, male scent as she caressed his silk-covered back beneath his gray jacket.

Pressing her lips against the base of his throat left bare by his open collar, she urged, "I'm ready to go. How about you?"

He issued a husky groan from deep inside his chest while momentarily tightening his hold around her. They exchanged a heated look. He whispered, "Yeah." With her hand clasped in his, he paused to drop a large bill on the table before guiding her out.

After retrieving their outerwear and hurrying through the cold to the car, instead of heading north, toward the suburbs, he stayed in town.

She quizzed, "I thought we were going back to your place?"

"We are, after a short detour." He reached over and gave her hand a quick squeeze.

The detour turned out to be a stop at Belle Isle, the city park that was an island oasis in the midst of the big city life, especially in the warmer months. The island housed a conservatory and botanical gardens, Great Lakes Museum, nature center, beach and picnic areas, yacht club, tennis and basketball courts, and baseball fields.

Jenna smiled as they passed stately, older three-story homes, many of which had been converted into nursing homes, office facilities, and even day-care centers. She knew where they were going as they drove across the MacArthur Bridge that connected the island park to the city.

She didn't have to ask why he had brought her here. During the warmer months, the two of them used to bike the park's numerous walkways and share romantic picnics and moonlit walks. Even during the fall, they'd enjoyed strolling hand and hand to the water's edge and gazing up at the stars and Detroit's fabulous skyline. It was a special place where they'd talked and dreamed of a shared future.

"Still beautiful," she mused, slipping her hand into his after he'd parked. "You've gone all out to make this day special."

Scott grinned. "I tried. We spent many nights gazing at the boats and sharing secrets and plans for the future. This is where you first told me about your family and your hope to find them. Remember?"

"Yes," she said, shivering from his caressing hand on her nape. "We were so poor, we had to put our pennies together just to have enough gas to get that old clunker of yours out here."

"Clunker? That was a classic 1970 Chevy Camaro in mint condition."

"It was held together with a ton of duct tape and prayers. The thing belched smoke and backfired, protesting every mile you forced out of it," she teased.

He was quick to say, "But it got us where we needed to go. We even went to Florida to visit my family. Talk about young and poor. We got lucky on that trip when we didn't break down on the road." He laughed.

"Yes, blessed," she corrected.

"And so much love," he said huskily, close to her ear. "Has it all gone, babe?"

"What?"

"The love, Jenna."

She shook her head. "I thought we agreed that rehashing our past mistakes would serve no purpose."

"Our mistakes? I was the one who left, not you."

"Scott, let's drop it," she said, edging away.

He caught her hands in his. "We need to talk about it. I take full responsibility for my mistake. I was a nineteen-year-old kid who ran toward a dream, not away from you. I was in love with you then, just as I'm in love with you now."

When Jenna released a startled gasp, he squeezed her hand. "That's right. I've never, not for one minute, stopped loving you. Of course I didn't realize it until I saw you again."

"Why are you telling me this?" she demanded. He was spoiling their magical day.

"Because it's important to me that you know the truth. I tried, believe me, I tried to get you out of my system. Nothing worked. And when I saw you in the cafe, all I knew was that I had to get you back. In the past weeks, I've done everything I could think of to show you how I feel, Jenna. My sweet love."

Jenna sat very still as she tried to absorb what he'd revealed. No, it couldn't be true. But what if it was true? What if he did love her? Jenna was floored by the emotions that came rushing over her as she considered the possibility. Bombarded by so many emotions, she didn't know what she was feeling.

He said, "You were busy fighting me every step of the way."

"I couldn't help it. I was afraid—"

"Shush." He silenced her by pressing a finger against her luscious lips. "I'm not trying to force a confession out of you, or even a commitment."

"Then why?"

"Because I need to level with you. Let you know what's going on inside of me. You know I wanted you back. I've made no secret of that. It's time you know that when I said my feelings haven't changed, I meant it. I want what I've always wanted. I want you to be my wife and the mother of my children."

Jenna strained to see his expression in the dim interior of the car. She felt like she'd been on an emotional roller coaster for the last few months. So much had happened that she couldn't even begin to sort out her feelings. She couldn't believe he was telling her all this. That he was forcing her to evaluate her own heart. It was too soon! She was just getting used to the idea of the two of them being back together. That had been enough for her.

Now he was rushing forward, talking about being in love, marriage, and children. Had he just proposed?

"I know this may seem sudden, but I've been thinking about it for some time. In fact"—he paused, then reached into his overcoat and pulled out a velvet-covered ring box—"I bought this for you." He opened the lighted glove compartment so she could see, then used his thumbnail to lift the lid.

Jenna's eyes went wide when she saw the large solitaire. The five-carat, cushion-cut, deep purple amethyst stone was surrounded by diamonds and set in a thin gold band.

Her heart thundered in her chest as she stared at the most beautiful ring she'd ever seen. It was exquisite . . . perfect for her. And it came with enough baggage to keep her caught in emotional knots well into the next century.

Scott tilted her face up toward his. His kiss was brimming with tenderness and sweet promise. Before she could formulate a single thought, he kissed her again, only this time it was hard, possessive.

When he pulled back, he whispered, "I don't expect an answer tonight. There won't be any pressure from me. All I ask is that you think it over, remember what we once wanted and meant to each other, as well as what we could still have if we're willing to work at it . . . willing to take the risk."

He held a fine gold chain. While she watched, he opened the clasp and threaded the ring onto it. Holding it up to her, he hesitated, then said, "I'd like you to wear it close to your heart until you decide. May I?"

For a long moment, she couldn't respond. She was

stunned, immobilized by a combination of disbelief and a healthy dose of fear that if she said no, she would lose him. She was just getting used to having him back, just starting to feel as if she could lean on him. This went far beyond being together. He wanted it all . . . love and trust . . . enough to last a lifetime.

"Jenna?"

She nervously worried the fleshy inside of her bottom lip. She needed time to think . . . to decide. The most she could manage right then was to nod her consent to wearing the ring around her neck. She silently assured herself that he had promised not to pressure her, give her time to decide.

Her hands shook as she unbuttoned her reliable black wool coat. She cupped the ring in her palm as his large fingers worked to secure the clasp. She shivered when the cold metal settled between her breasts, and then again when he moved her hair to press a lingering kiss against her throat.

"Thank you," he murmured. Once they were both buckled in, he turned on the defroster, then put the car into gear. But he kept his foot on the brake when he asked, "Your place or mine?"

"Yours," she said without hesitation, "but only for a few hours. I can't spend the night. I have loads of work waiting for me."

"You don't have to explain. I understand."

He hadn't said a word, but Jenna sensed his disappointment. She was doing her very best, trying to please both Scott and her sister. She'd called Leah several times to check in with her. She'd broken down and let Leah use her car, to make up for her daylong absence.

But it wasn't her demanding workload or feelings of guilt over neglecting her twin that was worrying her. She was doing her utmost to ignore the significance of the engagement ring on her neck. She marveled over all he'd done to make this day special. She couldn't help wondering how long he'd been planning the day. She tried not to dwell on his reason for proposing or the enormity of what it would mean to both of their lives if she was foolish enough to say yes.

Oblivious to the late-night traffic, Jenna's stomach was in a knot, and her eyes burned from a sudden urge to cry. He'd said he still loved her. That he'd never stopped. She stared at the passing scenery while wondering how long she had. How long would he wait for an answer? A week? A month? A year?

He'd barely turned off the car when Jenna, unable to express her emotions, gave in to the need to touch him. She caressed his cheek and strong chin. With her thumb, she outlined his full lips. Her breath caught when he playfully bit the tip of her thumb.

"You have such a sexy smile. Combined with those dark, sultry eyes, I melt inside when you look at me like you are looking at me now . . . hot with desire." She confessed, "The first moment I looked into your eyes, I was fascinated by you. I didn't understand it back then, but now I know I wanted you, just as I want you now. Take me inside, Scott, and make love to me."

He didn't respond verbally, but a muscle jumped in his jaw and his eyes smoldered with passion. Suddenly, Scott moved. He wasted no time in getting them inside the house with the doors locked.

His hot, hungry kisses stole her breath. Soon they were both shaking with urgency. He carried her into his bedroom. Unaware of the low lamp that glowed on the nightstand beside the bed, she focused on him and what he made her feel.

They quickly undressed each other. They didn't stop until there were no barriers between them. He caressed her from nape to hips, lingering on her full bottom. His touch released a mountain of need inside her. She launched a sensual attack by wrapping her arms around him and caressing his sleek, long spine. She stroked him as if he'd been a giant cat while pressing damp kisses over his wide chest and dark throat.

When she changed direction downward to place kisses on his taut midsection, he growled his enjoyment. But when she smoothed over the jetting curve of his shaft, he stopped her. He clasped her hands, holding them still, while he took Jenna's mouth in a hard salute.

He whispered, "Your touch feels so good. I won't be able to hold back if I let you pleasure me that way."

"The pleasure would be all mine," she confessed, then shivered when he distracted her with another tongue-suckling kiss.

Trembling with urgency and as if he was desperate to claim what was his alone, Scott dropped down on the bed, bringing her with him.

"Finally, I have you all to myself," he husked, lowering his head to tongue the sensitive spot on her neck. He sighed when she trembled, but he didn't ease up until Jenna moaned, her soft body trembling. He laved the hollow of her throat while cupping and squeezing her lush breasts.

When her moans turned into breathless gasps, he said, "That's right, my sweet love . . . enjoy, because I plan to give you all the pleasure you can handle and then some."

Scott took a pebble-hard, dark peak into his mouth. He sponged her nipple and groaned as he suckled and savored her.

"Your skin is like silk," he said, as if she was a drop of milk chocolate. He journeyed down to caress, then squeezed her plump mound. Knowing what she craved without words, Scott applied more suction, while parting her feminine folds. "You are so creamy, wet with desire," he whispered.

She needed him as urgently as he seemed to need

her. Instead of rushing, he slowly rimmed her opening. When she whimpered impatiently, he slid a finger inside her aching sheath, then another. When she released a keening wail, he switched breasts and continued his assault on her senses. By the time he moved a caressing thumb over her clitoris, Jenna's lush frame shook from her release.

"What are you trying to do to me?" she gasped, struggling for breath.

He chuckled. "Drive you out of your mind with pleasure and show you how much you mean to me."

Before Jenna could digest that information, she was once again spiraling out of control. Her second release was swift and extraordinarily sweet. Feeling as if she was floating on air, she was sated physically but empty deep inside. When he began lowering his head, she pressed her hands against his broad shoulders, as if she could hold him in place.

"No more. I mean it, Scott." She stared into his hot, molten gaze. "Find a condom, and make it quick, because I'm done with your sweet torture. I need you inside me . . . hurry."

His lips tilted upward in humor, but he didn't laugh or waste time arguing. He opened the drawer in the nightstand and pulled out a box of condoms. She noticed that his hands shook a bit as he ripped the foil, then covered his erection. She took pleasure in knowing that she had managed to ruffle his ironclad control. She'd been frustrated because he wouldn't let her pleasure him to distraction as he so enjoyed pleasuring her. It was a tiny victory, but a victory nonetheless.

She released a poignant sigh. Finally, he was there, filling her emptiness. Moaning his name, Jenna lifted her hips to meet his thrusts and wrapped her legs around his waist. She marveled at the sheer pleasure of their intimate connection and smiled as she listened to his appreciative groan. Scott eased back only to return again and again. Quickly caught up in a maze of sensations, Jenna welcomed his thrusts as he established a consuming rhythm that quickly had them both drenched in perspiration and panting for breath. Scott quickened the pace, moving them steadfastly closer to completion.

Eyes closed and heart pounding with excitement, she lost all sense of her surroundings. The mesmerizing strokes of his fingertips against her clitoris had her shaking with the sweetest pleasure. Jenna said his name, telling him that she loved him as she climaxed. Mere seconds later, Scott reached his own earth-shattering climax as his big body shook with the power of his keen release.

Shocked by her declaration, she bit her bottom lip to keep from breaking down and sobbing her frustration. All those weeks, she'd been denying what had been in her heart. She'd lost control and in that weak moment had revealed her unwavering love for him. The instant she'd said those three powerful words out loud, she'd known they were true.

She loved Scott Hendricks. Had she ever stopped loving him? She closed her eyes. It didn't matter. There was no longer any question that he was firmly rooted deep in her heart.

How could she have been so careless? So foolish? Evidently when he'd revealed his feelings for her, all her carefully guarded defenses had started to crumble. Before she'd realized the depths of her feelings, the floodgates had opened and she was pouring out a tidal wave of feelings for him.

As she rested against him, struggling for a measure of control, Jenna's heart ached. It wasn't fair!

She'd already made that mistake. Once should have been enough. Scott had shattered her world when he'd walked away. Yet here she was, handing over her heart, the very weapon that would destroy her.

She was nobody's fool, yet she had gone all weak inside because he'd said he loved her. Scott Hendricks wasn't offering any lifelong guarantees that he would stay this time around.

Suddenly, she was conscious of the weight of his ring pressing into the valley between her breasts. Jenna didn't need a reminder of the shattered dreams she'd foolishly weaved about them . . . the sweetest one being a family of her very own. She'd wanted his babies so badly.

He had crushed that dream like pieces of broken glass beneath the weight of his athletic shoes when he'd walked out of her life to enter the NBA. Basketball had always come first with him. He had claimed to love her back then, just as he said he loved her now.

"Wow!" He held her close, kissing her tenderly. "I still can't believe you love me."

Jenna's eyes burned from unshed tears. She said candidly, "I can't believe it either. I didn't know how I felt until the words came rushing out."

He surmised, "You don't sound happy about it."

"How can I be? You know the things that went wrong between us. We hurt each other badly. And I'd be a fool if I didn't have plenty of misgivings. I'm scared, Scott. How do I know you won't hurt me again?"

"I could be asking you the same question, but I'm not." He smoothed a hand up and down her arm. "We can't see into the future. We have no choice but to step out on faith. Take it one day at a time." Brushing his lips against hers, he said, "I don't intend to hurt you any more than I believe you intend to hurt me. Fear doesn't change what we feel for each other."

Jenna frowned, infuriated with her loss of control. Why couldn't she have kept her mouth closed? A glance at the bedside clock had her saying, "I'm sorry, but I can't stay."

He asked, "What harm can come from spending what's left of the night with me? I'll get you home as early as you'd like. Five? Six? I'm not ready for our special day to end."

She smiled. "It was very special."

He pressed a lingering kiss on her lips. "I'll set the clock for six. Okay?"

Weakening, she nodded. "Thanks."

"Thank you. I could use a shower. Interested in sharing?"

"I'd rather soak in the tub, but I'd probably fall asleep and drown."

"No worries. I'll keep you safe."

He soon had them relaxing in his large tub, the whirlpool jets soothing tired muscles. Jenna was nearly asleep when he dried them both off and carried her back into the bedroom. Once they were settled in the middle of his big bed, he curved an arm around her, easing her back against his front.

"Comfortable?" He kissed her nape.

"Mm . . ." she moaned, curling her fingers over his wrist, where it rested against her stomach.

The sweetness of their time alone drifted through her mind. There was nothing so urgent that it had to be resolved that night. As sleep claimed Jenna, her last thought caused a smile. Despite all that had gone wrong between them, he had said he still loved her.

Twenty-three

Jenna was busy dealing with finals and working to make her first semester as a full professor successful. She tried not to worry that Leah wasn't job hunting or even looking through the college catalogue she had brought home. She struggled to hide her increasing frustration at not knowing her sister's plans. Leah hadn't said if she was going to stay in Detroit or return to dancing in Las Vegas. She had skillfully managed to avoid Jenna's inquiries while spending her time catching up on her sleep after more nights out on the town with the new friends she'd met in the clubs.

No matter how often Jenna told herself she had no reason to be concerned, she disliked the way her twin vied for Scott's attention. Jenna did her best to ignore it, aware of her sister's need to be the center of male attention. The knowledge that her sister loved her and would never do anything to hurt her was what made her dismiss the worry. She flatly refused to give in to that fear, or let it rule her world.

On Friday evening Scott and Jenna drove to Laura's condo for a tree-trimming party. Jenna had been disappointed when Leah had refused to come, preferring to go clubbing with her new friends.

"What exactly does one do at a tree-trimming party?" Scott asked, opening the heavy glass door of the Riverfront Condominiums for Jenna.

"You mean besides eat, drink, and make merry?" she teased. "Oh, look! There's Sherri Ann." She called out, "Hey, girl."

"Hey, yourself," Sherri Ann smiled. She and her date were waiting in the lobby for the elevators.

The foster sisters hugged before Sherri Ann introduced them to Ben Edwards, her escort for the evening. By the time the couples reached Laura's front door, Jenna had surmised that Sherri Ann had no true interest in getting to know the handsome lawyer at her side.

Sherri Ann had made no secret that her career came first with her. She fully intended to make partner in a prestigious law firm before she reached her thirty-fifth birthday. Marriage and a family were going to have to wait until she reached her career goals.

"Well, it's about time!" Laura announced with a hand on her hip. She pointed to a large, bare evergreen tree in front of the picture window. Judging by the laughter and music playing in the background, the party was well under way.

The three hugged. Jenna and Sherri Ann handed over their gift-wrapped ornaments.

"Now we can get this party started," Trenna McAdams laughed. The nursery school owner was a mutual friend and a member of Laura's book club. She also had come with a date.

Newlywed Vanessa Grant Prescott, one of the founding members of Laura's book club, was with her husband, Ralph. Scott and Ralph were old friends and former college teammates. The two men greeted each other with warm grins and fist bumps.

The newcomers were greeted warmly by Maureen

Hale Sheppard. She owned and headed the Sheppard
Women's Crisis Center, where Laura worked. An avid
reader and book club member, Maureen never gave up
trying to convince Jenna and Sherri Ann to join their
group. And, like the others, she'd come with a date.

Laura had invited Craig Owens. The two were
friends and had met through work. Craig, a police detective, had investigated some of the rape cases that
Laura had been assigned. Craig was nothing like the
highly successful men Laura dated.

Jenna found it interesting that Laura only dated men
that met her financial requirements and also managed
not to become emotionally involved with any of them.
When challenged, she would laugh and insist she just
hadn't met the right millionaire.

Both foster sisters liked Craig and believed he'd
be great for Laura. Despite the intensity of his work,
Craig was easygoing, refusing to take himself or life too
seriously.

An elaborate spread had been set up in the dining
room, which was where Sherri Ann and Laura teamed
up on Jenna. Having just popped a shrimp canapé into
her mouth, Jenna blinked in surprise when Sherri Ann
took her plate and Laura grabbed her elbow. They ignored her protests that she was hungry and pulled her
into Laura's lovely bedroom.

With the door closed, Jenna looked from one to the
other. Annoyed, she complained, "I'm hungry, why'd
you take my plate?"

"Forget about food. We have important things to
discuss," Sherri Ann said.

Jenna asked, "Like what?"

"Like you keeping secrets! Leah let slip you've been
wearing an expensive ring on that gold chain. Well?"
Laura demanded.

"Are you engaged and forgot to tell us?" Sherri Ann asked, all business. Judging by the set of her mouth and her crossed arms, she was not backing down. She expected an answer.

Throwing her hands up in a show of helplessness, Jenna confessed, "I didn't tell you because I didn't think I had much to tell." Hoping to buy time, she sat down on the padded bench at the foot of the bed and crossed her legs.

"Did Scott propose?" Laura wanted to know.

"Why keep it a secret?" Sherri Ann quizzed.

Laura insisted, "Sherri Ann, will you hush and let her answer the question."

"Which one?" Jenna said impatiently. "I told you about the day Scott and I revisited many of the places we enjoyed while we were students." She smiled, recalling.

"The ring?" Laura prompted.

Jenna ignored the interruption. "It was such a wonderful day. We were parked on the island when he told me he'd never stopped loving me. Then he asked me to marry him. I wasn't expecting it. I didn't know what to say or even how I felt about it or him. He assured me that he didn't expect an answer. He promised not to pressure me but wait for my answer. He asked me to wear the ring on a chain, close to my heart, until I decide."

"I want to see!" Sherri Ann insisted.

Jenna pulled the ring hidden under her purple turtleneck sweater.

Her foster sisters gasped and began talking excitedly.

Laura gushed, "Wow!"

"Simply stunning," Sherri Ann marveled. "Well? What have you decided? Should we be congratulating you?"

"See, that's exactly why I didn't tell you two. I knew

you'd demand answers." Jenna frowned, holding the ring tightly in a fist. "I wish I knew."

Laura said, "We all know that you're still in love with the man. That's been apparent for weeks. Why else would you have crawled back into bed with him?"

"She's right," Sherri Ann said.

"It would have helped if one of you told me," Jenna snapped. "I didn't realize how deep my feelings went until I blurted it on Saturday night while we were making love. I felt like such a fool."

When Laura and Sherri Ann started laughing, Jenna hissed, "It's not funny." But soon she joined in. Once they'd sobered, she confessed, "I don't have a clue what I'm going to tell him when the time comes. Despite his promise, he expects me to say yes. I do love him, with all my heart. I just don't know if I can trust him not to hurt me again. I'm scared." She shook her head wearily. "I keep thinking that I'll say or do the wrong thing and he'll be gone again. He walked before."

Laura moved to sit on her right and Sherri Ann on her left, surrounding her with their loving support.

Sherri Ann said, "You're not going to lose him. He's back and willing to give you the time you need to make the decision."

Laura insisted, "We're forgetting what's important here. You two are in love. That's what matters. The problems can be worked out."

"She's right." Sherri Ann put her arm around Jenna's shoulders and gave Jenna a quick squeeze with a brilliant smile. "This is good news. Congratulations, sister girl."

Laura kissed Jenna's cheek. "Congratulations! Much love and happiness! And we'd better get out of here before my guests come looking for us and asking pointed questions. Scott's no doubt waiting for his lovely, soon-to-be fiancée."

* * *

Scott approached Jenna the instant she returned to the living room. Resting an arm on her shoulders, he whispered close to her ear, "Everything okay?"

"Perfect. Did you eat? I'm starving."

He smiled. "We'd better take care of that."

Even though Jenna enjoyed the party, she was relieved when Scott suggested they leave early, after they lit the Christmas tree.

She giggled when she saw him cover a yawn. "I'm glad I'm not the only one worn out by the hectic week. There's been too much to get done."

Unfortunately, her work wasn't the reason she'd gotten little sleep. Night after night, she'd lain awake holding his ring and wondering if they could have a future.

He grinned sheepishly. "It has been a struggle to get everything finished and turned in on time."

Laura only offered a token protest when they said their good-byes. During the drive back to her home, Jenna knew she didn't want the evening to end. She smiled as she watched him walk around the car to open the passenger door. She took his hand, enjoying, rather than needing, his help. They walked hand and hand to her lit porch. Once inside, she called out her sister's name. There was no response.

"It looks as if we have the place to ourselves," she smiled. After hanging their coats in the hall closet, she tugged him along with her into the living room. "You aren't in a rush to leave, are you?"

"I'm beat." Scott stretched out his long legs, settling back against the sofa cushions. Covering another yawn, he said, "Sorry, but I can't stay long. I don't want to risk falling asleep on your couch." He chuckled. "You wouldn't be able to move me without a forklift."

Jenna snuggled up to him. "Don't go," she said, covering her yawn. "Excuse me. I want you to stay the night."

"That's not a good idea," he said wearily.

"It's a wonderful idea," she said, closing lids too heavy to remain open. She had no idea how much time passed, but she stirred when she felt herself being lifted. "Scott? Where are you taking me?"

"To bed. It's late and there's no point in us both losing sleep."

Looping an arm around his neck, she didn't offer a single protest. When he put her down on the side of her bed, she couldn't rouse herself enough to comment as he systematically helped her undress.

"Where do you keep your T-shirts?"

She nodded, pointing to the dresser's top drawer. He returned with an oversized I love New York nightshirt. Stretching the neckband, he dropped it over her head and guided her hands into the soft cotton sleeves. He pulled back the flannel sheets and tucked her beneath the quilt. Jenna didn't rest against the pillows.

"You're staying, aren't you?" She pressed a kiss against his throat. "Please . . ."

"You sure?" he quizzed.

She patted the place beside her. "Yes, hurry." There was no doubt about it. "I want to sleep in your arms."

There was no holding back his smile. Scott stripped down and joined her, drawing her close to his side. A little later, relishing the sound of his deep, even breathing, Jenna heard her sister's footsteps in the hallway and her bedroom door close. Content, she sighed deeply. For the first time since he'd proposed, Jenna was able to sleep soundly.

Refreshed from a good night of rest, Jenna woke early. Scott was sleeping so peacefully that she didn't have the heart to disturb him. Hungry, she recalled the wonderful pecan cinnamon rolls they used to pig out on on lazy Saturday mornings back in the day.

On a whim, she decided to surprise him with the treat. The bakery was near their old upstairs flat close to campus. She quickly showered and dressed in a pair of comfortable black cords and a bright violet sweater. Dashing on a touch of makeup and taming her hair with her favorite hair butter, she ran a wide-tooth comb through her wavy curls. Jenna paused. She was momentarily captivated by the brilliant amethyst-and-diamond ring that hung from the fine gold chain. It was so beautiful.

She wanted it to mean that he would always love and cherish her. That he would always be there for her. She wanted that future with Scott. She desperately wanted to believe she could put her well-being in his care for safekeeping and know that he would never walk away from their love. He'd had his choice of the most beautiful women in the world, yet he'd asked her to be his wife. It was something that she couldn't dismiss.

Impulsively, she decided not to tuck the ring inside her top but leave it where she could see it, a lovely reminder of what they meant to each other. After collecting a pair of ankle boots, her purse, and keys, Jenna tiptoed out and closed the door softly.

As she put on her boots, she glanced at her sister's door. She started forward to tell her where she was going, then stopped. Leah was a late sleeper. There was no need to wake her.

On her way into the foyer, Jenna decided to make a stop at the market and pick up shrimp and crabmeat for a delicious seafood frittata to go with the rolls. Bundled in her down-filled parka, she jotted a note and left it propped on the table in the foyer. She smiled, imagining Scott's and Leah's faces when they woke to delicious smells filling the house.

She hummed as she waited for the car to warm. She

would have to stop at the gas station, since Leah had forgotten to fill the tank. It was a clear, cloudless day. In less than a week, Lincoln and his family would arrive for the holidays. Soon her dream of her family being united would finally come true. Jenna backed out of her drive knowing she had a great deal to be thankful for and even more to look forward to.

Sleeping soundly, Scott didn't immediately respond to the caressing hand on his chest, but the seductive lure of her nails teasing his flat nipple slowly roused him. Despite his mind being clouded with sleep, his body began to harden with desire.

"Jenna . . . my sweet love." He groaned groggily at the provocative feel of her breasts against him and the warmth of her lips at the base of his throat.

He'd wanted to make love to her last night, but he'd been too tired to do anything about it. With his eyes closed, he wrapped an arm around her and dropped his head to kiss from her temple down her cheeks to her throat. As his mouth opened to cover hers, he inhaled.

Suddenly, Scott realized that her scent wasn't quite right and her mouth tasted like stale wine. Confused, but before his sleepy brain could sort it out, he heard a loud scream and the crash of china hitting the hardwood floor.

Jenna, pleased with her culinary effort, used only one hand to balance the heavy tray braced against a hip as she opened her bedroom door. Her eyes widened as she realized that Scott was in her bed but he wasn't alone. Leah was wrapped around him and they were kissing. Shocked, Jenna wasn't conscious of making a sound or letting go of the tray.

Her hands went up to cover her face while she stared

in horrified disbelief. No! It couldn't be true! Her sister couldn't be in bed with her man!

For an endless moment, no one said or did anything. Scott was the first to react. He swore heatedly as he roughly pushed Leah away from him, giving her a hard glare before turning his attention to Jenna.

"Jenna, sweetheart! I don't know what's going on here, but it's not what you think. You have to believe me!" he insisted. "I was asleep! I thought it was you in my arms," he said, urgently swinging his feet down to the floor. The bed linens covered his nudity.

Leah rushed to say, "I came in here, looking to borrow a dress. He asked me—"

"Shut up! Both of you, just shut up!" Jenna yelled. Her hands were balled into taut fists on her hips. "I don't want to hear a thing from either one of you." She sent her twin a furious glare. "You have no business being in my room! Whether he invited you in here or not. None! Get out! " Jenna raged, taking a threatening step forward.

"It was a mistake!"

"Get your things! I want you out of my house! Now!"

Leah sent her twin an angry glare before she stamped out on bare feet, wearing nothing but a short gown. She slammed the door so hard that it rattled.

When Scott opened his mouth to speak, Jenna shouted as she pointed her finger at him. "No, damn it! I'm not interested in anything you have to say. I want you out now!"

On his feet, Scott began shoving his legs into his jeans. "You can't mean it. You have to let me explain."

"I don't have to do a blasted thing!" Shaking from the force of her emotions, she yelled, "I want you gone. Out of my house . . . out of my life for good! I should never have taken you back. It was a terrible mistake to give you another chance to hurt me."

"Jenna . . ."

"I said no!" Gesturing wildly, Jenna touched the engagement ring he'd placed on the fine chain around her neck. She grabbed it, yanking until the chain broke, then flung it at him. She hissed, "Get out and take this with you. I don't want to see it or you ever again!"

She turned her back to him, waiting for the sound of his retreating footsteps. It wasn't until he slammed her front door that she could breathe easily. Jenna couldn't bear to look at the bed or the mess on the floor.

She was hurting. How she hurt. Yet she didn't dare give in to the agony raging inside her. Instead she went into her office and sank into the chair behind the desk, to wait for her sister. She fought back tears, determined not to give in to the incredible anguish ravishing her heart. She had to wait until she was alone to give in to the crushing weight of their betrayal and her keen disappointment. First things first: she still had to get Leah out of her house.

When her twin appeared on the threshold of the room, Leah hesitated. Jenna motioned for her to come into the room, noting that though Leah's chin was up, she avoided eye contact.

"Jenna, I know it looked bad, but you have to let me ex . . ." Leah stopped when Jenna raised her palm for silence.

"I've told you, I'm not interested in anything you have to say. It's over. And I want you gone from my sight. Although I'd like you gone for good, I can't do that, especially not with Lincoln and his family arriving next week."

Unlocking her desk drawer, Jenna quickly wrote out a check. After tearing it off, she placed it on top of the desk. "That should be enough for you to stay in a motel. When Lincoln comes, you can stay here only as

long as he and his family are here. The minute he leaves,
I expect you to do the same. We may be twins, but as
far as I'm concerned, we're no longer sisters."

"You brought me here and now you're just going to
leave me—"

"Not another word! You crawled in bed with my
man! That means I don't have to listen to any excuse
you can come up with. There is no justification for what
I walked in on. Don't you get it? I no longer care about
anything you have to say or what you do. Hand over
my house key."

Jenna didn't so much as glance Leah's way as she
tossed down the key, snatched up the check, and hurried out of the room. Jenna lifted her legs until she could
wrap her arms around them. She leaned forward, resting her chin on upraised knees. Unshed tears burned
her eyes, but she held them back.

She waited until she heard the sound of a taxi's horn
blaring outside, then Leah slamming the front door behind her. Finally, Jenna was able to let go of the tight
hold she'd kept on her emotions. Anguish-filled sobs
tore at her. She was bombarded with despair, grief, and
an excruciating sense of disappointment.

It was hours later before she was able to call her foster sisters, confessing that she needed them.

Despite the mess she had left on her bedroom floor,
Jenna couldn't deal with it. She simply didn't care.
She remained curled in a pain-filled ball. She couldn't
make her way past the despair and the heaviness in
her heart.

She thought she'd gotten rid of the worst of it, but
when she tried to explain what happened, she realized
she'd been wrong. Huddled on the sofa between Sherri
Ann and Laura, Jenna felt her tears return full force. It

wasn't until she finished speaking that the tears slowed to a trickle.

"It's going to be alright, honey. Even though it doesn't seem like it now, you will get through this." Sherri Ann squeezed her hand.

Laura nodded. "She's right. It won't be easy, but one day you'll look back on all this and wonder why you shed a single tear over either of those two losers. They certainly don't deserve you. They're the ones who will be left without you in their lives. It's their loss."

Jenna appreciated her best friends' love and support. Even though her foster sisters did their utmost to console her, they all knew words couldn't erase the horror of finding her twin sister in bed with the man she loved.

"It could be worse," Sherri Ann put in. "At least you know that Scott was asleep and thought he was with you, not Leah."

Laura demanded, "And how does she know that? Because Scott said so? He's a man, Sherri Ann! When their male thingy takes over, who knows who's calling the shots. Besides, he's not a complete fool. He wasn't about to admit he lost control and for that moment didn't care which twin he had in bed with him."

"Laura Murdock, you are not helping! Jenna needs your support, not you throwing what Scott did in her face!"

"Jenna has to face the truth. Regardless of the reasons why, you tell me how's she going to get past walking in on the two of them in her bed?"

Twenty-four

"*I wish I knew,*" Sherri Ann confessed. "If only there was a way to salvage her relationship with Scott."

"It's not possible!" Laura insisted.

"Forget about it! And there's no point in going over it yet again," Jenna hissed. "Right this minute, I really don't care 'why' he was kissing her. None of that matters, because it doesn't change what I saw. That image feels as if it's burned into my brain. Unfortunately, it's not going away anytime soon."

Her foster sisters weren't ready to let it go. They went over every detail, trying to figure out what had gone wrong, what could have been done to prevent it, and why they hadn't suspected a thing. Had Leah planned it? Had she been after him from the first but had waited for the first opportunity to strike? Or had Scott secretly been attracted to Leah?

"Enough! I don't want to hear another word about it. I'm exhausted. All I want to do is sleep and forget," Jenna sighed. "I can't do that considering the food I left on the bedroom floor. The thought of getting into a bed that smells like the two of them turns my stomach."

"Don't worry about it. Don't worry about anything. Laura and I will take care of it."

Laura asked, "Have you even eaten today?"

Jenna thought for a moment, then shook her head.
"I wasn't hungry. I'm not even sure I can eat now, especially when I think of how stupid I was leaving them
alone while I went to make a special breakfast for them.
I feel like an utter fool."

"This isn't your fault. Stop berating yourself. You,
sister-girl, sit back and relax while Sherri Ann and I
clean up."

"You don't have to," Jenna protested.

Sherri Ann persisted, "We want to, so just rest. I'll
make you some hot sweet tea. Mrs. Green swore by the
soothing powers of sweet tea."

Her foster sisters cleaned the floor in her bedroom,
stripped both beds, and replaced them with fresh sheets.
They also cleaned the kitchen, doing their best to elimi-
nate all traces of the special breakfast Jenna had made.
They prepared a light supper of tomato soup and grilled
cheese sandwiches, complete with sweet tea.

Jenna managed to eat some of the meal. Later, she
swore she was okay and they'd done enough for one
day. But the ladies insisted they weren't going anywhere.

It was very late when the three of them climbed
into Jenna's bed to sleep, Sherri Ann and Laura wearing borrowed pajamas. Sharing a bed was something
they'd done growing up when one of them had had a bad
dream, or they'd seen a scary movie and had been afraid
to sleep alone.

Jenna was glad they were there. It helped. Years ago,
her foster sisters had spent the first night with her after
she'd broken up with Scott. This time was vastly different. She and Scott could never fix this mess. It was
finally over.

"This too shall pass," Sherri Ann assured her.

"Tomorrow will be a better day," Laura encouraged
her.

Jenna squeezed each foster sister's hand, acutely aware that in an effort to spare her further hurt and disappointment, they'd gone out of their way not to badly berate her twin. Although Jenna appreciated the sentiment, unfortunately it couldn't ease the incredible sadness that had taken root in her heart.

What hurt the most was that Leah had set out to hurt her. Jenna hoped she was pleased with herself, because Leah had succeeded beyond her wildest dreams. She had shattered Jenna's happiness.

Jenna couldn't fully understand why. As she closed her eyes in an attempt to block from her mind that hated image of the two of them, she accepted that the reason didn't matter. The knowing couldn't erase what had happened. The end results remained the same.

Jenna's hopes and dreams for a future with Scott were gone, buried beneath the crushing weight of her twin sister's high heels. Sherri Ann was wrong. There was nothing to salvage. Regardless of which twin Scott had believed himself to be in bed with, his male sexual needs had kicked into high gear. There was no mistake. He had been aroused. That realization was a blow to Jenna's battered heart. She felt wretched, her self-esteem and confidence hanging by a slender thread. How was she supposed to get beyond this?

Scott had been at her side when she'd found both her siblings. He'd supported her every step of the way. Having him there had meant the world to her. He'd said he loved her . . . claimed it had never stopped. He'd even asked her to be his bride and the mother of his children. And he'd given her the most beautiful engagement ring.

Jenna wiped away tears as she fully accepted the fact that the two people she loved the most had indeed betrayed her. The worst part was that she hadn't even seen it coming. She'd left this morning without realizing that she had given them the means to destroy her. How could they have done such a thing? If she'd live to be a very old lady, she would never forget it or get over it.

Just then, something Mrs. Green had often said when she'd been troubled flashed into Jenna's mind. She fell asleep silently mouthing the words, "Bad times don't last forever," again and again.

Scott had driven aimlessly for hours, unaware of the time as he'd struggled to come up with a valid reason for leaving town so close to the holidays. Fresh out of ideas, he'd settled on a version of the truth—he was tired and needed a few days away.

"What do you mean that you won't be here for the holidays?" Taylor nearly shouted at her brother. "You can't go to Aspen. Christmas is in a few days! Why are you doing this? Scott, what's wrong?"

Stalling for time, he carried several shopping bags full of gift-wrapped packages into her large family room, where the tree had been set up.

Startled by the agitation in his wife's voice, Donald looked up from the newspaper.

"Scott?" Taylor demanded, trailing after him.

Donald soothed, "Taylor, honey, if you give the man a chance, he'll answer your questions." He bumped fists with his brother-in-law in greeting. "We haven't seen much of you recently. Can I get you something to drink?"

"Naw, I'm straight." Scott wiped an unsteady hand over his damp forehead.

He was sweating, but it had nothing to do with the warmth coming from the heating system. He didn't remove his down-filled jacket. He didn't intend to stay.

His gaze darted from the logs burning in the grate to the large, flat-screen television mounted over the mantel. It came to rest on the grandfather clock ticking in the corner of the room. Was it really after eleven? Recognizing the late-night newscaster on the screen, Scott muttered a swear word. No wonder his sister had looked surprised when she'd let him inside.

Emotionally raw and fresh out of excuses, he was unable to meet his family's concerned gaze. Honesty wasn't an option. Hell, he still couldn't believe what had happened on Saturday morning, and he'd been there. He wasn't about to pour out his heartache in the hope his big sister could make it better, the way she'd done when he was a kid. No one could fix the hellhole he'd fallen into. He was in over his head and knew it.

A week in Aspen wouldn't take his mind off his troubles, but it was better than staying in Detroit and trying to suffer through the holidays with the help of the alcohol he'd been drinking the past few days to numb the pain, in order to sleep and forget for a few hours.

Nothing had made sense since he'd left Jenna's place that morning. He'd been so out of it that he'd run a red light and come close to hitting another car. He shouldn't have been behind the wheel, not when his thoughts had been so chaotic. He'd been forced to pull over to the side of the road until his hands had stopped shaking and he'd been calm enough to complete the drive home without injuring anyone else or himself.

There was no question about it. Leah had set him up. She'd gone after him in the hope of taking Jenna's place in his life. To make matters worse, he'd seen it coming. He'd known she'd been up to something. Unfortunately for him, he hadn't figured out how to put a stop to it in time.

He was shocked when he realized that for the first time in his life he was furious enough to want to do bodily harm to a female—a thought no man in his family had ever entertained. It was easier to blame her than admit that the true blame rested with him.

Sure, he'd been exhausted. And he'd ignored his instincts! He'd given in during a weak moment . . . given in to the need to be with his lady and spend the night with her in his arms. He'd let his hunger to be close to Jenna overshadow his common sense. He should have gone home.

That error in judgment had cost him what he valued the most. As yet another day had passed without word from his love, Scott's hopes of repairing the damage had dwindled a bit more. Unaware of the way his hands were balled into fists, he silently acknowledged that he might as well accept it. Jenna hadn't called, nor would she—not ever.

"Don't just stand there glaring into the fire. Scott Hendricks, you better start talking. Have you spoken to Mama about this? What about Jenna? I'm sure she isn't pleased, considering her brother and his family will be arriving on Christmas Eve."

His heart ached at the mention of her name. He snapped in a voice raw with emotion, "I'm a grown man. I don't need to clear my travel plans with anyone. I'm going. I'll see you after the holidays."

Before he could walk past her, Taylor caught his arm and held on. "Don't go. I'm sorry. I didn't mean to make you angry. I could see something was very wrong when I said Jenna's name. Did you two have a fight? Is that why you're leaving town?"

"Sis, believe me. Jenna has no objections to my leaving town. She'd like nothing better than to see me burn in Hell." In disgust, he added, "After what happened on Saturday, I can't blame her."

"What happened?" Taylor asked anxiously.

"Should I give you two some privacy?" Donald asked.

Scott shook his head, sighing dejectedly. "You might as well stay and hear the triple X-rated details." Yanking off his jacket, he tossed it over an armchair before he turned to face them. "Jenna threw me out of her house Saturday morning because she found me in bed with her twin sister."

"That's not funny, Scott. There is no way I'm going to believe you slept with Leah!" Taylor shook her head vehemently. "Don't get me wrong. You're no angel, but you're a long way from being that low-down."

"Man, that's nothing to joke about," Donald said.

"It's no joke. I didn't say I slept with Leah. I was asleep when she crawled in bed with me after Jenna had left to pick up some food. The little hussy has been after me since the day she arrived. My mistake was not seeing her as a genuine predator. I thought I could handle her. Thought I had her all figured out." He shook his head in disbelief. "I messed up royally when I underestimated Jenna's selfish twin."

A wealth of bitterness and resentment poured out in the single swear word used to describe Jenna's twin. Taylor gasped, but she didn't scold him as he paced back and forth between the fireplace and the decorated Christmas tree. Instead, Donald and Taylor sat quietly on the sofa and waited for him to elaborate.

"Jenna and I went to a tree-trimming party at Laura's, but we left early because we were both beat from the stress of finishing the semester. At first I turned down Jenna's invitation to spend the night at her place. Then I let her convince me to stay, knowing full well that Leah was not to be trusted.

"Not too long ago, she pulled a trick on me, pretending to be Jenna. She was dressed in one of Jenna's outfits. She somehow convinced Jenna it was a good trick to play on me, so Jenna went along with Leah. Leah had changed her hair and makeup and met me at the door. She rushed into my arms."

Donald asked, "Did you say Jenna went along with this?"

Scott nodded. "Jenna didn't see the harm. She said it was something they'd done when they were kids to fool their mother. Jenna teased me when I didn't recognize Leah immediately. I'd hugged Leah thinking it was Jenna and touched my mouth to hers. But the instant I looked into her eyes and smelled her perfume, I knew it wasn't Jenna. I got very angry, certain no good would come from it." He paused before he admitted, "It really bothered me. Frankly, I didn't trust Leah, but I knew Jenna wouldn't listen to criticism about Leah. How could I tell her I thought Leah was taking advantage of her? I could see that Leah resented Jenna's success and was jealous of her, but I didn't tell her. Jenna adores her sister, especially after waiting years to find her and have her back in her life."

"I can see why you kept silent," Taylor said.

"Even though it went against my better judgment, I kept quiet. I was more concerned with upsetting Jenna when I should have been figuring out a way to protect her. I would have put an end to it if I'd known Leah was capable of such deceit." He seethed with anger.

"Oh, Scott," Taylor sighed. "What exactly did Jenna see when she walked in?"

There was no easy way of saying it. He said through clenched teeth, "Like I said earlier, I was asleep. I felt Jenna's caress. She was stroking my chest, her breasts against me, and her lips on my throat. Naturally, I responded to her. I pulled her close even though I must have sensed something wasn't quite right. Hell, my eyes weren't even opened. I was just beginning to wake up when I recognized that she didn't smell the same. The scent was all wrong. Jenna doesn't use heavy perfumes. We kissed. That's when I knew something was definitely wrong. Her mouth tasted like stale wine. That's when I heard Jenna scream and dishes crashing to the floor. She'd brought in a breakfast tray." Scott let out a frustrated oath, rubbing an unsteady hand over his unshaven cheeks and bare scalp.

"I'm so sorry, Scott. So very sorry," Taylor said with tears in her eyes. "You and Jenna have been through so much. You two don't need any more heartache."

He nodded. Words weren't enough to ease the incredible pain of his loss. With a heavy heart, he knew that all he needed was for Jenna to believe in him and their love. At that moment, her trust meant everything to him, but as badly as he wanted it, Scott couldn't see it happening . . . not ever again. Jenna believed what she'd seen that morning.

"She wouldn't listen to your explanations?" Donald surmised.

"She wasn't interested in anything I had to say, not after seeing us in bed together. I suppose I should be grateful that Leah was wearing a nightgown and not in the nude.

"I was at the point of pushing Leah away, only I wasn't quick enough. Jenna saw us kissing. I wasn't even wearing briefs. I've never been more furious or felt more helpless in my life." He hung his head. "No matter what I said, Jenna didn't want to hear it. Not from either one of us. She wanted us out of her house . . . gone from her life."

He growled his frustration and impotent rage. "I can't even blame her. Nonetheless, I'm still disappointed that she flatly refused to hear me out. That's what hurt the most. She didn't give me a chance to explain."

"Goodness!" Taylor exclaimed. "It sounds more like

a scene out of one of Mama's soap operas than something in real life. How could you let yourself get caught in a situation like this? It's nasty."

"He didn't let himself do anything, baby," Donald said. "These things happen, especially when large sums of money are involved. That's what Scott was to Jenna's sister. Apparently when Leah looked at him, she saw dollar signs. She hasn't known him long enough for anything more." He asked, "Taylor, have you forgotten? Something similar to this nearly broke us up?"

Her eyes went wide. "That female fan who waited inside your hotel room, expecting to see you? Instead I came along. I assumed the worst. If you hadn't come after me, I honestly don't know if we could have gotten past that. I can only imagine how much worse this has to be for poor Jenna. She must be devastated. It's a nightmare."

Scott nodded. "Yeah, a nightmare. Only it's my life, and at the moment it reeks. I figured spending the holidays in Aspen will give me time to cool off, to stop feeling and start thinking. I'm a mess right now. Sis, you don't want me around this Christmas. Besides, if I'm out of town, I can't very well strangle Leah. You have no idea how much I want to go after that woman."

"Scott! Stop exaggerating. It's not funny."

"Sis, do I look amused? I'm dead serious. Until now, I've never actually considered physically harming a female. But considering what she did . . . man! I'm angry enough to want to do some serious damage. Leah has got it coming."

Donald said, "Leah isn't coming out of this unscathed. She has lost her sister. Or do you think that Jenna can ever forgive her for doing this? I'd say that was highly unlikely. It certainly isn't going to happen anytime soon, if ever."

Taylor frowned. "I don't like this talk of you hurting anyone, but the way I feel, I'd like to snatch that woman bald. That little witch! How could she do something so despicable to her own sister? It's outrageous. Jenna has shown her nothing but love. What more could Jenna have possibly done to please her?" Taylor didn't wait for an answer but rushed ahead with, "She opened her home and heart to that dreadful woman. Just look at how she repaid her. While Jenna's back was turned, Leah helped her fast tail to her sister's man. What did she expect you to do? Fall in love with her and throw what you felt all those years for Jenna into the trash? If you were that low-down, why would Leah even want you?" Taylor ended in an indignant huff, so upset that she was shaking.

"Honey, calm down." Donald placed his arm around her.

The men looked on as Taylor suddenly burst into tears. Wringing her hands, she said, "I'm sorry. I didn't mean to cry, but I'm just so angry. You and Jenna don't deserve this, especially not now. You two were finally finding your way back to each other. You bought her that lovely ring because you loved her and wanted her to be your wife. We should be talking about your wedding, not trying to wade through garbage like this."

After taking a seat near his sister, Scott took her hand. "I'm sorry to dump this in your lap. It's Christmas. You have a family to consider. Little Donnie and Brianna come first. They expect their mommy to be as excited as they are. See why I have to leave town? I don't want my problems to take away from the kids and your happiness."

"You're an important part of my family." Accepting the tissues Donald gave her, Taylor dried her eyes. "Besides, this isn't about me. I may be a little emotional, but basically I'm fine. You, little brother, look as if you haven't slept in days. And going off alone to Aspen isn't going to help. Maybe if we put our heads together we can come up with a way out of this catastrophe."

"Taylor's right, Scott. Flying off to Aspen isn't going to fix this. We'll find a solution together."

"Jenna hasn't returned any of my calls or answered my text messages. Like I said earlier, I can't blame her for being hurt. Hell, I would have done the same thing if our positions had been reversed." From the depths of despair, Scott grated bitterly, "I can't get past the fact that Jenna has walked away as if what we shared no longer matters. It's tearing me apart."

The possibility of losing her was something he still couldn't fully entertain. Damn it! He wasn't a quitter. There had to be a way of clearing up this misunderstanding. That's all it was—a horrific misunderstanding.

Why couldn't Jenna see that? He'd tried in every way he could think of to reach her, but she wasn't willing to listen to anything coming out of his mouth. He couldn't help being hurt because of it. Had her love and trust in him simply vanished in an instant? Why couldn't Jenna have a little faith in his decency as a man?

Frustration battled with hurt feelings and acute disappointment. Why had she had to walk in at that exact moment? If she'd only waited a few seconds, he would have been out of that bed and raising hell with her sister. He hated that she'd caught them at the worst possible moment.

Scott complained heatedly, "What would I want with Leah when I had Jenna? When I look at Jenna I see a heart of gold in her eyes. She loves deeply and gives freely to those she cares about. Leah is plain selfish. She doesn't come close to measuring up to the goodness in my Jenna. I'd be a fool to settle for less."

"All you have to do is to figure out a way to convince Jenna," Donald said, deep in thought. "Jenna does know you didn't actually have sex with Leah, right?"

"Absolutely. I tired to tell her that I thought I was in bed with her, not her twin. It wouldn't be so complicated if she'd let me explain my side of this compound."

"Scott! This not some chemical formula to be solved," Taylor snapped.

Donald advised, "If you want to save your relationship, you're going to have to find a way to sit her down and tell her in detail exactly what you did and did not do."

"How? She's not interested in the particulars. She's going by what she saw with her own eyes. That leaves me out in the damn cold! Don't I at least deserve a hearing?" He swore in frustration. "She broke it off with me saying that she's sorry she took me back. I'd like to know what happened to the love. How could she say she loved me and then days later take her lying sister's word over mine?"

Donald interrupted, "Well, you aren't going to get her to hear you out if you don't get a handle on your emotions. You can't let the hurt and disappointment get the best of you. You have to find a way to step back and think this through."

"Donald's right. You're upset . . . too close to the situation. Clearly, Jenna's not ready to talk, so you're going to have to back off for a while and give her some space. For goodness' sake, Scott, she caught you in her bed with her twin sister." Taylor insisted, "No matter how badly you want to straighten this out, you must respect her boundaries. Keep your distance for now. She has to heal a little before she can listen."

"You mean she needs time to find more barriers to put between us. She's got a truckload of them as it is.

Each day seems to shorten my temper and deepen my bitterness and resentment. Dragging this out isn't working for me."

Taylor threw her hands up in the air. "Knucklehead! Donald, talk to him. Maybe you can get him to see that if he pushes too hard, he'll only make things worse."

"Sis, you just said that a female fan tried to come between you and Donald. My brother-in-law didn't sit around twirling his thumbs until you were ready to listen. The man went after you and straightened things out."

"Which part doesn't Jenna have straight? That it was you wrapped around her sister? Or that you had a hard-on when you got out of bed?" Taylor challenged.

Twenty-five

Scott said, "Oh, man! Sis, I don't believe you said that."

Taylor lifted her chin. "No one is disputing that you have good reason to be upset, but so does Jenna. Giving your temper free rein isn't helping. You're making things worse. Jenna apparently needs time. And you have no choice but to respect that."

"I have a choice. I'm done with begging her to listen to me. Whose side are you on, anyway?"

"I'm on your side, but only because I've loved you since the day Mama and Daddy brought you home from the hospital. Don't go doing something you'll regret for the rest of your life. Why do you have to be so stubborn? First you're talking about going away for Christmas. Scott! Why are you punishing Mama and the kids? Or didn't you think they would notice you're gone? Are you sure you weren't dropped on your head when you were a baby?"

Scott gasped so suddenly that it made him swallow incorrectly, sending him into a coughing fit. Donald snorted, his large frame shaking with laughter.

"Now, honey," Donald soothed. "Scott's in over his head and knows it. Family's about all the poor man has left. This thing has hit him hard, and he's not thinking straight."

Scott frowned. He didn't like being discussed as if he hadn't been in the room. Yet considering how much he'd upset his only sister, he decided to give in.

"You win. Christmas is a time for family. Why should I upset Mama? Besides, I've been looking forward to going with you all to Christmas Eve service and hearing my favorite nephew recite his lines in the Christmas pageant." Scott smiled for the first time. "Donnie's so excited about Santa. He can hardly wait. Even baby Brianna is fascinated by the lights on the Christmas tree."

Taylor was right. Why should he go off as if he'd done something wrong? He hadn't had sex with Leah. The worst he'd done was kiss her, and he hadn't enjoyed it. The more Scott thought about the situation, the angrier he became.

For weeks, he'd been doing everything in his power to prove his love to Jenna. He'd gone out on a limb and told her how he felt. He'd even given her his ring. How much more could he have done to save what suddenly felt like a one-sided relationship?

Jenna had certainly never given them a clear shot at happiness. She'd fought him every step of the way. Why had she accepted his ring? She'd hidden it under her clothes, as if it had been a dirty little secret.

Judging by the way she'd flung it at him, she hadn't had any trouble turning her back on them. Did she know him at all? How could she just assume he would lie to save his own skin? She believed the worst because of something as common as a morning erection! He'd never forget the look of horror on her face when he'd gotten out of bed.

Hell, he was a man. His natural response had been to Jenna. An erection didn't mean he was prepared to jeopardize what they felt for each other and a lifetime of love. Scott was beginning to feel like a class-A fool for giving her another chance to break his heart. She'd nearly destroyed him emotionally when he'd entered the draft in the NBA and she'd turned her back on his first proposal. She hadn't thought that his offer to marry her and pay for her education had been a serious one. All he'd asked in return was that she take a year off college to travel with him during his first season. Her refusal had been crushing.

Now, more than ten years later, she was rejecting him again. She wasn't giving him the benefit of the doubt. Although her refusal was devastating, he wasn't going down on his knees to get her to listen to him. Nor was he about to beg for forgiveness. No way! He had some pride.

He'd made a fool of himself years ago trying to convince her to come away with him. Once was enough. He didn't need a sledgehammer upside his head to show him what had been there for all to see. Jenna didn't really love him. How could she, when she didn't trust him? Love and trust went hand in hand. It was time he faced the facts. Jenna wasn't going to trust him, not after finding him in bed with her low-life sister. It was over.

Breaking into his troubled thoughts, Taylor said, "I'm so glad you changed your mind about going to Aspen. That gives us time to figure out the best way to convince Jenna you didn't betray her. I could call—"

Scott interrupted, "There's nothing to figure out." His voice had taken on an icy calm. "It took me a while, but I've finally taken a hard look at what's right in front of my face. Jenna was never the right woman for me. I should have left it alone. Instead I attempted to repair a relationship that ended over a decade ago. I should have known better than to try again. It was my mistake. I apologize for dragging you two into my mess."

"Scott, no. Let us help. Now isn't the best time for

you to be making decisions about the future. You love Jenna. We all know it."

"Yeah, I do. But the problem is that feeling has never been mutual. It's time I accepted it." He rose to his feet. "I'd better get going. I'll see you tomorrow. I promised Donnie to take him Christmas shopping, help him pick out your gifts. I'd like to take him ice-skating afterwards, if that's okay?"

"Scott . . ."

"That sounds fine," Donald said. "Donnie is look forward to going. Right, honey?"

Taylor nodded, getting up to give her brother a hug. "Yes. We'll see you tomorrow. Come by anytime. You know you're always welcome."

Scott forced a smile. "Thanks. Bye." He pulled on his jacket before hurrying away, taking care to close the side door quietly behind him.

How could he have been so blind? He'd been so busy chasing after her that he hadn't taken into consideration what he really wanted, what he valued and needed from a relationship. Jenna didn't love him the way he needed and deserved to be loved.

Yes, he'd been wrong not to have shared his suspicions about her sister with Jenna, but the blame didn't stop with him. Jenna had also been wrong not to at least have given him a chance to explain. After all they'd gone through, she owed him that much.

It hurt like hell knowing that Jenna wasn't deeply in love with him. Regardless of how much it hurt, Scott was fresh out of options. When all was said and done, he was George Hendricks's son. He would deal with the gut-wrenching truth like a man. Then he could put it behind him and get on with the rest of his life.

Trying to recapture the past had been a colossal error in judgment. It was an error that had apparently left a bitter taste in her mouth and a hole the size of a basketball court in his heart. In the end, they'd both suffered and lost.

"Lincoln, at the rate you're downing that punch, Jenna's going to have to make a bucketful," Carolyn laughed.

Lincoln grinned. "Can't help it. Jenna's got me working up a sweat to earn my keep," he teased from where he was reaching up to put the ceramic angel on the top of the Christmas tree.

"You call decorating the tree work?" Carolyn quizzed, hand on hip.

"I do, especially when you consider the drive to the country, and then hiking through the snow to find the perfect tree. When you ladies finally made up your minds, I had to cut the darn thing down with a handsaw. Jenna's idea of an old-fashioned Christmas was a workout," Lincoln complained affectionately. "Isn't that right, Sis?" He smiled at Leah, who was stringing popcorn from where she was seated on the sofa.

Leah smiled. "Lincoln, you always were a big old tease. The day was like something out of one of those old picture books Mama used to read to us when we were little. Remember the time you took off my baby doll's clothes and hid them?"

While the others laughed, Jenna averted her face. She sat on the floor, helping Corrie place ornaments on the lower branches of the fragrant pine tree. In an effort to keep the mood festive, she said, "Lincoln, you were always tickling or chasing us. You might as well admit it. You enjoyed chopping down that tree. Lucky for you, big brother, I'm on my way into the kitchen to check on the pies in the oven. Only because I'm such a generous person and wonderful sister, I'll bring you another cup of punch." She nestled Corrie's baby-soft cheek. "Would you like more punch too, sweet pea?"

Corrie shook her head vehemently. "Cookie!" she said, clapping her small hands.

Laughing, Jenna scooped up her niece in a hug. "See! Someone likes my sugar cookies." She blew loud bubbles against the little girl's tummy until she broke into a fit of giggles. After placing her onto her tiny feet, Jenna called from over her shoulder, "Anyone else want more punch?"

"I'll take more," Leah said, "but I'm going to add my own kick." She referred to the bottle of rum on the side bar.

"I'd also like some," Carolyn sang out, patting her swollen tummy. "Since I'm eating for two these days. Need any help, Jenna?"

Holding back the angry retort for Leah to get her own punch, Jenna had to concentrate to remain calm. She said to her sister-in-law, "After the long trip here and taking care of Corrie and Lincoln, my dear Ms. Carolyn, you need to relax and conserve your energy. Santa may need your help later, getting things set up."

"Santa has two left thumbs and definitely needs all the help he can get," Lincoln volunteered, squatting down to steady Corrie as she placed another ornament on the tree.

"Turn that up, Carolyn. I love that song!" Leah began dancing to the Temptations' Christmas song "Jingle Bell Rock."

Jenna mumbled beneath her breath, "I can do this . . ." as she hurried into the kitchen. She clenched her teeth to keep from screaming her frustration. She'd been planning the Gaines family Christmas gathering for weeks, down to the smallest detail. What she hadn't counted on was feeling as if she'd like to slap her twin senseless and order her out of the house again. Not for a moment had she believed that having Leah back would be easy, but it was proving to be a lot harder than she'd anticipated.

Knowing how much Lincoln and Carolyn had been looking forward to spending time with Leah, Jenna hadn't had the heart to disappoint them. So for their sake, Jenna had chosen to take the high road and pretend all was right in her world. After only one day, Jenna's nerves were stretched thin and her temper even thinner. Plus she hadn't slept well in nearly a week. She yearned to crawl beneath the covers, pull them over her head, and shut out the world. Unfortunately, hiding from her problems wasn't an option.

Soon after Lincoln and his family had arrived, Jenna had told them that she and Scott had broken up. Both Lincoln and Carolyn liked Scott, and they'd admitted being disappointed by the news. Though Leah had been out of the room, Jenna had been unable to explain, and she'd quickly changed the subject before she revealed too much.

Jenna had assured herself that reuniting her family was more important than her personal heartache. Lincoln and Leah hadn't seen each other since they were small children. She had also feared that Lincoln would change his mind about driving such a distance if he'd known about the rift between the twins. Having him and his family here for the holidays was a huge comfort to Jenna, and one she'd been unwilling to forgo.

Even though Laura and Sherri Ann pointed out that by keeping quiet, she was protecting her sister, Jenna was determined to stick to the plan. This Christmas was special for their family, and she refused to let Leah take anything else from her. Surely she could put up with her twin for a few days and remain silent?

"That smells wonderful."

When Carolyn joined her, Jenna nearly dropped the

mug she was filling with the fragrant brew from a large simmering pot on the stove.

"And it tastes better than it smells," Carolyn continued. "You have to give me the recipe."

Jenna nodded. "I'm glad you like it. Mrs. Green used to make it on Christmas Eve. It doesn't feel like Christmas without it. Aren't you supposed to be relaxing?"

"I'll relax once Lincoln has put together Corrie's kitchen and stove set. I know we should have left it for her to see when we got back, but Lincoln and I were the excited ones who couldn't wait. This will be the first Christmas that she will really know what's going on. She knows Santa." Carolyn laughed, but then sobered as she studied Jenna. She placed a comforting arm around Jenna's waist and gave her a quick hug. "How are you really doing, kiddo? The breakup can't be easy."

"I'm fine." Jenna forced a smile as she handed Carolyn the cup. "It's alcohol free. No worry about harming the new baby."

"Thanks. Jenna, if you need to talk, I'd be happy to listen," she offered softly. "Lincoln and I had our ups and downs before we got married. Maybe you and Scott can—"

Unable to explain that it was more serious than the normal emotional swings many couples experience, Jenna shook her head. "I appreciate your wanting to help. It's not our first breakup, only this time, it's over." Eager to change the subject, she asked, "I'd like you and Lincoln to feel at home. I do appreciate the sacrifice you two made to spend Christmas here instead of with your families."

"Being here isn't a sacrifice. You and Leah are family. The three of you really deserve this special time together, especially after being apart for so long." She hesitated before she said, "Lincoln and I are a little worried about you. The breakup came at the worst possible time. Plus you have to put on a happy face for us. Jenna, what I'm trying to say and doing a terrible job of, is that I care about you. I hope we can be friends. I'd really like to help."

Jenna leaned down and gave her petite sister-in-law a hug. Taking comfort from the embrace, she said, her voice thick with emotion, "Thank you. We haven't known each other long, but I don't want you to think my reluctance has anything to do with my not trusting you. I'd also like us to be friends. Tomorrow is going to be the best Christmas ever, especially with you, Lincoln, and Corrie. She is such a sweet baby. I'm doing my best not to spoil her rotten, but it's so hard."

Carolyn laughed. "I know what you mean. It's hard not to give in to the urge to give her any and everything she wants. But Lincoln and I are determined to raise a strong, generous woman, not a selfish little brat." Glancing at the clock, she said, "I'd better get Corrie into bed, or no one will enjoy the day. By the way, you forgot Leah when you said you wanted all of us to have the best Christmas. I still can't get over that you two really are identical. Lincoln warned me, but I'm still amazed. Yet when it comes to personality, you and Leah are opposites. Thanks for the punch," Carolyn said before she went to collect her daughter.

At the mention of her sister's name, Jenna automatically stiffened. She had to make a conscious effort to uncurl her balled-up hands and even out her breathing. Jenna hadn't forgotten Leah. She'd purposely left her twin's name out. Jenna still loved her twin, but she no longer liked or trusted her. They would always be twins, but as far as Jenna was concerned, they weren't sisters.

As she peeked at the browning sweet potato pies and peach cobbler, Jenna's brow creased in a frown. She recalled the apple cobbler she'd made for Scott on Thanksgiving.

"Doesn't matter," she mumbled aloud. He wasn't on the guest list, and she wasn't going to waste time thinking about him or wondering where he was and what he was doing.

Scott had destroyed any fragile hope or lingering doubts she might have had. While he claimed he hadn't known it was Leah in bed with him, his sizeable erection had screamed the truth. Leah hadn't been the only one in the wrong. Scott shared responsibility for what had happened that morning.

Lincoln and his family were staying until the end of the week. Jenna hoped she would be able to keep it together until they left, but she wasn't making any promises beyond Christmas Day.

After filling the mugs and arranging them on the tray with a plate of sugar cookies, Jenna ran out of reasons to delay. She whispered aloud, "This too will pass," in the hope of bolstering her ego.

"My head hurts," Leah moaned as she took a sip from the open bottle of wine left over from the evening meal. After yet another fortifying sip, she put the bottle on the bedside table.

Curling into a ball, she mumbled, "I should not have come." Anything was better than being back at Jenna's, even that dreary cheap motel room she'd holed up in since her twin had put her out.

It wasn't like she hadn't known what to expect when she'd returned to the house. Yet she had come anyway. Her only excuse was that it was Christmas and she didn't want to spend the holidays alone. Plus, she was eager to see her big brother and spend time with him. She was also looking forward to getting to know Carolyn and her little niece.

The reunion with Lincoln had gone well. It was a lot better than she'd anticipated, since Jenna had kept quiet and not revealed Leah's part in the breakup. That in itself had been a real shocker. While she didn't fully understand why, she was grateful for it. It meant Lincoln could get to know her before he learned the truth.

Their big brother had turned out to be a real hunk, and he was smart as well. Like Jenna, he was well educated. There was no doubt that he was going places.

"My big brother is a big-shot attorney," Leah grinned with pride.

It was odd that she hadn't been proud of her twin. Jenna's success hadn't thrilled Leah at all. She couldn't explain or control her feeling of resentment when it came to her twin's good fortune. Nor could she stop comparing her own life to Jenna's. Her sister had it all—beautiful clothes, lovely house, a good job, and her own car. It wasn't fair, especially when it came to Jenna's man. Scott was the kind of man Leah had dreamed about having in her life.

Unfortunately, Leah had messed up big time. She'd lost control, given in to her emotions. She'd been so caught up in her own needs that she foolishly hadn't taken her twin's feelings into consideration. Nor had she taken time to consider the repercussions of her actions. Only now that her twin sister wasn't speaking to her did Leah fully realize just how much she loved and needed Jenna.

Leah didn't have a clue how to make it up to her twin. If only she had thought it through before she'd acted. Leah hadn't expected it to hurt herself when she'd seen the pain she'd caused. She hadn't been thinking when she'd gone into Jenna's bedroom that morning. It hadn't been planned. Hunger pains had driven her out of bed that early. She'd seen the note and simply taken advantage of the situation.

Yeah, she'd been a little high from the drinking she'd done that night. She'd been reckless, acting on sheer bravado when she'd gotten into Jenna's bed. She'd assured herself that once Scott realized he preferred Leah, Jenna might be disappointed, but she'd get over him and move on. Leah had been convinced that her twin hadn't really been in love with Scott.

"Stupid. . . . Stupid!" she whispered as tears ran unchecked down her cheeks.

What was she going to do? Once her brother learned what she had done, he would hate her, too. She only had a few days to make things right, but she didn't have a clue how to even start.

"Why did I do something so damn stupid?" she sobbed unhappily. Now her twin sister hated her, and very soon so would her beloved brother. What was she going to do? How was she going to fix it?

Leah cried herself to sleep, unable to find an answer.

Twenty-six

After yet another long, restless night of too much thinking and not enough sleep, Jenna said a quiet prayer of thanks. It was time to get up and celebrate the reason for the season.

On her way into the kitchen, she paused to turn on the Christmas tree lights and marvel at the bounty of toys waiting for Corrie. With a smile, she put on the coffee and began preparing breakfast for her family.

While she was whipping up some eggs, both of her foster sisters called to wish her a merry Christmas. Jenna heard the concern in their voices. Determined to keep busy, she made a big breakfast and had it warming in the oven by the time everyone was up and laughing at Corrie's giggles of delight. She'd also prepped the honey-glazed ham and prime rib before they sat down for breakfast.

Amidst Lincoln's good-natured teasing, Carolyn's cheerful banter, and little Corrie's enthusiastic joy, Jenna found pleasure in the day. She basically ignored Leah. It also helped that Sherri Ann and Laura arrived earlier than planned. Her foster sisters came loaded down with gifts, side dishes, and good cheer. Their unfailing support helped keep a smile on Jenna's face.

No one mentioned Scott's name. While Jenna appreciated their consideration, it was a real struggle for her to keep him out of her thoughts. Her heart was weighed down with the knowledge that this would have been their first Christmas together in more than ten years. She should have been on top of the world, knowing that Scott loved her as much as she loved him. They should have announced their engagement and begun planning their wedding and a future filled with happiness and promise.

Today, Christmas Day, should have been a true celebration, coupled with finally having her family back together after years of separation. Instead of being overjoyed, Jenna was fighting not to cry, was struggling to keep her grief and disappointment on the inside.

Every time she glanced at her twin she wanted to unleash the fury simmering just beneath the surface. It took every bit of self-control she possessed to continue the pretense that nothing was wrong.

By seven o'clock that evening, Jenna was exhausted from the strain. Her little niece had also had enough excitement for one day. She'd missed her afternoon nap. This, combined with all the attention she'd received from the adults, the tired little had girl crawled into her father's lap. She promptly went to sleep with her thumb in her mouth. Lincoln carried her into the bedroom while Carolyn rushed ahead to help.

For the first time that day, Leah was alone with Jenna and her best friends. The festive mood in the living room had disappeared and been replaced with tension.

Leah shifted restlessly from one hip to the other as the others stared at her. She braced her hands on the padded arms of her chair and crossed her legs.

"Nothing to say, Leah?" Laura said, breaking the silence.

Leah snapped, "Why bother? You three have already condemned me without bothering to listen to my side. You aren't interested in anything I have to say."

"Give her a gold star," Sherri Ann quipped. "We're not interested in your explanation. Someone as low-down as you doesn't deserve a loving, caring sister like Jenna. The loss is yours. I'd bet once Lincoln knows the truth about you, he'll turn his back on you also."

"Amen to that. What I don't understand is why you brought your deceitful self back here. Did you think that because today was Christ's birthday, Jenna would forgive and forget what you did to her? Our sister has a generous heart, but she isn't wearing a halo, like that black angel on top of the tree," Laura said, her voice rising.

Ignoring her twin, Jenna stood and said, "Let's drop this for tonight. She isn't worth the effort." As she linked arms with her foster sisters, she said, "You two have to take home some of the ham and prime rib. Laura, your scalloped potatoes were fabulous, as usual. Sherri Ann, that coconut cake was simply delicious. You did Mrs. Green proud." They walked into the kitchen without a backward glance.

Once they were in the next room, Laura said, "Enough about food. How are you holding up?"

"Yes, how are you?" Sherri Ann asked.

Jenna shrugged. "Not as well as I would like, but better than I expected, all things considered. I'm glad it's almost over. A few hours more, and I can say good-night and call it a day. When I woke up this morning, I wasn't sure I was going to keep it together." She smiled at them. "You two helped so much. I don't think Lincoln suspected anything was wrong. He seemed to really enjoy having the Gaines family together."

"Group hug," Laura requested.

The three of them wrapped their arms around each other and gave a warm squeeze.

"Thanks," Jenna said around a sigh.

Laura said, "Now that you've accomplished what

you set out to do, how you managed it is still a mystery to me."

"You should go to bed as soon as we leave. If you'd like, we can stay over so you don't have to deal with her at all," Sherri Ann offered.

"You've done enough. And I don't intend to spend what is left of the night hiding in my room. This is my house. I've done nothing wrong. If my twin's uncomfortable, that's her problem, not mine."

Sherri Ann laughed. "I like your attitude. She's the one who doesn't belong."

Laura joined in. "Well, ladies, let's get busy."

The three of them worked swiftly and efficiently to clean the kitchen, store leftovers in the refrigerator, and pack enough food so that Laura and Sherri Ann would have no need to cook the next day. They were finishing up when Carolyn joined them.

"Oh, no! I'm too late to help," Carolyn complained.

Laura giggled. "That's supposed to be a relief."

"Laura's right. You've been helping out all day. It's time to kick your shoes off and put your feet up." As Jenna ushered them out of the kitchen, she asked, "Is Corrie settled for the night?"

Carolyn smiled. "She didn't even stir when I sponged her off and got her into her pajamas. She was like a rag doll, all limp arms and legs. She's getting too big for me to manage on my own. But then, she's a daddy's girl. And Lincoln is so good with her." Realizing that Sherri Ann and Laura had collected their gifts and were preparing to leave, she said, "Surely you don't have to go so soon?"

"Soon?" Sherri Ann shook her head as Carolyn walked them into the foyer. "We've been here for hours!" Shoving her arms into the coat Jenna held for her, she said, "Thanks again for the silk scarf you and Lincoln gave me. I love it."

"And I love my red leather gloves. They fit perfectly," Laura said as she buttoned her coat.

"You ladies aren't leaving already? What? Do you have hot dates?" Lincoln teased, joining them.

"We wish." Laura laughed. "It was great seeing you two again. Jenna, everything was perfect. Thanks for having us."

"It wouldn't be Christmas without you two." Jenna gave each of them a final hug. "Thanks for everything."

"Since I can't persuade you two to stay, I'll walk you out," Lincoln said as he quickly pulled on a jacket and collected their bags of gifts and food.

Jenna, her foster sisters, and Carolyn had made plans to spend the next day bargain hunting. Jenna and Carolyn stood in the doorway, waving and calling a final Merry Christmas.

As they waited for Lincoln, Jenna hoped that Carolyn hadn't noticed that Leah hadn't bothered to even say good-bye.

"Wow, it's cold out there." Lincoln came in rubbing cold hands together. After he locked the door, he placed an arm around each of their shoulders and urged them into the living room.

Leah still sat in an armchair, her feet tucked beneath her. She was cradling a mug of eggnog. Judging by the open bottle of rum on the coffee table, Jenna assumed it was spiked.

"I take it your guard dogs have finally gone home. Not a moment too soon," Leah announced, raising her mug for a long sip.

Jenna stiffened. Then she said, as if her twin hadn't spoken, "I'll put on some coffee. Excuse me." She turned, silently congratulating herself on not reacting to the dig, when Lincoln stopped her.

"No, Jenna. Don't leave. What's going on?" Lincoln asked. "Don't bother denying it. Both Carolyn and I have picked up on the tension between you twins. Christmas is over. The baby's asleep. So let's stop tip-toeing around it and put whatever it is out there." He pointed to the sofa. Once Jenna and Carolyn were seated, he said, "Leah? Jenna? Who'd like to go first?"

The twins' gaze locked for the first time that day. For a prolonged moment, the twins really looked at each other. Leah was the first to look away. Jenna remained silent.

"Well?" he prompted.

With her lips compressed and her arms crossed tightly beneath her breasts, Leah snapped, "Go ahead, Jenna! You know you're dying to tell him."

Jenna clasped her hands tightly in her lap. "If that were true, I would have told them the instant they walked through the door." She hesitated before she said, "Last Friday night, Laura gave a tree-trimming party. Scott and I went. Rather than going with us, Leah decided to go out clubbing with friends. When we came back, she was still out. Both Scott and I were exhausted from the mad rush to get everything done at the end of the semester. I invited him to stay over. The next morning, I got up early to make a special break-fast. I went out to pick up rolls from the bakery and a few items from the gro—"

Leah swore impatiently. "Will you get to the point, Ms. Drama Queen? Why do you have to make a big production out of everything? Just tell them that you found me in bed with your blasted fiancé."

"What?" Lincoln shouted.

"You can't be serious," Carolyn said at the same moment.

"That's what happened." Jenna unconsciously folded her arms the same way as her twin. Her eyes burned from unshed tears.

"Leah! How could you?" Lincoln wanted to know.

Leah hung her head. "I didn't think. Okay? I just did it!"

Jenna said candidly, "I didn't wait for an explanation. I put both of them out of the house. The only reason . . ." She paused to point at her twin. "Leah's here now is because of you."

Swallowing to hold down the sob rising in her throat, Jenna paused to give herself time to gain control of her emotions. She would not cry in front of her twin.

Eventually, she said firmly, "I couldn't let her spoil our family reunion or Christmas. She's done enough damage as it is."

"Would you stop talking about me as if I'm not in the room?" Leah hissed, rising so she could glare at her sister. "I know I was wrong to go into your bedroom. That doesn't give you the right to treat me as if I'm invisible, as if what I think and feel doesn't matter. That's exactly what you've done the past two days," Leah accused hotly. "Your two friends were even worse. Acting as if I'm lower than dirt."

Lincoln and Carolyn exchanged a look before turning disbelieving eyes on Leah.

"After what you've done, you expect me to care that you don't like the way I've been treating you? Tough! You're extremely lucky that I'm willing to let you inside my home. Forget about speaking to your deceitful behind." Jenna stared pointedly at her twin. "When Lincoln leaves, you leave."

"I told you I was wrong! What more do you want from me?"

"I want you gone. And I don't care where. You can take up residence in the Dumpster in the alley for all I care. You no longer matter to me," Jenna hissed.

"Quiet! Both of you have said more than enough," Lincoln snarled, all traces of his good humor gone. He ran a hand over his close-cut natural and shook his head. "This is insane. After years of being apart, we've finally got our family back. We can't let anything come between us." He began pacing in front of the low-burning fire in the grate. "Somehow, we're going to sit down together and talk. And we're going to keep on talking until we've worked this out."

Wringing her hands in frustration, Carolyn said, "Lincoln's right. You can't let this come between you. We have a new family member coming soon. You've got to find a way to fix this. But not tonight. We're all tired." She was clearly upset as she rested a protective hand on her swollen midsection.

"Tomorrow . . . the next day . . . a year from now isn't going to clean this up. How am I supposed to forget I saw her having sex with my boyfriend? Tell me how?" Jenna said hotly.

Leah angled her chin up, saying through clenched white teeth, "We didn't have sex! We were kissing when you walked in. The instant he saw you, he forgot about me."

"Is that supposed to help ease my mind? That you hadn't gotten around to doing the sexual act?" Jenna jumped up, placing her hands on her hips. "Why am I even talking to you? You don't exist as far as I'm concerned. You stopped mattering to me that awful day, Lenna Marie. I don't want to look at you. I don't even want to be in the same room as you."

Carolyn came over and placed a supporting arm around Jenna. "I know you're upset and hurting right now. But it's not going to fix the problem. Remember, Jenna, you're the one who brought the family back together."

"Obviously, a huge mistake. We're way beyond the fixing stage. Nothing is going to make this better. She thinks because I didn't catch them doing 'the nasty' that it's supposed to make a difference? Well, it doesn't stop me from feeling as if my flesh and blood has stabbed me in the heart!"

Jenna went to stand in front of her twin so she could look her in the eyes. "You stopped being my little sister the moment you placed your big toes over the threshold of my room. You crossed the line of decency." She shook from the force of her emotions. "And to think I brought you here because I loved you and wanted to give you a fresh start. Just look at how you repaid my trust and faith in you."

Jenna paused to take a breath before she said, "Biologically, we're identical, but deep inside where it counts, you and I are nothing alike. It would never occur to me to hurt someone I loved in such a hateful way. My three sisters are Carolyn, Laura, and Sherri Ann. There won't be another Gaines family Christmas. This was the first and the last. If you're there, then I'm leaving."

Lincoln came over to Jenna and gave her a comforting hug. He said, close to her ear, "It's going to be alright. You're going to be alright. We're going to get past this."

Carolyn joined them also, putting her arms around Jenna and offering her support. "Both Lincoln and I love you. Jenna, you did nothing to deserve this."

Resting her head on her brother's shoulder, Jenna fought back the tears. She couldn't break down, not in front of Leah. Reeling in distress, she said, "I can't just let it go as if it didn't mean anything. It meant everything to me. I loved him! I was going to marry him! He gave me an engagement ring. And she took that away from me for no good reason!"

Lincoln's head shot up, a puzzled frown creasing his brow as his soothing hand moved over Jenna's shoulder. He kissed her forehead and ushered her back to the sofa. Then he turned a piercing gaze on Leah. "Why? Why did you do it? Scott was in Jenna's bed, so he didn't come after you." He waited expectantly.

Hands clenched at her sides, Leah's eyes darted around the room. Eventually, she said, "What difference does it make now? I was wrong, and I already said so. I can't change it or make it go away. Why can't we leave it at that?"

"That doesn't explain why you came into her bedroom. Or how you got from the doorway into the bed? Was Scott awake when you came in? Did he invite you inside?" Lincoln asked pointedly.

Having heard and seen more than enough, Jenna hissed, "Leave it alone, Lincoln. His physical reactions to her speak for him. I can't get over that I welcomed her into my home and she took everything I offered. Only she didn't stop with things. She helped herself to my man. The why's don't count."

"But Jenna—" Carolyn injected, but before she could say more, Jenna interrupted.

"I don't care why!" Jenna cried as she jumped up. She kissed her brother and then her sister-in-law. "Good night. I'm going to bed."

"Sleep well," Carolyn called.

Jenna didn't see the anguish on Leah's face, or the way her composure crumbled, or the silent tears that trickled down her cheeks. Nor did Jenna notice her brother's troubled gaze as it rested on Leah's bowed head.

Jenna walked with her head held high and her spine straight until she reached her bedroom. Once the door was closed, the rigid control she'd clung to during the long day vanished. Unable to bear the weight of her unhappiness, her shoulders hunched forward, sending her off-balance. Her trembling knees gave out completely. She slumped into the chair like a forgotten rag doll.

The emotional storm triggered by the traumatic

events of the last week caused her to sob against an upraised arm. She cried until she couldn't cry anymore.

Afterward, she slowly got ready for bed. For so long, she'd believed their first breakup had been wretched, that nothing could have been more painful. She'd been wrong. This time around was worse. The difference was in the depth of her love for Scott.

Her twin's involvement added to Jenna's suffering. Finding them together had hurt her to the core. A week had passed, but it hadn't gotten any easier. She assured herself that as soon as Leah was gone she could get her life back on track. This time when her twin left, it would be for good.

At least things were finally out in the open; there were no secrets or pretense. Now that their brother knew the truth, it was up to him to manage his relationship with Leah.

Jenna sighed unhappily. When she'd begun the search for her siblings, she hadn't expected it to end badly. The good part was that she'd found her brother, and gained a wonderful sister-in-law and a precious little niece. For that Jenna was deeply thankful.

She smiled as she thought of Carolyn and their plans to go shopping the next day. Along with her foster sisters, they would hit the malls early, looking for the best after-Christmas sales. It would also get Jenna out of the house and away from Leah for a couple of hours. Lincoln had agreed to entertain Corrie.

As Jenna squeezed her pillow, she realized she'd done it. She'd gotten through another day without Scott. She'd better get used to not seeing him on holidays or any other day.

Lincoln was wrong. Knowing why Leah had come to her bedroom didn't change what had happened. Nothing could make this wrong right.

Twenty-seven

On their last evening in Detroit, Lincoln insisted on taking the family out to dinner. In deference to Corrie's bedtime, they dined early. Jenna would have preferred a quiet meal at home, where she had become practiced at ignoring her twin. She'd gotten so good at it that she could get through a meal without directing a single glance or comment Leah's way.

Her composure was put to the test when she spotted Scott with his family across the restaurant. Judging by the sympathetic glances Carolyn sent her way during the meal, Jenna assumed she'd done a poor job of hiding her unhappiness. It was a relief when Lincoln asked for the check.

After they returned to the house, Jenna was following Carolyn and Corrie into the bedroom when Lincoln called her name.

He said, "This is our last night together. I'd like for the three of us to sit down together as a family and talk." When Jenna hesitated, he said with a smile, "Pretty please."

Reluctantly, she nodded, slowly returning to the living room. She sat beside Lincoln on the sofa.

Seated across from them in one of the armchairs,

Leah asked, "What is this about, Lincoln? You can't blame me because Scott was at the restaurant."

"Hardly. That was an unfortunate coincidence. If we'd left a half hour earlier, we probably wouldn't have seen him." He gave Jenna's hand a squeeze. "You okay?"

"Yes. What do you want to talk about?"

"I want you to know that while you and Carolyn were out shopping, Leah and I found her a furnished one-bedroom apartment. We also stopped in to see an old friend of my father. He has a law firm here in Detroit. He offered Leah a job as a favor to me." He waited for Jenna's response. When there was none, he said, "I've done what I could to help give her a fresh start. The rest will be up to Leah. Right, Sis?"

Leah nodded. "Jenna, you will be pleased to know I'm moving out tomorrow. Lincoln is giving me a lift to my new place. I start work on Monday."

Jenna didn't expect to be pleased, but she was, for her twin's sake. She merely said, "That was kind of you, Lincoln. I hope she doesn't disappoint you."

"I won't, I promise," Leah was quick to add.

Jenna had doubts, but she kept them to herself. It was sad that none of the things she had done to help Leah had worked. Leah would have been better off if Jenna had left her in Las Vegas. Leah had had a job then, and Jenna had had Scott. She quickly changed her mind. She was better off without him. No woman wanted a man she couldn't trust. It wasn't worth the inevitable heartache.

Lincoln said, "Leah has something she wishes to say to you. Some things she believes you should know about that morning."

"No!" Jenna cut him off. "I've been through enough. I've put up with her being back in my home. You can't expect more from me."

"Calm down, Sis." He caught her hand before she could leave. "I know this has been extremely difficult for you, but I honestly hope you will let Leah explain her side. It's important that you understand why she did this." When Jenna shook her head no, he interjected, "Please, hear her out. Our parents are gone and all that's left of them are the three of us. No matter what happened, we're still blood. Jenna, you can't just walk away from this family because Leah did something incredibly thoughtless and selfish."

Jenna lifted her chin. She stubbornly clung to her belief. "Lincoln, I don't care why. She did what she wanted to do. I was the one hurt and left to deal with the aftermath."

He surprised her when he admitted, "We all make mistakes, honey. I'm ashamed that I didn't do what I could to find you both years ago. I had the means to find you, but I was so selfishly caught up in my own life that I did nothing. That was wrong. You could have held it against me, but you didn't. Jenna, you can't know what happened that morning. How can you, when you haven't heard all the facts? Please, just hear Leah out. That's all I'm asking, please."

Although she tried, she couldn't harden her heart enough to dismiss the plea in her brother's voice. "I can't."

He persisted, "I wouldn't ask if I didn't think it was important."

Jenna sighed heavily. "I'm doing this for you, not her."

He kissed her cheek. "Thank you." Then he urged her back to sit beside him.

Jenna didn't so much as look at Leah. She waited with her hands tightly clasped in her lap.

Leah hesitated, looking nervously at Lincoln. He encouraged her, "Go ahead. Tell her what you told me."

Slowly, Leah got to her feet. She crossed to the side table where Jenna kept the hard liquor. She opened a bottle of rum and poured it into a shot glass.

"You don't need that," Lincoln said.

"I need something." Her hands were shaking as she lifted the glass to her mouth. After a sip, she put it down. "You're right. I just need to say it."

Jenna compressed her lips while crossing her arms beneath her breasts. Her body language spoke for her. She didn't want to hear a single word of what her twin had to say.

"Leah, this is your chance to—"

"I know, Lincoln. It's what I said I wanted to do, but I didn't know it would be this hard. Look at her! She alrea—"

"Just tell her why you came to her room."

"I woke up hungry. I was on my way into the kitchen when I saw the note. I knew it was my chance." Her voice was laced with bitterness when she said, "I was upset because you have it all. Everything I wanted for myself."

"What?"

"That's right! I was jealous!"

"Of what?" Jenna asked.

"Everything!" Leah threw her hands helplessly into the air. "Just look around. You own this beautiful house. It's full of pretty things. You have gorgeous clothes. Everything about you is perfect, including your friends and education." Leah said pointedly, "You even had a rich, good-looking man in love with you and wanting to marry you. Compared to you, I had nothing. I hated it!"

Eyes wide in disbelief, Jenna asked, "That's why you went after Scott? That's why you hurt me, because of a bunch of stuff?"

"It's more than stuff. From the moment we met, you

were practically shouting, 'Look at me.' You showed up at the club in expensive designer clothes, in an outfit that was straight out of *Vogue* magazine. That handbag you carry cost the earth. I saw a movie star carrying it in red in *Style* magazine. It's made in Paris. Did you think I was too stupid to recognize the real thing? At first I assumed Scott must be taking care of you, but you quickly set me straight. You let me know you paid your own way and were proud of it. Jenna, you even came to Las Vegas in a private plane, for heaven's sake!"

Leah didn't wait for a response but rushed on, "How do you think that made me feel? I was taking my clothes off for a bunch of strangers while you're with a rich, good-looking boyfriend throwing money left and right. You even bragged about how smart you were. How you weren't adopted and had worked your way up." She sneered, "Little Miss Perfect.

"And when I came here, you never let me forget that you not only finished high school but that you have a bachelor degree, a master's and doctorate . . . all of them hanging on your wall behind your desk. You went on and on about your high-class friends. You made sure I knew they were your real sisters, not me. Only it didn't stop there. You started in on me the moment I arrived, letting me know that I wasn't good enough. My job didn't have a future. I needed to go to college so I can get a career like yours. Nothing about me seemed to suit you, even the way I talked. You encouraged me to come here so you could make me over, just like you. The longer I was here, the more you harped on me to change. You never asked what I really wanted to do."

Leah glared at her twin. "Finally, I had enough. I was tired of feeling like a loser. I saw how you neglected Scott. He was the kind of man I dreamed about having in my life. You certainly didn't appreciate him. Your man came last on your list, behind your work and your best friends. More often than not, you were here with me rather than with him. He wanted to take you away for a romantic weekend. You wouldn't go! You hardly ever spent the night with the poor man."

Jenna hissed, "Are you done?" She had clearly had enough.

"I'm just getting started, sister dear." With a hand on her hip, Leah announced, "Scott needed a woman who can appreciate him. Someone who knows how to satisfy him and keep him coming back for more. So when the opportunity presented itself, I acted. I was on my way into the kitchen when I saw your note. I didn't give myself time to worry about right or wrong. I went after him." She ended the rant with, "I'm just as pretty as you and had just as much to offer. Probably more, considering I didn't have a career or friends to get in the way. I might have been a little high, but I'm not using it as an excuse for what I did."

Unable to stay seated a moment longer, Jenna stalked over to her twin. She didn't slap her face or even pull her hair out in clumps. She merely looked at her. The clock on the mantel was the only sound in the room. Leah was the first to drop her lids.

Jenna shook her head, her voice dripping with disgust. "I can't believe you did this. And you did it because I have a house full of secondhand furniture and clothes bought off the sales rack? That's right, Leah. I don't think I own a single piece of furniture that cost three hundred dollars. I bought every piece from one of the hotel liquidators. The only furniture I ever bought new was the bed and a mattress I bought with Scott."

Jenna wanted to laugh at her twin's stunned look, only it hurt too much. "Close your mouth, little sis. It's true. I never could afford brand-new furniture out of the showroom, not when I had to put myself through college. Lucky for me I like to sew, shop, and hunt down a good bargain. I also like traditional furnishings, because it's what you mostly find in those kinds of places. The coffee table was twenty-five dollars because of a scratch on the top. I sanded it down and stained it. It was one of my first projects. The sofa and love seat are covered with slipcovers I made myself. I've had them for years. I hated the brown tweed fabric, but I loved the lines of their rolled arms and the high back. I used a very expensive ivory jaguar silk that I got on sale. See?" Jenna squatted down and lifted the skirted, perfectly pleated edge. "Done the correct way, you can't tell, especially with certain styles. I upholstered the armchairs for less than a hundred dollars after taking a class. I stayed away from loose cushions on the sofas because it was a dead giveaway.

"The rugs in the living and dining room match because I bought them on clearance when the store was going out of business. They were marked way down because they were floor models. Oh yeah, I did buy the drapes and throw pillows, on sale. I also padded and covered the headboard in the guest bedroom. Decorating is a hobby of mine. I never told you about it because I didn't think you shared my interest. I'm forever watching the HGTV Channel on cable."

Jenna swallowed the scream of rage and frustration building inside her. She went on tightly, "As for my expensive clothes, I love certain designers. I'm guilty of having expensive taste and liking the high-end stores." Jenna laughed without humor. "I lived in New York City. I know how to find a deal. I can't afford to buy during the season, so I wait for the sales. The lower the price, the better. Why do you think Laura, Sherri Ann, and I braved the malls the day after Christmas? We went to no less than three malls. The sales are phenomenal." She admitted, "I'm not above hitting the consignment stores where the very rich ladies drop off their gently worn designer goods. I've come across some real finds. I got that leather jacket I wore in Vegas on a clearance rack while I was in New York. It was marked sixty percent off because of the rip in the lining. I repaired it.

"As for that really expensive bag you were drooling over, it was a birthday gift from my foster sisters. We pull out all the stops when it comes to birthdays. I've wanted that bag for a long time. I've only had it a year, but you better believe I take excellent care of it. Not because of the cost, but because Sherri Ann and Laura sacrificed to give it to me. We're sisters . . . willing to do anything for each other. Sherri Ann and I are saving up to buy Laura a new piece of that well-known designer's luggage she adores for her birthday. You'd recognize his signature logos done in brown and beige the instant you see it. It's about love and family and loyalty. But you wouldn't know a thing about loyalty, would you?"

The last comment seemed to hang in the air.

Jenna confessed with tears in her eyes, "All those years we were apart, I felt as if a part of me was missing. You were my twin, my sister. No one could take your place. I was so happy when I finally found you. I always loved you. I desperately wanted you back in my life. I might have gone about it the wrong way when I encouraged you to go to college. But I was trying to help. I didn't mean to put you down," Jenna ended unhappily.

Leah's face crumbled. "I'm so sorry, Jenna. I never meant to hurt you. I wasn't thinking about you at all, only about what I wanted."

Jenna raised and lowered her hands in a display of helplessness. "I suppose I should count myself lucky that you didn't decide that you're in love with him.

Who knows what you might have done under those circumstances."

"It's true! I'm really sorry. I love you. I wasn't thinking," Leah insisted.

"Well, you hurt me . . . badly. And you can't just make it up to me by telling me why you did what you did. The facts speak for themselves. I'm not likely to ever forget finding you in my bed with Scott. There is no explaining that away."

"But I—"

"You had your say. Now it's my turn to talk and your turn to shut up and listen," Jenna interrupted, shaking with fury. "I didn't have the advantage that you and Lincoln had, because I wasn't adopted. I had to work for everything, especially my education. All things considered, it worked out well for me. I've had some rough times and some breaks along the way. Looking back, I have no regrets. I'm certainly glad I've never felt the need to hurt someone else because I was jealous of what they have or who they have in their lives. I don't think I'm better than you because I finished college. No one needs to point out that it has to do with the way we were brought up. We're identical. It's more than circumstances that differentiate us. We were both smart when we started kindergarten and first grade. Intelligence runs in our family. Look at Lincoln. He was always at the top of his class."

Jenna didn't wait for a response. "From the investigator's report we know that both our parents went to college. And that Mama dropped out because she was pregnant. Daddy quit college when they got married to support the family, but evidently he couldn't handle the responsibility of being a husband and father, because when we were little he gave up and walked away. Poor Mama never recovered from his leaving."

She paused before she said, "Our folks had problems, but they were both educated people. You had the same opportunity to do something with your life as Lincoln and I. Why you decided not to go to college no longer concerns me. I see now that you never wanted my help. I won't make that mistake again. Your life is your concern, not mine. Now that we've got that settled, my part in this discussion has ended."

Lincoln kissed her cheek. "Thank you for hearing Leah out. At least you know that Scott didn't come on to Leah. He's evidently the innocent party in all this."

Jenna's entire body tightened, as if someone had poked her with a pin. "Innocent? No way. From where I was standing he was guilty as sin. He had her wrapped in his arms. And he looked as if he was prepared to finish what Leah started."

"Jenna, come on. You can't hold the fact that he reacted as a man against him."

"Yeah, I can and will."

"Leah was all over him."

Jenna snapped. "So what? He wanted her. That's fine with me. He can have her. I'm not going to stand in his way."

Lincoln insisted, "Scott thought he had you in his arms."

"You don't know that," Jenna shot back.

"That's what you told me."

"It's what he said, but I don't believe it. He said what he thought I wanted to hear at the time. He was aroused, Lincoln. His body told its own story," Jenna said, fighting her turbulent emotions.

"Come on! So what if he was aroused? That could have happened for a number of reasons . . . a woman in bed with him or a normal morning reaction. Or it might have been exactly what he told you at the time. What if he re-

ally was asleep and thought he was making love to you?"
Lincoln paused before he said, "There's only one sure way
of finding out. Ask him what really happened. You trusted
him enough to sleep with him. Why won't you trust him
to tell you the truth about what was going on with him?"
When she didn't respond, he prompted, "Jenna, have you
forgotten that you were considering spending your life
with him? Scott didn't strike me as being either a coward
or a liar. Why would he suddenly change?"

Jenna's heart began to pound from the possibility that Lincoln might be correct. Had she misjudged
Scott? He'd tried to explain, but she'd cut him off, refusing to listen.

Leah said, "I was telling the truth. I never meant to
hurt you. Scott was also telling the truth. He was asleep
when I got into bed. He didn't wake up until I pressed
against him and started kissing his neck. He called your
name when he pulled me close and kissed me. Then I
heard you scream and the sound of dishes crashing to
the floor. That's when I got scared and panicked. I'm
not even sure what I said to you. I just made up some
crazy excuse for my being in your room. What I'd done
had finally hit me. By then, you were ordering me out
of the room and the house. Nothing has been right for
me since that moment. I lost more than a place to stay,
Jenna. I lost my sister. Because of the resentment and
jealousy, I didn't think about how you'd feel." She said
unhappily, "I didn't think you really loved him. It was
too late when I figured out I not only hurt you but myself. I feel so bad. I know now that I was so wrong."

"Why are you telling me all this now?"

"I'm really sorry. I want to make it up to you, make
things right between us. I hate how things are between
us. It hurts. I want my big sister back. I'm hoping that
someday you might find it in your heart to forgive me,"
Leah ended miserably.

Jenna frowned. "You're sorry? Well, it's too late. What's done can't be undone. You can't expect to make nice and I'm supposed to forgive and forget. I can't do that. I don't want to. You destroyed two relationships."

Leah shocked Jenna when she said, "It doesn't have to be over between you and Scott. Go and talk to him. Give him a chance," she begged. "I owe it to him to try and fix things if I can. He will probably never speak to me again. But he's a decent guy and deserved better than he got."

"Leah is right. Scott deserves a chance." Lincoln squeezed Jenna's shoulder before he got up and stretched. "Think about it, Jenna." He walked over to Leah and kissed her cheek. "Good night, ladies."

After Lincoln left, Leah said softly, "I don't expect you to believe me, but I really would like to make it up to you." Jenna didn't respond but stared into the grate. Leah sighed heavily before she said, "Good night." Then she quietly left the room.

Deep in thought, Jenna absently turned off the lights before she went into her office and closed the door. She flicked on the lamp, then plopped down in the chair behind the desk. She drummed her fingers on the desktop. Had she been misjudging him? Had she overreacted in the heat of the moment?

She slowly opened the middle drawer and flipped over the framed photograph that had been lying face-down. With a trembling finger, she traced Scott's firm jawline, then sighed unhappily.

Jenna closed her eyes, imagining Scott's response if she showed up at his door. He'd glared at her when he'd spotted her in the restaurant. He was furious.

She'd seen it in his eyes when their gazes had briefly locked. Consumed by her own hurt, she'd quickly looked away. She certainly hadn't thought that a few hours later she might be wondering if she was wrong about what she'd seen that Saturday morning. Or that she might have to go to him for clarification.

"This is crazy!" she mumbled in misery. She'd been the one wronged, not the other way around. But what if she'd been mistaken? What if he hadn't been making love to her twin sister? What if he hadn't desired Leah?

Since Lincoln had forced her to listen to Leah's explanation, she realized she should at least hear Scott's version of what had transpired that morning. It was the only way of clearing away the doubt. She would have to go to him. There were no other options. And what if she'd been wrong? Would she be woman enough to apologize?

Until now, she hadn't been able to imagine anything worse than seeing her twin in her bed with her love. If she'd been wrong about what she'd seen, she had no way of making it up to him, of making it right. He was already so angry with her. Would he even hear her out?

"Why does everything have to be so darn complicated? Aren't there any easy solutions out there?" Jenna whispered as she covered her face with her hands. She'd be lucky if he didn't slam the door in her face.

Suddenly furious, she wanted to scream. Or throw something. She had done nothing wrong. She hadn't orchestrated this situation. Why did she have to always be the one trying to do the right thing? It wasn't fair.

At first he had called several times and sent text messages, trying to explain. Then there had been nothing from him. Hurt beyond measure, Jenna had been unable to bear hearing excuses for what she'd seen. Naturally, she'd tried to protect herself from further hurt and disappointment.

Once her family left in the morning, she would have nothing pressing to occupy her thoughts. The university wouldn't be back in session until well into the new year. There was nothing to stop her from going to see him. There was nothing but fear to stop her from finding out the truth.

She held out little hope of straightening out their difficulties or of their finding their way back to each other ever again. Her heart was so heavy because she knew they'd never really repaired the damage caused by their first breakup. They'd lost something vital. They'd lost faith in each other a long time ago.

Twenty-eight

Scott was working out in his recently completed home gym when the doorbell sounded. He scowled, focusing on his anger and resentment. It was Jenna. She'd called to request a meeting.

Last night's unexpected sighting across the crowded restaurant had firmly crushed the sliver of hope that had lingered despite his best efforts. Hope that she would think better of him. When their eyes had locked for that poignant moment, he'd known beyond doubt that she still believed he'd betrayed their love. Everything she knew and thought of him as a man had been boiled down to that single defining incident. And it hurt like hell.

What he couldn't figure out was why she had bothered to come. What could she possibly have to say?

Dressed in navy sweats, Scott's legendary smile was absent when he opened the door. The frosty late December day matched his cold, dark eyes as he looked down at his lost love. She'd broken his heart—not once but twice. He had no one but himself to blame for giving her yet another opportunity. Never again, he vowed, no matter how good she looked.

"Come in," he said, with no preamble.

He led the way into the den, gesturing toward the sitting area, while he remained standing. He waited until she removed her coat and draped it over the back of a sofa before she sat down. She was dressed in a lavender sweater set, black jeans, and high-heeled boots. She crossed her long, shapely legs.

"Well?" he asked, his entire body tight with tension. He refused to let his gaze linger on her beautiful features or her enticing curves. He wanted this over and her gone.

"I apologize for intruding on your time. But I have a few questions that only you can answer," Jenna said candidly.

"Why now? You weren't interested in hearing anything I had to say before. What changed?" With teeth clenched, a muscle jumped in his cheek. Although he saw her look of reproach, he chose to ignore it. He wasn't going to make this easy for her.

"I've had time to calm down and think. I've also talked it over with my brother. Lincoln attempted to offer the male point of view."

"Thank him. I mean, for pointing out there are two sides," Scott retorted, his voice laced with sarcasm.

"You can't blame me for being upset, Scott. You were in my bed with my twin."

"Oh, I blame you. Just as much as you blame me," he snapped impatiently. "I know how bad it looked. But because you said you loved me, I thought that meant you cared enough to listen to what I had to say."

"I'm here now, aren't I?"

"Only because your brother suggested it, and not out of any consideration for me."

"Perhaps I was wrong in not giving you an opportunity to explain."

"Perhaps?"

"Okay! I apologize for that. But I was devastated. I still can't get that image out of my head."

She hadn't been alone. He'd shared her devastation and shock as he'd recalled the look of sheer horror and disbelief on her lovely face. If she had only listened—then or even later that night or the following day—then maybe they would have been able to get to the truth.

"Would you please just tell me what happened?"

"Not until you tell me why it suddenly matters to you. How did Leah explain her actions? I'm assuming you gave her that much consideration?"

Jenna jumped to her feet, hands balled at her sides. Reluctantly, she said, "I listened to Leah last night after Lincoln convinced me to hear her out. As you know, I put her out. I only let her come back the day Lincoln and his family arrived. He wants to help. He doesn't want us to remain estranged."

Scott said nothing, his only acknowledgement that he heard her a slight nod of his head. He was deeply wounded by her lack of faith in him. It had left a bitter taste in his mouth.

As the silence stretched on, Jenna finally said, "Leah admitted she was jealous of me and what I had, especially you. She saw my leaving the house that morning as an opportunity to show you that you picked the wrong twin. She claimed she didn't think, just acted."

His frown deepened as he crossed his arms over his chest, but he made no comment.

Jenna rushed ahead, saying, "She said you were asleep when she climbed in bed with you. That she pressed against you, kissed your neck. Then you kissed her. Is that true? Is that what happened?"

Scott was shaking with fury. Jenna had been willing to listen to her unscrupulous sister, and now had the nerve to want his confirmation. Her willingness to listen had nothing to do with what the two of them felt for each other.

The realization cut into his very core, highlighting as nothing else could their differences. She claimed to love him, yet she didn't trust him or believe in his decency as a human being. Her hurtful comment that she should never have taken him back flashed through his mind, fueling his brooding anger and hardening his heart.

"Yes, it's true. But I told you that much. Naturally, I thought I was holding you, kissing you. My eyes weren't opened. It wasn't until I tasted her stale, wine-laced breath and smelled her skin that I knew I was in bed with the wrong woman. I would have pushed her away then, but that's when I heard your scream."

He fumed. "You saw my erection as a betrayal, rather than what it was—a man's natural response first thing in the morning. You didn't want to listen then or when I tried to call you and text you later. You ignored all of that. It was pointless to go to you and try to get you to listen."

Exasperated, he needed a few moments to collect his thoughts. "Frankly, I don't get what you hope to gain by coming here today. We both know you trust me about as far as you can throw me. Your lack of faith in me ended it for me. I deserve a hell of a lot better than what I got from you."

When he saw her lush, dark-pink-tinted mouth tighten and her hazel eyes fill with tears, he looked away. "You were right, Jenna. You never should have taken me back. It only raised both our hopes that we could make it work the second time around." He shook his head wearily. "I was so damn hopeful when I saw you in the cafe. All I knew was I wanted you . . . more than ever. Like a lovesick fool, I was willing to go to any length to win back your love." His laugh was harsh, packed with bitterness. "What a waste of valuable time, energy, and effort."

"You can't mean that."

"I do," he said without hesitation. "You were reluctant from the first, not even wanting us to be friends. I was so busy trying to convince you we had a future that I couldn't see what was right in front of my face. It couldn't work no matter how hard I tried. What I don't get was why I didn't learn from the past. It would have saved us so much heartache. Hell, it wasn't like I didn't know how you felt, that you didn't trust me. You came right out and told me."

Scott laughed bitterly. "When I entered the draft, you felt as if I broke my promise to finish college and marry you, but I saw it as a once-in-a-lifetime chance to make a dream come true. I invited you along for the ride. I never set out to hurt you, but that's what happened."

He stopped as he stared down at his athletic shoes, as if they'd held the answers. He took a breath. He didn't look at her when he said, "Who knows which one of us was right or wrong about that. It doesn't matter anymore. What's important was that your trust and faith in me were never the same after that. Because of it, you stopped believing I was a man of my word."

She surprised him when she said, "I wanted to believe. I wanted you. I wanted us to work this time, so badly. And I was trying to forget the past as we moved toward the future. I was so close to making a commitment to you, but then I saw . . ." She broke off.

Scott finished for her, "When you saw me in bed with Leah, all the old doubts and fears came right back. And for a good reason. You don't love me, Jenna. Without trust there can be no lasting love. Sure, we said we loved each other, but evidently not enough to make it through the tough times."

He admitted, "I saw this thing with Leah coming, but I wasn't sharp enough to put it all together. I knew she was after me and that she didn't respect our boundaries. She was giving off signals left and right. I should have warned you, but I knew you'd think I was over-reacting. When it came to your sister, you saw her the way you wanted her to be, not the way she really was. So I kept my mouth shut. I could see that she resented you, and it bothered me. But it never occurred to me that she could have gone as far as she did. That error was costly."

"You should have told me," Jenna insisted.

He nodded. "I realize that now. I was furious when she pretended to be you, but you just went along with it. You were so happy to have her back, you couldn't get past it. She could do no wrong in your eyes. I had a bad feeling that night, knew I should have gone home, but I didn't."

"Scott, I knew she flirted with you. I didn't like it, but I said and did nothing to stop it. We've both made mistakes. I readily admit that."

"It was much more than that. I realize now that I need a different woman. A woman who believes in me and trusts me to never deliberately hurt or betray her. I want that kind of trust." He said vehemently, "Your sister didn't break us up, you did. I was convinced that you were the woman I needed and deserved. I know now that I made a huge mistake. I'm sorry about that, just like I'm sorry about a lot of things."

Scott's eyes burned from unshed tears, and his heart was heavy with grief for what could not be. Just because he loved and believed in her didn't mean she loved him back with the same intensity. It kept coming back to that one point. She'd been right all along. They were good at hurting each other. They didn't belong together.

"Good-bye, Jenna. Let yourself out."

He walked out of the room and didn't look at her. He couldn't. It hurt too damn much.

"There's just no way we're going to let you stay home moping on New Year's Eve," Sherri Ann said over the telephone. "So get up, comb your hair, and put something pretty on. Come on over to my place. We're having a girlfriends' night in. Don't say no. Trenna and Maureen are coming. We're going to eat, drink lots of champagne, talk trash about men. Doesn't that sound like a good time?"

Jenna sighed unhappily. She'd been doing just that, moping at home. She hadn't stepped out of her door since the day she'd gone to talk to Scott. She'd thought she'd been prepared for all possibilities when she'd arrived at his place.

She'd gone over everything so many times, her conversations with her siblings before going to see Scott. She'd tried to recall exactly what she'd said to him. Her expectations hadn't been lofty. She'd gone seeking answers, and he'd given them to her. The result had been devastating.

She'd misjudged what she'd seen. His culpability began and ended with him being in bed with her twin. He hadn't invited Leah to join him. He'd been asleep until she'd climbed in and tried to seduce him into making love to her.

It had taken her too long to understand what had really happened that morning. She believed Scott when he said he would have pushed Leah away the instant he'd recognized he'd been holding the wrong twin. The truth had been as clear as his disillusionment and disappointment in her when he'd looked directly into her eyes and answered her questions.

Unfortunately for Jenna, the truth had come too late to repair their relationship. The damage had been done when she'd refused to listen to his explanation. That failure had convinced Scott she didn't love and trust him, not enough to build a future together.

What they'd discovered so long ago on U of D's campus was finally over. That small glimmer of hope buried in her heart had been ultimately dimmed. There had been no loud argument, no heated exchange. It had ended with Scott walking out of her life.

Jenna had been too stunned to do anything but stare after him. The realization had finally hit her in slow, painful degrees. She had wanted to curl into a ball of utter misery and howl her anguish. Pride had saved her from making a complete fool of herself and had stopped her from going after him to plead for his forgiveness. Pride had been the only thing that had gotten her out of his house and into her car without falling apart.

Scott had made his decision. She had no choice but to respect it. She didn't recall the drive home. Once she'd gotten inside her home, she'd given in to the emotional turmoil. She'd done nothing but cry, pouring out her grief. The worst part was that everything he'd said had been painfully true.

She'd placed the blame for their original breakup squarely on his shoulders. She'd believed that by following his dream, he had deliberately set out to hurt her. She hadn't realized the truth, not until he'd pointed it out. His actions hadn't been calculated. Yet they had seemed that way to her because of the hurt they had caused her when he'd broken his promise to her. Scott was correct. She'd treated him as if he'd intended to harm her, while she'd ignored his proposal that they marry and share this new chapter in his life.

At an early age she had learned there weren't a lot of

things she could count on in life. That was why promises had always been important to her. She made a point to keep hers and expected no less from those she loved.

Scott was wrong about one thing. She did love and trust him. It was no accident that she'd welcomed Scott's support or that he'd been the first person she'd told when the private investigator had found Lincoln. Scott had been there for her every time she'd needed him.

"Jenna? Are you still there?"

"Yes, I'm here. I was just thinking. Sherri Ann, do you believe what they say? That hindsight is always perfect?"

"Jenna, please stop beating yourself up about Scott. You had no way of knowing what he was thinking or feeling the morning you found him with Leah. You did your best under drastic circumstances. You weren't at fault!"

"I could have listened to—"

"Jenna! Forget it for one night," Sherri Ann begged. "Please."

"It's cold outside," Jenna said halfheartedly. She wasn't eager to inflict her miserable mood on anyone else.

"It's winter in Michigan. It's supposed to be cold. Get dressed."

"It's also snowing."

Sherri Ann sighed. "Does that mean you aren't coming? Because I will come and get your uncooperative behind. I'm not letting you spend New Year's Eve alone."

Jenna sighed. "You can't leave your own party to come after me."

"Then I suggest you get your butt in gear. Or I'll bring Laura with me. You get yourself over here. You've got an hour and a half. If you're not here, expect us at your door, missy."

Jenna laughed. "Missy? I'll get dressed. Has anyone told you that you're bossy?"

"Yeah, you. So what else is new? I mean it, Jenna Marie."

"I'm coming. Give me an extra half hour. I need to take a shower first."

"Not a minute longer. Bye."

Still brooding, Jenna was slow to move. For weeks she had doubted her ability to hold onto him. Scott had come a long way from being the gangly young man she'd first fallen in love with. She'd had no defenses against the sophisticated, debonair man who had pursued her with intensity. He was an accomplished man with striking good looks, a great deal of masculine grace, and wealth. Naturally, he drew male and female attention wherever he went. Scott didn't have to do much—just show up and he was mobbed for autographs. It was the way women flocked to him that Jenna found particularly disturbing. He had been involved with some of the most glamorous women in the world.

That morning she'd been very close to accepting his proposal. Yet all the old insecurities had rushed back the moment she'd seen him in bed with Leah. Jenna knew she was pretty, but she wasn't outgoing or strikingly beautiful. She didn't spend hours on her hair, nails, and makeup. She didn't wear curve-hugging clothes, and her experiences with men were limited. She'd only slept with one man. It hadn't been a stretch for Jenna to believe he preferred her sexy, flamboyant twin.

Scott had assumed that her lack of faith in him proved she didn't love him. What Jenna lacked was confidence in her feminine appeal. It wasn't something she could gain from a textbook. Her problem had nothing to do with how she felt about him.

Jenna sighed. She didn't want to spend hours pretending to be excited about the upcoming year. It would be a year that wouldn't include Scott in her life. Despite all that they'd been through and all the hurtful things that they had both said and done to each other, she still loved him. And it hurt.

A glance at the bedside clock sent her hurrying to get ready. Hoping to at least look festive, Jenna teamed a glittery silver-beaded sweater with a long black velvet skirt. She'd just pulled on a knee-length black boot when the telephone rang.

Grabbing the telephone, she said, "Sherri Ann, I'm heading to the garage to warm up the car right now."

"Hi, Sis. Looks like I was lucky to catch you at home."

"Lincoln! It's good to hear your voice." Jenna's voice wobbled. "How are you? Carolyn? And little Corrie?"

"Wonderful."

Brother and sister visited for a few minutes. Then he insisted on knowing how she really was holding up. Brushing away a single tear, Jenna quickly recounted her meeting with Scott. She admitted to being a little down, but in the hope of ending their conversation on an upbeat note, she told Lincoln of her plans to ring in the new year with friends. After telling Jenna about his plans to spend a romantic evening at home with Carolyn, Lincoln told Jenna that Leah was going out with friends. Jenna held back an angry retort. She quickly ended the ˙call, cheered by her brother's promise to phone the next day.

Bundled in a long wool coat, muffler, gloves, and hat, Jenna hurried out and nearly took a spill on an icy patch on her way into the detached garage. Grumbling all the while, she lifted the lid of the aluminum garbage can where she stored rock salt, then tossed some onto the spot.

Once the car was warm, she backed out of her recently shoveled driveway, thanks to the neighbor's teenage son. The snow was steadfastly falling, and the wind was fierce. She shook her head as she drove past the neighborhood liquor and convenience store. It was brightly lit, and, judging by the number of cars in the lot, the party was on.

As she maneuvered around a deserted car left on the side of the road, she took her foot off the accelerator. Rather than slowing, the car picked up speed as the tires spun on a sheet of black ice. Thanks to Scott's tutoring during their college days, she knew better than to apply the brakes. Instead, she focused on staying calm and loosening her death grip on the steering wheel.

"This makes no sense. I'd rather be at home in my nice, warm house celebrating with a pint of triple caramel chunk ice cream," Jenna complained aloud.

The wind was howling and the snow wasn't letting up. Despite the front and rear defrosters going full blast and the windshield wipers moving at top speed, she was having trouble seeing.

"Oh, Scott . . ." she sighed, recalling the things they'd done together when they'd first fallen in love. Even though he'd given her driving lessons, he hadn't liked her being out alone at night. He'd often picked her up from her night class so she wouldn't have to take the bus home.

Deciding it was too slick to chance the steep incline at the entrance to the expressway, she stayed on the well-lit street, even though it would take twice as long. Jenna began to relax as she approached the Wayne State University area, still several blocks from Sherri Ann's condo. If she got stuck around here, she could get out and walk. She giggled. At this rate it might be after midnight by the time she got there.

As she neared the busy intersection, she began to slow even more, anticipating the traffic light changing to red. Suddenly an SUV moving too fast for the elements was behind her with horn blaring. Rather than decreasing speed, it seemed to pick up speed as the driver came barreling toward Jenna.

She tried to speed up, but her tires were unable to gain traction on the slick pavement. The SUV's brakes screeched as it plowed into the back of Jenna's dated compact car. The impact sent her car hurtling through the red light and into the intersection. She swerved to avoid hitting an oncoming car, while her car seemed to pick up even more speed on the ice. Struggling to gain control of the car, Jenna screamed as the car crashed into a lamppost.

Twenty-nine

"Something's wrong. She should be here by now," Laura said as she listened to the repeated ring of Jenna's telephone.

"Stop that! You're scaring me, making me think something's really wrong," Sherri Ann complained, her forehead creased in a frown.

Laura said, "It's not like her to say she's coming and then not show up! She hasn't answered her home or cell. It's nearly eleven."

"Laura's right. Jenna should be here by now," Maureen said.

"Maybe she and Scott made up? And she hasn't gotten around to calling," Trenna suggested hopefully.

The ladies were seated around Sherri Ann's living room, with a bounty of food laid out on the large coffee table and the champagne chilling in an ice bucket.

Sherri Ann shook her head. "That's not likely, considering how she sounded earlier. She wasn't expecting him. But even if he had shown up at the last minute, she would have called."

"Well, I can't just sit around, doing nothing but worrying. I'm going to drive over to her place to check on her." Laura got up, heading into the foyer for her coat and boots.

"Wait! I'm going with you," Sherri Ann called, then turned to her guests. "You don't . . ."

"Don't worry about us. You two go. Trenna and I will stay here in case Jenna suddenly calls or shows up," Maureen volunteered. "She might be having car trouble, especially with the weather being so bad."

"You don't mind waiting?" Sherri Ann straightened from putting on boots and reaching for her hooded coat.

Bundled up in a down-filled coat, Laura waited with car keys in her hand. "We'll call as soon as we get there," Laura said.

"Drive carefully." Trenna waved from the open doorway. "Don't forget to call!"

"We will," Laura called back. While she started the car, Sherri Ann grabbed a long-handled snowbrush and scraper to clear away the snow.

Neither foster sister voiced her fears as they sat waiting for the defroster to clear the windows. They began to retrace the route Jenna normally took. They were nearing the busy intersection a few blocks away from Sherri Ann's condo when Sherri Ann shouted, "Slow down. There's been an accident. Oh, no! That looks like Jenna's car against that post!"

Shaking with fear, Laura managed to slow the car to a crawl and ease over to the side of the road. "Are you sure? I can't see anything!" Snow was falling, and the windshield wipers were going full blast.

"Come on, Laura. We've got to go see if it's our Jenna."

A policeman was there directing traffic away from the accident while the approaching EMS vehicle blared in the background. Surrounded by sirens and a growing crowd, Laura and Sheri Ann hurried toward the dark blue car. Tears of fear and disbelief were racing down their cheeks as they neared the scene.

"Let us through!" Laura yelled over the din of sirens and curious onlookers. "That's our sister!" They pushed their way to the front of the crowd.

"She's not moving! Laura, she's not moving!" Sherri Ann sobbed, unaware that they were clinging to each other for support.

"She's going to be alright! She has to be!" Laura insisted, wiping away blinding tears. "That's our sister! We have to get to her!" She tried to rush past the authorities blocking the way. "Why aren't they doing anything to help her?"

"Ladies, you have to stay back. They're doing everything they can to get her out of the car."

"What if she's . . ." Sherri Ann broke off, unable to say the word.

The two foster sisters hung on each other, quietly praying. They watched anxiously as the men went to work. They had to pry the car open in order to reach her. The paramedics quickly checked her out and soon were wheeling her into the flashing lights of the waiting ambulance. Through it all, Jenna never moved or opened her eyes.

"Come on, Sherri Ann. We've got to follow them to the hospital."

While Laura drove, Sherri Ann called Maureen and Trenna. They agreed to meet them at the hospital. Then she reluctantly called Leah on her cell phone. She told her what had happened and asked her to relay the message to her brother, Lincoln.

Laura asked, "Why did you call her instead of Lincoln?"

"She's here and she has a right to know. Besides, we may need a blood relative to authorize treatment," Sherri Ann pointed out.

"Always the lawyer. Who are you calling now?"

Sherri Ann said into the phone, "Hello, Scott. This is Sherri Ann. Jenna's been in a car crash."

Laura listened as Sherri Ann answered one question after another. When she broke the connection, Laura prompted, "Well?"

"He sounded as upset as the rest of us. He's meeting us at the hospital."

"I don't know, Sherri Ann. Jenna's going to be upset when she finds out that both Leah and Scott are at the hospital."

"Sounds good to me. She was too still. I can't wait to hear her yelling at us. Maybe that will mean she won't be badly hurt."

Sprinting through the snow-covered parking lot, Scott entered the emergency room with a gut-wrenching fear unlike anything he'd ever experienced. It was an all-consuming fear that dominated every thought and emotion.

While his family had been busy celebrating the holiday, he'd been home brooding, actively nursing his righteous anger and feeling justified for every harsh truth he'd thrown her way two days ago. He'd kept a mental tally, recalling in detail the smallest slight she'd shown him since the day he'd paid for her lunch in the cafe. He'd been determined to prove to himself that he was right, and she was wrong.

One telephone call and that unrelenting anger had been instantly shoved aside.

The news had come out of nowhere and struck with an incredible force that had left him reeling from the impact. The crushing weight had momentarily cut off his ability to breathe. No! Not his beautiful, sweet Jenna. She had to pull through this. She just had to!

"How is she?" he asked without preamble when he

spotted Laura and Sherri Ann in the crowded waiting room.

Jenna's foster sisters were dressed for an evening out on the town, while others, like Scott, were dressed casually in jeans and turtleneck sweater. Judging by the hoopla being broadcast over the TV, the glittery ball had dropped in New York. It was after midnight.

"Look, that's Scott Hendricks!" a teen fan shouted, then rushed over for an autograph.

For the first time in memory, Scott ignored the fan. "How is she? Laura? Sherri Ann? Has she regained consciousness?"

"She's with the doctor. So we're still waiting for news," Sherri Ann volunteered.

Dejected, he scowled. He'd been hoping for word, some news. He yanked off a knit cap and shoved it into the pocket of his heavy jacket.

"You might as well take a load off and relax. It's gonna be awhile," Laura advised.

Scott nodded, then suddenly recalled the teen he'd brushed off. He crossed the room to the embarrassed teen. "Sorry about that." After offering his hand, he reached into his inside pocket and pulled out one of the postcard-size basketball cards he always carried. Pen in hand, he signed the card.

"Thanks, man. I appreciate it."

"No problem," Scott murmured.

He took the empty seat beside Laura. He nodded, acknowledging the other friends he remembered meeting at various functions. When his eyes touched on Leah, he bristled.

He glared at Jenna's twin. "Who called her?"

"I did," Sherri Ann said tiredly. "Like it or not, she's Jenna's twin and has a right to be here."

Scott dismissed her. Shoving himself to his feet, he

shrugged out of his jacket and tossed it over the back of the chair. Restless, he began pacing the short hall outside the waiting area.

"Would anyone care for coffee or something to drink from the cafeteria?" Maureen asked.

"I'll go with you," Trenna offered.

Scott shook his head, unwilling to move from the area.

"I'm going to see if they've forgotten we're out here waiting," Laura said, jumping to her feet.

Scott said nothing, but walked with her to the front desk.

Laura smiled at the receptionist. "We're part of the Gaines family. Can you please tell me if there's been any update in Jenna's condition?"

"Sorry, no. The doctor is still in with her, Ms. Murdock. Hopefully it won't be too much longer."

"Thank you, Anita," Laura forced a smile.

Scott wasn't surprised that Laura knew her name. Laura was no stranger to the city's emergency rooms because of her work with rape victims.

"Does anyone know how this happened?" he asked.

"She was on her way to Sherri Ann's to ring in the new year with friends. The police and eye witnesses said it wasn't her fault. She was hit from behind. An SUV was driving too fast for the road conditions and plowed into her, sending her through the intersection and into the lamppost. It's a miracle she didn't hit anyone else. She's lucky to be alive."

Scott swore, then caught himself. "Sorry. She didn't deserve this."

"She hasn't deserved a lot of things she's had to deal with lately," Laura said pointedly. Then she walked off in a huff.

Scott swallowed a bitter retort. This wasn't the time

or place to get into an argument with Jenna's foster sister. He was lucky they'd called him. Maureen and Trenna returned with the drinks.

A doctor dressed in scrubs entered the waiting area. "Jenna Gaines's family, please?"

They all came forward. No one bothered to mention that Leah was the only genuine Gaines family member present.

"Hello, Dr. Andrew," Laura said as she came forward. She quickly introduced the others. Finally she introduced Scott as their brother.

Impatient, Scott quizzed, "How is she?"

Dr. Andrew shook his head. "Ms. Gaines came in with head trauma, a broken left arm, and a great deal of bruising to her shoulder and face. We've only been able to set the arm and make her comfortable. The head injury is what concerns us. She hasn't regained consciousness. We can't treat the head trauma until she wakes up. We're going to admit her into the hospital. We need someone to complete the paperwork and a family member signature. Most of the information was gained from the contents of her purse."

Scott flexed his hands, feeling helpless and hating that he had no rights where Jenna was concerned. He'd had to stand there and lie about being her brother just to hear how she was doing. Not so long ago, he'd asked her to be his wife. Right about now he'd trade everything he owned just for the right to see her.

"I'll do it," Sherri Ann volunteered.

"How long until she wakes up?" Leah began crying. "She's going to wake up, isn't she?"

The doctor looked stunned when he said, "I didn't realize she had an identical twin. We can't say how long she'll be unconscious. There was no air bag to cushion the impact. She hit her head hard. She may have a concussion, but we won't know until she wakes up. We're hoping it will be soon."

"When can we see her?" Laura asked anxiously.

"Not until she's been settled into a room." After fielding a few more questions, Dr. Andrew excused himself and left.

It was four o'clock in the morning before Jenna had been given a room and the family was allowed to see her. She still hadn't regained consciousness.

Scott was the first one to go in to see her, as if he had the right. He walked in with his heart aching from a combination of dread and anticipation. He didn't bother trying to analyze his emotions. They were all over the place. It didn't matter—nothing mattered but seeing for himself that she was still among the living.

Overwhelmed with relief, he stared at Jenna from the foot of the bed. He marveled at her incredibly beautiful face despite the bruises and swelling and the cast encasing her upper left arm, cradled against her side in a sling.

He was deeply thankful that she'd been wearing her seat belt, since her car hadn't been equipped with air bags. She could have been killed instantly by the impact.

As he stood staring at her, he didn't say a word. He couldn't get a sound past the constriction in his throat. He longed to cradle her close to his heart and simply hold her until the fear of her dying finally went away. He didn't dare so much as reach out a hand to touch her as he fought to control conflicting emotions.

This wasn't about them and what had gone wrong between them. It was so much bigger than that. It was about Jenna. All he wanted was for her to open those gorgeous hazel eyes. Then everything would be alright again, and he could breathe easy.

As the others came in one by one, he settled into the

corner of the room. From there he could wait and watch over her as he silently chanted, "Wake up, sweet love."

The first day of the new year passed painfully slowly without any change in Jenna's condition. The hours seemed to drag as one day slipped into the next. The ladies took turns sitting at her bedside, holding her hand. They softly pleaded with her to open her eyes.

Her foster sisters and Leah took turns going home for a change of clothes, a meal and rest. Scott stayed. Mostly, he stood with his shoulder braced against the wall as he silently prayed and watched over her. He only left for nature's call or when the doctors or nurses asked him to step out. He didn't go when Taylor stopped by and urged him to go home and get some rest. Although exhausted, he flatly refused to leave, but he accepted the food and change of clothing she brought for him.

By the wee hours of the third day, they were all displaying signs of strain, even Scott. He was just returning from a bathroom break when Laura and Sherri Ann met him in the hallway with the news. Jenna was awake and asking for him.

Overcome with emotion, weak from exhaustion, Scott's vision blurred. Blinded by sudden tears, he bowed his head. After a silent thanks to God, he nodded, then turned and walked toward the elevators. Lucky for him, he was wearing his jacket with his car keys in the pocket. He left the hospital with Jenna's foster sisters calling his name.

From the moment Jenna had opened her eyes, she'd been surrounded by family and friends. Although only two people were allowed in the room at a time, she was never alone. She'd also been poked and prodded by a team of nurses and doctors and lab technicians. She'd also received a battery of X-rays, blood draws, and medical tests.

She couldn't remember the accident. She didn't remember much beyond getting into the car on New Year's Eve and waking up in the hospital. The doctor had assured her that it was perfectly normal, along with the headaches.

She couldn't quite believe what she'd been told, that Scott had stayed at her side until she'd regained consciousness. She'd struggled to conceal her disappointment when he'd left and hadn't returned. When she'd asked for him, both Laura and Sherri Ann had been quick to say he was getting some well-deserved rest.

Jenna didn't say it, but she hadn't expected him to return, especially recalling the way they'd parted. Yet that hadn't stopped her hopeful glances whenever someone new had entered the room. She was thrilled to see her brother.

"You should try to get some rest, Sis." Lincoln gave her hand a gentle squeeze.

"I can't sleep, not with this headache."

"Why won't they give you something for it? What about the pain in your shoulder and arm?" Sherri Ann asked. "I can go and talk to the head nurse. Maybe the doctor will reconsider?"

"They already said they are holding back on using strong medications because of the concussion. It's not too bad. Besides, I agree with the doctor. I'd rather suffer a little pain than risk going to sleep and not being able to wake up again."

Lincoln patted her hand. "You're doing so much better than you were twenty-four hours ago. You had us worried."

"I know. I'm sorry you had to turn around and come all the way back to Detroit."

"Stop it. I'm just glad you are getting better. That's all any of us care about." He leaned over and kissed her forehead. "Be good. I'll see you in the morning."

Closing heavy lids, Jenna promised, "I will. Bye."

Sherri Ann said, "I'm leaving, too. You get some rest. We want you out of here," she added, kissing Jenna's cheek.

"Good night," Jenna said tiredly.

The silence was welcoming. Although exhausted, Jenna knew she wouldn't be able to fall asleep easily. She settled for trying to relax her bruised and sore body. More important, she tried not to worry about why Scott had even come and then stayed so long, only to leave without talking to her. Every time she thought about it, her head would pound unmercifully, and she would be forced to push the questions away.

Eyes closed, she shifted, then whimpered from the pain. She lightly pressed fingertips to her aching head.

"Is it bad?"

The deep, familiar male voice instantly caused her heavy lids to lift and her lips to part in surprise. She whispered, "Scott . . ."

Thirty

He shrugged out of his jacket, then tossed it over the back of a chair. "Your head, does it hurt?"

"Yeah," she admitted.

"And the arm?"

"I'm better than I was when you left." Suddenly she was aware of the way his powerful frame filled the small room. "At least I'm awake."

"So Laura and Sherri Ann told you I was here."

"That's right. We ladies have to stick together."

"You had us all scared with that sleeping beauty routine."

She felt, rather than saw, his dark eyes moving over her bruised and swollen face. She was grateful that Sherri Ann had brushed her hair, although she was keenly aware of how beat up she must look. She quickly said, "Hardly a beauty, more like puffy and bruised."

"It's nothing a few weeks of rest won't cure. You were extremely lucky, Jenna. It could have been a lot worse."

Using her uninjured hand, she smoothed the blanket covering her legs. "They said you were here watching over me the entire time I was unconscious. Is that true?"

When he remained silent, she finally looked at him.

It wasn't until their eyes connected that she felt the full force of his personality.

"It's true."

"But why? We both know how bad things were the last time we talked. You didn't want to stay in the same room with me. Why did you come? And why did you stay away all day and then come back tonight?"

He laughed without a trace of humor. "You don't ask for much, do you? Just put it all out there, why don't you?"

"Why waste time? A brush with death will do that for you." She tried to ignore the way her heart hammered in her chest and the way her head pounded as she waited for his response.

"The last question is easy. I was exhausted. When I left here, I went home and crashed. I came back tonight for the same reason I came when Sherri Ann called. I had to see for myself that you were alright. We've meant too much to each other, far too long, for me to ever just stop caring about you, Jenna."

Determined to conceal her relief and keen disappointment, Jenna nodded her head. But she quickly regretted it. Shooting pain had her wincing and cradling her cheek as if to contain the misery. She blinked away tears that temporarily blinded her.

"Sweet thing, are you okay?"

"No, I'm not okay!" she snapped, and then spoiled it by moaning pitifully. "And don't call me sweet thing. It's condescending and sexist."

"I'll call the nurse. Tell them to get you something for the pain." He moved toward the door.

"No. Don't call anyone. I'm fine, or at least I will be as soon as they let me out of this place and I can go home." Aware that she was at a distinct disadvantage, not even close to looking or feeling her best, she took a calming breath before she said, "It's late, and as you can see, I'm on the mend. So there's no reason for you to stay. Goodnight, Scott. Thanks for coming."

She nearly said, don't bother coming back, but she caught herself just in time. She didn't have to be told that she sounded like a petulant child who'd been denied her favorite toy. She resented it. No, she resented him for not loving her enough to at least try and work things out.

Scott stiffened but didn't leave. Instead he dropped into the chair beside the bed. Leaning forward, he studied her. "Your head hurts, you're tired. And you're upset. Why, Jenna?"

"Just go away, Scott. I'm not up to a debate about anything, certainly not my feelings. You lost the right to question me when you kicked me out of your house." She absently rubbed her injured arm as she fought the urge to cry. If she wasn't careful, she'd beg him to take her back, to love her again.

"Not one of my finest moments. I was disappointed and angry." Scott shrugged.

"You were furious! You blamed me and refused to listen to what I had to say. And you were wrong!" she shouted, although she immediately regretted it.

"Wrong about what, babe?" When she refused to look at him, he rose to his full length. "Okay. I'll go. I'll see you tomorrow. I will come in the evening when you don't have so much company. How long will Lincoln be in Detroit?"

"He leaves tomorrow. Scott, I said don't . . ."

"I heard you, but I'm not going away. I'm staying for the duration of your time in this place. And I'm not pretending there's nothing going on between us."

"It's over. We agreed," she insisted.

"That was before you almost died, damn it. I love

you. That didn't end because of your manipulative twin sister. Nor did it stop when I ordered you out of my house because I was hurting. It almost ended when you crashed your car into that lamppost." He stood with his feet braced and his hands at his side. "Your accident really got my attention. It hammered into my thick scalp as nothing else could how much you mean to me. Thanks to God, we still have time to deal with our problems . . . but later."

He placed a tender kiss on her bruised forehead, another on her nose. At the sight of tears pooling beneath her lashes, he sank down onto the bed and tenderly gathered Jenna against him.

"Don't cry, sweet love. It's okay. Whatever is wrong, it's going to be okay. We'll fix it together."

Overcome by the wealth of her emotion, Jenna cried harder. She made a bit of a protest when he first cradled her against his chest. He still loved her. Would they ever get it right? They'd made so many mistakes.

"Please don't cry. Talk to me, Jenna," he urged softly.

She sniffed. "I'm crying because you said you still love me despite all that has gone wrong. I love you so much," she confessed, using her good arm to wrap behind his neck and pull his head down to hers. They shared a long, tender kiss. "I didn't know what to think when they told me you were here but you left just when I woke up."

"Believe me, you didn't want to see me then. After three days without sleep, I was an emotional wreck. Mostly, I was so darn thankful that you were alive and going to get better. Plus, I was still so angry with you for letting me down, letting me get close enough to realize that I'd never stopped loving you. Then you yanked the rug out from under me, babe, when you refused to believe in me . . . to believe I'd rather cut off a body part than betray your trust by going after your twin."

He gave her a hard kiss. "When I first returned to the city, everywhere I went I thought of you and what we shared. I was miserable without you. I used alcohol to mask the pain. Then Taylor told me you'd moved back. Suddenly I had a reason to get my life back on track. When I ran into you on campus, I was a goner. I wasn't going to let anything stop me from getting you back."

He moved a caressing hand down her cheek. "You gave me hope when you agreed to let me go with you to find your family. When you made love with me, the first time, I knew we could make a go of it this time around. You gave me a slice of heaven that night." He smiled. "I knew we had a future when you agreed to wear my ring close to your heart. I was devastated that morning, knowing you believed the worst and not being able to get you to even hear me out."

"Scott, I'm so sorry. I never meant to hurt you that way, but I thought . . ." She stopped. "You know what I thought."

He lifted her hand and placed a kiss in the soft center. "You had every right to be upset. You were also hurting. Neither one of us asked for Leah's interference. But man, did we suffer because of it. I kept thinking this looks so bad, but we can get past it. I believed that until . . ."

"Until what? You started believing that I didn't trust you because of the past?"

"Yeah," he reluctantly admitted. "I was so angry, I couldn't see past it."

"You were wrong about me not trusting you," she insisted softly, lacing her fingers with his. "It wasn't only about you. I didn't believe in myself. I was shattered when I saw you with her. I needed time to get past it . . . to think. But you weren't backing down. You insisted I listen to you right then. I couldn't! It hurt too much, like a nightmare that was never going away."

He nodded, kissing the back of her hand. "Logically,

I accepted that, but I also knew that if I didn't reach you then, I'd lose you. I was right. Your sister really did a number on us. And for what?"

Scott swore bitterly. "Jenna, it was all about the money. It was never really about me. She didn't even know me. She should have told us straight up what she wanted. Believe me, I would have made it clear that there was only one woman for me. And that was you. I didn't want a look-alike, a poor imitation, or any kind of substitute for you, my sweet love. I want you . . . only you, Jenna Marie Gaines.

"When she realized she couldn't have me"—he paused, his voice brimming with disgust—"she should have asked for cash. Leah wants the easy way. If I'd only realized that it meant so much to her that she was willing to destroy us to get it, I would have gladly dropped a million on her sneaky behind." He snapped his fingers. "Just like that, she would have been gone. Problem solved."

"No way," Jenna hissed.

"Oh, yeah. I would have. And it would have been worth it, especially if it could have saved us the heartache. Look what she did to us! Just look how you are laid up in a hospital, all battered and bruised." He gently kissed her swollen cheek. "I can't stand that you're suffering this way."

Jenna smiled. "I know, my sweet man. But you can't blame Leah for the accident. That had nothing to do with her. If I had anything to say about it, you would absolutely not be giving her a red nickel. She doesn't deserve to be rewarded for bad behavior. At least now she finally gets it. She hasn't been happy with the way things turned out."

"How do you figure? She wanted us to break up. She won!"

"She didn't win. She didn't want me to hate her. She

didn't plan to get thrown out of the house. In fact, she didn't plan any of it. From what she told me, it was an impulse that she quickly regretted. You should have seen her at Christmas. She was as miserable as I was."

"That makes three of us. I don't want her anywhere near me. You better believe that I was watching her when she sat with you while you were unconscious. Leah caused this, and I can't see myself forgiving or forgetting that. When I saw her in the waiting room, I really wanted to tell her a few things. We should have left her in Vegas. Hell no, I'm not interested in how she suffered," he snarled.

Jenna pressed closer to him, smoothing her cheek against his cashmere-covered chest. "I know."

"When I think of all you did to welcome her into your home, to help her in every way to build a better life for herself. . . . You used your savings just to find her and then spent your hard-earned money to bring her here so that your family could be together for the holidays. You could easily have left her dancing topless in that club and living with a man who steals from her. You were willing to help her get a college education. And she didn't thank you for any of it." Scott scowled. "She had the nerve to go after what was yours for no good reason. No, I'm not likely . . ." He stopped talking abruptly.

He raised her hand to place a kiss in her soft palm. "Enough about Leah. The more I talk about it, the angrier I get. Tonight is about you and me finally finding our way back to each other."

"Finally . . ." she repeated around a yawn. "I'm sorry."

Scott smiled down at her, smoothing her cottony-soft hair away from her face. He kissed each of her eyelids. "I can take a hint. You need your rest. When are they letting you out of here?"

"I have no idea, but it can't be soon enough to please me." When he shifted, she begged, "Don't go. The nurses will let you stay. The females on staff are already half in love with you," she teased.

"What made you say that?"

Jenna giggled. "Laura told me how often they came in here to get a good look at you, my brother. Then when Lincoln showed up, you told them I was your fiancée." She kissed the side of his dark throat. "Please stay. I want you here with me until they put you out. Promise to stay?"

He smiled. "I promise. So you heard about the fiancée thing, hmm?"

"Oh yeah, I heard. There are no secrets, especially with 'eagle-eyes' Sherri Ann and 'nose-to-the-ground' Laura around," she giggled.

"And you're not upset because of it?" he quizzed.

"No, why would I be?"

"You've forgotten the way you threw that ring at me? Babe, you tried to take my eye out."

"I did," Jenna readily agreed, jutting her chin out proudly. "I'd do worse if I ever caught you near a bed with any female. Got it?"

"Got it," he echoed. He moved until he could look into her beautiful hazel eyes. "I want to put this behind us. I want us to make that final commitment to each other so there will be no doubt in anyone's mind about how we feel about each other and that we belong together." He hesitated, and then said, ". . . including your own."

She nearly shook her aching head but stopped just in time. "Yes, including me. I had so many doubts about my ability to hold on to your love that it was downright easy for me to assume that you were attracted to my vivacious, prettier twin."

"Prettier? No way!"

She smiled. "My lack of trust wasn't all about you. I lacked faith in me."

Scott said firmly, "When I look at you, I see all I want or need in a woman. It's more than your physical appearance." He placed his palm over her heart. "It's the beauty on the inside that shows through. I love who you are, how you think and feel. Your unconditional loyalty to those you care about. In short, I love everything about you that makes you you, Jenna. There's no one like you."

Jenna blinked away sudden tears. "That's so sweet. Unfortunately, because of my doubts, it wasn't hard for me to believe that you picked Leah over me."

"But why? I don't get it." His brow creased. "You're a beautiful, well-educated, classy lady."

"Thank you, but it goes deeper than how I present myself to the world. You have to remember a lot has changed in the years we were apart. You weren't the same nineteen-year-old jock that fell in love with a twenty-year-old studious college student. We have both changed in countless ways. While I gained confidence in my intellectual abilities in the financial and academic arenas, I also knew I wasn't like the worldly, glamorous women you dated. Scott, you have traveled the globe, and have dealt with all kinds of challenges over the years."

"For those women, the attraction was the sport and the glamour of being in the spotlight—it wasn't me."

"You, gorgeous man, are a huge part of the attraction. I accepted that. Things were cool until you asked me to marry you. It forced me to face the fact that we were not the two people who fell in love years earlier. I wondered if I could hold on to you, especially considering my very ordinary, mundane life. I'm a college professor, for heaven's sake."

"But sweet—"

She pressed her fingertips against his lips to stop him and said, "Let me say this. It's important." When he nodded, she said, "I'd reached many of my personal goals. After we broke up, I concentrated on school. Emotionally, I was empty. I didn't feel as if I had anything to offer a man beyond friendship. I would pull back the instant things got even remotely serious, forget about being intimate with a man." She kissed his cheek while inhaling his scent. "The first time we made love again I didn't want you to know that I hadn't been with another man."

"Jenna." He cupped her face lovingly, then said in a throaty whisper, "I knew or suspected. Your body told your secret. I was just as overwhelmed from being with you again. I realized I was in danger of falling in love with you, all over again. Even though you wouldn't talk about it, knowing you'd held back gave me hope that you might still have feelings for me. I was desperate for any little crumbs I could get."

Jenna confessed, "I did have feelings for you, but I held them inside. I used our past as a shield to keep my feelings at bay. I was scared. I kept remembering the promise you broke when you left school and me. I was afraid you'd walk away again. Only weeks later, when I realized you wanted to get married, I thought of all the rumors and stories I'd heard about you and those beautiful women. Scott, you dated Darah Michelle for months. I saw the pictures of the two of you at one of her Hollywood premieres, for heaven's sake. You took her to one of those big awards shows. Then there was that *Sports Illustrated* swimsuit cover model."

"But sweetheart—"

She interrupted, "If you can leave someone as gorgeous as Darah Michelle, how was I supposed to hang on to you? So when I saw you with my sexy, outgoing twin, naturally I believed you preferred her."

"I got it, baby. You couldn't help what you felt any more than I could help my body's reaction to waking up with what I thought was you in my arms. Both responses were inevitable. We have to accept that so we can put this whole incident behind us."

He brushed her soft lips with his tongue. "Yeah, I've dated famous women. I also dated several businesswomen, as well as an attorney and a doctor. At the time, I was busy living my life. I didn't love any of them. They didn't make me feel what you make me feel, Jenna, my sweet love. I gave my heart to you a long time ago. I may have tried to get it back a time or two, but it never worked. No matter how angry or hurt I was, it didn't stop me from loving you." His gaze locked with hers when he said, "Even as I told you it was over, if you think back, I never said I'd stopped loving you."

"Oh, honey." Jenna sighed with happiness.

He whispered into her ear, "I gave my heart to you a long time ago. Maybe the first moment I looked into your eyes that day at the computer lab. I'd just left basketball practice, so I was hot, sweaty, hungry, and broke. I'd stopped in to borrow a couple of bucks from my sister. I forgot all of that when I looked at you.

"Do you remember, babe? You were working on one of the computers, so engrossed in what you were doing that you didn't even look at me." He chuckled huskily. "I thought you were the most gorgeous female I'd ever seen. I couldn't take my eyes off you. And when you walked over to where Taylor was working at the desk, I was hooked. You had it all—shapely, long legs and dangerous feminine curves. No way was I leaving that room without finding out your name and digits."

She laughed, her heart filled with love.

"Let's get it right this time, Jenna. Let's not leave room for mistakes, doubts, misunderstandings, or outside interferences. We've proven that time and distance can't stop our love. Let's prove we aren't about to let anyone or anything keep us apart. Please, be my wife, so I can be your husband. I can't get enough of you, my love. I want to see you grow round with my babies."

"I want that, too," she whispered.

"Marry me?"

"Absolutely!" Jenna beamed.

"Absolutely," he echoed. "How soon? We've already wasted enough time."

"As soon as the cast is off my arm and the bruises are gone. I plan to be a beautiful bride."

"You will be." He kissed her. "Now close your beautiful eyes and get some sleep so you can go about the business of healing. Not to worry, I'll take care of all the arrangements while you recover."

"You?"

"That's right. All you have to do is pick your dress and tell me when, where, and how you want it. I'll get it all done. I promise that from this moment on, I will never give you reason to doubt my love and devotion to you. There won't be any regrets for either one of us. I've always been yours, just as you've always been mine. We've got a lifetime to look forward to . . . together."

"Together . . . always," she confirmed softly, closing her eyes.

Jenna quickly slipped into a deep, restorative sleep, wrapped in Scott's protective, loving arms.

At Avon Books, we know your passion for romance—once you finish one of our novels, you find yourself wanting more.

May we tempt you with . . .

- **Excerpts** from our upcoming releases.

- Entertaining **extras**, including authors' personal photo albums and book lists.

- Behind-the-scenes **scoop** on your favorite characters and series.

- **Sweepstakes** for the chance to win free books, romantic getaways, and other fun prizes.

- Writing **tips** from our authors and editors.

- **Blog** with our authors and find out why they love to write romance.

- **Exclusive content** that's not contained within the pages of our novels.

Join us at
www.avonbooks.com

A V O N

An Imprint of HarperCollins*Publishers*
www.avonromance.com